LAY

YOUR

BODY

DOWN

ALSO BY AMY SUITER CLARKE

Girl, 11

LAY YOUR BODY DOWN

A Novel of Suspense

AMY SUITER CLARKE

WILLIAM MORROW
An Imprint of HarperCollins*Publishers*

Epigraph from *A Year of Biblical Womanhood* by Rachel Held Evans (2012)

This is a work of fiction. Names, characters, places, and incidents are products of the author's imagination or are used fictitiously and are not to be construed as real. Any resemblance to actual events, locales, organizations, or persons, living or dead, is entirely coincidental.

HarperCollins books may be purchased for educational, business, or sales promotional use. For information, please email the Special Markets Department at SPsales@harpercollins.com.

FIRST EDITION

Designed by Bonni Leon-Berman

Library of Congress Cataloging-in-Publication Data has been applied for.

ISBN 978-0-35-841831-3

23 24 25 26 27 LBC 5 4 3 2 1

To Peter, Emery, and Asher.

And to the church girls: past and present.

If you are looking for verses with which to oppress women, you will find them. If you are looking for verses with which to liberate or honor women, you will find them. . . . If you want to do violence in this world, you will always find the weapons. If you want to heal, you will always find the balm.

—*Rachel Held Evans*

ONE

Noble Wife Journey: a blog
Title: The Calling
Published: September 14, 2011

There is a message being delivered in Bower, Minnesota, and the world needs to hear it.

I want the same things as any other teenage girl: romance, love, adoration. I want a boy who will claim me as his own, who will win my heart and spend every day trying to keep it. But I know the way to find these things is not what the world tells me is so.

The secular world tells us to be selfish. It tells us to go after our own desires, seek pleasure, chase success, embrace what they call progress. And what are the results of this?

Broken families. Disease. Poverty. Despair.

What if there is a better way?

My church may be small, but my pastor's gifting is powerful. And with his permission, I am sharing his message with the world. This blog might reach ten people or ten thousand, but my purpose is clear: we are sharing a way for the next generation to learn from the mistakes of our elders.

So much of what is wrong with the world today is blamed on men. Like their centuries of achievement should be canceled out by the terrible actions of the few. As if my namesake, Eve, were not the first to eat the forbidden fruit.

No. If I want to see this broken world heal, it starts with me—with us. Women. In pursuit of the equality the world has told us to desire, we have sacrificed our very nature. We have corrupted ourselves, turned our softness into hard angles, filled our gentle mouths with harsh rhetoric. We have stripped off our strength and dignity in favor of anger and bitterness.

That stops with us. There is a movement among the girls in Bower, and we invite you to join it. We are setting aside the glossy magazines full of women with impossible figures we are taught to emulate. We are turning off the movies and TV shows that tell us to be more seductive, more carefree, more independent.

Pastor Rick tells us women are created to serve, to be pure, to submit, to be a delight to their husbands. Who are we to deny the very nature our Creator has built within us?

"A wife of noble character who can find?"

We will be found. We are the future.

I am following the lessons in Pastor Rick Franklin's revolutionary series. Every girl between fourteen and sixteen is invited to do the same in our church, and we meet weekly to go through the lessons. However, there is no age limit on this wisdom. If you want to, I will make it as easy as possible for you to follow along.

Subscribe to watch my journey, and you will see the results for yourself. I have faith.

We each have it within us to be a Noble Wife.

TWO

I AM GOING TO KILL my boyfriend. The carbonara on the table in front of me has taken on the sheen of lightly scrambled eggs, and his hard lump of steak has a pool of fat hardening in the center. Halfway through my second glass of red wine, and he is still not here. Word has spread with the waitstaff, because every time one of them passes, I see them steal another glance at the uneaten food before casting their eyes on me in pity.

I would hate them if I hadn't done the same thing back when I tended bar.

I haven't been stood up, I want to snap. *My boyfriend just has lots of things to do.* We've been together seven months, which is the longest I've made a relationship last in a while, and it's because I don't complain about meaningless stuff like him being an hour late to our dates. Although that has been happening more often than not lately.

Dan is very important. A medical student, he is always sure to mention.

A mumbled "There you are, Del" announces his arrival. His hand scrapes across the dark blond stubble on his jaw as he sits down, meeting my gaze across the movie-set-cold plates of our dinner.

I say nothing.

"What's wrong with you?" His tone is curious.

"You told me to order almost forty minutes ago."

Dan sighs. "I know, I was on my way out and Dr. Freedman caught me."

"You didn't tell him your girlfriend was waiting?"

His mouth tightens as he pours himself a glass of wine from the half-drunk bottle. He hates when I use labels. My question apparently doesn't warrant a response.

I stick my fork in the pasta.

"Don't eat that. We'll send it back."

"We can't send it back, Dan. They didn't do anything wrong."

He shows me his palm. "Calm down. I'll just explain the situation. They'll understand."

Heat stings my face as I watch him look around for a server. At last, he spots someone and waves her over. "Hi there. I'm sure you noticed our food has gone cold. I got caught up with something after she ordered. Can we get you to remake it for us?" He smiles the same way he did when we first met, when he came looking for a pair of shoes. Even in the too-bright fluorescents of the department store where I spend thirty hours every week, that smile hooked me like one of my dad's brightly colored fishing lures.

It's working on the waitress, too, annoyingly.

"It's fine, it's not your fault it's cold," I tell her. As much as I don't want to eat gluggy pasta, the thought of them rewarding Dan's behavior by making us fresh meals is worse.

He glares at me for half a second before turning the charm back on. "It would be such a big favor. Long day at medical school, and I could sure use a hot steak."

He hasn't apologized; Dan never does. The "sorry" is implied in his tone but carefully not stated. That way he can get you to do what he wants without ever admitting he's wrong. It took me a few months to notice.

The woman hesitates for a valiant three seconds before her shoulders relax in her starched white shirt. "Of course, I'm sure there's something the chef can do. I'll be right back." She picks up our plates, and then she's gone.

"Seriously, what is the matter with you, Del?" he asks.

"Me? You're the one who's demanding special treatment. If you don't want to eat cold food, don't be late." A warning snags somewhere inside me as I hear the venom in my words. I'm being too harsh. I try to dial it back. "I know you didn't mean to, but it seems unfair to ask them to throw out what was perfectly good food a half hour ago."

"I'm going to tip well."

That's true. He does do that, at least. I let out a tight breath. Nothing I want to say will make him happy.

"You know, you're being pretty dramatic. She said it was no big deal."

"She has to say that; you're the customer." My fingers close around the stem of my wineglass, and I tip another gulp of red into my mouth.

We sit in silence until the food comes. Dan thanks the waitress effusively before sawing into his steak. I twirl my fork in the glossy pasta, betrayed by my growling stomach.

"There, now isn't that better?"

It tastes divine, but I can barely swallow around the knot of anger in my throat. That tone. My lips pull up in what I hope is a convincing smile. Maybe if I keep eating, he won't try to talk to me. I take another bite, and another, and another, trying to drown my irritation with carbonara. But I can't drown out the sound of his knife squealing against the plate, or his mouth masticating that steak with the repetitious insistence of the animal it came from.

He picks up the knife to cut off another knob of meat, and I'm struck with the urge to reach across the table and stab it into his hand instead.

"You could at least say thank you."

I blink at him.

He gestures at my plate. "For not letting you eat that shitty pasta."

My lips part, but I can't force the words out. Instead, I pick up my fork and shove more food into my mouth, staring at him as I chew.

After another minute, he sets down his cutlery with a sigh. "You know what? I don't need this. I told you I don't like girls who are all emotional."

I say nothing.

His voice is calm, casual. "If this is how it's going to be, then I'm out."

"What? Dan."

That hand goes up again. "Don't. I've been thinking about this for a while, and you just made the decision really easy. We're done. Now finish your pasta, and don't make a scene."

And then I do the worst thing I've done all night.

I do what he tells me to.

"I'VE GOT EXCITING news!" my roommate, Jess, says before I can even get our apartment door shut behind me. Her face falls when she sees the tears on mine. "What's wrong?"

"Nothing, go on. I could use some exciting news. What's happening?"

She's obviously trying to look concerned, but her smile splits her face wide open. "Simon and I are moving in together!"

I freeze for a second. "Oh. Oh, that's great. Congratulations!"

Jess nibbles on the corner of her lip. "I know, I know. We should have talked about it first. But it just kind of happened. He asked me tonight, and I said yes before I could really even think about it."

I shake my head. "It's fine, Jess. So, are you moving out?" I shed my winter coat, drop my purse on the counter, and open the fridge to hunt for a bottle of hard lemonade. It's way too cold for a drink like that, but it's the only alcohol I've got in the house. Unscrewing the cap, I take several slow gulps before I notice she hasn't answered me.

When I lower the bottle, she isn't meeting my gaze.

"Jess." Then my shoulders drop. "You want me to move out, don't you?"

"Not right away! I mean, you don't have to. We can find a place for ourselves. It's just, you know, I've lived here for a few years and it would be easier if . . ." She looks up at me.

I stare back over the bottle and take another drink. "It would be easier if I stopped mooching off you and found another apartment."

"You're not mooching, Del. I've never thought that."

"But I only pay a third of the rent, and I'm guessing Simon can go full halfsies." I set down the bottle and sigh. "I'm sorry. I'm excited for you, and you're right. I only moved in here last year. It makes sense for you guys to stay."

Thirteen months ago, I found Jess through an ad at my favorite café. She had just started work as a law associate at a high-powered firm in downtown Minneapolis, so she could have afforded the apartment herself but didn't want to live alone. I called her, we met up for coffee and hit it off. I moved in two weeks later. Most of the roommates I had before her were various levels of civil acquaintance; she and I had actually turned out to be pretty good friends. Just over a year, and it's the longest I've lived in any apartment since I moved to Minneapolis. I shouldn't be hurt, but I didn't think she'd want to get rid of me so easily.

Jess's cheeks pull up in a smile that is distinctly more pitying than the one from a few minutes ago. "There's no rush, though. Really." She rubs my arm. "And you don't need to apologize. I'm sorry for springing this on you when you've obviously had a bad night. What happened?"

"Oh, nothing. I'm just tired—going to call it a night." There's no point in ruining her excitement. I can tell her all about Dan dumping me over waffles and coffee tomorrow.

Simon pokes his head out of her bedroom door. "Coming, babe? Oh, hi, Del."

I return his smile and look back at Jess. "Go on. I'll talk to you more in the morning."

She doesn't need much convincing. A few minutes later, she's safely shut away with her boyfriend in her bedroom, and I'm on my own with music playing, my laptop open, and a full bottle of hard lemonade in hand. I am tired—that part wasn't a lie—but I'm too wound up to go to sleep. A quick apartment search yields results too depressing to deal with tonight, and I quickly shut the tabs. I open Facebook next, scrolling through my timeline as I drink the sour alcohol.

It's been days since I logged in. The people on my account fall into four main categories: those I grew up with, extended family, people I went to college with, and coworkers from the various jobs I've had since I graduated. Dozens of girls have gotten married and changed their last names, and I don't even recognize half of the profile pictures on my timeline. It's why I barely ever log on here anymore—the word *friend* has lost all meaning.

I'm just about to close out the tab when I scroll to a picture that makes my heart tilt. It's been years since I've seen it in person, but the face hasn't changed: strong chin that never managed to stay free of stubble, full lips, light brown eyes. Lars Oback smiles at me from the screen. When I tear my eyes away from his face, I see the caption.

*Can't believe I just saw you last week, and now I never will
again. You were a bball legend and an even better friend. RIP
Lars. Gone too soon.*

Something hollows out inside me. Breathing hard, I click to view the
comments. It's more of the same: people sharing memories, broken-heart
emojis, RIP after RIP, and promises to pray for his family. When I get to
the end, I search his name. There are dozens of posts, almost all of them
by people I'm connected to from Messiah Church, where I grew up. It's
not a mistake, it's not a joke.

Everyone is saying the same thing: Lars Oback is dead.

My hands shake as I open another tab, searching for the local news
in my hometown. There is one short article, posted around noon today.

> Twenty-eight-year-old Bower resident Lars Oback was shot
> and killed while hunting early yesterday morning. The Green
> County Sheriff Department attended the scene and assessed
> the circumstances of the death, providing a brief statement to
> the public this morning.

A video is embedded in the article. I click play. Sheriff Wilson stands
behind a cheap-looking podium, florid cheeks shaking as he talks into
the microphone. "As you all know, our community was hit with the
tragic loss of a godly young man yesterday. Our department responded
to a 911 call from Lars Oback's hunting companion early yesterday
morning, saying that he had been shot. Upon attending the scene, our
deputies sadly confirmed that Mr. Oback was already deceased. They
interviewed his friend and spent hours investigating the scene. We have
determined that this was a tragic accident—a stray bullet, likely from a
passing hunting party."

The sheriff looks up from his notes. "Lars Oback was a husband, a
father, and a beloved member of Messiah Church, where many of my
deputies and myself enjoyed fellowship with him. Our pastor, Rick
Franklin, would like to say a few words as well."

Something moves at the edge of the screen, and then he's there, on camera. He steps up to the microphone next to Sheriff Wilson with his trim shoulders wrapped in an expensive suit, black hair frozen in carefully styled waves. Pastor Rick's jaw and cheekbones are sharper than I remember, but my nightmares have made it impossible to forget that voice.

"It is difficult to capture the depth of our sorrow, but fortunately the Word of God is here to help us. Psalm 118 says, 'In my anguish I cried to the Lord, and he answered by setting me free. The Lord is with me; I will not be afraid. What can man do to me?'"

He looks at the camera, and I feel his gaze slicing through me. I can't breathe. "I would like everyone to know that counseling services are available from the church at any time. Free for members, of course, and at a very generous rate for anyone in Bower who is struggling. We are here to help our community grieve and process this terrible, tragic accident."

The video ends there. A line of text appears below.

Services are as yet unconfirmed but will likely be held at Messiah Church, where Lars was a member along with his wife and baby daughter.

I stare at the screen until the words blur, becoming a fuzz of black on glowing white. It's real. Lars is dead. Lars is dead, and Pastor Rick has somehow managed to make it an advertisement for Messiah Church. Lars is dead, and my mother didn't even have the courtesy to tell me.

She let me find out on social media like he was just another person, some random resident of Bower, Minnesota, instead of the only man I've ever loved. I would have known something was wrong the second I saw her name come up on my phone. I could have used those seconds to prepare myself, to brace to hear her voice for the first time in months, not to mention the message she would deliver. But she never called.

Maybe it's for the best. I can't imagine her delivering the news without somehow implying it was my fault.

If you'd just been able to keep him happy, who knows how differently things could have turned out? Maybe you two would have been on a winter vacation and he'd still be alive.

My mom somehow believes that even my worst experiences were God's will, but also that they could have been avoided if I made better life choices.

I go back to Facebook, look at the photo of Lars again. It must be recent; he has aged since I saw him six years ago, but it suits him. The angles in his face are more defined, his eyes sharp and wise. His mouth is the same, and I'm struck by the memory of his lips on my neck. It's so strong that I close my eyes, momentarily drowning in it. I once thought I'd spend the rest of my life with him. I fell for him weeks into my freshman year at college, but it didn't seem strange at the time. Most of the girls I knew were married by junior year. For us, going to college was much more about earning the MRS degree.

It might have been years since I saw his face, but it hasn't been that long since I heard him speak. The voicemail he left only four days ago is still on my phone. I never returned it.

Guilt hits me viciously, too fast to stifle the moan of grief that escapes my lips. I swipe to my voicemail and open the message Lars left last week. Last week, when I thought things were fine with Dan. Last week, when I lived with a roommate I liked and felt like I was finally settling into some sort of rhythm. Last week, when he was still alive.

"You have one saved message."

Then his voice is there, the rich baritone that sent a shock of longing through my system when I first listened to it. I know that's really why I didn't return the call. I couldn't bear the fact that a part of me was clearly still in love with him after all this time.

"Delilah," he says, his tongue wrapping around my name in a way that used to give me goosebumps, "call me back. I need to talk to you. You . . . you were right. I'm sorry."

I stare at the screen as the robot asks if I want to save or delete the message. I end the call. Those are the last words I will ever hear him say. They're six years too late, but they're something.

I'm sorry.

THREE

Noble Wife Journey: a blog
Title: The Tenets
Published: September 15, 2011

There are five core tenets we are taught to live by in our pursuit of becoming Noble Wives, all outlined in Proverbs 31. Every lesson we learn will be in service of developing these traits now, so that we are well practiced in them by the time God blesses us with a husband.

They are so simple, yet so powerful. Pastor Rick says each one has the ability to change our entire lives if we let it. I wonder if you'll do them with me?

1. Be positive. Don't add to his daily burdens with trivial problems you can handle yourself.
2. Be pure. Purity extends past the wedding day: in all you do and say, live above reproach to avoid bringing shame on yourself or your husband.
3. Be caring. Showing care looks like keeping a tidy house, making delicious meals, and meeting the needs of your family.
4. Be hardworking. Your body and mind both require consistent work to stay strong and agile—don't waste time just because you're not "on the clock."
5. Be loving. You are the brightest spot in your husband's life; do everything you can to make him feel loved, respected, and cared for. Make yourself worthy of his praise.

Pastor Rick suggests we practice these at home with our families, especially our fathers and brothers if we have them, since we do not yet have a husband to try them with. That is what I will be doing this week: showing my father how positive, pure, caring, hardworking, and loving I can be.

Join me, will you?

FOUR

IT TAKES AN HOUR TO stop sobbing long enough to pull my face away from the pillow. I don't know if it did anything to muffle the sound, but Jess hasn't come to check on me. Probably too busy celebrating with Simon.

The memories keep crashing over me, like a wall of water I've been sandbagging for years finally breaking free. The first time I heard Lars's voice: the warm, open, West Coast vowels, so different from the nasally flat ones I had gotten used to in Minnesota. The first time he pushed my hair behind my ear, letting the pad of his finger trail down my cheek so lightly I wasn't sure if I imagined it. The first time we sat next to each other at a movie and his fingers edged closer until they brushed against my knuckles, testing for permission. Eventually, his rough palm was pressed tight against mine, sending a jolt of unrecognizable heat straight to my middle in a way I now recognize as lust.

I had so many firsts with him. He should have been my first everything. Now, he is just the first man I have loved to die.

Rolling over, I look at the patchy paint job on my ceiling through swollen eyes. In the corner, a daddy longlegs is huddled in a frail crouch. I've been meaning to kill it for days, but it won't be long before it starves, releasing its grip on the wall and gently floating to the ground to be picked up by the vacuum.

The newspaper article says the services for Lars will likely be at Messiah, and I think that's inescapable. My desire to be there for his funeral wars against my promise never to go back to that place again. I can usually avoid thinking about the last time I was there, except on the nights when I'm trying to go to sleep and my mind decides to feed me my most embarrassing memories in short, heated bursts. It would be bad enough to walk into that building again. Seeing Eve would be even worse. She'll be surrounded by members of the church, dozens of people fussing over her, ready to respond to her every need. As if she is the only person devastated by Lars's death. Her feelings are the only ones that matter.

That's how it's always been.

I moved from Boston to the small town of Bower, Minnesota, the year I turned thirteen: the worst possible time. I'd been there twice for Christmas at my grandparents' house, and then the trip for my grandpa's funeral the year before. My grandma struggled to live on her own but refused to move to a nursing home no matter how much my mom begged. She flew to Minnesota for weeks at a time to care for her mother until finally my dad found work at the biggest employer in the area, a local power company. They bought a house down the road from my grandma, and we moved in the last week of summer. I had six days to prepare for starting eighth grade in a new school. Junior high is a nightmare in the best of circumstances, but being the new kid in a town of two thousand—where the rest of the school had grown up doing summer sleepovers on each other's trampolines and celebrating every birthday together—was a catastrophe.

Then my parents sprang church on me. We'd never missed a Sunday as long as I could remember, but I thought my parents would at least give me a week to catch my breath.

I was wrong.

Messiah (which I would later learn nonmembers in the area called "the Mess") was the church my mom grew up in, but since her time in Bower, it had exploded. When Rick Franklin took over after the founding pastor's diagnosis of dementia a couple years before we moved, he turned it from a modest congregation to a wannabe megachurch that had merged with several of the other congregations in the town until almost half the residents attended.

Our first Sunday there, I slipped from the car in my black Skillet hoodie ("They're Christian!" I had told my mom that morning) and pulled the hood over my dull sandy ponytail to hide the zit that throbbed red and humiliating on my cheek. Mom strode eagerly ahead, modest heels clicking on the pavement, and I trudged behind in my worn, off-brand canvas sneakers.

Inside, the church was a riot of noise and sleek wood floors. It was a shock to the system, something I'd never seen before. There were children everywhere, running around in groups of four or five, playing hide-and-go-seek behind tables where people working in some sort of ministry were talking over Styrofoam cups of coffee. Mom was quickly sucked in by a woman in a white turtleneck with a simple green necklace around the collar. I ducked to the right toward the coffeepots.

It had only been a few months since I'd convinced my parents I was old enough to drink coffee, and I was relishing my newfound caffeinated liberty. Cup full, I searched the containers until I found powdered hazelnut creamer. There was only a light layer left in the bottom. I scraped together a scoop, then two spoonfuls of sugar, stirring them in. The steaming liquid transformed from murky brown to honey gold, and I blew across the top before taking a sip. I stepped away from the pots, looking around the room from under my lashes.

I was used to our old-school church in Boston—all disturbing Jesus-on-the-cross paintings and hard pews and maroon carpet. This one was completely different. It looked like a fancy conference center. It was light and open and full of people, and the coffee was good. I took another long drink.

"Aw, who took the last hazelnut?" a delicate voice behind me asked.

Prickles danced across the back of my neck. My eyes dropped to the liquid in my cup, and for a second I considered downing it even though it was way too hot. There was a poke at my side, and I whirled to see a girl my age, dark brown hair swept in a perfect bun with two strategically loose curls framing her petite face. She had a spray of freckles across her nose, which turned up adorably at the end. I had always wanted a nose like that instead of my own, which came to a stubby stop like Play-Doh that hadn't been fully pressed into the mold.

She stepped close to me and sniffed my cup, a mixture of mirth and something darker glinting in her blue eyes. "Aha! You're the culprit."

Then she laughed, curls dancing against her jaw with the movement. "I'm only kidding! Hazelnut is the best flavor. You have good taste."

I shuffled, trying not to make it obvious I was backing away from her. My own laugh was shaky as it burbled from my tense lips. "Oh, thanks. Um, sorry, I shouldn't have used it up."

The girl set her coffee cup back on the counter and shook her head as she looked at the rest of the choices. She wore a long black skirt that hugged her small waist and flared stylishly around her slim calves. Her top was pale pink, with a modest collar and capped sleeves that showed off her summer tan. I tried not to stare, but something sharp lodged itself under my rib cage as I looked at her. She was everything girls on TV were like, everything I would never be, and I missed most of what she said as her fingers hovered over the containers of creamer until she selected the amaretto.

"I'm Eve," she said, turning back to me. "You must be Allison Morrow's granddaughter?"

"Uh, yeah." I told myself to stop saying *uh* like an idiot. "You know my grandma?"

Eve lifted her cup to her perfect ruby lips and looked at me over the lid. "Of course. Mrs. Morrow has been a member here since before I was born. I'm on the rotation to visit her every week. She plays a mean two-handed whist."

"Oh." I blushed. This girl had seen my grandma more than I had.

Music swelled from the sanctuary. Like it was choreographed, everyone in the room stopped what they were doing and started toward the open double doors. Eve took a quick sip of her coffee and threw the cup in the trash, mostly full. "Time to head in," she said. Then she took mine from my hands, that glimmer in her eyes, and drained the last half while I stared.

"What the . . ."

Eve licked her lips and smiled, then let out her tinkling girlish laugh again. "Ah, that's what I wanted." Without another word, she linked her arm through mine and led me toward the sanctuary.

That wasn't the last time Eve took what she wanted from me. And now that she's lost the husband she worked so hard for, she's going to be unbearable.

But it's Lars. When I walked away from him for the last time, I swore I would never see him again—but I hadn't really meant it. I always believed we might have another chance.

No matter what happened between us, I can't just skip his funeral.

Finally, I sit up and grab the box of tissues by my bed. After blowing my nose a few times, I venture out of the bedroom to wash my face in the bathroom I share with Jess. My skin is puffy and red in the harsh light. In the kitchen, I pour myself a glass of cold water and drink it in long, slow gulps. I should just go to bed, but I can't imagine sleeping right now. I'm drained from the long, awful night, but my mind is racing.

It just doesn't make sense. Lars was more alive than anyone I ever knew. He wanted to be a pastor, wanted to live in Los Angeles or New Orleans, wanted to travel the world. Even when I had the opportunity to leave Minnesota again—return to the East Coast or go somewhere new altogether—I ended up only applying for a college that was twenty minutes away from Bower. Lars's parents encouraged him to dream big, but they still supported his choice of a small Christian college, even moving to the area so they could be closer to him. They had the kind of money that allowed for tropical vacations and European tours, while my family's biggest splurge was the time we rented a camper van and drove to Disney World. I'm twenty-six years old, and I've still never been on an airplane—a fact that would baffle Lars if he knew.

If he could know anything at all.

There are no more tears left in my body, but there's a fresh ache in my eyes and throat as I walk back to my bedroom. I open my closet and pull out the boxes on the top shelf. I don't have a lot of stuff. My wardrobe is mostly black T-shirts and jeans, with a dress or two for special occasions. Even though I've lived here for a year, the walls in my room are bare except for the theater programs from plays I've seen on rush tickets. When I started college, most of my stuff stayed at my parents' house, where I could come home and do laundry and pick up anything I needed after church on the weekend. The day I left Bower for good, I left my things too. I sometimes wonder if my parents kept them or if they put them out at their annual garage sale, trading my Christian rock CDs and emptied photo albums for a quarter.

The only stuff I still have from childhood is in this box, the diaries I wouldn't risk leaving behind. I'll never know if my mom read them when I was growing up. It wouldn't surprise me; there was no such thing as privacy in the Walker house. But I doubt she did, because there's no way she wouldn't have confronted me about what was inside. And the ones I wrote when I was at college never saw the inside of my parents' house. They remained locked in my dorm drawer until the day I threw everything else that I owned into two suitcases, sorted out my transfer paperwork, and left Moorhead too. In my twenty-year-old Plymouth, I blazed a trail of rage and loud music all the way to St. Paul, where my cool older cousin let me crash on her couch.

And that was how I started my new life. This life. A barely earned college degree that I don't use, a series of minimum-wage jobs, and seven apartments in six years.

Rubbing my eyes, I reach into the box and pull out the diary on top—the one from 2014. That was the year I started thinking I would marry Lars Oback, the year he would leave me halfway through. Almost every page in the second half of this diary is a mess of scrawled anger and bitter tears. I set it aside. Just for tonight, I want to remember the good times. I want to remember Lars the way he was when he loved me back. I pick up the 2013 diary, my freshman year at college. The first semester, Dr. Kirk's English class. This diary has been read more than any other, thumbed through on the nights when I felt loneliness like a physical lack: a gap in my chest, a phantom limb.

I might never recover from the boy I met today. He sat next to me in English, our very first day, and Dr. Kirk told us where we had sat would be our assigned desk for the class. I almost did a dance in my chair. The most handsome guy I've ever seen will be sitting next to me every Monday, Wednesday, and Friday for the whole semester. We didn't talk, but I know he noticed me too. When I looked around once, while Dr. Kirk was talking about expository essays, I caught him look-

ing at me. Not in a weird way. And he didn't look shy or embarrassed, like I would have. He just smiled and tilted his chin a little, nodding. I smiled back. He had his name written at the top of his notebook. *Lars Oback.*

Lars. I have whispered the name to myself a few times. I like the way it sounds, the way it feels on my tongue. I wonder what it would be like to say it to him.

Dr. Kirk probably thinks I'm stupid because I didn't speak up in class at all, even when he asked questions I knew the answers to. But all I could think about was the boy sitting next to me with the dark brown hair and the slightly crooked nose, like maybe he's broken it once before. I want to ask him what happened. I want to hear his voice. I want to know if he's happy he's sitting next to me too.

But obviously I can't make the first move. I just need to make sure I look good on Wednesday. I know what I'm supposed to do, and I'm not going to make any more mistakes. The ball is in his court. I'll wait for him to come to me, and hope that he wants to.

FIVE

Today, I made one of the stupidest mistakes of my life. I knew it was stupid during the whole drive from my dorm in Moorhead to Messiah, the first time I've made the trip since Lars dumped me last year. I knew it was stupid when I checked myself in the mirror, making sure every hair was in place and my makeup was flawless. I knew it was stupid when I got out of the car and walked across the slippery parking lot to the church office building, where the grooms always get ready.

But I went anyway. I was invited.

By sending that card with their hands overlapping, stunning diamond shimmering from hers, they knew what they were asking for. They knew what they were doing to me. Rubbing their happiness in my face, bringing me close enough to touch what they have without letting me have it. Well, I wasn't ready to just let them have it either.

Something came over me in the walk between my car and the office door. I stopped shaking, stopped worrying about what he would say. My anger boiled. I have never shown Lars how angry he made me. How much his rejection didn't just hurt—it infuriated me. When he left, I just let him go. Maybe if I showed him that I could be passionate too; I could write poetry and make him good meals and give him a warm set of arms to come home to every night. I could be everything Eve was, and more. He owed me that. He made me think that he loved me, and at the first sight of another woman—a better woman—he left without giving me the chance to fight for us.

That's what I was thinking as I strode past groomsmen and cousins and uncles until I got to Pastor Rick's office, where Lars was straightening his already-perfect tie in a large gilded mirror.

Seeing me in the reflection, he whirled around in surprise. Words lodged in my throat as I took in his handsome face, neatly shaved for once. A deep blue suit settled perfectly on his broad shoulders, his narrow hips.

"Del, I'm so glad you came," he said. His smile seemed genuine, but it wasn't the smile I had come to expect from him. It contained none of the old admiration, the love it used to radiate for me. Somehow, as kind as it was, that smile was the thing that knocked down all the confidence I'd built up in the past few minutes.

"Don't marry her," I said, tears falling freely. I shut the door behind me, grasping at my final chance to be alone with him. My feet carried me toward him, my arms reaching out. My whole body ached to be touched by him again. "There's still time to back out. I know you don't love me anymore, and that's okay. But don't do this. You will regret it if you marry her."

Sadness fell across his features, heavy as a stage curtain. He had stepped toward me, but now he paused, his outstretched hand drifting back to his side. "Del, please. You're better than this."

Even as the words sliced through me, I met his gaze. "I am not. I am never better than when I am loving you."

He sighed in exasperation. "You just can't say stuff like that to me anymore! We are not together. It's inappropriate."

"What kinds of things did she say to you when you and I were together?" I asked. My tone was too sharp; I know that now. But I couldn't help it. Esha told me Lars and Eve sent each other letters the summer before last, when he and I were supposed to still be together. It was Esha's last real act of friendship.

At least he looked a little bit ashamed. He knew he had done me wrong, even if he wouldn't admit it out loud. "That's in the past. Eve is about to be my wife, and if we've made any mistakes to get to this point, then God has forgiven us."

"What about my forgiveness? Is that not something you even care about?"

His gaze hardened. "Pastor Rick says that we can't force others to forgive us. A grudge only hurts the person who holds on to it, not the one it's directed toward."

I stared at him for a long time. "You're quoting Pastor Rick now?" For the first time ever, he sounded just like all the guys I grew up with. He sounded like a Messiah boy. He even had that same fervent glow in his eyes, that reverent tone when he said Rick's name. I was the one who had brought him here in the first place, but this transformation—that was Eve's fault too.

"It's not Pastor Rick; it's the Bible, Delilah. 'Love covers a multitude of sins,' remember?"

One of the pastor's favorite verses to use when shutting down intermember disputes. "It *is* Pastor Rick. I don't think you realize how much you've changed since you started going here, Lars. Messiah isn't good for you—it's not good for anyone. And Eve is not going to be good to you either. She only cares about herself. She loves herself. She will hurt you, I promise you that."

It was the most critical thing I'd ever said about the church, and in the pastor's office no less. I looked up at the corner of the ceiling, as if there might be a camera recording me. When I looked back at Lars, anger glinted in his eyes, a spark so rare I had only seen it a couple times when we were together.

"Get out," he said. "How dare you speak about her that way? Leave. Now. And do not come to the ceremony."

My mouth fell open, a fresh wave of tears streaming down my face. Someone must have heard the anger in his voice through the door, because it opened and then there was a firm hand on my arm. Caleb, Lars's cousin. He was gentle but insistent as he pulled me out into the hallway. The mortification I should have felt at being dragged away from my ex-boyfriend on his wedding day was overcome by the pain stabbing into my heart from all sides.

It took me a long time to be able to drive, but once I did, I didn't stop. I drove straight through Moorhead and Fargo, on and on until I got to Bismarck. I could have kept going. I could have driven to the Black Hills, to Montana, to Washington. I could have driven to the Pacific Ocean and seen it for the first time before just driving right in. But finally I turned back around. By then, I knew what I wanted to do.

I packed up all my things at college, sent an email to the registrar's office with the form to transfer, and called my cousin Alexis. And now I'm here at her house in St. Paul, more than two hundred miles away from everyone I know, wishing it was farther. But at least I've finally done something. I'm starting fresh.

I am never going back to Bower, Minnesota.

SIX

I AM GOING BACK TO Bower, Minnesota.

The last straw happened yesterday at work. I've been barely scraping by selling shoes thirty hours a week at Lou's Threads, a modest department store wedged between a Whole Foods and a Panera Bread right off I-694. I was halfway through my shift yesterday when the manager announced that they were making budget cuts, and that meant everyone would lose one shift a week until sales improved.

Maybe it was the fact that Dan dumped me this weekend, or the news about Lars, or that I'm about to be homeless, but something snapped.

"Actually, don't worry about cutting back everyone's shifts," I said. Then I took off my tacky purple uniform vest and dropped it on the floor like I was Norma Rae. "They can take my hours. I quit."

And I walked out before Chris and his creepy, barely there mustache could say anything in reply. It was the most powerful I've felt in years, and I got to enjoy it for approximately nine minutes before I completely freaked out.

It's not hard to get a job in retail right now, but the terrible pay and complete lack of benefits are the same everywhere. Still, I've got a tiny bit of savings, and if I move out right away, I won't owe Jess rent next month. I've got enough to scrape by for a little while, if I eat crap and don't go anywhere.

Which is why it's stupid that I'm already halfway through driving the three hours to Bower, but I can't help it. I have to be at Lars's funeral.

A Smashing Pumpkins song blasts from my car stereo. Because I was only allowed to listen to Christian music as a kid, I didn't discover the Pumpkins and a hundred other nineties and early-aughts bands until after I finished college. Unlike other people my age, I don't listen to these songs to relive nostalgic memories.

I listen to them because now I can do whatever I want.

A green truck flies past me on the left, even though I'm going ten over on the freeway. People around here drive whatever speed they think they can get away with. In my rearview mirror, partially obstructed by boxes in the back seat, the road is clear.

Everything I own is in my car. It took me less than two days to pack it up, since all the kitchenware, decorations, and furniture in our apartment belong to Jess. She gave me a tight hug and even had misty eyes when she said goodbye, but I was too wrung out emotionally to do anything but smile and make a lukewarm promise to visit soon. I don't know if I really will.

That's how it goes for me. Most of the friends I've made since college are relationships of convenience. I run into them in the places we met: work, shared living spaces, theater. And we make no effort to see each other outside of that. The only reason I even saw Dan again was because he came in to ask me out three days after he bought that pair of shoes. It's the most romantic thing he ever did for me.

Bower is small enough that the road signs only mention it when you're getting close. The one that tells me I've got twenty miles to go sets off the warning in my gut. To get there, I'm passing through Elden, which is where I've booked a cheap motel to stay the night. I couldn't stomach the idea of staying in Bower. I'll backtrack to Elden after the funeral, which I expect to go late. Messiah Church doesn't do any ceremony fast.

Ten minutes later, I crest a hill and see the broken-down farmhouse on the right that's been there since I was a kid.

A two-exit town with no visible businesses from the freeway, it's easy for folks to drive right past Bower. I turn on my blinker and take the first exit, passing a truck stop famous for its venison roast.

I run a hand through my short, bleach-blond hair, fingers coming away sticky with the styling wax I used this morning. It's even more defiant and spiky than usual, miles away from the long sandy hair I had when I lived here. While my mom would call my hair and makeup garish, my one concession to the Messiah culture is the simple black dress and black tights I'm wearing. It's too cold for anything that shows skin, and I'm going to be dealing with enough sidelong glances as it is. There will be new people at the church, after all this time—people who don't know who I am. But the core attendees from my childhood will all be there too.

Hardly anyone leaves the Mess. Not voluntarily, anyway.

Every Sunday, a thousand or more people gather across three services in the morning and one at night. Bower itself is a town of only a couple thousand, plus another few hundred on farms in the surrounding area, and almost no one drives farther than ten miles to attend. Basically, if you live in Bower, you either go to Messiah . . . or you have a really good reason not to. Almost all the other church options in the area have disappeared in the past few years, closing due to lack of attendance or merging with the Mess.

Pastor Rick always said the church is the Body of Christ. But when it comes to Messiah, I know better than anyone the rotting, porous skeleton underneath the healthy facade.

A chemical taste fills my mouth—the coppery tang of blood even though I haven't bitten myself. As I drive into the first residential neighborhood within the town limits, I see the large houses separated by massive swathes of open land. Trucks parked in wide driveways, swing sets and basketball hoops in front yards. Even though it's below freezing, there are still kids out in their yards: kicking a soccer ball, riding bikes, playing tag. No adults in sight. Helicopter parenting was never really a thing here. When kids go out, they always come home.

I slow the car as I pass Hamilton Park. The playground equipment has changed in the decade and a half since I last played on it, not surprisingly. They got rid of the metal slide that burned a layer of skin off your thighs in the summer and the jungle gym that went so high it's a wonder no one ever broke their neck. Esha, Eve, and I used to play here when they came over, since it's only a five-minute walk from my parents' house. I glance down the road that would lead me to them.

They still haven't called to let me know about Lars. For all they know, I'm still unaware of his death. My dad and I haven't spoken in over a year—Mom and I even longer than that—but I still can't believe they didn't tell me. As much as I wish I could avoid them completely, I'm sure I'll see them at the church. The building is big, but my mom doesn't miss a thing.

I have some time, so I turn down their road. The lights in the house are off, and the garage door is open, the car gone. I'm sure if I walked up to the house, I would find the door unlocked, just like it always was growing up.

"That's the thing I missed the most when we lived in Boston," my mom used to say. "Trusting people. Around here, everyone knows you and you know everyone. You don't have to worry about anyone trying to hurt you."

It didn't take long for me to find out that wasn't true.

I take a few side streets to get back to the main road. Election Day was last week, but several lawns still proudly display campaign signs. I recognize a few of the faces, people who have been in local politics as long as I lived in Bower. There's a new mark on some of the signs, though. I squint, pulling my car over so I can read one near the road.

FRANKLIN ENDORSED appears in the top left of most of the signs. The only ones missing the logo are for people I don't recognize—presumably people who aren't members of Messiah. I snort, trying to shrug off the unease clutching at my shoulders. Just like a lot of evangelical pastors, Rick Franklin plays a little fast and loose with the laws around churches getting involved in politics. A quick search on my phone shows the results of the last election. Every Franklin-endorsed candidate for the city council won by a landslide, and Messiah members now make up two-thirds of the school board.

My phone vibrates, reminding me the funeral starts in thirty minutes. With a deep breath, I start driving again.

Messiah is in the center of the town, the building and parking lot taking up an entire city block. Even though I'm early, the place is already packed. Volunteer parking attendants are out in their matching jackets and orange visibility vests, waving sticks like they work on an airport tarmac. I follow their directions and squeeze into a spot that seems like it's a mile away from the entrance.

Clusters of families and friends approach the church from their own vehicles dotted around the parking lot. Getting out of my car, I huddle my chin in the light scarf wrapped around my neck, but it still feels like there's a spotlight following me. This is something I should have gotten used to at the Mess, but I never did.

The automatic doors whisper open as I get closer, and a blast of heat hits me in the face. Messiah welcomes its guests with a huge, diamond-shaped foyer featuring high ceilings and glossy wood floors. This place is always full, with groups gathered around bar-style tables drinking the free beverages offered by the kitchen, children zooming in and out of adults' legs, and several strategically placed greeters who blend in with the everyday churchgoers until they break away to welcome newcomers to the fold. The acoustic effect is extraordinary.

On Sunday mornings, with the welcome music floating through the speakers and several hundred congregants fueling up on coffee before the hours-long service, this place sounds like a stadium before a big game. It's exciting, electric. It makes you feel like you're part of something.

Today, the mood is much more somber, although there are even more people than the last Sunday service I attended. There is no requirement in evangelical churches to wear black to a funeral, but movies and TV have done their job influencing our behavior, and almost everyone is. So the one person in the room wearing color stands out like Goliath on the battlefield.

Eve Oback is near the entrance to the sanctuary, a cerulean dress pulling at her shoulders, nipping in tight at her hips, which are more rounded than they were when we were teens. A young girl with white-blond hair sits on her hip, clinging to her. I know from her posts that she had a daughter a little over a year ago: Emmanuelle. The Noble Wife blog is still going strong, with thousands of loyal readers all over the world, obsessed with following the story of a woman who completely devoted herself to the Noble Wife philosophy and received every reward that it promises. She got the perfect life, the perfect marriage, now the perfect daughter. And I'm one of the few who know what she destroyed in order to get it.

Our eyes meet across the room, and her full lips part in surprise. She tries to hand off her daughter to the woman standing next to her, but the girl shrieks and buries her face in Eve's neck. I turn away like I didn't notice her. Even though I'm already jittery, I walk toward the coffee station. Something about the way Eve looks bothers me. Blue was Lars's favorite color, so I'm not surprised she chose it for his funeral. But something is off; I just can't think of what it is. It's been years since I've seen her. She was bound to look different than I remember.

On the other side of the room, Lars's parents are talking to a couple I don't recognize. The sight of Susan Oback with tears running down her face makes me ache. It's been years since I spoke to her, but I still feel protective, as if she was the second mother I always thought she would be to me. As far as I know, the Obacks never became members of the Mess; I can only hope those are tears due to grief rather than a passive aggressive comment from some church member.

I dump a spoonful of sugar and enough milk into my cup to cool the infamously lavalike Messiah coffee, stirring it around. Over the lid, I glance around the lobby. So far, Eve is the only one who seems to have noticed my presence. By some miracle, my parents are nowhere in sight. Maybe they're visiting my dad's family in Pennsylvania. I can't imagine any other way they'd miss this.

The service will start in a few minutes, and I'll sit in the back. Maybe I'll manage to get through the whole thing without anyone else taking notice.

Only problem is, I won't be able to find out why Lars called me last week without talking to Eve.

For the first time, it occurs to me that she might not even know he did. Embarrassingly, it makes me smile. I might know something about Eve's husband that she doesn't. Something that could hurt her. A betrayal. Wouldn't that be interesting?

"Delilah? Delilah Walker?"

My skin heats at the sound of my full name. I've gone by Del ever since I left the Mess. I always liked *Delilah* when I was a kid, but like so many things, the people here ruined it for me. The week after we moved to town, we had a meeting with Pastor Rick to welcome back my mother to the community. I remember the way his lip curled after my parents introduced me.

"Delilah? We're going to need to do something about that."

Despite her unquestioning respect of pastoral authority, I could see my mother bristle. She and three friends in Boston had all been pregnant around the same time, and they wanted to use biblical names, of course. The only problem was, every other kid in the church was a Mary or Hannah or Joshua or Luke. They wanted to be more unique, so they made a pact to reclaim the names of some of the less reputable characters in the Bible by raising children who would give them new life. I became Delilah, and my best friends were Judas, Rahab, and Magdalene.

"Delilah is a good girl," my mom had insisted.

Pastor Rick waved her away. "It will make some of the other parents uncomfortable, understandably. You might not have had any issues yet, but she's a teenager now." When his eyes settled on me, my skin buzzed unpleasantly. "You need to be vigilant."

My dad said nothing, which was his way. Adam Walker, the quiet husband.

Finally, Pastor Rick tapped his desk. "Still, of course, I'm aware she's gotten used to being called something her whole life. So we won't change it too much. *Lila*, how's that? Pretty, isn't it?" The way he stared at me, I knew I had to respond.

"Yes."

That week in youth group, I was introduced as Lila. And from then on, no one—not even my parents—called me Delilah.

Not until I was sixteen.

Shaking off the memory, I turn to find the source of the voice. Colette James, one of the youth leaders in charge of girls back when I was a teenager, is standing behind me. She looks much the same: weak brown hair in a frizzy braid over one shoulder, small bladelike nose making her pinched face look even sharper. I never knew a woman who wanted to get married as badly as Colette did, nor one who was less likely to find a man who lived up to her high standards. A quick glance at her empty ring finger shows me I was right.

"Hi, Colette," I say, lifting my head. I realize I've been hunched down in my scarf this whole time, trying to hide. Can't have her noticing that.

"Well, what do you know?" she says in a voice that must carry halfway across the growing crowd in the foyer. "Aren't we blessed to have you back in the house of the Lord? It's been way too long."

The words are as pointed as her nose. They sound friendly, welcoming, but I know they're chosen carefully. It's much more satisfying to call someone a backsliding heathen to their face, but that's not how things are done here.

And that's certainly not how things are done at a funeral, which I intend to remind her of. I force my expression into a sad smile. "Yes, such a shame it isn't under more pleasant circumstances. I still can't believe what happened. Poor Lars."

Colette's gleeful smile cracks lightly around the edges. "Oh, absolutely. We have had a twenty-four-hour prayer chain going since Saturday. Such an incredible tragedy."

"What happened?" I ask, wishing I didn't have to get this information from her. Giving Colette any chance to feel like she knows more than I do is a mistake. "The sheriff just said it was an accident."

She sighs, one hand clutched to the gold cross necklace dangling from her buttoned blouse collar. "That's right. He was out hunting, and someone must have been going for a deer nearby. Such a terrible tragedy."

My forehead creases. If someone thought Lars was a deer, wouldn't they have gone looking for it after they took a shot and realized what they'd done? "I don't understand; was he not wearing orange? Lars was always so careful when he was hunting . . ."

"It's natural to want an explanation when such an awful thing happens, Delilah. We don't understand the Lord's plan, but that's what faith is for, right?"

It's a way to shut down my questions and a test at the same time. Do I still have enough faith to say the random freak death of a man I loved could be part of God's master plan? I don't, but not for the reasons she thinks.

Despite everything I went through in the Mess, I still believe in God. I just don't believe he decides whether we live or die. The way we were taught, everything that happens is part of God's plan, so if you die, it's because he "chose to call you home" for some reason. When I was a teenager, I asked one of the youth leaders if that meant God was using serial killers and mass shooters, and I got sent home for being impertinent.

Finally, I answer her. "I've gotten used to accepting there are a lot of things I don't understand." It's noncommittal, but I'm done with this fake conversation. It's only been three minutes, and my skin is already crawling.

Fortunately for me, the ushers choose that moment to open the sanctuary doors. A flood of music pours out. Among other things, Messiah is known for fostering incredible musical talent. The stage is decked out with people holding various instruments—even more than there were last time I was here. The song they're playing is gorgeous: sad but hopeful, tender while still holding its power. It has that quality of all great worship songs, making me feel like both weeping and conquering the world.

"Going to find a seat," I say to Colette, and then I walk toward the sanctuary. By now, I can definitely feel other eyes on me.

Colette's attention has gotten me noticed.

SEVEN

Noble Wife Journey: a blog
Title: Purity
Published: September 16, 2011

On the subject of purity, the Bible is very clear. Women have been given an incredible gift, and with that comes a terrible responsibility. Our bodies are created to be ravished, adored, enjoyed. But only by one man—our husband.

Pastor Rick explains this with an object lesson, which he likes to do. He says that's because Jesus taught all his greatest lessons in the form of a story.

He takes two pieces of construction paper: one cut in the shape of a man, and one cut in the shape of a woman. On the woman, he runs a stick of glue over the center of her. Then, he joins the two paper bodies together.

"This is what happens when you give your body to a man," he says. "Sex binds us to the other person because it's a spiritual union as well as a physical one."

After a few minutes, he picks up the paper people again. "Now, imagine this is a dating couple. They have gone against the Word of God and joined together physically before being married, and now they decide they aren't right for each other. So they separate." He tugs at the papers, trying to pull them apart. Even though he's careful, the two pieces rip, and parts of the bodies are still stuck together.

"When you have sex with someone, a part of you always stays with them. Now, imagine you do this again and again while you are searching for your partner. Imagine the souls and bodies of other men building up on you, never to be scrubbed away. That is why it is so important to be pure, to wait."

The day he did this object lesson in our Noble Wife class, all seventeen of us girls followed along in the purity pledge Pastor Rick taught us. We promised to keep ourselves virtuous and holy until our wedding days, so we could present ourselves to our husbands without the residue of other relationships clinging to us. We were blessed with rings commemorating this incredible ceremony. I wear mine on the ring finger of my left hand, where it will stay until my future husband replaces it with his own.

The purity pledge isn't just about sex, although that is important. It's also about how we dress and carry ourselves in church and school. Pastor Rick explained that our bodies have been perfectly designed by God, but because of the Fall, they also represent one of men's most difficult temptations. That is why we have such a strict dress code at Messiah Church. When he explained the way boys think, the way their minds take photographs of our bodies without being able to help it, only to tempt them again and again, it all made sense. I'll never complain about having to wear shorts over my swimsuit or not being allowed to wear tank tops again.

We're girls now, but our bodies are becoming those of women. It is our responsibility to be sure we aren't causing our brothers in Christ temptation. Doing this will set us apart, prepare us for the next step. Get us ready to become Noble Wives.

EIGHT

I DO MY BEST TO blend into the crowd of mourners making their way to the main event. While everyone starts for the chairs on the ground level, I make a right and go up the stairs to the balcony. There are only a few people up here so far. I ignore their glances and walk through the shadows to a seat at the front left corner. From here, I can see the stage and the first several rows of seats below.

In the center of the altar area at the front of the stage, a polished black coffin sits surrounded by white and yellow roses in large vases. Even from a distance, I can make out the waxen quality of Lars's skin, the unnaturally neutral expression on his face. It's all wrong. Lars was passionate, intense, excitable, hilarious. He made me laugh more than anyone I've ever known. It's unfair of me, but I'm furious at whoever got him ready for this. They have sucked all the life out of the man I loved, and I know that makes no sense considering the situation, but I am struck by the urge to run down there and slam his coffin shut rather than look at that unrecognizable face one more time.

I can't believe Eve would let this happen. She claimed to love him so much, to be so much better for him than I was, and she couldn't even protect his dignity when he was at his most vulnerable. She is easy to spot in the front row, a splash of blue in an ocean of black and gray. Her parents are sitting on one side of her, her sister, Esha, and daughter on the other. They are all facing forward, not talking to anyone.

That's when I realize what was bothering me earlier. I haven't been to many funerals. People here seem to live forever. But in the few that I attended, the grieving family was always surrounded by members of the church, making sure they had water and tissues and a hand to hold. That was one of the things I actually liked about belonging here: you never had to look far when you needed someone.

But just as she was outside the sanctuary, Eve is practically alone by the church's standards.

I don't understand. Eve and Lars were Messiah's poster couple for the Noble Wife movement. Up until a couple years ago, he was the worship pastor here, and everyone knew her from the blog. More famous than anyone else in the church besides Pastor Rick Franklin, they were a huge part of driving the attention and donations the Mess received. While a thousand people attend in person every Sunday, Messiah's messages are live-streamed online and often watched by church congregations all over the country. Pastor Rick's message clearly resonates with people, and Eve is a big reason for that.

And now the whole Messiah community seems to be holding back from her. It's not something a nonmember would probably even notice, but I know what it looks like when this church starts to turn its back on you.

Before I can consider what she might have done to warrant this kind of rejection, the music evolves into singing, and the congregation stands in a chorus of rustling clothes so familiar it makes me sweat. I haven't been inside a church, any church, for three years. I tried a few places in the Cities after I moved, but I only lasted a couple weeks before I started ignoring my alarm clock and spending the morning in front of the TV like the heretics I'd grown up judging. Everything was just too familiar. The music, the language, the overeager smiles. I had determined to leave that behind when I drove away from Eve and Lars's wedding, crying so hard I could barely see.

Yet here I am.

I stand, stiff, with my hands in fists at my sides as the worship team goes through several songs. Messiah treats funerals like any other church service, and I know it won't be long before Pastor Rick comes up to deliver a message and talk about Lars's life. Anxiety is already tearing its way through my gut. I taste acid in the back of my throat.

I should never have come here. Even after all this time, I wasn't ready. As if to torture myself more, I look back at the coffin again, at the cold face of my ex-boyfriend. Something inside me shatters. It isn't right, him being there. His baby daughter squirming next to his wife, whose mouth is open in song as if her husband isn't lying dead right in front of her. It makes no sense.

There's a box of tissues on the floor in front of me for just this reason. I reach down and grab a handful, lowering my chin as I wipe my face. I can feel that there are more people behind me now, that the balcony is filling up, but no one has come into my row. I'm sure I should be offended by that, but instead I'm thankful. I don't want to be close to any of these people. I don't want a reassuring hand on my shoulder, the whispered prayers of a stranger in my ear. I just want to be alone, but I know if I walk out now, it will be worse than if I stay.

After a few minutes, the final words of the song taper off, and I see movement from the corner of the stage. Pastor Rick is climbing the stairs, face a solemn rock under his perfectly coiffed hair. In a sharp black suit and silver tie, he's much more dressed up than he would be on a Sunday morning, where his tailored jeans and untucked collared shirts make him every inch the cool, Gen X pastor.

My stomach flips as he makes his way onto the stage, weaving between members of the worship band who are still gently playing their instruments. When he reaches the front, the music fades. It's a finely honed production, but it feels effortless. Like the music is naturally coming to an end to make way for his words.

"Today, we are not grieving," he starts.

His voice rings through the speaker above my head, beating against the blood pumping in my ears. It's that same firm, chiding tone he used on me in his office when I was sixteen. That same stoic expression he had when he spoke the words that were a rope thrown into the tempest of my life.

"Confess to me."

And I can't do this. I can't sit here and listen to it. I shift in my seat, ready to fake a coughing fit so I have a pathetic excuse to run out, but suddenly there's a family of seven filtering into my row. It must be the last available spot in the balcony. With the wall on my left, I'm trapped. I sit back, my breath coming in sharp gasps.

Pastor Rick continues. "Instead, we are celebrating the life of a dynamic young man. Someone many in this church family were proud to call a friend, a brother, a son. It is never easy to lose someone we love, least of all someone with so much life ahead of them. But the Bible tells us that our earthly lives are only temporary, that the eternal paradise with God is what our spirits are longing for at all times. That is why this world is so imperfect, why it is so easy to feel anxious or discontent. Our spirits are missing our heavenly home. Lars is home now, with his Father, and he would not want us to mourn. He has gone to the place we all yearn to be, the place where our hearts will finally know true peace."

I hold a tear-soaked tissue to my mouth, trying to control my breathing before I get sick. The message shouldn't surprise me—I've heard it several times before. But after years away from the church, it now seems cold. Lars was an elder here. He came to Messiah as a young adult, first as a visitor with me before becoming a member when he started dating Eve. The last I knew, he was a close confidant of Pastor Rick's. Christians have always struggled to tread that fine line between grieving someone they've lost and acknowledging they're now in eternal paradise, but this just seems heartless.

"There have been a lot of questions about what happened, as there always are when someone so young is called home to Jesus. God has created us with curious, inquisitive minds, and there is nothing wrong with that. However, I'm saddened to see that some rumors and untruths have made their way through this congregation. As we well know, gossip is a sin like any other, and something we should all condemn when presented to us. I know these stories have caused the Oback family great pain, so let me be clear. Last Saturday morning, long before dawn, Lars bid his loving wife, Eve, and beautiful daughter, Emmanuelle, goodbye, and he went hunting. I know a lot of you were out in the woods yourself—it's almost sacred, that first weekend of deer season. I had to miss out this year due to a speaking engagement, but my brother promised to split his venison with me when he got one, praise God."

A low chuckle goes through the congregation, turning my stomach.

Making jokes from the pulpit to lighten up serious moments isn't unusual, but it seems especially cheap to do it at a funeral.

Pastor Rick's smile fades. "Sadly, Lars was struck by an errant bullet, and he passed away before help could arrive. It was a tragic, terrible accident. The sheriff is a member of Messiah, as you all know, and he has reassured me that his men are doing everything they can to make sure nothing like it happens in the future."

My mother would say it's because I'm biased. I've got a reputation for distrusting what Pastor Rick says, in her opinion, "just for the sake of it." But it's strange that he's spending several minutes of a funeral sermon reassuring the congregation that Lars was killed by accident. I can't be the only one who thinks that.

Hunting accidents are rare, but they do happen, especially when people go to a crowded hunting ground. Lars was always cautious, wearing all the right gear and sticking to his section, but that doesn't mean someone else wasn't reckless.

Still, it just doesn't feel right. Everything Pastor Rick says sounds suspicious to me now, his message ringing hollow in my ears. Ten years ago, I would have been comforted by the idea that a person I loved was dancing in heaven instead of suffering here on earth. But right now, I can't accept that he's gone, despite the deathly mask in the coffin below. I just want to talk to Lars. I want to rewind the clock and call him back the night I got that message. I want to know what he was going to say to me. What I was right about.

Now I'll never get the chance.

NINE

Delilah's diary

I was wrong. Wrong about everything. It's over.

TEN

THE FUNERAL SERVICE SEEMS TO go on for hours, but finally, the closing music trails off and people start to file out.

At the bottom of the stairs, I'm greeted by the savory aroma of roast chicken and scalloped potatoes. My mouth waters; I was too nauseated to eat breakfast this morning. I should just get in the car and go to the motel, but I'm here now. I committed to honoring Lars. If I stay, I might get the chance to talk to his parents, see if they have any hints as to why their son called me. And a free meal is not something I'm in a position to say no to at the moment.

I scan the foyer, which has been set up with round tables of eight during the service. There are two long buffet tables stuffed with food, and people are already lining up. Eve and her family are standing off to the right, deep in conversation. Her sister, Esha, looks up and catches my gaze. Even from several yards away, I can see that her deep brown eyes are red with tears. As far as I know, Esha still lives in Minneapolis, where she went to college. She's one of the few people in my grade who isn't still a member of the Mess. Like Eve, she was adopted as a baby, but unlike her, she has golden brown skin that makes her unmistakably *not* the biological child of her adoptive parents. She never talked about whether she was bullied for being South Asian, but I would be shocked if it didn't happen. It can't have been easy for her to grow up here, with only a handful of people of color around. Even though she always seemed devoted to the church, I'm not surprised she left Bower for good when she went to college.

But she's here now, and she looks absolutely shattered in a way that tugs at my chest. Esha had mostly been kind to me, and I hate to see her in pain. I attempt a small smile, which she briefly returns before someone steps in front of her to offer their condolences, blocking my view.

The Obacks are standing close to the Thompsons, receiving handshakes and embraces from everyone passing by. While they're busy and the lines are still short, I head toward the buffet.

Potlucks at the Mess are nothing to sniff at. Part of being a good Noble Wife means learning how to cook, and most of the girls I grew up with not only make tasty food, but they have their own signature dishes they bring to every event. As I walk down the line with my plate, I see Angela Culpepper's caramel rolls, Celia Brown's taco hotdish, Barb Smith's loaded potato skins, and Jessie Nichols's seven-layer salad, which for some terrible reason has both mayonnaise and marshmallows in it. I never settled on a dish of my own before leaving; it's the kind of thing most girls establish after they get married.

I take some of everything that doesn't mix candy and salad dressing, and then I turn to find a table. My plate comes an inch away from running into someone.

"Mom." The word is snatched out of my mouth before I can hold it back. She's gaping at me, fingers clenching a coffee cup that looks like it might break under the strain.

"What are you doing here?" she asks.

The words sting, no matter how much I deserve them. "I had to." My voice sounds sticky. I take a sip of the punch in my left hand, swallow hard. "I had to say goodbye."

"So, this is what it takes to get you home," she whispers after a subtle glance around to make sure no one is within earshot. "Good to know what the standards are, if I ever want you to return one of my calls. Someone has to literally be dead."

My lips settle in a hard line. "What calls? You didn't even call to tell me Lars was dead. I had to find out on Facebook."

Her gaze flicks down, then back up to my face. "You look thin."

I say, "Thank you," and immediately hate myself for it. It's not a compliment, even if she means it as one.

She eyes my plate. "You didn't take one of my brownies."

"Oh, I didn't see them." That, at least, is true. My mom makes the best brownies in the church; I'd never skip one on purpose.

Ignoring the line, she strides to the buffet table and picks a brownie off a green platter in the center before returning to plop it on my plate. "There."

"Thanks." I glance around, looking for an escape.

Noticing this, she grabs my arm and starts walking. "You'll sit with us."

"Oh, Mom, I was going to find—"

One sharp look over her shoulder shuts me up. "Young lady, I will not have my daughter return to church after six years and not sit with me."

Letting out a breath, I follow her and take a seat at a round table with three other people: my dad and an older couple I recognize but can't name.

Dad, at least, greets me with something resembling warmth, but that might be for their friends' benefit. "Delilah! You're here."

"I'm here." I set down my plate and walk around my mom's chair to give him a kiss on the cheek. It's rough, familiar with the scent of his shaving cream.

He smiles at me briefly, then turns back to his friends. My mom stays seated for approximately three minutes, saying nothing as I start to pick at my plate. Then she's up and walking around again, chatting with people and making sure everyone gets food. Ironically, this is as close as I could get to my wish: eating alone.

For a moment, I watch her talk to an elderly woman wearing a crocheted vest weighed down by a gaudy brooch. My mom's face has transformed in the moments since she stopped looking at me: she is all light and passion and joy now. This is how she's always been at church, but especially at Messiah. These are the people who supported her when her father died, and again when her mother passed a few years after we moved here. This is her second home, her second family, but it was never her second priority. When she wasn't at church or in one of her prayer groups or Bible studies, she was talking about it. My dad was never quite as zealous, but he supported her completely. We were a church family, and besides that blip when I was sixteen, I was happy to be part of it. Until I wasn't.

When I look at church through my mom's eyes, I can understand her love for it. Her closest friends, her unwavering faith, and her most meaningful life moments—all wrapped up in one place. When she needed a meal or advice when I was sick or help with something around the house, she had hundreds of people she could call who would drop everything to be there for her.

It was nice. Is nice. The constant support and encouragement are the best parts of belonging to a church. As long as you don't do anything to screw it up.

"Delilah?"

I set down the last bite of my dinner roll at the sound of Susan Oback's voice. Lars's parents are standing behind me, teary-eyed and pallid but smiling. I push out my chair and stand to give them both a hug.

Mrs. Oback clings to me, and I sink into her embrace: the closest thing to a mother's hug I've had in years. Her hair smells like cookies. Baking was always her response to nerves. The night Lars brought me over to meet them, she had two different cakes and a tray of snickerdoodles ready to greet me.

"Hi, Mrs. Oback." I was raised to call any married adult by their title and last name.

"Susan, please," she says, pulling away. "Nathaniel and I hoped you would be here, although we would have understood if you decided not to come. We always felt you were part of our family."

I always wanted to be. I bury the thought in a dark corner of my mind.

Nathaniel Oback pats me gently on the shoulder. "It's nice to see you, Delilah."

"You too, Mr.—Nathaniel."

We take a few steps away from the tables, toward a quieter part of the lobby. "Do you come home often?" Nathaniel asks.

"No." I lower my gaze for a moment. "This is the first time since . . . since their wedding."

There is a hint of pity in his eyes. He knows what happened at Lars's wedding, then. Of course he does. Lars told his dad everything. Nathaniel looks around the room, wincing. "I never did understand what Lars saw in this place. No disrespect, but it just always seemed so incestuous."

Susan puts a warning hand on his arm. "Nathaniel."

"Well, I'm sorry, but it's how I feel." He crosses his arms, shaking her off. The shoulders of his dark suit bunch around his neck. His voice is lower when he speaks again. "I don't like this, Susan, and maybe Delilah is the only one who will understand."

"Understand what?" I ask, matching his quieter tone. "What's going on?"

He leans in closer. "No one is telling us anything, that's what. Everyone keeps saying how sorry they are, how it's such a terrible accident that happened, and we can't even get a meeting with the medical examiner to ask about the autopsy. The sheriff told us Lars was shot in the chest from less than a hundred yards away, but he can't explain how they don't know who did it."

"Wait, they don't know who shot him?" That can't be right. "I assumed they just weren't telling the public."

Nathaniel shakes his head. "Not as far as we can tell. Lars and the guy he was with were hunting on private property, so no one else should have been around. The sheriff says they've cleared his friend, but he won't tell us who Lars was hunting with, and nobody else seems to know. We can't get a straight answer out of anybody. Seems like every time we're at the station, that pastor is there too. All just going on about *how sad*, they'll have to post some more safety ads on the hunting groups on social media. It's not that we think anyone wanted to kill our son, but everyone's acting like they're hiding something."

Susan's hand rests between her husband's shoulders, rubbing back and forth slowly. "I'm sure they have their reasons, Nat. It's only been a few days. We have to let them do their jobs."

His chin drops, just in time for a few tears to fall, splashing the wood floor. "I guess. I don't know. I'll never get used to the small-town life. Everyone knowing each other just makes me feel like they have more reason to keep secrets."

Tell me about it. I nod sympathetically, words lodged in my chest. Nothing I can say would be particularly helpful right now. As far as I'm concerned, Nathaniel is right not to trust the people in Bower. It would make sense for the sheriff to protect the identity of whoever Lars was hunting with, but he should at least tell the family.

Susan speaks again, her voice gentle. "You'll have to forgive Nathaniel. We're both a bit fragile when it comes to Messiah at the moment, considering everything Lars went through the past few months."

My gaze snaps to hers. "What was he going through?"

Tears pooling in her eyes, she says, "We don't know that much. Lars didn't want to speak poorly about the church, but he seemed really down the last few times he called us. A couple weeks ago, he told us he'd been formally removed from his position as elder."

"What?" I forget for a second to keep my voice down. Becoming an elder in Messiah is a big deal. I still remember Eve's blog post from the day he was welcomed into the role, a little over two years ago. The way she dripped with pride at his accomplishment. Men were only removed from elderships if they or someone in their family committed a grave sin.

"*You were right*," he said on my voicemail. Maybe he was talking about something to do with the church.

"Do you know why he was removed?" I ask.

Susan dabs at her eyes with a crumpled tissue. "He never told us. Just said he didn't want to talk about it, but he thought we should know."

"I know why," Nathaniel says, his voice gruff. "It was that pastor, Rick. I'm sure Lars said something to challenge him, and the man couldn't handle it."

"Now, we don't know that," Susan says.

"Susan, Nathaniel," a familiar voice cuts in. My heartbeat picks up. Pastor Rick has appeared beside us, and even though Nathaniel was whispering, I'm sure that he heard. My face feels hot, and I can see Susan's is red also, but Nathaniel is unapologetic, chin lifted high. "I thought I'd come see if you want one of our young people to prepare you a plate of food."

I keep my gaze down, trying to edge away.

"Delilah." He turns to me. "How wonderful to see you. It's been far too long."

The dig is expected. "Hi, Pastor Rick."

"Nice of you to join us, although I wish it could be under better circumstances. We will miss Lars so much."

My mouth is too dry to respond.

Pastor Rick looks back at the Obacks. "What can we get you? Some chicken? Potatoes? Mrs. Henderson makes a wonderful green bean hotdish."

"I'm not hungry, thanks." Nathaniel's tone is clipped.

"Maybe later, then," Pastor Rick says, not losing his preacher's smile. "If you need anything, please don't hesitate to ask. We're here to serve you." For a moment, his blue eyes fix on mine. I'm struck by the sudden urge to go to the kitchen, put on a white apron, and start clearing plates. When you're a teenager in Messiah, you don't get to enjoy any of the after-service lunches. You're there to fill drinks and clean dishes. I realize that today is the first day I've sat at one of these round tables with a plate of food; we always ate in the kitchen after the adults had been served.

My feet stay planted on the floor, and finally, Pastor Rick gives me one sharp nod and walks away. I let out a breath that had been stitched in my throat since he arrived.

Nathaniel grabs my wrist, so tight that I gasp. And then he's pulling me out of the foyer, down the hall toward the Sunday school rooms. I have to jog to keep up.

"Nat, what are you doing?" Susan races after us. When I look back, I see dozens of heads swiveled our way, taking in the afternoon entertainment.

We round a corner and Nathaniel pulls me into an empty room. There are rows of chairs set up, facing a small stage. This is where the drama club used to meet, where I practiced skits that delivered Gospel messages to people who already believed them.

Nathaniel's eyes are bright, almost manic. I glance at Susan as she pulls the door closed behind us. Her husband draws me close, his face only a few inches from mine. "Delilah, please. You know what it's like here, what the people are like. There must be a reason you left and didn't come back until now. Something isn't right. Can't you see that?"

"I . . . um . . ."

"Nathaniel, you're scaring her. Stop it!" Susan pulls her husband's arm, trying to get him to let me go.

"If this was just an accident, why is everyone acting so strange? Why hasn't Eve even called us since it happened?"

I gawk at him. Eve never wrote much about her in-laws on her blog, and looking in Nathaniel's eyes, now I know why. Apparently, there's at least one other person in the world who doesn't think she's God's gift to womankind.

I came here for answers, and it turns out the parents of the man I loved have even more questions. Tears burn in my eyes. "He called me last week," I whisper.

"What did he say?" Susan asks sharply.

"I don't know. I was at work and . . . I never called him back." Shame washes over me at her stricken expression, but I do my best to push it away. After Lars dumped me, I called him and called him, left a hundred messages. He never returned one. I hadn't intended to leave him unanswered forever like he did me, but I thought he could deal with being made to wait. It was spiteful, petty. The kind of behavior my mother would identify as the reason I can't keep a man.

Hoarsely, I say, "He just left a voicemail. I was hoping you would know what he wanted to tell me." I take my phone out. Lars's voice makes all of us tense up, as if he has just walked through the door.

"Delilah, call me back. I need to talk to you. You . . . you were right. I'm sorry."

After staring at my phone a moment, I look up at them. Susan has buried her face in Nathaniel's shoulder. He has one hand wrapped around her, stroking her hair, as the other wipes the tears off his own face. "I wish I could tell you what he meant, but I don't know," he says. "All I know is that something isn't right here. You can feel it, too, can't you?"

I nod, slip my phone back in my purse.

"You know we didn't even find out about what happened until six hours after Lars was killed?" Nathaniel's fingers rub his forehead. "The sheriff waited until Rick Franklin could drive back into town from some conference. He wanted the pastor next to him when he came to our door. As if that would provide any comfort."

I use the sleeve of my dress to pat my face; it comes away soaked with tears. "I'm so sorry."

The pain in his eyes is almost unbearable to see. "My son was dead for *hours*, and because of the people in this church, I didn't even know. My gut tells me there's more that they're hiding. Lars made it clear to us over the years that they don't trust outsiders. That's why he always wanted us to come here, be part of his church family too. But we just couldn't. The church isn't supposed to be a place of exclusion. We never saw eye to eye on that, and now it's—" He cuts himself off, trying to rein in his emotions. After a moment, he says, "We know you're not a member any-more, but can't you see if anyone will talk to you?"

"She's not a detective, Nat," Susan murmurs.

He steps away from her, raking a hand through his thinning gray hair. "I don't know what else to do, Susan! Trying to get anyone in this town to open up is like trying to walk on water."

"I'm not a miracle worker either," I say. "I haven't been to Bower in six years. I barely talk to my parents anymore, much less anyone else here. I don't think anyone would trust me with their secrets."

"But you do think they have them."

My laugh is bitter. "Oh, yeah. No one has more reason to keep secrets than someone who goes to Messiah."

His gaze holds mine, heavy with grief. "I just want to know what happened to my son. If, God forbid, someone killed him on purpose, he deserves justice."

My vision blurs with tears. All I want is to run out of this room, out of this church, get in my car, and keep on running. It's what I'm good at.

"I want to know what happened to him too," I whisper. "But I don't know if I can help."

"Please." His hands rest on my shoulders, gentle this time. "Please, try."

I look between him and Susan, take in their broken faces. They were always kind to me. Susan even called me the week after Lars ended our relationship. She told me she thought he was making a mistake, that I was welcome in their home anytime. It was one of the few things that helped me feel like I wasn't totally out of my mind for thinking he and

I were supposed to be together. His mother had seen it too. They were there for me in my darkest moments.

Suspicion of Messiah is nothing new for me, but the way everyone was acting around Eve today was bizarre. Nathaniel is right; I know what these people are like, and there is something more going on here than just a simple hunting accident. I doubt that I will be able to find anything, but I have to at least try. For the Obacks and for myself. I want to know what happened to Lars, what he was going to tell me when he called. But I'm not ready to make any promises yet.

"I'll see what I can do."

Nathaniel closes his eyes in relief, and Susan smiles grimly. "Thank you," she says. "Now, you go ahead and get back out there. I'm going to stay here with him for a few minutes, see if we can't calm down."

I nod. "I'm so sorry, again. For everything."

As they walk toward a pair of folding chairs, I head out the door. If I turn left, I'll soon be out in the lobby with the hundreds of mourners again. Or I could turn right and sneak out the back exit next to the nurseries. A crappy motel bed and cable TV are calling to me.

I turn right. The wide hallways pass several Sunday school rooms and the largest restrooms in the building. There's a private prayer room that's mostly used by the elders when someone needs individual counsel and a breastfeeding space that I've never been in.

Rounding the corner, I start for the nurseries, which won't be occupied today. Parents keep their children with them for funerals. Something about facing the reality of our temporary existence on this earth. I'm just about there when I hear murmuring, and I freeze.

Just ahead of me, a door is half open. I would continue past, but I recognize one of the voices. The delicate, just-shy-of-whiny tone. It's Eve. And whoever is answering her is a man.

Holding my breath, I inch toward the door. I pause just outside, peer through the crack under the hinges. Eve is standing in profile, arms wrapped around her body, head bowed and tears on her cheeks. That part isn't a surprise. The man who's with her is.

He's just as tall as he was when we were teenagers, but he's filled out enough to be intimidating instead of scrawny now. I knew him as Keith

Rivers, a senior when I was a sophomore and Eve was a freshman, a guy all the adults thought was well-behaved when most of us knew he was just good at getting away with things. Now, most people know him as Pastor Keith—the associate pastor and Rick Franklin's protégé.

And he's leaning in close to Eve, pulling her to him, one arm around her waist and his other hand on the back of her head, cradling it against his chest. He glances in my direction.

My lips part in shock, and I stumble away from the door. The hallway is dark and the crack I was looking through is tiny, but there's still a chance he saw me. Without pausing to look back, I race toward the exit. There's no sound to indicate I'm being followed, but I burst through the door and run into the cold fading light as if the hounds of hell are after me.

ELEVEN

Noble Wife Journey: a blog
Title: Provision
Published: September 17, 2011

Sisters, do you ever find yourself stressed? I am only fifteen, but I see the drawn faces of some of my female teachers and the shadows under the eyes of the women working the cash register where my mom and I shop.

All this time, energy, and effort we have put in for the better part of a century, just to be allowed to work. Are women really happier now that they can do the same jobs as men? Does it satisfy us, clocking in and out or working the standard nine-to-five, leaving our homes and lives vacant while we're away?

I don't see the appeal, and I'm glad to be told that there is another option. A better one, in fact. One that is as ancient and timeless as the wafer-thin pages of the holy book on my desk.

The Noble Wife series instructs us that if we have married a godly man, he should be able to provide for us. That means instead of padding the pockets of another executive, we wives can pour our energy and richness into our own homes. That is why women were created, our perfect design.

What a gift we were given—one that the world has spent centuries trying to convince us to squander.

Our work still has meaning, even if we don't receive money for it. We are paid in the gratitude of our husbands, in their cheerful provision for us, and in the pride of seeing the direct results of our efforts in our own homes. Healthy meals, clean and beautiful living spaces, happier families.

Not that you can't also earn money. I am personally teaching myself how to make jewelry, which I might one day figure out how to sell online or in the local stores. The woman in Proverbs 31 makes clothing to sell in the market.

She laughs without fear of the future.

Now, doesn't that sound better than going to a minimum-wage job with a boss who doesn't respect you and coworkers who don't share your values?

TWELVE

ELDEN IS A FIFTEEN-MINUTE DRIVE from Bower, and I spend every one of them trying to think of another explanation for what I saw. Pastor Keith was counseling Eve. He was praying for her. He was comforting her after the sudden death of her husband. All those excuses would make sense to an outside observer, but I know better. In Messiah, a woman is never supposed to be alone with a man who isn't her husband. There is an exception for pastors—I certainly had my share of one-on-ones with Pastor Rick—but they were always in his office, with his secretary just a few yards away on the other side of the door.

Not that she protected me.

Patches of dirty snow pass by in a gray-white blur as I speed down the highway. It's not that I can't believe Eve would have an inappropriate relationship with another man. The flawless purity she projected was always a facade, just like it was for all of us. But sneaking off with another man at her own husband's funeral? That never made the list of terrible things I thought she was capable of. Apparently, I've underestimated her.

A curl of suspicion starts to form in my gut. Lars died under mysterious circumstances, and his wife is cuddled up on another man just days later? That is not a coincidence.

I take the exit for Elden just as the sun slips down past the horizon.

Shaped like an L, the motel is just off the highway. The main office sports beige siding a shade lighter than the rest of the building, and the light in the sign that announces "Free WiFi" is flickering. Inside, there's a worn sofa in front of a coffee table that has several people's initials scratched into it and a half-full jug of filtered water with paper cups in a dispenser on the side. The reception desk is the nicest thing in the room—a giant mahogany antique that looks like it's been here since the town was founded.

Behind the desk sits a plump Black woman with her hair in tight white coils. Besides Esha, she's the first person of color I've seen today. It's been so long since I spent time around here, I forgot just how white rural Minnesota is. Maybe Elden has started to become more inclusive; from what I've seen, Bower certainly hasn't.

"Hi, dear, need a room?" she asks, peeking over the top of the desk. The blue light of her computer reflects off square-framed red glasses.

I smile at her. "I made a booking. Del Walker?"

She types something and nods. "Here you are. Room seven. That's our best one." She winks, handing me a metal key attached to a wooden disc with the number seven on it. "Just staying the one night, then?"

I take a breath. Something is going on with Eve, with the church, with this whole situation. Seeing her alone with Pastor Keith made that clear. I don't know if I'll be able to find out what it is, but at least I've got enough distrust of Messiah and the people who belong there to not take whatever they say at face value.

"I know I only booked for one night, but I might need to stay a little longer. Is that okay?"

"Sure, baby girl, we're never fully booked unless there's some kind of event in town. Just let me know by nine a.m. each morning if you're planning to stay another night so I can tell our housekeeper. If you stay longer than three nights, the rate goes down to forty per day."

I let out a breath. I should have asked Nathaniel for some money, although that would have been humiliating. Reluctantly, I hand the woman my credit card. "You can put it on this. I'll be staying at least three nights, so if I can get the lower rate, that would be great."

"Can do." She swipes the card, gets my signature, and hands it back. "I'm Harriet; me and my husband, Bobby, own this place, so don't hesitate to ask if you need something. There's cold cereal and coffee right here in the lobby every morning from seven to nine. Vending machine's outside to your left. And if you're looking for a hot meal, you can't go wrong with Elaine's. Don't even have to get back in your car; it's just two buildings down, the place that looks like a little yellow cabin."

"Thank you." I wheel my bag out, smiling at her over my shoulder. The doors to each room are along the outside walkway, which is bordered by a planter box full of cold soil.

I don't know if number seven really is the best one like Harriet said, but it's warm at least. The decor is classic seventies—orange carpet and dark green walls—but it looks and smells clean. I heave my bag onto the luggage holder and check the bathroom. There's a wrapped bar of soap and a tiny shower, with a thin white towel on the rail.

Satisfied that I'll be able to sleep here, I run some gel through my hair, trying to make it look less flat, and then I head back out into the darkening November night. I'm not that hungry, considering my heaped plate of potluck food, but I would kill for a strong drink.

As soon as I walk through the door of the brightly colored restaurant, I'm greeted by the warmth of a wood-burning stove in the corner and the spicy aroma of home-cooked marinara sauce. Sure enough, an A-frame black chalkboard advertises spaghetti and meatballs as tonight's special. A short man in his sixties pokes his head over the glass display case in the entry, which is filled with a dozen or so pies in various stages of wholeness. The chocolate peanut butter is clearly the most popular, with only one slice remaining. It's got my name on it.

"Just one?" he asks.

"Yes, please. A booth if you've got one."

He leads me there, and I take the side that faces the door. Even though I'm in the next town over, there are plenty of Messiah people who come to Elden for dinner out or a chance to shop at one of the big-box stores that Bower lacks. The man drops a menu, says he'll be back with water, and walks away.

Shrugging out of my coat, I look around. I'm not sure who Elaine is, but she clearly couldn't decide between a diner or a bar, so she made her place a blend of both. My booth is in the center of the room, next to a wall with a large glass window that stretches almost the whole way across the center of the restaurant. On my side are booths and tables, with several people enjoying an evening meal. Through the window, there are smaller booths and high-top tables, as well as a glossy bar lit by hanging lamps with colorful glass shades. There's almost no one on that side, but it's early yet. A guy in a blue flannel shirt stands behind the bar, writing something on a clipboard.

The host brings me a glass of water. "Your server will be with you soon."

"Hey, can you save me that last piece of chocolate peanut butter pie?" I ask.

He winks at me. "Yes, ma'am."

I smile back, then turn to the menu. Most Midwestern diners rival the local paper with the number of pages in their menus, but Elaine's is an exception. They offer six options for breakfast, ten for dinner, and a small selection of appetizers and bar snacks. The sign when I walked in said they'd been around since the eighties, so everything must be good. There's a waffle dish with bacon and burnt butter ice cream that I make a mental note to order when I come back hungry tomorrow.

After a few minutes, a woman in jeans and a black T-shirt stops to take my order. I ask for coffee and a strong rum and Coke, making sure she knows about the pie.

I pull out my phone. There are a few missed calls from my mom. She'll be mad I ducked out without saying goodbye. She left a voicemail, but I delete it without listening. Jess sent a text to check on me, which I reply to with a thumbs-up emoji.

There are no messages from Dan. A little part of me has hoped he would call or text for the last few days, but I know he won't. Dumping me was not something he needed to stop and put any real consideration into. Dan always trusts his gut. He's done.

I should be relieved. I know what it's like to love someone, to be infatuated with them. Thinking about them every spare moment, wanting to tell them all the random stuff that happens to you throughout the day. That's how it was with Lars. Even when we weren't together, we spent hours on the phone or texting every night.

But that was seven years ago. I'm ready for it to happen again, and with every ended relationship, I feel like it never will.

"You look like you could use the bottle."

The bartender stands next to my table, a tall glass with brown liquid in one hand and a bottle of Captain Morgan in the other. His smile is cocky but warm, flannel shirtsleeves rolled up to the elbow. He sets the drink in front of me.

"What gave me away?" I ask.

"Well, for one thing, I know how boring it is to eat alone. For the other, you're dressed all in black and look like you just got smacked upside the head by life."

I chuckle and take a long drink. "You're not far off."

"I hope you've got someone to keep you company, then."

It should be embarrassing, admitting that I don't, but the way he's asked makes me think he doesn't hope that at all. I shake my head. "Nope."

"Hmm. That's a shame." His smile is a beacon on this dark, awful day. "Do you . . . *want* company?"

My heart hammers. I wish I could be cool, that I knew how to handle a man's attention with something that felt like more than just desperate gratitude. "You won't get in trouble?"

"Boss won't care." His grin gets wider as he plops into the seat across from me, producing a lowball glass from under his arm. He pours himself a shot. "Cheers. To the end of a crappy day."

After hesitating a moment, I clink mine against his. "Amen to that."

"What did you order?"

"Chocolate peanut butter pie."

"Mm, good choice." He takes a slow sip of his rum, full lips hugging the rim of the glass.

I try not to stare, but having worked in about a thousand food service jobs, I can't help being nervous for him. Never in my life would I have sat with a customer when I was bartending, much less shared a drink with them. Any boss I've worked for would have had a coronary.

Finally, I can't hold it in anymore. "Are you *sure* it's okay for you to sit with me?"

The kitchen door opens, and a woman walks out carrying a plate with the pie and a scoop of vanilla ice cream, as well as a steaming mug of coffee. She sets them in front of me. "Enjoy. This guy isn't harassing you, is he?"

"No, no, he's fine," I say quickly.

"Finn, when you get a chance, Joe says that right burner is on the fritz again."

The bartender nods, taking another drink. "I'll have a look at it later. Thanks, Denise."

"Don't let him keep you from your pie, now," she says, and then she walks toward another table to clear the dishes.

The guy she called Finn gestures at my plate. "You'd better listen to Denise. That ice cream is homemade; try it with the pie, there's nothing like it."

"So, you must be the manager or something," I say, cutting a thin slice of the fudgy pie with my fork. I dip it in the ball of ice cream, then slip it into my mouth.

He smirks at what must be a look of pure delight on my face. "Owner, actually. Family business. I took over from my parents a few years ago. Good, huh?"

I chase the bite with a sip of rum and Coke. Binging on sugar is its own kind of therapy. "Delicious."

"My grandma's recipe. The famous Elaine."

"God bless her." I swallow another bite, keenly aware that he's just sitting there, watching me eat. "Um, so, did I really look that pathetic before?"

"Not pathetic. Just sad. Like maybe you needed to talk to someone. I'm having a quiet night, and I've been told I'm a good listener." He takes another sip of his drink.

I pause. Maybe it's the booze warming my blood, but I feel bold. "So, you came over and offered me a free drink because you were bored. That's the only reason."

"Who said it was free?"

I look from my glass back to him and laugh. "Come on."

"Okay, okay. You want honesty? I work here six days a week, sometimes seven, and almost all my shifts are at night. Elden has about fifteen thousand people and I feel like I'd recognize every single one of them. I don't get a lot of chances to meet a beautiful woman. Is that what you want me to say?"

My cheeks warm further. "I mean, only if it's true." I can barely believe the words coming out of my mouth. For once, flirting feels natural. Like something I'm almost good at. With Lars, I had no experience at all. I barely made it through our first few conversations without hyperventilating. Every guy since has taken the lead. The most I've ever done to put myself out there was the three weeks last year when I caved and joined a dating app. Even then, every chat with a guy felt stilted and awkward. They either came on way too strong, sending crude emojis or worse, or they could barely keep a conversation going because they were even more shy than I was.

This feels different. I'm comfortable, relaxed, even with this good-looking guy watching me eat and calling me beautiful. I wrap my fingers around the mug, take another drink.

Finn sits back, the pad of his pointer finger tapping slowly on his glass. His eyes are on my mouth. Without stopping to overthink it, I lick my lips, tasting a hint of rum but thankfully no chocolate that would indicate I had food on my face. One side of his mouth turns up in a smile.

Twenty minutes later, we've covered family dynamics, jobs, and favorite TV shows. Finn pours a shot of rum into my coffee cup. I cheers his glass again, and we both take a long drink.

"So, I see my grandma's pie has improved your mood. But you really did look upset when I came over here. Want to tell me what that was about?"

"I'm fine. Just a bad day. I . . . Did you grow up here?"

He blinks, lower lip pushed out. "Yep. Like I said—family business."

"Well, I just visited the town where I grew up for the first time in more than six years, and for the worst possible reason. An old friend of mine died. I just came from his funeral."

Finn's eyebrows rise. "You were in Bower. For that guy—the one who got killed in a hunting accident."

My jaw tightens. "That's the one."

"Wow, I'm sorry." His gaze lowers to the glass in his hand. "It's been in our paper here too. Just awful."

"It is," I say carefully. If there was anywhere rumors would spread that the accident wasn't really an accident, it would be the next town over. "It's also hard to believe. I knew Lars pretty well. He was always really careful, and he was on private property. There shouldn't have been anyone else there besides his friend, and the sheriff apparently cleared him."

Finn's tongue runs across his top teeth, and he holds my gaze for a moment, as if considering what to say next. Finally, he says, "I don't know the details, obviously, but I guess if someone was illegally hunting on private property, that would be a pretty good reason not to come forward. Especially if they knew they'd killed someone, even if it was an accident."

"That's true." I take another sip of rum. The answer is simple, but it's not satisfying. That's not a good enough reason to disregard it, though. "You said it's been in the paper here. Do they have any theories?"

Finn shakes his head. "A friend of mine is a journalist there, and she interviewed the sheriff. All they'll say is they're confident it was an accident and they hope to eventually find out the circumstances of the shooting. They don't plan to release the name of the friend he was hunting with or whose land they were on. All she knows is it was a farm about fifteen miles south of Bower."

My mind races, trying to think of who owns a farm in that area. Dozens of Messiah families live out in the country, and half of them would call their places farms even if they don't actually grow anything besides their own vegetables.

"They're hiding something," I say.

"Who?"

"The sheriff's department. My mom has told me a thousand times that I see everything that happens in Bower as some kind of conspiracy, but you agree with me, right? It doesn't make any sense for them to keep the identity of the person who was hunting with Lars that day a secret."

Finn's lips tighten into a grimace. "I don't know. Maybe they don't want anyone thinking he did it if they've already cleared him. I guess I can understand that."

That's never seemed too important to police before, though. I've seen plenty of stories where the full names of witnesses or friends of victims were provided, with the justification that they were simply the facts of the case. Especially in a small town, surely there were people who already knew who Lars was hunting with that day. It would only be a matter of time before word got around, unless someone was actively trying to stop that from happening.

That's what I'm worried about. Because the only person I know who wields that kind of influence in Bower is Pastor Rick.

Even thinking about him knocks the wind out of me. I push my coffee cup away, tears filling my eyes. I should never have promised Nathaniel Oback that I would look into what happened to his son. I've given him false hope. If Pastor Rick really is pulling strings to hide what happened to Lars, I will never be able to find out the truth.

"Hey, you okay?" Finn reaches across the table, his warm hand pressing into mine. "I'm sorry—I shouldn't have said anything. We can talk about something else."

I shake my head. "No, it's not that." A wave of emotion surges through me, so overwhelming I almost can't breathe. In the span of five days, I've been dumped, pushed out of my apartment, quit my job, had a snippy argument with my mom, and lost the only man I've ever loved. I keep shoving down the despair, hoping it'll just go away, but that clearly isn't happening. Instead, I'm now three drinks in and ready to lose it in front of a nice guy I barely know.

"Oh, crap, I'm sorry." The words are barely out before I'm hunched over in the booth, arms on the table with my face buried in the sleeves, tears already soaking through. I try to breathe through my nose to avoid making this any more embarrassing by actually wailing out loud.

A moment passes before I feel a gentle hand on my shoulder, warm fingers rubbing circles. It's too intimate, too soon, but I'm surprised at how good it feels. Finn is quiet as I let the sobs have their way for a while, until I can finally breathe normally again. Before I lift my head, I reach for a napkin and wipe my face, hoping I've cleared away the worst of it. Then, I look up at him.

The pure kindness of his smile makes my heart hurt.

"Well, that was humiliating."

He waves it off. "Psh, you're like the third person to have a breakdown in here today. The first one was a waitress, and she stormed out, which means I'm coming in at four a.m. tomorrow. The other guy was a customer. He threw a chair across the room because we skimped on his whipped cream. So, you're pretty low on the drama scale, actually."

My laugh sounds wet. I grab another napkin, blow my nose. "Well, if you need someone to fill in until you find another breakfast waitress, I make a mean pot of coffee."

Finn pauses. "Are you serious?"

I look up at him. I had been joking, but it isn't the worst idea. At least this way, I could pay for my motel without destroying my savings account.

"Sure, I guess. At least for a few days. I'm not sure how long I'll be in town, but I could use the tip money while I'm here."

"Have you waitressed before?"

I smile darkly. "I'm a twenty-six-year-old with a useless college degree. What do you think?"

Finn smacks his hand on the table. "You're hired."

THIRTEEN

Delilah's diary

The summer is almost over! I never thought I would be excited for the last days of July, when I'm usually soaking up hours of sun at the lake with Esha and Eve, eating our weight in watermelon and putting on way too little sunscreen. We didn't get our usual summer, though. Esha only visited from college for a few weeks and spent the whole time with her family, and Eve has been acting weird around me. I know she went to a prospective student night at MCC a few months ago, and I wonder if she feels like she'll be tagging along now that she's going to the same college I do.

Whatever. I'm just excited to go back. It's been seven whole weeks since I saw Lars, and I can't wait for him to wrap me in his arms again.

I've never been the world's best journaler, but I feel bad for not updating this more. Looking back, I guess I mostly tend to write when I'm sad, and I haven't been sad for like a year. But one day, when Lars and I are married and looking back on our relationship, I'll probably wish I recorded everything that happened. All the sweet, impossibly adorable things he said to me. All the times we stayed up late into the night, talking about what we wanted for the future and where we'd like to travel together. We used to do that all the time, even when only a few buildings separated us at the dorms in Moorhead. But now, with his summer job as a youth pastor, he's barely had any time to be on the phone. We get by on a few emails a week, sometimes with a late-night Messenger chat thrown in. I can't wait until we're back together and pick up where we left off at the end of spring semester.

We talked for over an hour tonight, and I still feel like my whole body's glowing. He said he's been thinking a lot about the calling on his life, and the ministry work he's done over the summer has really clarified what he wants to do. He plans to finish college next year and pursue a job in the church somewhere. Maybe as a worship leader! I think that's perfect, and I told him so. Listening to him sing in our college group was one of the reasons I fell in love with him. Not only that, but it made me fall in love with worship again. The energy that pours from his guitar when he's on that stage, eyes closed, face turned toward heaven. It's nothing short of divine.

He told me that to do what he feels called to, he needs a partner who will love and support him in good times and bad. He needs someone who will be willing to live on not very much money, who will take care of the house, who can find creative ways to scrimp and save. When he was saying all this, I swear I was grinning from ear to ear. It was like he was describing me. One of the first things we talked about when we were becoming friends was the outfits I wore to class. I never buy anything full price. Every item of clothing is from a thrift store or a sale rack, but I am an expert at making things work.

I think that was what he was saying to me on the phone tonight, confirming that he knows I am the woman for him. This is his last year of college, and I can take the hint that he will be ready to settle down after that. That means he will want to get engaged soon. We've only been together for eight months, but that's longer than a lot of my friends' relationships. There were plenty of couples at Messiah that got married at nineteen, and they still seem blissfully happy. There's no point waiting when you know it's right.

I still have three years of college left, but who knows? Maybe I'll need to drop to part-time so I can support him while he gets started in whatever ministry job he can find. Associate pastors don't exactly rake it in, but that's okay with me. I would be content to live in a tiny studio and put together delicious meals on dollars a day as long as I could be with him. I will show him what an incredible wife I can be.

Three weeks. Three weeks until I head back to Moorhead and we can be together again. I wonder if he'll propose right away. I wonder if he's already talked to my dad. Oh, shoot. Now I'm going to find it impossible not to look for hints every time we talk over the next few days! I can do it, though. I want to be surprised. I don't want to ruin whatever moment Lars has planned for me.

FOURTEEN

DRIVING AROUND TOWN IS A tour of my past. There's the candy store I used to ride my bike to every Saturday, the ice cream shop my parents and I visited after church on the first Sunday of each month, the burgers-and-shakes joint that gave me my first job when I was fifteen. Bower provided us endless opportunities to fill ourselves with sugar and fat when we were young and active twelve hours a day, when most of us couldn't put on a pound if we tried, and the few girls who had to worry about weight before they hit high school were deemed failures in yet another way.

I'm too keyed up for sugar, though. I've been up since before 4:00 a.m., when I started my first shift at Elaine's. It was busier than I expected, full of truckers taking a break from the interstate for a hot meal and a good cup of coffee. After being given a quick rundown of the point-of-sale system and the menu, I jumped straight into the fray and worked a solid five-hour shift, serving pancakes and coffee and bacon until my stomach was stitched with hunger. Thankfully, I got half-price breakfast out of the deal when I clocked off, not to mention the hundred-plus I made in tips. Not a bad start.

Now, I'm free to spend the rest of the day nosing around Bower.

I'm not exactly sure where to start. I've watched enough detective shows to know that most of what they do is going around talking to friends and family of the victim after they were killed, trying to figure out what led up to it. If the police think Lars was killed in a hunting accident, they probably wouldn't have done that. I spent a few hours combing social media last night, seeing if anyone was talking about who Lars was with, but either nobody knows or they were all doing a great job of keeping it a secret.

I guess I might as well start with talking to his coworkers. According to his profile, Lars was working at an accounting firm in the center of town.

I park on the street in front of a strip of shops and office buildings. Prosperity Accounting is sandwiched between a workout studio called Just for Kicks and a Christian bookstore my mom loves called Holy Words. The names in this town always trend from corny puns to the overtly religious. There's a black plate added to both signs that I haven't seen before. In bold white letters, it proclaims "Owned by Messiah Ministries."

The words aren't threatening, but I feel them like a heavy object over my head. A quick scan of other businesses on the main street shows several with the same black plates, even ones I know have been around since before Messiah Church was planted. Most of the business owners in town go to the church, just like everybody else, but this is new. When I lived here, Messiah ran a private high school and a coffee shop—that was all. Now it seems to own half the businesses in town.

A soft bell dings when I step into Prosperity Accounting, and a young woman looks up from the polished desk at the front. Her blond hair is in a braid crown that would have made fourteen-year-old me jealous, and her crisp blue shirt is buttoned to the collar.

Her eyes light up, as if I'm a friend she's just welcomed into her home. "Hello there!"

I unbutton the top of my jacket. "Uh, hi." I hadn't even planned what to say. This is a mistake. But I'm here now. "I'm looking . . . I'm wondering if I can talk to someone who worked with Lars Oback."

"Oh, I see. Who can I say is asking?"

I straighten up. "My name is Del. I'm an old friend of his."

Recognition dawns on the woman's face. "Delilah?"

Reluctantly, I nod.

A strained laugh bubbles from her lips, the smile still plastered on her face becoming tight. "Oh, wow! You look so . . . different. I'm Annabelle. I was—well, am—four years younger than you, so we were never in the same groups, but I knew of you."

There are two types of people in Messiah who are known *of*. People like Eve, who inspire a smile of adoration when discussed, and people who are spoken about in hushed tones by concerned parents. Everyone knows which type I am.

I shift my weight from one foot to the other. "Anyway, so is there someone I could talk to? Even just for a few minutes?"

Annabelle studies my face, curiosity in her pale blue eyes. But that Messiah training goes deep, and one thing you're not supposed to do is question your elders—not even ones who are probably considered heretics like me.

After a moment, she stands, smoothing the front of her long, cream-colored skirt. "I'm sure Henry would. He was Lars's manager. Hold on a moment." She walks around her desk and disappears through a door with a frosted-glass pane.

While I wait, my gaze travels around the reception area. There's a small leather sofa with a glass coffee table in front of it, several Christian magazines artfully spread across the surface. The local worship station plays softly through the speakers. On a side table, there is a vase of fake flowers and a plastic stand full of pamphlets. My muscles tense when I see Pastor Rick's headshot in the top right corner, with the words *Messiah Ministries* underneath. The pamphlets cover a variety of topics, from the practical guidance of saving for retirement or writing a will to the more church-related things like the value of tithes and honoring God with your finances.

I'm starting to feel like Messiah is everywhere I go in this place, even more so than I remember. My fingers run across the tops of the papers.

"Looking for some financial guidance?" a deep voice asks. I turn to see Henry Tanner, one of the elders of Messiah who always seemed larger than life when I was a kid. Even as an adult, I still feel small with him standing over me. I set down the pamphlet I had grabbed, one about setting up a joint bank account after marriage.

My uncomfortable laugh spills out before I can stop it. "Nah, you can't ask for financial guidance if you don't have finances in the first place." At his stern expression, my smile fades and I clear my throat. "I was wondering if I could ask you some questions about Lars."

"That's right, you used to be a friend of his." The word is chosen carefully. Men at Messiah start with a clean slate in each new relationship. All the dirty buildup of previous romantic entanglements only seems to apply to women.

"I'm just trying to understand what happened."

Henry gestures to the sofa and I take a seat. His broad frame takes up well over half of it when he squeezes in next to me, his body angled toward mine. "An absolute tragedy, that's what. We're praying for his wife and child every day."

I nod, my eyes solemnly on the floor. "Was he still working here before—"

"Yes, we had just celebrated his two-year anniversary with the company a couple weeks ago, in fact."

"I know Lars studied accounting in college, but I always thought he was going into ministry."

Henry straightens the cuff of his right sleeve. The smell of his cologne wafts over me. "As I understand it, that was his path up until he applied here."

I consider that. "So, he quit being the worship pastor around the same time he became an elder?"

He meets my gaze. I try to find some hint in his eyes of knowing more than he's saying, but there's nothing. "It was a few months after he became an elder that Lars came to me and asked whether there were jobs available. I was looking for someone to help me manage one of our largest accounts at the time, so it seemed like a good fit."

That piques my interest. For such a small town, Bower has its share of wealthy people. A lot of Messiah members who work in the corporate world build their mansions within the city limits here to take advantage of the low property costs, then make the easy commute to Fargo/Moorhead. If Lars was working on a major account, he could have been privy to some big secrets.

I know if I show any sign of suspicion, Henry will shut me down and walk back to his office. So, I just say, "Wow, he must have been so honored you trusted him to work on a big account right away." Genuine emotion rises in my throat, thinning my voice. "I still can't believe what happened to him. It was so sudden."

He nods, mouth set in that distinct line of sadness and acceptance that men his age seem to have mastered. "Such a terrible accident. We were all shocked."

"Somehow, it's always harder to lose someone without any warning. You're going along and everything is normal, and then one day they're just gone."

"It is. Of course, the Lord always knows what's coming, but we don't have that benefit of foresight. Lars was a little agitated the last time I saw him, but I know that God is forgiving. He will look at the whole measure of a man's life, not just his final days on earth, on Judgment Day."

"Agitated? Hmm, I wonder why," I ponder.

Henry crosses his arms and leans back into the sofa cushions. "Could be any number of reasons. They still have a young baby in the house, bless her, and increased responsibility at work can always put a burden on a man. Especially if his home life is already challenging."

I force my expression to stay neutral, but Henry and I both know that he overstepped there. Messiah Church members are never shy about holding women accountable, but there's an unwritten rule against talking about other people's marriages.

Rather than apologize, which I know he won't, Henry claps his hands on his knees and pushes himself to a standing position. "Well, that's about all I have time for. It was good of you to come back for the funeral. I know your parents have missed you."

I know they haven't, but the comment still hurts. Shaking it off, I stand up and offer him a pleasant smile. "Thank you, Mr. Tanner. It was nice to see you."

"You too, Delilah." He takes one of my hands in both of his, holding it tightly as he meets my gaze. "Watch your step out there, now."

Oh, I will, I think, pulling my hand away. I know exactly how thin the ice is.

THE TEN MINUTES I spent with Colette at the funeral was enough to tide me over for another half a decade, but I can't avoid visiting her after what Henry said. If Eve wasn't the perfect Noble Wife she portrayed on her blog, there is no one more likely to be aware of that than the person who made it her job to know every woman's business at the Mess.

If Eve is the poster child for the ideal Noble Wife love story, then Colette is the cautionary tale. Seven years older than me, Colette was an established youth leader and Noble Wife mentor when I moved to Bower as a teenager. As much as she obeyed every rule, as much as she stuck by the tenets of the Noble Wife teachings, it never led to a relationship. By the time I left the church, she was twenty-seven and single: basically a spinster by Messiah standards.

She isn't bad-looking—a little sharp in the features, blue eyes too beady to be pretty—and she has the modesty and demure nature down pat, but she has never managed to snag a man. I don't even remember anyone being interested.

Considering how miserable she made my last two years of high school, I can't say I feel sorry for her. The number of one-on-one sessions I had to deal with before and after youth group, listening to her read the same verses over and over, telling me how I fell short of everything expected of me.

No, I'm not surprised no one ever wanted her. Not that I'm much better off.

I swing my car into the parking lot of the biggest bank in town, where there's always guaranteed to be a free space. When I was younger, the streets were easy enough for parking. But the stores have gotten busier over the years, bringing in more people from out of town, even on weekdays.

In addition to being a favorite of Pastor Rick's, Colette can take the credit for putting Bower on the business map in western Minnesota. She owns a little shop on Main Street, selling her homemade candles, as well as bespoke crafts and artwork made by other people in the town. But her biggest success was starting the weekly farmer's markets on Saturdays. With its quaint, old-fashioned setup and proximity to the city, the market has made Bower a tourist draw. Hipsters and visitors from Fargo/

Moorhead make the twenty-minute drive to shell out money for local produce and anything that promises to be one-of-a-kind or handmade. She might not have a handsome, godly husband, but Colette is a natural entrepreneur.

Just that on its own is still not enough for people here to think of her as a success.

When I open the door to Colette's Crafts, the place is bustling. Rustic wooden tables are laid out with various wares: candles, soaps, lotions, and bath bombs; jewelry made of polished stones and twine; picture frames in all shapes and sizes, next to a sign explaining they're constructed of recycled wood; and various accessories knit from the softest wool I've ever touched.

At the counter, facing a line four people deep, Colette is beaming from behind the cash register. After finishing with a customer, her gaze flicks to mine, and her expression shifts. She doesn't look surprised to see me, but she's not happy either.

"Excuse me," a voice says. I turn to see a middle-aged woman with a loose perm pointing at the preserves on the table in front of me. "Can I have one of the chokecherry jellies?"

"Sure." I hand her the jar. When her fingers close around it, I notice the label, and a chill creeps up my spine. She walks off, and I pick up another jar. The sticker on the front is innocuous, advertising Joyous Jams and Preserves. But on the back, there's the Messiah Ministries logo, with a snippet of a Bible verse next to it.

YOU WILL KNOW THEM BY THEIR FRUIT.

I set the jar back down. It's supposed to be cute, I'm sure, but that verse was used to chastise me enough times that I can't see it that way.

"Try this."

Colette is next to me, having abandoned her post at the counter to one of her salespeople, and she's holding up a cracker with something red smeared on it. I'm not sure I can eat anything, but turning her down feels like a bad way to start this conversation, so I let her push the food into my mouth. At least she's wearing disposable gloves—something she never did the hundreds of times she gave us communion in youth group.

The cracker is buttery and delicious, the spread tart and sweet. I instantly want more, but I'm not going to say so. At least I don't have to fake my enjoyment. "That's great. What is it?"

"The chokecherry jelly you seem so fascinated with." Colette's eyes travel to the jar I just set down.

I swallow hard. "Yum."

"I assume you want to talk about something? Or are you taking in the sights while you're in town? A lot has changed."

I nod, looking around the room in a subtle gesture. "I know. I've heard all about the farmer's market you started, and your shop is adorable. Looks like you've done well for yourself."

"I've been blessed." Colette's smile walks that delicate line between exhausted and satisfied, like a new mother's.

"That's great. I'm happy for you." *I'm happy you got one thing you wanted, and I'm happy it's not the thing you wanted most,* I think. "And yes, I would like to talk to you if you have a minute."

"Follow me." Colette leads me around the counter, through a beaded curtain that my mom would find too New Agey to be appropriate, and back to a closet-size office that smells like lavender and lemons. There is no desk, just two wooden chairs and a small table holding a laptop.

Colette sits and gestures for me to do the same. We look at each other for a moment. Somehow, I've forgotten everything I came here to ask. Sitting in front of her, in a cramped office, I'm sixteen again, my face burning as she tells me how disappointed she is in me.

Finally, she says, "When did you cut your hair?"

My lips part. "What?"

"It's much shorter than when you were in Messiah. I was just curious when you cut it off."

I finger the blunt strands self-consciously. "Oh, um. A couple years ago. I just wanted a change."

"Sometimes change is good." From her tone, I can tell this isn't one of those times.

I take a deep breath. "So, I know it's been a while since I was here, but something happened at the funeral yesterday. Ever since, it's been"—I search for the word that might endear me to her, remind her that I used to be part of the group too—"on my heart. I felt like I needed to ask someone about it, and you were the first person who came to mind."

The lines in her forehead smooth out, and she leans forward. "Oh? What was troubling to you?"

I bring my hand to my chest. I'm about to do something I can never take back, and it might ruin Eve's life more than it already is. But I need answers. "When I was leaving, I walked past one of the nursery rooms and I saw . . ." I clear my throat. "I saw Eve with someone. A man—Keith Rivers. It just seemed strange, and I know you two are close, so I thought maybe you could set my mind at ease."

Colette is quiet for a long moment. I worry I've messed this up already, but then she taps her thin lower lip and something sparks in her eyes. "What were they doing?"

That's when I know I've got her. For all her high-and-mighty behavior, Colette never could resist a good gossip. "Just talking, I guess. Oh, it's probably nothing." I cut my eyes to the ceiling, as if annoyed at myself for even bringing it up.

"Probably," Colette agrees, but her tone gives away the lie. She's practically salivating. "Keith *is* the associate pastor. Maybe Eve was finding the reception difficult, and he was helping to guide her through it."

"Is that part of his usual role? I'm not sure I know what he does," I say.

Colette twirls a limp strand of brown hair around her finger. "Odds and ends. He's taken a few adult Sunday school series over the years and occasionally leads Sunday night prayer. I think Pastor Rick mostly brought him on to help with some of his duties during the week, like visiting sick members and conducting funerals. Oh, and he does some counseling too."

Counseling. The word brings me straight to Pastor Rick's office, sitting in that small chair across from his massive oak desk.

"Tell me where you let him touch you. Don't leave out any details."

I force the memory away. "What kind of counseling?"

Colette pauses, then says, "Relationship, mostly. Pastor Rick still officiates all the weddings, so he does the premarital counseling as well. But Keith did a minor in marriage and family therapy at seminary, so he helps married couples who are struggling." As she's saying this, I can tell something has occurred to her.

"What is it?" I press. "Do you think Lars and Eve were having trouble?"

Her gaze darts to the side, then back to me. "It was obvious they were. Ever since their daughter was born, Eve had been different. She seemed worried all the time, like she was just waiting for something bad to happen. I sometimes wondered if she should have quit her job at the church. Just to focus on being a wife and a mom, you know? She was only working three days a week, but it seemed to be taking a toll on her."

She'll no doubt be beating herself up for giving in to the sin of gossip later, but for the first time, I'm grateful for Colette's big mouth.

"Why do you think she kept it?" Eve had never talked about wanting any specific career when we were friends. For as long as I knew her, her one life goal was to get married and be a mom. It didn't make sense that she would cling to a part-time job if it was making her unhappy.

"Well, you know how committed she is to the church. Plus, she didn't always seem to dislike the job. Keith hired her a few months after he started, oh, three years ago? She took several months off when Emmanuelle was born, so she'd only recently gone back. She's officially the church secretary, but sometimes she acts more like his personal assistant. I think she found it a natural fit, you know? Eve was always very good at anticipating other people's needs."

The needs of men, you mean.

"Do you think Keith is the reason she stayed even though she wasn't enjoying it anymore?"

Colette pauses. The sallow skin on her cheeks turns pink. "I don't know."

"But you have a guess."

"Guesses are not truth, and I shouldn't say."

"You have good instincts, though."

Her eyes flash as she looks up at me. "Why do you want to know, anyway? What are you even doing here? You barely stayed after the funeral, and now you're going around town asking questions about Eve and Lars's marriage?"

I should have expected the cordiality wouldn't last, but I'm annoyed at how quickly her tone makes my body tense up with memory. It's exactly how she used to talk to me when I got pulled aside for some offense or another in my teens. Talking to boys too much, wearing shorts that were slightly higher than the one inch above the knee we were allowed, wearing a T-shirt over my bathing suit that was too sheer.

"I'm not trying to do anything except understand what happened," I say carefully.

"What happened is that Lars was killed in a terrible hunting accident." Colette pushes her chair back and stands up. "Whatever was going on with him and Eve they would have worked it out in time. Every marriage has rough patches, but they had a firm foundation and it would have only made them stronger. It's heartbreaking that they'll never have the chance."

"How do you know it was an accident, though?" I ask, my voice barely a whisper.

That's too far. Colette walks around the table and yanks open her office door. "I have to get back to work, Delilah, and I don't want to keep you from your drive home."

I pause on my way out the door, meeting her gaze. My throat is dry, but my words come out strong. "You always thought you were keeping us safe, Colette. I wonder when you'll realize we weren't the ones you were protecting."

FIFTEEN

Noble Wife Journey: a blog
Title: Submission
Published: September 18, 2011

Like so many other aspects of the Noble Wife theology, the idea of wives submitting to their husbands is not popular in today's society. We are told we should want equality, a balanced scale. But I would ask you: What has equality gotten us? Divorce has skyrocketed, sexual diseases have spiraled out of control, women have children by multiple fathers and rely on the government to keep them alive.

Is this really what we want?

I say no.

The Bible clearly outlines that men are the head of their households and wives must submit to their authority. God has gifted them with wisdom and discernment that go beyond ours so they can fulfill their calling. If you have found the right man, you will be blessed to follow his leadership and let him drive the two of you toward success.

For now, I submit to my father's leadership. I live in his house, so I abide by his rules. One day, when the Lord brings the right man into my life, I will do the same with him and be confident that he won't steer me wrong.

What about liberation? you might say. To that, I respond: What greater liberation is there than having the weight of huge, life-altering decisions removed from your shoulders?

I have my own mind and my own knowledge, and it is biblical too for a woman to share her thoughts when invited by her husband. Pastor Rick reminds us that a healthy relationship involves trust and communication. So, we shouldn't feel that we can't share our thoughts or what the Spirit is saying to us. But, at the end of the day, the decision belongs to our husband and it is our joy to support him. If he is wrong, we can trust that God will convict him and fix any situation.

Be free, my sisters.

SIXTEEN

THE PARKING LOT OF MESSIAH is surprisingly full for a Friday morning. The Mess has activities going on every day, making it easy to keep the flock in line. Growing up, I was usually here several times a week. In the summer, we had Vacation Bible School for two solid weeks—the church giving parents a break from out-of-school madness by taking the kids off their hands every day from nine to three. As a student of the private high school run by Messiah, I basically lived and breathed the church. Turned out that wasn't enough to keep me holy.

But I would be lying if I said I didn't love it at the time. All my friends were members, part of my class. I got to spend hours every week with them, playing games and doing skits and eating way too many potato chips from large plastic bowls on the folding tables that furnished the youth room. The Mess is where I learned to do cartwheels, to French braid hair, to whistle, to play piano. It's where I met my first crush and where I learned to keep secrets. It's where I formed my first understanding of God—although now I don't think he's anything like the vengeful, punitive authoritarian I was told about.

Esha and Eve were the first people to make me their friend. Although Eve was a year younger than Esha and me, the three of us were basically inseparable from the time they invited me over for dinner a month or so after I moved into town. Eve was this great mixture of funny and wise, and Esha was gorgeous and fashionable and taught me how to put together an outfit. I should have disliked Eve for stealing my coffee on my first Sunday at the Mess, but the way I saw it, she paid attention to me before anyone else at church knew I existed. I think that being adopted, she and Esha knew better than anyone else how it felt to be an outsider.

I pull into a parking space several rows away from the other cars and turn off the ignition. The ostentatious, vaulting entrance looms overhead.

"Wealth is nothing to be ashamed of. Express your blessing. How can you show the rest of the world what they're missing out on if you don't have anything?"

Express your blessing. One of Pastor Rick's many catchphrases that I never questioned when I lived here. When I went to college, I took the beliefs that had been ingrained in me by Messiah. Every time a fellow student opted out of ordering pizza or going to a movie, claiming they couldn't afford it, I'd judged them. It was only after a few embarrassing confrontations and naive questions answered by friends who were far too gracious with me that I realized the damage a seemingly innocuous saying like that had done. For five years, I was basically taught that poverty was a sin. That people who didn't have money were evil or somehow deserved it. That even at a Christian college, surrounded by people who supposedly believed the same religious text I did, I was better than others because I always had cash. Never mind that it came from my parents.

It has taken years to deprogram messages like that.

My eyes refocus on the archway of Messiah. I'm not going through the front doors today. If I can avoid it, I never will again. I take a deep breath and get out of the car. My boots grate against the ice and sand as I cross the parking lot. Minneapolis hasn't had a snow so far this winter, but Bower is in some kind of strange weather vortex, and a storm dumped several inches on them a few weeks ago—rare, but not unheard of for November.

The church offices are in a separate building from the main campus: a beige, one-level sprawl the size of a five-bedroom ranch house. I try the handle, but the door is locked. A look through the glass door reveals an empty reception desk. I wonder if anyone is filling in for Eve. Or if she's even planning to come back. Without Lars's income, I'm sure she'll have to.

Scanning the buzzer on the wall, I find the name I'm looking for. Pastor Keith is one of seven extensions listed. Pastor Rick's isn't there, but his office is in this building. I've been there dozens of times. One can't just buzz him, though. Anyone who wants to talk to him would have to go through the secretary.

Now that I'm here, I'm second-guessing myself. What if Keith and Eve saw me through the crack in that door? Am I just walking into the lion's den by being here? It's either this or going to see Eve, though, and I'm not sure I'm ready to face her yet.

I punch in four numbers, and a metallic ringing sound is emitted from the speaker.

"Hello?"

My mouth feels sticky. I clear my throat. "Uh, Pastor Keith, hi. It's Delilah Walker. I'm wondering if you have a few minutes to talk with me about something?"

There's a brief pause. Then: "Of course, we always have time for a former member. Come on in. My office is third on the right." He hangs up with a click.

A moment later, the door buzzes and I pull it open. He knew right away who I was, but that's no surprise. Even though he was three years ahead of her in high school, he was always obsessed with Eve, and I was one of her best friends. At least, I hope that's why he remembers me. The other possible reason makes my cheeks burn.

The lobby is tastefully decorated with rich brown walls and off-white trim. Two cream sofas sit across from each other, with four olive green armchairs scattered throughout the rest of the waiting area. A wooden coffee table displays copies of Pastor Rick's books.

Thankfully, I don't see any sign of him. If I'm lucky, that means he's out doing one of his house calls or holed up in his office writing yet another manual for Christian living that tens of thousands of people will buy.

I walk past the reception desk and turn right, where the third door is open and casting light into the gloomy hallway. My head pops around the doorframe first, and I knock lightly on the wall. Sitting behind a modern glass-top desk with a black iron frame, Pastor Keith raises his head. His smile is warm and curated: the practiced smile of preachers and politicians.

"Delilah, welcome." He stands halfway, gesturing to the seat across from him. "Come in, come in. Feel free to close the door if you like, but I think everyone's gone for lunch."

"You can call me Del." Trying to hide the fact that my body has started trembling, I clench my hands together and plop awkwardly into the chair. "Not joining them?"

"Brought my own today. A salad with grilled chicken." Keith chuckles and leans back in his office seat, patting his stomach. "I'm trying to be good. Are you hungry, though? I can offer you a coffee, and I think we have some cookies stashed away in the office kitchen."

He's being friendlier than I would have expected if he knows I saw him and Eve together. I shake my head, squeezing my hands between my thighs. "No, I'm fine, thank you. I've already had way too much today."

He offers an open-mouthed smile. "You sound like me. It's one of the areas where I still have to work on some self-control."

I smile politely. When I don't say anything more, Keith does not press. His expression is relaxed, his gaze focused on mine but not probing. If I didn't have reason to be suspicious of him, I might actually like him. He definitely has the makings of a good associate pastor. The kind of person troubled members of the flock would seek out for comfort, a listening ear. Keith seems to be the perfect calming counterpart to Pastor Rick's audacious firebrand. It can only be intentional. Everything Rick does is a strategy, and that includes bringing Keith on board.

This conversation would be a whole lot simpler if I outright hated him.

Finally, after what could be seconds or full minutes of silence, I find a place to start. "So, you know I used to go here."

Keith nods. "Sure, I remember you. You moved to Minneapolis a few years back, right?"

"Yeah, I finished my degree there." By some silent agreement, we don't mention why. I'm grateful for that.

"I see. What do you do now?"

I release my hands. My fingers are tingling, almost numb. "Retail, mostly. Sometimes food service. Still trying to figure things out."

He seems to process that information neutrally enough. Now that my hands are gripping the armrests of the chair, he can see my naked ring finger. No real job, no husband. Clearly no wealth, considering I'm wearing frayed jeans and a flannel shirt.

I take a deep breath. Every part of my body is rejecting being here right now. I might as well get straight to the point. "Anyway, I was hoping to talk to you about Eve Oback."

The name has a subtle but instant effect. While his smile doesn't fade, the skin around his mouth tightens. "Oh yeah?"

"Yeah. I don't know if you remember, but we were really good friends for a while: her, me, and Esha."

Keith's forehead creases and he nods, as if understanding. "I see. Is that what brings you to town? Several of her old friends have come in, looking to help in whatever way they can. It's such a tragedy. Such a terrible—"

"Accident, yes," I finish, trying to hide my exasperation. It's like they were all given the same line in a play. A strange, bitter taste settles on the back of my tongue. I wish, suddenly, that I had asked for a glass of water. "Eve and I used to be really close. We shared everything: clothes, jewelry." *Boyfriends.*

He nods sympathetically.

My eyes flick to his. "I understand you know her pretty well too."

"Of course. I know everyone in the congregation, but Eve works in the church office." Keith glances past me at the open door, as if remembering the sight of her there, letting him know he had a visitor in the waiting area or a phone call on line three. "I've been busy with other matters while Pastor Rick took care of the funeral arrangements, but I know we have members taking turns making meals for her family. Do you want me to put you in touch with some people?"

It's almost funny. The things that are best about the church can also be the ones that infuriate me most: the interconnectedness, the chain emails and phone calls and group chats. Everyone in everyone's business all the time. It's great in times of crisis, when you need a hotdish to pull out of the freezer or a ride to the hospital. It's terrible when you're eighteen and trying to figure out who you are away from this close-knit group of people who all act like they believe the same things and think the same way.

If I were still a member of the Mess, I know I wouldn't have to worry about my hours being cut or finding another job. All I would have to do is ask, and someone would help with my résumé, while others would write letters of recommendation or put me in touch with their brother or uncle or cousin who's hiring. Then again, if I still went to the Mess, I'm sure I would have married by now and have a man to support me in exchange for doing all the housework and totally giving up on any dreams of my own.

Not that I have any dreams, really. But at least I can, if I ever decide to.

"That's okay, thanks," I say at last. "I'm actually here to talk to someone who knew her these last few years. She and I sort of fell out of touch after my first year of college. Someone mentioned you and she seemed to get along pretty well."

Keith sits forward in his chair, elbows on the desk, fingers of each hand folded together in an earnest prayer pose. "Hmm, that's interesting. I wouldn't say I knew her better than anyone else I work with regularly."

"So, she was just a colleague?"

"Of course."

"You didn't see her outside of work?"

A hint of frustration ripples across Keith's face. "What exactly are you implying, Delilah?"

Seeing him falter, I ask the question I came here for. "Were Lars and Eve doing marriage counseling with you?"

This catches him off guard enough that he can't control his expression. I see the answer on his face before it settles into a tight mask of indifference. So, Eve and Lars *were* having marriage problems. I wonder if it was because Eve was attracted to Keith, or if that attraction came out of long, intimate sessions where she discussed all the ways in which Lars fell short. Either way, it seems obvious to me that Keith still had a crush on her—which makes him the worst possible person to try to help them make amends.

I take a leap, knowing I'm about to get kicked out anyway. "Was it because of infidelity? It wouldn't be the first time Lars was unfaithful." The words are supposed to misdirect Keith, but I feel terrible saying them, even if they are true. I'm sure Lars would never cheat on Eve, but I can't let Keith know I actually suspect him.

"That's an incredibly offensive question."

"I notice you're not defending him, though."

His hand slams on the desk, and I jump, words dying in my throat. "It's not my job to defend him to a nosy, jilted ex-girlfriend. Lars was an imperfect man and an imperfect husband, but he doesn't deserve to be slandered after his death. What went on between him and Evie is absolutely none of your business."

We glare at each other in silence for a moment. Then something seems to click in Keith's brain, and he sits back in his chair. His expression transforms into neutral interest once again, as if given a silent command. It sends a chill across the back of my neck.

"Delilah, I'm afraid I'm going to have to ask you to leave," he says. "We have a strict policy about not speaking ill of any member of our congregation to outsiders, and you have already pushed me far too close to that line for my liking."

Outsiders. Of course I know that's what I am. That's what I want to be. But the word still slices through me. When I stand, my legs are gelatinous. Silly as it might seem, I don't feel safe turning my back on the pastor. He might call himself a man of God, but the fury in his eyes seconds earlier was unmistakably violent. Not knowing how to respond, I say nothing as I back toward the door.

When I reach it, he stands suddenly. His height is intimidating as he unfolds himself from that chair—surprisingly muscular for someone whose job it is to sit inside and listen to people talk most of the day.

I freeze as he opens his mouth, but moments pass and no words come. Is he going to threaten me? Beg me not to say anything about this encounter? I glance over my shoulder. A dark hallway stands between me and the sunny day outside.

Finally, he just says, "Don't come back."

I waste no time walking out of his office, shutting the door behind me. It's only when I lean against the door, taking a deep breath, that I realize something.

He called her Evie.

SEVENTEEN

Noble Wife Journey: a blog
Title: Who I am
Published: November 6, 2011

I am delighted to see the Noble Wife message resonating with so many
people, as I knew it would. Pastor Rick has been called to Bower,
Minnesota, but he has a word for the country—for the world, if they will
listen. He is working on a book to help with this, and I can't wait to do
whatever I can to get it in the hands of as many readers as possible.

It has been a few months since I started the Noble Wife blog, and
other than my hometown and my name, I have revealed very little about
myself. This has never been about me, but it's becoming clear that many
of you would like to know more. After all, that's becoming the thing to do
these days, isn't it? Reveal all the secrets about yourself online?

I'll be brief.

My name is Eve, and I am adopted. I grew up in a small town in
Minnesota, which you already know. My sister and I were both babies
when we came to our parents: me from a poor white family in Wisconsin,
and her from an Indian American teenager in Minneapolis.

Esha taught me how to be adopted before that was even a thing I
knew I needed to learn. One year older than me, she knew the questions
I was in for when I started school, and she stood by me every day.

They weren't trying to be cruel, of course. Many of my classmates
and friends from church read this blog, so I want to be clear. I know they

didn't mean to hurt us, but Pastor Rick always says acknowledging a mistake is the first step to forgiveness. The things we got asked as kids were a mistake, the most common one being: *"Who's your real mom?"*

Esha got it more often than I did, and other questions I never experienced, like *"Where are you from?"* With her brown skin, she was different from almost every kid in our school—different in ways I would never understand. I could "pass" as being our parents' bio kid, but Esha never could.

But we are their children, no matter how different we look or whose blood runs through our veins. My dad says our family is like the family of God—people from different backgrounds, coming together to love and serve and cherish each other. The way we unite as one family despite our differences is what sets us apart in the world.

And that is how we are all called to be.

No matter who you are, where you are, the next time you're tempted to ask a person *Where are you from?* based on how they look, I hope you'll remember that.

I am from Bower, Minnesota. I am from my parents—my birth parents and my adoptive ones. Most importantly, I am from heaven, and the world is my temporary home. Now you know where I am coming from. How about you?

EIGHTEEN

THE DRIVE BACK TO ELDEN feels eternal. I'm being paranoid, but every time a car comes up behind mine, I slow to see if it's following me. When the driver inevitably passes at the first opportunity, laying on the horn, I feel stupid all over again.

I wonder if Keith knows that I know about his affair with Eve. If he does, he has every reason to make sure that information doesn't go any further. The affectionate nickname was the final straw, but I knew the moment I saw them embracing in the church. I wonder if Lars knew too. Maybe that's what he was going to tell me when he called.

You were right.

You were right about Eve. You were right—I regret choosing her.

Tears blur the road in front of me, and I blink them away quickly. As much as I hated the idea of them together, thinking about Eve throwing her relationship away to be with a pastor makes me sick.

She can't possibly have thought it would work. People don't get divorced in Messiah Church. They certainly don't get divorced to be with other people.

Then a horrible thought snakes its way into my mind: she doesn't need to get divorced. With Lars dead, now she is free to be with whoever she wants.

Of course, that should have been obvious to me from the start, but up until this moment, I figured that everyone in Messiah was covering for Lars's hunting buddy. It made the most sense that whoever was with Lars killed him, whether by some kind of negligence or on purpose.

Now, I'm not so sure. I never had any doubt Eve was capable of being a terrible wife, but I didn't think she would physically hurt Lars. It's just a little too convenient, him dying and leaving her free to pursue a relationship with Keith—a pastor, just like she always wanted.

I grip the steering wheel. There's only one way I'm going to get the answers I need. I'm going to have to talk to her myself.

But not today. I take the Elden exit and drive into the parking lot of my motel. The sunset makes the modest building look beautiful, bathing it in pink and golden light. I resolve to do a little social media snooping until I'm ready for dinner at Elaine's. I should go somewhere else now that I work there, but the promise of an employee discount can't be passed up. Plus, I wouldn't mind the chance to talk with Finn more.

My face is warming at the thought as I unlock the door and walk into my room. I stop on the entryway rug.

The sheets are ripped back from the mattress, tangled up with the comforter on the floor. My suitcase—which I haven't bothered to unpack—is turned over, with all the contents spilled out. As soon as I can get my muscles to move, I walk around the room, trying to determine if anything is missing. The only thing of value I have is my laptop, which I'd brought with me since the hotel didn't provide a safe to lock it up. It looks like whoever ransacked the room didn't find what they were looking for, but that doesn't make me feel any better. I glance over my shoulder at the exit, half expecting whoever it was to be standing there, waiting for me.

As I walk past the bathroom, a hint of red catches my eye. There is writing on the mirror. *John 15:6.* One of my lipsticks is laying open on the sink, the tip crushed.

In my time at Messiah, I must have memorized hundreds of verses. We played games and had contests to see who could remember more. The first part of John 15 was Jesus talking about being the vine from which all Christians grow, giving us life and allowing us to bear fruit— evidence for the world to see that we belong to him. Generally, the verses are full of love, a beautiful metaphor for how he sustains us and helps us flourish. But verse six is the one where he tells his followers what will happen to those who do not stay with him—the vines that wither and bear no fruit.

Such branches are picked up, thrown into the fire, and burned.

My eyes glaze as I look at the scrawl. I blink, and my own reflection comes into focus behind them. It looks like the Scripture reference is written across my face.

Legs shaking, I stumble out of the bathroom. I pause for a moment, looking around the room in a daze, before finally deciding to go to reception.

Harriet stands up behind the desk as soon as she sees me. "I could swear none of our rooms are haunted, but it looks like you're about to prove me wrong."

"Robbed." I clear my throat, lean against the raised edge of the desk. "I mean, not robbed, I guess. Someone broke into my room."

Her forehead bunches with concern. "Oh, dear. Are you okay?"

My nod is a lie, and we both know it. "I wasn't here. I just got back, and my stuff is all over the place."

"Okay, okay." Harriet taps her fingers on the desk. "I have a nephew who works for the sheriff's department here. I'll give him a call." She picks up the phone.

I walk over to a small table in the corner, which is laid out with coffee and tea. After choosing a mug with Snoopy on it, I fill it with hot water from the large percolator and drop a chamomile bag in. Something to calm my nerves.

Harriet hangs up the phone and walks out the door toward my room, presumably to survey the damage. I huddle on the couch, sipping my tea, until the police arrive.

When they do, it's in a single patrol car with no sirens or flashing lights. I guess it's not really an emergency. Harriet enters the lobby first, followed by a man in his thirties who shares her nose and kind brown eyes. "That's her, Wallace. Del, are you all right to take my nephew through what happened? There are a few guests poking their heads out, so I'm going to do a walk-around."

"Sure," I whisper. I take another drink of tea, trying to loosen my throat, and then stand.

Wallace is short, only an inch or two taller than me, but his stocky frame makes up for it. With his tan deputy uniform and belt full of weapons and restraints, there is no mistaking his presence in the room. "Miss Walker, why don't you tell me what happened? Can you show me to your room?"

"It's number seven." I lead him out and down the path to my room, where the door still stands open. Wallace takes note of the damage as I recount when I got back, how I discovered it, that there didn't seem to be anything valuable taken. When he looks into the bathroom, I feel a familiar blaze of humiliation. Even if he doesn't know the verse by heart, he'll definitely be looking it up later.

"I used to live in Bower. I went to Messiah Church."

He meets my gaze. "I see."

The response is just cryptic enough to make me unsure whether he goes there himself. Not a lot of people of color do, which Pastor Rick is always quick to insist is due to local demographics rather than his style of teaching. What he's never addressed is how communities don't become homogeneous by accident; targeted intimidation and terrorism make it happen, and carefully written laws and policies make it stick.

Wallace is writing on a form. Watching him, my blood starts to race under my skin. Whoever did this obviously wants me to leave. They don't like that I'm asking questions about Lars's death. They want me to tuck my tail in shame and run away again, like I did after he married Eve.

That's not going to happen.

Even though he's not looking at me, I gesture at the badge on his chest. "Green County Sheriff. That's the same county Bower is in. Do you know anyone investigating what happened to Lars Oback?"

His thick eyebrows draw together. "That's not still under investigation, to my knowledge. It was ruled an accident."

I push my lip out innocently. "Oh, I see. I thought they might still be looking into it, considering what was going on with his marriage. Kind of weird timing."

Wallace's pen pauses on the form. He looks up at me. "I'm not sure I know what you mean."

Shrugging, I sit on the edge of the rumpled bed. My face is carefully arranged into a neutral expression, my fists squeezed tightly between my thighs. The fear I felt thirty minutes ago has shifted into rage. And rage makes me reckless. "Just seems odd that right when rumors have started about Eve having an affair with one of the church pastors, her husband dies in a freak accident."

For a moment, he stares at me. Then he looks back down at the form in his hands and continues to take notes as he speaks. "I wouldn't worry too much about rumors, Miss Walker. You know how those things can get out of hand in small towns like ours." When he meets my gaze again, his eyes are hard. There is no mistaking it. He is done answering my questions.

"Now, just add your contact details and sign, please, and I'll get this filed."

I write in the information. "What are you going to do?"

"We'll file the report and take pictures for my auntie's insurance, in case there's any damage she needs to fix. And I'm sure she'll move you to another room. But since there's nothing missing, we don't have anything to recover. All I can do is say I'm sorry for what you've gone through, and we will let you know if we find the person who did this."

"But you won't." I hand the clipboard back to him. At his tense expression, I smile and try to lighten my tone. "I mean, I know you'll try, but statistically it's not likely you'll find the person who broke into the room—especially since they won't have any of my stuff to prove it."

Wallace lifts his chin, folds the clipboard under his arm. "We'll do our best. Now, have a nice day, Miss Walker. If you don't mind, I'll just take some photos and then you can gather your things."

I cross my arms over my chest, holding myself together. With a nod, I walk out the door.

NINETEEN

Delilah's diary
APRIL 27, 2014

Today was the best day of my life.

I can barely keep my eyes open, but I have to write this down! I don't want to forget a single moment. Lars and I have been getting more serious these past couple months, especially since he met my parents and we took them to our church in Moorhead. But last week, he decided it was time he visited Bower. He said he wanted to see where I grew up, to visit the church that was such a huge part of my life these last five years.

I've never been more nervous or excited about anything. I don't think I slept a wink, and my alarm went off early so I could spend lots of time getting ready. It's been a couple months since I went home, and I wanted to look my best. Show how much I've changed for the better since starting college.

I chose a modest blouse and flowy black pants that were perfect for the warm spring day. My hair was curled, soft and fresh around my shoulders. Lars told me three times on the drive to Bower how beautiful I looked, and by the time we got there, I was practically floating. He parked and came around to open my door, taking my hand.

We walked into Messiah Church together.

And when I tell you every eye was on us, it is not an exaggeration.

I suspected word had gotten out that I was in a relationship, since the only person more excited about it than me is probably my mom. But it was clear from the awed expressions on so many faces that nobody thought I would be able to snag such a handsome, charming man. Lars greeted everyone I introduced him to with his firm handshake, gorgeous smile, and unique ability to be genuinely interested in what everyone has to say. During the service, he lifted his hands and sang his heart out, with that astonishing voice I still can't believe belongs to the man I love. After the service, Pastor Rick found us in the lobby and introduced himself, and we had a good long chat. When he learned Lars was interested in becoming a worship pastor, Pastor Rick insisted he come and play in Messiah one Sunday.

For the first time since I was sixteen, I felt like I truly belonged again. This perfect man was by my side and blew away everyone in my church with how amazing he was. If someone like him saw me as worthy of his love, then maybe the rest of the church would again too.

Lars wants to go back next week. Maybe, with him by my side, it can finally feel like home again.

TWENTY

FINN TAKES ONE LOOK AT my face when I sit at the bar before he picks up a large, curvy glass. "I make a mean Long Island."

"Sounds great." I open the menu, even though I already know what I want. My hands still feel shaky.

A moment later, he sets the amber-colored drink in front of me. "Don't tell me you've been needing that since you finished your shift this morning." He grins in that way men do when they want to make you smile.

I reward him half-heartedly. "No, no. That went fine. I just . . . Someone broke into my hotel room, actually."

His eyes widen. "Are you okay? You're not hurt?"

I take a long drink, then shake my head. "No, I'm fine. They didn't even steal anything. Just messed up the room and . . ."

A customer walks up to the bar, takes a seat three stools down from me. Finn puts his hand on my arm. "Hold on one sec." He goes over to take the man's order.

I use the moment to get myself together. Between sweet sips of my drink, I study Finn, the confident way he moves around the bar. The muscles in his arms tense and strain as he lifts up a rack of glasses, shakes a drink, wipes the counter.

Finally, he comes back over. "Let me put your food in. It's on me tonight. What are you having?"

"You don't have to do that," I say.

"I own the place, remember?"

"Thanks, Finn. I'll have the loaded fries." If anything will make me feel better, it's heaps of fried potatoes and cheese.

He opens the computer to enter my order.

"How old were you when you started working here?" I ask, trying to take my mind off the day.

His fingers continue tapping on the screen as he glances up at me. "Fifteen, officially. But my parents had me on dishwasher duty a few hours a week when I was thirteen to earn my allowance."

"Did you ever think about leaving?"

He pours a glass of water and grabs a rolled set of silverware out of the bin behind him, setting both in front of me. "Not really. By the time I graduated from high school, my mom was sick and couldn't work anymore, so they needed my help to keep the place running. Besides, I didn't have the kind of grades to get into college."

I nod. "Is she okay now?"

The flicker of sadness in his eyes makes my heart sink. "Not really. My dad takes care of her pretty much full-time."

"I'm sorry."

His lips curve into a small smile. "It's all right. I like being here for them. I know a lot of people who grow up in small towns only dream of leaving, but I never really did."

The words give me a small stab of guilt, even though I know that wasn't his intention. Sometimes I wonder if I always had one foot out of Bower when I was a teenager, if that's why I couldn't make things work there no matter how hard I tried to fit in. People in small towns can tell if you think you're too good for them. I hope Finn doesn't get that sense from me.

He squeezes my hand for a moment, then leans back against the counter. "Anyway, back to you. You said someone messed up your room, but they didn't take anything?"

I shake my head. "Not that I could see. But I don't think they were planning to rob me, actually. I think they wanted to scare me."

"What makes you say that?"

The alcohol has made its way to my muscles, unwinding some of the tension from the day. "You know how we talked about the whole hunting accident theory for Lars Oback's death being kind of weird? Well, I have been looking around town today, talking to some people, and I don't think everyone in Bower appreciates that. It looks like one of them was bold enough to let me know."

"I see." Finn crosses his arms. His sleeves are rolled up, exposing faded black ink in swirling patterns curling from his right wrist and disappearing under the fabric bunched at his elbow. "So, what, they just threw your stuff around and left?"

I run a finger along the glass, making a clear path through the condensation. "Not exactly. They wrote something on the bathroom mirror." I don't look up at him, and he doesn't say anything. Finally, I continue. "John 15:6. It's the part about . . ." I trail off, not sure I want to say.

"He is the vine and we are the branches."

My gaze flicks to his face in surprise; he looks away. "Yeah."

"I grew up in church too."

"I guess most people around here did." Whoever wrote that verse reference knows me, might even have been following me. I haven't belonged to a church in years. Days go by where I don't even think to pray. My Bible is in the back seat of my car, gathering dust and road dirt. What fruit do I have to show for my life? Maybe I am due to be picked up and thrown into the fire. Shame curls in my stomach.

"So, what are you going to do?"

I take a long drink, chasing the calm buzz I know the alcohol will provide. Finally, I put my hands down on the bar in what I hope looks like a determined stance. "I'm not going to let them chase me out of town. If they don't like me asking questions, that just proves they have something to hide, and I'm going to find out what."

He nods for a moment, considering. Then he murmurs, "Del, you used to go to Messiah, didn't you?"

Stirring my drink with the straw, I meet his gaze. There's some fierce emotion in his eyes I can't quite pin down. "I left six years ago."

"And they aren't especially kind to people who move on."

My eyes burn. "There's a reason there are so many lifelong members there. The only really acceptable reason to leave is if you have to move for your job or college, but even then, most of the kids I grew up with came back with their degrees and live in the town still."

Finn shakes his head. "There are a lot of churches here in Elden, but they don't demand lifelong loyalty. That place is a cult."

Like muscle memory, the instinct to fight against accusations of being in a cult is automatic—something I did dozens of times as a kid. Even though I went to the church's school, I still played sports with the local high school, and those kids had plenty to say about us. Of course, the more we fought against their claims, the more we seemed to reinforce them.

Sensing my discomfort, Finn raises his eyebrows. "I'm sorry, did I offend you? I didn't mean to. I thought—"

"No, no. You're right." I take another long drink. "I know other churches aren't like that, in theory. But I haven't really been able to find one."

His laugh holds a touch of bitterness. "I work every Sunday morning, but even if I didn't, I'm not sure you'd find me in church. It's hard to go back once you've been burned."

I want to ask more about that, but I know how hard it is to open up about religious trauma, and I'm not sure I'm ready to share my own with him yet. Maybe we'll get there eventually.

"I get that, for sure. And obviously someone in Messiah doesn't want me snooping around. I'm pretty sure I know why."

My voice has lowered, and he leans in closer. "Why's that?"

I chew on the corner of my lower lip. Finn is obviously no fan of Messiah, but there is a phantom of loyalty to the church that keeps tripping me up. I don't know enough yet to prove what I'm thinking, but I have to run this by someone.

Finally, I scoot forward on my stool so my face is just a few inches from his. A shiver of excitement spreads across my skin at the proximity, but I push that away. "I think Eve was having an affair with one of the church pastors. And I think Lars might have been killed so she could be with him instead."

The words were whispered, but they ring in the space between us. Finn looks stunned. Neither of us moves for a moment.

Then, like a spell is lifted, Finn straightens up and runs a hand through his hair, eyes bright. "Holy shit."

"I know!" I'm a mixture of terrified and smug, and it makes me giddy.

One of the waitresses brings out a plate piled high with crispy fries smothered in cheese, barbecue sauce, and ranch. As I take a bite, I notice Finn is still watching me intently, ignoring the drink tickets gathering on the printer behind him.

Swallowing, I finally continue. "I can't prove anything. But I saw them embracing at the funeral, and they were very close. Then when I went to speak to the pastor about his relationship with Eve, he was really angry. Like, he looked like he might hurt me. Plus, he called her by a nickname." At his doubtful expression, I rush on. "I know this doesn't sound like anything, but you have to trust me. Women in our church are basically taught from the time we're girls to never be alone with a man unless we're related or married to him. Seeing her off in a dark corner with another man at the funeral for her own husband is about as scandalous as you can get in Messiah without, you know, consummating the thing right there in the hallway."

Finn doesn't laugh at my poor attempt at a joke, but his face is alight with excitement. "This is perfect," he says.

"What do you mean?" I pop another fry in my mouth.

He pauses for a moment, like he's trying to work something out in his head. Then he leans forward, arms resting on the bar. "You know how I told you my friend is a journalist here in town? Well, she is kind of known as the person who wants to take down Messiah Church. She's never had a really big break, though. If you told her this, she would freak out. It's got all the potential to be a great story, and if the affair is connected to what happened to Lars, it could be huge."

"I don't know." I look down at my food, stalling by taking another bite. I should jump at the opportunity. No one else is going to help me. Harriet's nephew or not, I could tell Wallace wasn't going to do anything about the break-in at the hotel. Nobody in Messiah would believe me if I claimed Pastor Keith and Eve were having an affair. And even if I could prove that they were, I doubt it would be enough to get the police to change their minds about the way Lars died. It would take some kind of explosive, undeniable evidence for them to go against Pastor Rick's messaging.

Finn leans across the bar, his gaze intense. "Come on, Del. I don't know the story behind why you left Messiah, but I can tell that finding out what really happened to Lars is personal for you. Let me talk to my friend about what you found. She's a good reporter; if there's nothing there, she'll tell you."

After another moment, I nod. "Fine. But I want to keep my name out of it. I'm an anonymous source—that's all."

With a wide grin, he squeezes my arm. "I promise. Good for you. It's about time someone tried to expose some secrets at the Mess." Finally, he turns his attention to the printer, pulling up the string of tickets for drink orders.

I sit forward on the stool, elbows resting on the bar as I stare at my fries. I'm really doing this. It's not just about my promise to Nathaniel Oback anymore. I want to find out what happened to Lars, but airing Messiah's dirty laundry to a journalist will do much more than that. Especially if I really tell them everything. With the right reporter and the right evidence, I could shine a light on all the toxic, controlling messages Pastor Rick has been preaching for years. I could expose the dark underbelly of the Noble Wife movement. I might even be able to show how his propaganda has infiltrated every corner of the town.

I could be the one to end his legacy, destroying a mighty man by betraying him to the people he sees as the enemy.

I am Delilah, after all.

TWENTY-ONE

Noble Wife Journey: a blog
Title: Role model
Published: January 3, 2012

This post is coming to you a little later, but that's because the girls at Messiah have been given an extraordinary blessing. We attended a six-day camp last week, led by Pastor Rick's wife, Hillary, and our youth leader Colette. We didn't have to go far. The Franklins have returned much of their financial prosperity back to the church by building a resort ten miles outside of Bower, complete with six cabins and a huge main house, where we held daily meetings and Bible studies, and devoured some of Mrs. Franklin's incredible cooking.

We learned so much, but I was inspired just by watching Mrs. Franklin. She is the person who lets me know it's possible to be the kind of woman the Bible calls us to be. Every morning, when we stumbled to the main house, our hair still sticking up all over the place and melted frost clinging to our sweatpants, she was already in the kitchen putting the finishing touches on breakfast. I've included a picture of her and Pastor Rick below, but it doesn't do her beauty justice, as far as I'm concerned. She is such a wonderful mother figure to us. She and Pastor Rick often tell us that since God has not blessed them with their own children, they consider all of us their own.

When I complimented her on her outfit one day, she not only accepted with absolute grace, but she then changed up her planned

Noble Wife lessons to show us how she gets ready every day. We all clambered after her upstairs to her bedroom, where she walked us into the most amazing closet I've ever seen. Pastor Rick's shirts and trousers hung on the right, pressed and ready for his days at Messiah. She told us she does laundry every day and irons everything once a week, even if it hasn't been worn, to make sure it stays sharp. Her own clothes were on the left, organized by occasion then color. Every pair of shoes was neatly in its place on the rack, and there was an array of scarves and hats hung artfully on pegs on the wall.

One of the girls asked her how much time it took her to keep things like this, and she just laughed. "I've lost count!" she said. "But because of Rick's work, I don't need to be outside the home, so I have plenty of time to make sure things stay tidy. That's also why I get up so early and get dressed and make breakfast, while he does his Bible study and gets ready for work. I don't want the first thing he sees in the morning to be his wife looking like she just rolled out of bed. I want him to have a glimpse of what he's coming home to, because that'll make him work harder and be more excited to see me at the end of the day." She winked at us.

It was one of the many lessons the camp reinforced this week. Mrs. Franklin and Colette took us through Bible studies every morning, and the afternoons were set aside for learning life skills that would help us after we leave home. I'm proud to say that my mom already taught me and my sister how to cook and do laundry, but this week I learned several new recipes for hotdishes that can be prepared to share at potlucks and with sick or bereaved members of the church, and I can finally sew a tight seam!

But my favorite lesson of all was that day Mrs. Franklin told us why she gets up so early and does her hair and makeup first thing in the morning. For all our talks about purity and waiting for marriage, Pastor Rick never lets us forget how much he enjoys his wife. He proudly calls her his "stay at home model." Their marriage is one of the main reasons it's so easy for me to wait. I want a man who longs for me the way Pastor Rick does for Hillary, even years after being married to her. I want to be the kind of wife a man thinks about all day after kissing her goodbye in the morning, unable to wait until he can get home to be with her again.

I want to be the kind of wife who feels like a reward.

TWENTY-TWO

THE NEXT MORNING, I WAKE with a light hangover and a sense of trepidation. I'm in a new room at the hotel, and I slept with a cheap kitchen knife under my pillow, but I still don't feel safe. As long as I'm here, the person who wrote that message on the bathroom mirror has reason to be pissed. And that means I have reason to be afraid.

I don't have a shift at Elaine's today, so I can't justify the cost of a hot breakfast, even at half price. In the motel lobby, I chat with Harriet over cereal and a desperately needed cup of coffee. She has no updates on the break-in but seems more confident than I am that whoever did it will be caught.

Once I manage to reassure her that I'm fine and don't need any extra security in my new room, I throw on my coat and start my cold car. At least I don't have to go back to Messiah, but the alternative isn't a whole lot better.

I can't put it off anymore. I am going to see Eve.

It's been a while since I did any acting. I was an extra in the spring play during my freshman year at Moorhead Christian College, and Lars came all three nights. He told me I was the prettiest one onstage, which was a nice lie. The star was a willowy brunette with a stunning voice and perfect skin, but I didn't look half bad in my nineteenth-century dress and hair in shiny ringlets. I'm going to need to pull on any reserves from that one semester of drama training when I see Eve today.

It takes a little trolling through the private Messiah Facebook groups that I never left, but eventually I find out where everyone is sending the sympathy hotdishes and flowers. Eve lives in a sun-soaked two-story cabin on the outskirts of Bower. The neatly trimmed lawn died elegantly, a stretch of cream-brown in the crisp November air. The whole place is surrounded by clusters of trees, which have kept most of the snow out and make it feel private—far removed from the highway I turned off to get here.

A dog barks as soon as I step out of the car; I freeze, but the black Lab saunters around the house with a wide-mouthed, panting grin, thick tail wagging.

"Hello, bubba," I say, offering the back of my hand for a sniff before I pat its glossy dark head. The dog buries its nose in my jeans, searching for a treat.

"She won't hurt you," a voice calls from the house. I look up to see Esha standing halfway out the open screen door, long black waves held in a loose ponytail at the base of her neck. Her face is clear of any makeup, the skin around her eyes red. She doesn't seem surprised to see me here. I would guess people have been stopping by unannounced for days.

Still, the reception is not exactly warm either.

Esha is obviously grieving, but she looks more at peace than I ever remember seeing her as a teenager. She was always a devout member—not the kind of girl who got pulled aside by the youth leaders for being too promiscuous or disobedient. But I wasn't surprised when she told Eve and me she was applying for universities in the Cities, where she would be too far away to attend Messiah anymore. Everything about her was always too much for Bower: her dreams too big, her excitement too high, her feelings too powerful. I wonder if she feels the walls of the town closing in on her like I do. Love brought us both back: hers for her sister, mine for Lars. It won't be enough to make either of us stay, though.

"It's good to see you." And I really mean it.

The corners of her lips turn up slightly. "You too."

"Can't believe it's almost Christmas." I gesture to the wraparound porch, where a string of white lights is strung along the banister, woven through a green garland. At night, it's probably magical.

"Eve always decorates early. She and Lars put them up the day after Halloween. It's made the house seem a little more cheerful during . . ."

I shift my weight from one foot to the other, trying to hold back a shiver. "Is your husband here?"

Esha and I have stayed friends on social media, so I saw the pictures from her wedding a few years back. She looked like a goddess in white satin, her husband beaming in a dark blue suit.

"No, he had to go back to the Cities for work. I'm staying for a few weeks to help Eve out with the baby." She glances over her shoulder, then back at me. "I suppose you're here to see her?"

I nod. "I know it's not the best time, but I was hoping we could chat for a few minutes if she's up for it." *Chat* makes it sound like I just want to catch up. I suspect I'll be kicked out pretty quickly once I've asked the questions I've come to ask, but if I tell Esha why I'm really here, I won't even get through the door.

After another moment of consideration, Esha nods at the entrance. "All right, come in. I've got chai on the stove. Eve is resting, but she should be up soon."

The fragrance of cardamom and cinnamon reaches out to me, a comforting arm around my shoulders. A metal coat stand is just inside the door, a white wool peacoat dangling from one of its hooks. It's otherwise empty but for an artfully placed umbrella that looks like it has never been used.

"Feel free to hang up your things," Esha calls over her shoulder as she walks off, presumably toward the kitchen.

After toeing off my boots, I hang my bright red Walmart jacket over the bottom hook, looping the purse I got at a thrift store ten years ago on top of it. Next to the designer coat, my stuff looks even shabbier than usual. I take my phone out and slide it into my jeans pocket, then follow Esha.

The gray hallway walls are decorated with perfectly spaced print photographs in thin black frames. The sight of Lars's face beaming back at me is a swift kick to my chest. He's in almost every photo, except one where Eve is pregnant and standing in a field, holding her baby bump and looking down at it in admiration. In the rest, they are together, caught up in each other's gaze or cuddling Emmanuelle. The photo at the end of the corridor is the biggest of them all: Lars and Eve, holding each other under an archway of flowers on their wedding day.

I remember the first time I saw them together. My first week of sophomore year at MCC, Lars told me we were through. He didn't think we were "called to be together." As devastated as I was, I took that to mean he wanted to focus on finishing college, getting into seminary. A few days later, I summoned my strength to drive back to Bower and attend Messiah, like I had been all summer. I dreaded telling my mom, knowing she would probably take it even worse than I did. I would wait until after the service.

It turned out I didn't need to. The moment I walked in, there was a hum of excitement about the place. People were murmuring and looking around, smiling even wider than usual. I saw my mother across the lobby, and even from a distance, I could tell that she knew.

A cluster of people near the coffee station parted, and then I saw them. Lars had his hand in Eve's, their fingers wound together. She was saying something to Pastor Rick, and Lars was watching her lips as she spoke, mesmerized. I hadn't doubted his attraction to me when we were together, but he never looked at me like that. Their bodies had familiarity, magnetized together, faces flushed with new love.

That's when I knew. There was a reason Lars hadn't visited me all summer, made excuse after excuse not to come back to Moorhead or attend Messiah. He wanted distance from me, from us. He knew that the next time he'd be here, it would be with her. And he wanted our separation to appear as if it had been longer. I knew for sure in that moment: he had dumped me a week earlier, but he had chosen her long before that.

A throat clearing jolts me out of my memory. Esha is at the end of the hall, watching me. She turns without saying anything, and I follow, cheeks burning.

In the doorway to the kitchen, I pause. The room belongs in a magazine, all steel appliances and forest green tiles and russet timber countertops. A large island in the center of the room holds a bowl bursting with fruit: bananas and apples and kiwis and oranges just waiting to be devoured. Fake sunflowers stand tall in a silver vase, round faces brightening the room. The fridge is clean, free of the unpaid bills and magnets from the auto shop and pictures of cousins' kids that I'm used to having on mine. An appliance that's supposed to do everything from bake a loaf of bread to cook the perfect sous vide steak gleams on the counter under a glass-doored cabinet neatly lined with a variety of crystal drinking glasses.

The fit out of the kitchen probably cost more than my parents' whole house. It's got Eve written all over it—Lars was much more conservative. I wonder if that's why he decided to step back as the Messiah worship pastor, so he could afford to give Eve the things she demanded.

Aware I've been gawking, I snap my attention back to the reason I've come. Esha stands at the stove, stirring a medium pot with a large metal ladle. After a moment, she lifts it to her lips, blows across the surface, and takes a sip. I watch as she adds a few spoonfuls of sugar, my mouth watering. The smell is divine—somewhere between Thanksgiving pies and the milky black tea I buy from the boba shop downtown.

"Have you had chai before?" Esha asks.

"Um, yeah, I think so. At Starbucks."

Esha laughs. "So, no."

I don't like being laughed at, but I guess Esha doesn't like her culture being bastardized by a corporate coffee chain, so I chuckle too. "I guess not. It smells incredible."

"I made friends with a girl from India in college." Esha pulls two clay mugs down from the cabinet next to the stove and ladles in creamy brown liquid from the pot. "She taught me how to make it properly, her own mom's recipe." She hands me the mug.

Having to learn about your culture from people other than your family—I never thought about how much that would hurt. As far as I know, Esha loves her parents still. But the relationship must be complicated.

The chai tastes even better than it smells: warm and spicy and sweet. A pop of ginger heats the back of my throat, wakes up my sinuses. "This is amazing. Starbucks be damned." I regret the swear word the second it's out, wondering if the Thompson girls are still too good for bad language.

But then, the first genuine smile spreads across Esha's face, an uncomfortable laugh bubbling up. "Thanks." She ladles two more cups full and then nods toward the doorway behind me. "I thought we could talk in the living room."

"Sure, whatever you want." I follow her into a cozy room with Merlot-colored walls and thick white carpet that feels like moss through my thin socks. I sit in the charcoal gray chair that Esha nods to, mug clasped in my fingers.

Esha sets her two teas on the coffee table in front of her. Her eyes travel to the ceiling, as though listening for her sister.

I follow her gaze. After an awkward silence, I ask, "Are your parents here?"

"No, they went home for the day to get some rest. They've been here round the clock since last Saturday."

"Mm." I take another drink.

Footsteps sound above us, and Esha perks up. A moment later, Eve walks into the room.

My face flushes, my heart thrashing in my chest. I just saw her a couple days ago, of course, but she looked put together for the funeral. Now that I'm up close and she isn't slathered with makeup, I can see how much she's changed.

What used to be round, cherubic features have hardened into sharp cheekbones and hollows under her eyes. Her skin is sallow, dotted here and there with stress acne. Her old lustrous brown hair has fallen flat and greasy with inattention.

I always knew that Eve and Lars weren't meant for each other, that she had taken him from me in a way that was wrong. But I never doubted that she felt she couldn't live without him. That's how she looks now, like she doesn't want to continue living. In my darkest moments, I wrote about this day in my diary, even though I had no idea when it would come or what exactly it would look like.

I wrote about the day when Eve would be punished for what she did to me.

My gaze lowers in what probably looks to the Thompson sisters like shame. Really, I do it so I can be sure that I won't smile.

"What are you still doing here?" Eve asks. "I thought you wouldn't be able to get out of Bower fast enough."

She sits on the sofa next to Esha, their knees touching. I remember the three of us being together like that, sharing seats or beds at various church camps over the years. Legs intertwined, covered in blankets, chewing on whatever candy I'd managed to convince my mom to buy. Esha and Eve's parents didn't let their kids have sweets, but in that respect, mine were more lenient. I remember the warmth of their skin, the casual intimacy, the sugar-laced breath in my ear as we whispered secrets back and forth when we were supposed to be paying attention to Colette or Mrs. Franklin or whoever else was teaching that day.

The ache for that time is sudden and sharp, like a bee sting. Even though I'm sure it's reflected in my own, the hostility in Eve's gaze breaks my heart.

I don't owe her an explanation for my presence, so I don't offer one. "I'm still in shock, honestly. I can't believe he's gone. No one will really tell me what happened, so I thought I would ask you."

Esha puts a gentle hand on her sister's thigh, the other raising the mug to her lips. Eve's hand closes over hers as she meets my gaze.

"He was in a hunting accident. What more do you need to know?"

"Who was he hunting with?"

"We're not supposed to say."

"But you do know."

She stares at me.

I run my tongue across my teeth, choosing my words carefully. "Have you talked to Susan and Nathaniel? At the funeral, they said they still didn't have any information. Don't you think Lars's parents deserve the whole story?"

"It's not my business what the sheriff tells the Obacks." Her voice is as sharp and cold as an icicle.

"How can you say that?" I whisper. I imagine the years of Susan trying to show her daughter-in-law love—the baked goods, the invitations to dinner, the offers to babysit—only to be met with Eve shoving them all back in her face.

"You have no idea what you're talking about, Delilah," Eve says. "You can't come here after disappearing for six years and pretend you know anything about my family."

My hand tightens around the mug. "You're right; I don't know anything about your family. But I do know the Obacks, and they deserve the truth about what happened to their son. If the sheriff is telling you stuff he's not telling them, you at least owe them that. How can they even be sure it was an accident?"

Eve's eyes blaze. "I don't know, Delilah. Unlike you, I trust the police. I trust the church. I'm trying to deal with the fact that a week ago, I kissed my husband goodbye, not knowing I'd never see him alive again. I'm trying to wrap my mind around the fact that I'll be raising our daughter alone."

The emotion in her voice is raw, pulsating. Forced. I grind my teeth. "So, that's it? They told you it was an accident, and that you're not supposed to tell anyone where he was hunting or who he was with, and you just accept that? You can't give me any more information?"

She stares into the middle distance, as if she's a sailor's widow watching the sea. "There is no more information. Why does it matter who did it if it was an accident? Finding the guy isn't going to bring Lars back, and it's just going to ruin his life."

On my way here, I'd promised myself I would give her a chance to explain, but she's stuck with the same church lie like everyone else. A terrible, tragic accident. No one needs to take responsibility. Most people know better now than to say it was God's will, but the implication is still there. Everyone in the church seems comfortable to let Lars's death slide by, but I'm not going to let them. I'm not going to let Eve get away with what she's done.

She might not have killed Lars, but that doesn't make her innocent. If she had an affair with Keith and he murdered Lars to have her to himself, she's culpable. And I'm going to make sure she pays for it.

"I saw you at the funeral. With Keith Rivers."

Neither of the sisters says anything, but tension arcs through the room.

"You two seem very close now. He must love that, considering what a huge crush he had on you in high school."

Esha's neck jerks like she's been slapped, and Eve leans forward, glaring at me. "He was comforting me. My husband just died. What is wrong with you?"

"Whispering in your ear is how pastors comfort widows now?" I can't keep the disdain out of my voice. "Holding you close in a dark room away from prying eyes?"

Eve laughs sharply. "You know, you haven't changed at all. You're so focused on finding fault with me that you can't see the gaping holes in yourself. No one likes a bitter woman, Delilah. Why do you think Lars chose me?"

The jab is an expert stroke. I suck in a breath. "I don't know. Clearly you had no interest in living the modest pastor's life he dreamed about. I mean, look at this place." My eyes travel around the giant living room before settling back on her. "I warned him he was making a mistake. Turns out I was right. He'd still be alive if it weren't for you."

"I see you haven't changed. Still no control over your tongue." Tears fill her eyes as if they've been summoned. "There is absolutely nothing going on between me and Keith. It's offensive for you to suggest otherwise." Even with the muted, warning tone, her voice is pitched slightly higher. Eve is a good liar—too good to be appropriate, as far as the church is concerned—but the voice gives her away.

Her expression shifts as something occurs to her. "Is that why Keith has been calling me? I've been too busy with Emmie today to check my messages. Did you go talk to him already? Accuse him of having an affair with me?"

I lift my shoulders in a casual shrug. "I thought I had a better chance of getting the truth from him. Don't worry, he told me nothing was going on. But he's not as good a liar as he thinks he is." I meet her furious gaze, leaning forward. "*Evie.*"

As if yanked by a string, Eve jolts to her feet. "Get out. Get out of my house!"

Esha crosses the room to stand by my chair, as if she might push me out if I don't move. I spare her that decision, standing myself.

"Thanks for the chai, Esha. It was good to see you again, really." I meet her gorgeous brown eyes for a long moment. She seems shaken, and

I wonder if she had any idea about her sister and Keith. But her loyalty to Eve is unquestionably intact.

"Get out!" Eve shouts again.

I nod, making my way down the hall past the pictures of Lars with the family he chose over me. I slide my feet into my boots and toss my coat and purse over my arm, not bothering to put them on before opening the front door. I'm in such a hurry that I run straight into the solid frame of Pastor Rick Franklin.

TWENTY-THREE

Delilah's diary

Today was different than the rest, but it started the same. I woke up, did my Bible study, and showered. I ate cereal and drank coffee with too much sugar. I curled my hair and put on two coats of mascara and that new scarf that my mom just gave me for my birthday. It's getting colder here. By the time I made the walk between Anderson Hall and the Roberts Building, I knew my face was red. I pulled out a mirror before I went into English, but luckily the cold just made me appear as flushed and excited as I felt. It wasn't a bad look.

In my hand, I carried his umbrella. He walked in five minutes before class was due to start. It might have been my imagination, but I thought he looked even better than usual. Like he'd shaved right before class and chosen an especially flattering pair of jeans.

"This looks cleaner than I remember it," he said when I handed him the umbrella.

I tried to make my laugh sound carefree. "Oh, I wiped it down." Slight understatement. I had spent all last night meticulously removing every speck of dirt.

"I like your scarf," he said.

I could have floated. He'd noticed. I told him thank you, and then he asked the question I've been dying to hear since we first sat next to each other five weeks ago.

"Are you doing anything for lunch today?"

I tried to respond, but Dr. Kirk chose that moment to walk in and start his lecture. But I didn't want to leave Lars hanging, so I just nodded, trying to show him I was excited without being too overeager. I could tell I got it right when he grinned, settling back in his desk like he'd just aced a test.

I did not hear one word of that lecture.

Our class ended at eleven, so we were at the early shift for lunch. That was fine with me. This is a small enough college that we would definitely be seen by people we knew, and I didn't want to deal with all the questions and sideways glances we'd get. For just a little while, I wanted Lars all to myself. I've had enough of people staring and talking about me behind my back for a lifetime.

Lars used his own credits to pay for my lunch, even though I told him he didn't need to! We talked about college, and I found what I'm hoping was a nonweird way to ask why a junior was in freshman English. Apparently, a couple of his required courses were only offered every other year, so he had done them in the first two years rather than waiting and risking that the classes might fill up. He'll do English 102 next semester. I didn't say so, but I'm hoping we might sit next to each other again.

If things go well, maybe by that point I wouldn't even need to ask. :)

The whole time we talked, a part of my brain was running that I kept having to shut off. It's like a warning bell, flashing above me every time I get close with a guy. It's been over a year since everything happened with Noah.

Anyway. I should be over it. It was the worst time in my life, but I guess that's only because I've had a pretty lucky life. My roommate's mom has cancer. A girl I met in public speaking class lost her brother in a house fire. People deal with terrible stuff all the time, and like my mom says, it's our choice whether we dwell on it.

I wanted to smash that warning light with a hammer, but I just sat there with Lars and kept talking, and eventually, it went away. He makes everything else fade away. We're doing lunch again after class on Friday. I want to tell my parents, but I think they'll be too excited. No, I'll keep this a secret until I can bring him home. Until I can introduce him to all the people who matter.

Until I can walk through the doors of Messiah with my arm through his and my head held high.

TWENTY-FOUR

"WHOA, THERE." PASTOR RICK'S HANDS close around my upper arms. The movement keeps me on my feet, but I pull away from his touch as quickly as possible. He doesn't look surprised that I've just crashed into him, but over his shoulder, I see Pastor Keith gaping at me.

Of course. Eve probably hasn't gone a day since Lars's death without a visit from the pastors, checking on her well-being. Especially when she's the pet project of one and the likely mistress of the other.

Pastor Rick's eyes glide between me, Eve, and Esha, observing every frustrated breath, twitching facial muscle, shifting stance. Within ten seconds, I'm convinced he understands exactly what happened between us during the past half hour, even though I know that's impossible.

"Pastor Rick, welcome." Esha's smooth voice finally cuts through the awkward, electric silence.

"Yes, please come in," Eve says deferentially. I don't look up, but I can feel the fire of her gaze. "Delilah was just leaving."

"Of course. Keith, you go on ahead." Pastor Rick claps his protégé on the back. "I'll just walk Delilah to her car. I haven't had a chance to see her since she came back to town."

That's not true. The words refuse to take shape in my mouth. I can't contradict him. We are never supposed to do that. I remember once, after church, he told my mother that his wife was allergic to walnuts so she wouldn't put any in her brownies for the next potluck. But I had seen Mrs. Franklin eat walnuts in a salad at one of our retreats, and she was fine. I mentioned it to my mom on the way home from church, and she scolded me.

"He made a mistake, Delilah. Even pastors make mistakes, and we are to cover them over, not expose them and cause our leaders embarrassment."

I look at Pastor Rick now, and the question in his eyes is unmistakable. He's testing me. I wonder if the other incorrect things he's said over the years weren't mistakes. Maybe he lies to measure his congregation's loyalty.

At last, I find my voice again. "Oh, you don't need to do that. My car is right there." I point at my old faithful Plymouth, beating back the urge to be embarrassed at the state of it.

"Won't take a minute."

Everyone else has already gone inside. A breeze kicks up, and I shiver.

"Are you going to put that on?" Pastor Rick looks at the ratty jacket hanging over my arm.

Quickly, I slip it on, then make my way down the steps. I want to race to my car, but that feels unacceptably rude, even though I can't stand the thought of spending any more time with him than I need to. I settle for a brisk, determined gait.

Pastor Rick easily keeps up with it. "Nice of you to visit your old friends."

I nod, words jammed in my throat. My arms are wrapped tightly around myself. His hands are loose in the pockets of his spotless black coat, his shoulders relaxed. We reach my car in silence.

"Well, thanks." I fiddle with my keys, unsure if I can just get in and drive away with him standing here. I'm doing everything I can to avoid his face, that confident jaw that tightens perceptibly when he's disappointed, the piercing eyes that make even the most stubborn sinner want to confess.

As I reach to put my keys in the lock, his hand comes out against the door. The muscles in my legs turn to liquid. I put my own hand on the window to steady myself. Ears burning, I stare at the glass. His reflection looks back at me.

When he speaks again, his voice is low—not a deep growl, but rather the firm tone one uses when training a dog. It instantly transports me back to his office, back to those long sessions, recounting every sinful thought or desire I'd ever had—and then making up new ones when he demanded more.

"When are you going to learn, Delilah?"

My whole body is shaking. "Learn what?" The tears are obvious in my voice, even as they start to fall from my eyes.

He grips my chin, turning my face toward him.

Scream. Push him away. Run. My body cannot obey my mind, somehow both frozen and elastic at his touch.

There is a glint of amusement in his eyes as he speaks. "You never belonged here, no matter how desperately you tried. And really, you did try."

I close my eyes, sending more tears racing down my icy cheeks.

His fingers are still tight under my chin. "Somewhere along the way, you must have realized you weren't right for this community. Lars realized that too, but he *was*, and that's why he chose Eve. It was ordained that way. You were meant to bring him to Messiah, and he was meant to marry his true Noble Wife."

It's far from the first time I have stood still, allowing him to shred me with his words. I've been on my own for years, working multiple jobs and never asking anyone for anything. I may not have my life together, but I am an adult. Yet five minutes in his presence, and I am a helpless teenager again.

He lets go of my chin, and I stumble back, gasping as I try to force myself not to sob.

Pastor Rick dusts off his hands, puts them back in his pockets. "When will you learn, Delilah?" he asks again, my name a frustrated sigh. "When will you learn that no one can tear apart what God has put together?"

TWENTY-FIVE

Noble Wife Journey: a blog
Title: Anniversary
Published: September 14, 2012

One year. One year ago today, I asked you all to take the Noble Wife
journey with me. Since then, the audience for this blog has grown from
a few friends in my hometown to thousands of you across the country—
and even some sisters around the globe.

The world is starved for voices who will speak the truth. I am filled
with joy that Pastor Rick's message could reach all of you. One month
ago, his book on the Noble Wife movement was published. Although
he's something of a legend around our part of Minnesota, he tells me
that its spot on the bestseller lists is all because of this blog. He is not
a man of many compliments, so I accept it with grace—especially since
this blog only exists due to his teachings.

Sadly, it is not all celebrations. During this time, as much as I have
seen our movement grow, I have seen sisters fall away. I have seen
people I love stray from the Word. I have also received the occasional
nasty comment or email, which I am quick to remove from anywhere
public so that it won't harm those of you who are vulnerable. The Bible
teaches us to expect critics in our midst, that one of the ways the devil
works is by making us doubt ourselves. I am always sad when I see it
is other women doing this in our comment section. It breaks my heart

to know how much they have bought into the world's lies about who we should be.

The temptations of this world are many, and the faithful are so few. Nevertheless, our movement is resilient.

As a newly minted junior in high school, I have officially completed Noble Wife classes, and I feel more prepared for the next phase of my life than ever. If you've been following this blog for a while, you know my adoption story. While I was only a baby when I came to my parents' home, they wanted to give me plenty of time to adjust. I could have been young for my grade or old for it, so they decided to wait and let me start kindergarten just a few months before I turned six. As a teenager, though, I have always been told I am wise beyond my years. Now I am nearly seventeen, on the cusp of adulthood, looking to the future ahead of me.

I have followed every rule, obeyed every instruction. I have seen the results with my own eyes: members of Messiah growing up, staying chaste, falling in love, and giving themselves only to each other. I see the adoration in their eyes as they lean in for their very first kiss on the altar after committing to their spouse for eternity.

That is what my heart yearns for. I know this is the same for so many of you.

Hold fast, sisters. Our time is coming. Follow the path, stay firm in your convictions, and don't let the world distract you.

TWENTY-SIX

IT'S ONLY WHEN I'M IN the car, miles down the road from Eve's house, that I finally break down. My sobs come harsh and ragged, so violent that I quickly pull over on the side of the highway and collapse over the steering wheel.

"We know who is at fault here, Delilah. Anyone with eyes could see you tempted him."

Just like in my dreams, I see myself in Pastor Rick's office, like a camera filming the scene from above. I see my bony arms folded across a chest I was doing everything to flatten, my thin hair tucked behind my ears—bright red from the words he is saying.

"Confess to me."

Eventually, the humiliation passes, giving way to anger. I straighten up in the driver's seat. Three days is all it took to wipe the last six years of effort rebuilding my life away. Less than a week, and that man has me convinced I'm nothing but a gossipy bother interfering with a devastated widow's grief. I'm tempted to turn the car around, drive back, and finally tell him exactly what I think of him.

But I know that the moment he appears in front of me, all my bravado will vanish yet again. The best way to wipe that arrogance off his face is to prove him wrong. So, that's what I'm going to do.

When I get back to the motel, I open my laptop and go to Eve's blog. I was sixteen when she started writing it. At first, the only readers were in the church and our school, and we all knew the teachings anyway. But it was still fun to see someone write about our Noble Wife lessons on the internet, where anyone could read it. Then it started getting attention, and Pastor Rick quickly took advantage of the opportunity.

In the late aughts, the Christian purity movement had begun to fade. All the books promoting abstinence at all costs and courtship over dating that had sold millions of copies were no longer as popular. There was a gap, an opportunity for a new kind of teaching about dating and relationships for Christian teenagers. Focusing almost exclusively on one chapter in the Bible, Proverbs 31, Pastor Rick's Noble Wife message fit the bill. Although it was often referred to in both his youth group and Sunday morning services, the tenets of Noble Wife were taught in a special series over the course of two semesters on Wednesday nights. Freshman and sophomore girls went to those classes for an hour before our normal youth group.

I click back to the start of Eve's blog. It would take me days to get through her decade of posts, but I want to at least skim some of the beginning. She walks through the key aspects of Pastor Rick's lessons, but it's impossible to encompass everything he taught. He did that later, with his own book on the subject that went on to be a bestseller since thousands of readers were primed for it, thanks to Eve.

The words creep under my skin as I read. It's all straight from the Bible, which is the genius of it. No one could argue that what he was teaching wasn't scriptural, like they could with many of the relationship books that came before it. There was actually no biblical basis for telling teenagers they couldn't kiss or talk to each other alone like those other books did, but saying that a woman should submit to her husband and take care of the household—that was straight out of the Bible, even if it was arguably misinterpreted. And I signed on for it, maybe not as wholeheartedly as Eve did, but close. Sure, it was restrictive, but I was promised a perfect marriage and a lifetime of happiness if I complied. When I was a teenager, that was all I wanted in the world. That's why it was so easy for my parents and Pastor Rick to convince me that what happened with Noah was my fault; I had strayed from the teachings on purity, and that was the result.

It was only when Lars dumped me for Eve that I realized what a lie it had all been. He clearly felt like he didn't owe me anything, and why would I expect him to? By then, he was a committed Messiah member, attending when he could and following the messages online while he was away at ministry camp. In his teaching, Pastor Rick focused almost entirely on scriptures about the behavior of women. The Bible does tell wives to submit to their husbands, but it also says men should lay down their life for their spouse. The way Pastor Rick explained that verse was to say this was why men were called to war, to own guns that would protect their homes, to literally kill if necessary in order to protect their family. There were no weekly classes for men, no instructions for how to sacrifice their desires for us, to treat us with love and respect, to be good husbands and fathers. As best I can remember from youth group services, the boys in Messiah were taught not to get caught in temptation by being alone with us, and when they didn't succeed at that, it was the girls who were blamed for not saying no or running away.

I know that better than most.

I scroll through some of the comments on Eve's one-year blog anniversary post.

> This movement has changed my life. Thank you so much for bringing it to our attention. God bless Pastor Rick!

> I started studying Proverbs 31 and following the Noble Wife tenets you've laid out only six months ago. Since then, I have met an amazing man and we're now engaged! I can't thank you enough for this.

> My feminist mom hates it, but I'm learning to sew, and I just started canning my own vegetables from our garden. I feel like a whole new person—someone with purpose.

I exit out of the tab, breathing hard. I wonder where these women are now, if they still subscribe to the movement. If their marriages are everything they hoped, if they have lots of pretty babies and a husband who holds them as they fall asleep every night.

Only the good Noble Wife stories made it to the blog, for obvious reasons. There are rebuttal blogs and articles, of course, but they never garnered the same attention as the original. A quick search turns up the most recent one from two years ago, by a female journalist in Los Angeles: "I Lived as a Noble Wife for One Year and All I Got Was This Lousy Apron."

The piece is funny: a little bitter and sarcastic, which I like, but mostly focused on how annoying it was to learn to cook and go without casual sex. It's not the kind of thing that would have any impact on the target audience for Eve's blog. An unmarried, non-Christian West Coast journalist in her thirties trying on a chapter of the Bible like a sweater isn't exactly the type of piece that cuts through around here.

It's not just that Eve shares only the good stories of others on her blog. After a few hours of reading, painfully poking at my own scabs by going through some of her posts about her relationship with Lars, I can tell she shares only the positive side of being married to him too. I am caught up to the current year, and so far there have only been hints of discontentment, always expertly glossed over with reassurances to her reader (or herself) that marriage is worth it.

As I was warned, there are times when he makes a decision I don't necessarily agree with. There are times when he wants to do things I don't care to. But that is where submission comes in, where I take a step back and honor his authority. And oh, what beauty there is in that. How it draws us closer together. I see the love brimming in his eyes when I support him, when I uplift him, and it makes every moment worth it.

Being a wife is the most difficult, powerful, rewarding, heartrending thing I have ever done. It dismantles you and rebuilds you every single day. It holds a mirror up to yourself, exposing your flaws and showing you how to be better. And no one wants more for me, believes better of me, than my husband.

There is no struggle, no dimension, no reality. It would be so easy to think that she really did get everything she was promised by following the Noble Wife philosophy: a perfect, happy marriage.

Except she cheated on him and now he's dead.

I can't shake the image of her sitting on that couch, saying, "Why does it matter who did it?" Lars dumped me six years ago, and it seems like I care about what really happened to him more than his own wife does.

In high school, Eve's blogs were a topic of conversation in our girls' groups. Especially once she started getting subscriber numbers in the tens of thousands, a lot of the girls in my grade and hers treated her like some kind of role model. Her depiction of life in Messiah, of what it was like to be a teenage girl following Pastor Rick's teachings, was nothing but rosy. She often stretched the truth, embellishing a story or encounter that I'd witnessed myself and knew wasn't completely true.

If she did that then, there's no reason she wouldn't now. I study her three latest blogs, the last one from nearly two months ago, which is a little strange. Eve was always a ritualistic blogger. She wrote one a week, every week, after her initial burst of posts outlining the Noble Wife philosophy in 2011. Her most recent one doesn't mention anything about going on hiatus or slowing down her publishing schedule.

It's about her baby's dedication, and it seems normal enough. The language is a little less dreamy and excited than usual, but I could be reading into it. There isn't a lot of text at all, actually, mostly pictures. Messiah doesn't believe in baptizing infants; baptism is something that can only be done by someone with the mental capacity to make the choice for salvation. Instead, babies are dedicated to the church—sometimes in groups, sometimes alone, depending on the number of new kids around. Looking at the pictures, I can tell Lars and Eve managed to snag their daughter a solo dedication spot. Pastor Rick would have formally dedicated her to the church, charged the congregation with the spiritual care of the baby, and prayed over everyone after. I always thought the ceremony was nice, when I went there. Like the church was one big family welcoming a new kid.

Now, it makes me feel dizzy. Not because the dedication actually locks her into anything, but because I can see from the pictures that something is wrong. The ones Eve chose for the blog are perfect: in one prechurch snap, Lars is holding his daughter in her cream-colored dress, their faces close in profile, noses nearly touching as a wide grin splits his face. There are a few with Pastor Rick after the ceremony, which Eve says were taken by her dad.

But it's in the comments where I find the photo that chills me. A member of the church has uploaded all her own shots from the day, obvi-

ously believing Eve would want to see how she captured every moment
of the ceremony. In one, Pastor Rick has his hand on the baby's forehead.
Lars's head is bowed, and Pastor Rick's eyes are closed, clearly praying.
But Eve's eyes are wide open, staring at her baby. I see something in her
expression that is frighteningly familiar.

I saw it on my own face last night, when I looked at the mirror with a
Bible verse written in my own lipstick.

She looks haunted.

Henry mentioned Eve had started to change after she became a
mother. I skim the post titles until I find the one she published just after
her daughter was born. It stands out as being more raw than the others,
her words less carefully chosen.

Motherhood does something to you, twists apart and wrenches open
something inside you that you didn't even know existed. My heart has
expanded, large enough to wrap around this tiny body that was built in
my womb.

The days are long, and the nights are longer. I never knew it was
possible to hold the whole world in your arms. What a gift—awesome in
the truest sense of the word—it is to be her mother.

As grateful as I am, I am also overwhelmed by the responsibility.
Going out, which before seemed so safe and comfortable here in our
small town, now feels fraught with danger. Right now, everything that
happens to her and every move she makes is overseen by me. I am her
food, her safe place to sleep, her favorite person. It won't always be that
way. One day, she will have other voices in her ear besides mine. She
will be taught how to live by the church, just like I was.

But for now, I will stay here, curved around her body, vowing every
moment to keep her safe.

A SCRATCHING SOUND wakes me. I sit up in the dark motel room, lit only
by the glow of my laptop. I must have fallen asleep reading Eve's blogs.

My fingers find the lamp switch, turning it on.

There it is again. Like someone is slowly running their fingernails across the door.

Throat aching with a repressed scream, I slide out of the bed. The best I can do in terms of a weapon is the Gideon Bible on the bedside table. I'm too keyed up to laugh at the irony.

I aim for a shout, but my voice comes out high and strangled. "Who's there?"

The scratching stops. After two more shaky breaths, I open the door with the chain lock still in place.

Nobody.

I listen for a moment, sure I will hear whoever it is breathing just around the corner and out of sight. But there's nothing, only the sound of distant cars on the freeway. I slide the chain out of place and open the door wide, stepping outside. I whirl around, but no one is behind me.

A piercing ring makes me scream. It's the landline in my room. Stepping back inside, I lock the door and rush to the bedside table, picking up the receiver.

"Hello?"

Someone on the other end of the line lets out a long, annoyed sigh. I slam the phone down.

The unmistakable feeling of being watched is icy hot on my skin. This is C-grade horror movie stuff, I know, but it's effective. Bobby and Harriet live just blocks from this place. I could call them if I wanted, get Bobby to check the grounds for an intruder. Or I could call the police again.

While I'm debating, my cell phone vibrates. I look at the message on the screen from an unknown number.

You'd better get out while you can.

I throw it on the bedspread. Within minutes, everything I brought with me is tossed in my suitcase and I'm out the door.

I'm a few miles down the highway before I realize I don't know where I'm going. My rearview mirror reveals a pitch-black sky unbroken by other headlights. At least I'm not being followed. It's eleven o'clock at night, and I am exhausted, but I can't go back to that motel. I need some-where safe to sleep.

Finally, I pull over, take out my phone, and dial Nathaniel's number. He answers on the first ring. "Hello?"

"Hi, Nathaniel, it's Del. Delilah. Sorry I'm calling so late."

"No, it's okay. I was hoping I'd hear from you soon. How are you?"

"Oh, me?" My voice trembles. I watch the mirror for any movement, but nobody is coming after me. "I'm doing okay."

It all seems so silly now. The lipstick on the mirror, the scratching on the door, someone breathing on the phone. It's clearly someone from Bower who's pissed I'm here and doesn't have any better ideas than to scare me away. And I'm just letting them.

"Are you sure? Did something happen with your investigation?"

He makes it sound so formal that I almost laugh. "Um, no, sorry. I don't have any clear answers yet, but I'm making progress." I scramble for a reason to claim that I called him. "I just wanted to know, did Lars say anything to you about him and Eve the past few months? Like that they were having trouble or anything?"

There's a long pause. Then: "No, but he wouldn't have told us. Lars wasn't the kind to talk about private matters out of turn."

"Did you suspect anything? You must have spent a lot of time with them, especially with a new grandkid to look after."

Nathaniel's voice softens. "Yes, Emmanuelle. We watched her every Tuesday night. That's when they have . . . when they had their prayer group." He clears his throat, and I wait, not wanting to interrupt his thought. "I would love to say that I noticed something, to give you some information to help. But the reality is, as much as my wife and I never re-ally got along with Eve, she and Lars seemed to make each other happy. She was a little different after Emmanuelle came along, but that's nor-mal. Motherhood changes everything."

The image of her shadowed eyes in that picture from the dedication flashes in my mind.

I could tell him about the suspected affair with Pastor Keith, but somehow that feels premature, even though I've already mentioned it to other people. Nathaniel will treat that revelation differently, though. I'm not sure what he'd do, but it wouldn't be pretty.

Realizing I've been quiet for a while, I clear my throat. "Well, I guess I just wanted to let you know I'm trying, even though there are definitely some people in Bower who want to make sure I don't find anything."

"What do you mean?"

I glance at the mirror again. Even though it's embarrassing, I absolutely can't drive back to that motel. "The room where I'm staying was broken into. Someone left a threatening message on the mirror. I'm okay, nothing was stolen, but it's obvious someone doesn't want me snooping around. That has to mean there's something to find."

"My God, I'm sorry. I feel responsible."

"You're not responsible for the crappy behavior of someone else. I'm fine." My shaky voice betrays me. "It's just, I think whoever it was came back tonight. There was this scratching sound, and then my phone rang . . . I got in my car and left." As I say it all, it sounds so ridiculous.

"Where are you now? Did you find someplace else to stay?"

"No, I'm parked on the side of the highway."

"What? Del, please." I'm struck by how much he sounds like my dad when his tone changes. "We live ten minutes from Elden. Come stay with us. We won't charge you anything, and no one will bother you here."

"Oh, I couldn't do that."

"Don't be silly, it's done. Do you want me to come get you tonight so you can follow me back? It gets dark driving in the country." I hear him rustling around, like he's already putting on his coat.

"No, that's okay." Despite my embarrassment, I smile. Someone is trying to take care of me. "I can make my own way out. Can you text me the address?"

"Done. I'll see you soon."

TWENTY-SEVEN

Delilah's diary

I am in love with Lars Oback. I know I'm getting ahead of myself, and obviously nobody knows this but me and God . . . but it's true. We have talked here and there in Dr. Kirk's class since we met last month, but after today, I just know things are going to be different.

It was all because of a rainstorm. This afternoon, I was rushing from the dorm to the Freeman Building, holding my hood over my head with one hand and my book bag with the other. A red car pulled up next to me, and a window rolled down. It was him.

He asked if I needed a ride. Colette's chiding voice played in my head, telling me never to be alone with a boy, but I was shivering and wet and exhausted from running. If anything, I was sure that getting into a car with him would only set back my hopes of a romance after he saw me looking like a drowned rat.

I got in. He offered me a gym towel that he promised was clean, cranked up the heat, and we were on our way.

"No umbrella?" he asked.

"I haven't bought one yet."

His smile was warm, understanding. "Yeah, it's hard, isn't it?

Starting a whole new life at college? I remember what it was like, my first year here."

I was still breathing fast—from running or being alone with him, I wasn't sure. Probably a combo of both. "It is hard. I keep going to the cabinet to grab something, like a sponge or a bottle of cleaning spray, and then realizing I never bought any. My mom always seemed to have everything we needed plus a backup. Like, there were always spare toothbrushes in the drawer if one of my friends decided to stay over. When do you get old enough to keep spare toothbrushes in the drawer?"

I paused, realizing how long I'd been talking. I don't think I've ever talked that long to a boy. Just when I was sure he was going to pull over and tell this crazy lady to get out of the car, he chuckled.

"I don't know, but it's not when you're twenty, I can tell you that. I don't even have an extra set of sheets. Don't ask how many times I've slept in a sleeping bag because I put them in the washer and forgot to switch them to the dryer before bed."

"Hey, at least you wash your sheets." As soon as the words came out, I clapped my hands over my mouth, face on fire.

But instead of being offended, he burst out laughing. "I lived with a guy freshman year who didn't wash them once."

I made a face. "Ugh, this is why I brought a mattress protector. Who knows how many people slept on my dorm bed before me."

He glanced at me, his eyes glowing. He really has the most beautiful brown eyes. "Good idea."

And then, he pulled up in front of the Freeman Building. I wanted more than anything not to have to get out, but I had less than five minutes until class started.

"Thanks," I said.

He reached behind him and felt around for a moment before handing me an umbrella. "Here."

"Oh, that's okay. I can just run in, and besides, I'm already soaked." Again, I think my face was probably as red as his car.

"Take it. You can bring it to me on Wednesday."

That's when I did something bold. I looked him right in the eyes, forcing myself not to look away. And I saw the thing I've been longing for since I was thirteen. I saw a man who wanted to be close to me—who enjoyed it and was not ashamed.

I mustered up all my courage and said, "Looking forward to it." And then I took the umbrella and ran inside to my class.

Wednesday cannot come fast enough.

TWENTY-EIGHT

I'M WRAPPING UP MY MORNING shift when Finn arrives at the restaurant. His tall frame is hugged by a pair of well-loved jeans and a plain black T-shirt, light brown curls still wet from a shower. He smiles when he sees me, walking over to slide into the booth where I'm counting my tips. Mentally, I kick myself for being so excited about this basic level of attention. I've only known this guy a few days, but already I crave a glance from him like my favorite dessert. It reminds me of how I felt about Lars at the beginning—a thought that inspires both guilt and excitement.

"Morning, Del. How was it today?"

I stack the weathered bills on the table in front of me and slip them into my purse. "Not bad. We had a pretty big rush about two hours ago, but things settled down enough that Maxine cut me a bit early."

"How are you feeling since the other night? No issues in the new room?"

"Oh, actually, I'm staying with some old friends now. It wasn't Harriet's fault, but I just didn't feel safe there anymore. I called this morning to check out."

Finn's brow furrows. He reaches across and touches my hand, warming my skin. "Glad you found somewhere else, then. Are you still in town?"

He's probably asking because he doesn't want to be down another waitress so soon, but a little part of me hopes it's because he wants to keep getting to know me. I'm terrible at reading men, but so far he doesn't seem *un*interested.

I smile, leaning my cheek on one hand. "Staying nearby. You'll have to put up with me for a little while longer."

He chuckles, glancing to the side. "That's a burden I'm happy to bear. So, listen, my journalist friend—Parker—she's really excited to meet you. I thought you'd maybe like a break from our food, so I told her to meet us at one of the cafés in town. I'm supposed to call when we're leaving. Do you have time now?"

I smell like fried food and too many cups of coffee, but one of the drawbacks of no longer having a room right next door means I can't do much about that. "Sure. Just give me a few minutes." I pick up my purse and hustle to the bathroom. After running a brush through my hair, spritzing some body spray, and redoing my lipstick, I feel slightly less greasy, which is as good as it's going to get. With a final deep breath, I make my way back out of the bathroom.

Finn's gaze roams my face appreciatively. "You look nice."

I smile and lower my eyes. "Lead the way."

His car smells like him: a deep, spicy scent like Christmas cake or cinnamon gum. At a stoplight, he puts on the radio, and a soft rock song filters through the speakers.

"If you don't mind me asking, what's the deal with you and this case? You said Lars was an old friend, but this seems like a lot of work to go through for just an old friend."

I look at him, but his eyes are trained out the windshield as the light turns green. "He's my ex, actually. We broke up in college, years ago, but his death hit me hard. I don't know how to explain it. Someone dying after you break up . . . it's like losing them twice."

He nods, hands adjusting on the steering wheel. "Did you still talk to him?"

The question fills me with guilt. I would have, if I hadn't ignored the message he left me just days before he died. "No, but I still cared about him. And I just don't believe this act that no one wants to know how he really died. They either know more than they're telling, or they have their own suspicions and everyone's just too polite to say anything." Even as I say the word, I'm not sure it's accurate. When it comes to being silent about a murder, politeness is a pathetic excuse. It's either deception or fear.

Finn is quiet for a moment, and we drive on. The roads are gritty and brown, coating every vehicle in a sheen of scum. We pass the museum, a few streets of houses, a couple of banks.

Finally, he glances at me. "I think that's amazing. I don't have a lot of exes, but I can't imagine any of them trying to find out what happened to me if I died. You're pretty special."

My heart leaps, but I do my best to keep the reaction off my face. I need to be modest, humble. I settle for a small smile. "Thank you."

I may not know what I'm doing, and everyone in town clearly wants me to mind my own business, but at least one other person thinks that my investigation is important. Not just important, but *good*. Valuable.

Finn pulls into the parking lot behind a strip of shops and restaurants. We enter the café through the back. The place is crowded and loud, tables full of young parents trying to share smashed avocado on toast with toddlers drinking babyccinos. Finn leads me to a small private room off to the right, where a woman a few years older than me is sitting with large headphones over her ears, typing on a laptop.

When we pull our chairs out, she looks up with a start, then smiles. "Oh gosh, sorry! Sit down, sit down. I was just trying to finish this edit." She tucks a strand of reddish-brown hair behind her ear and rubs her pale forehead with the tips of her fingers.

"Feel free to keep going," I say.

After typing a few more words, she closes the laptop. "It can wait. Hi. Hi! I'm Parker." She extends her hand across the table, and I shake it. "Thank you for meeting me. Finn says you have some *very interesting* information about one of the pastors at Messiah Church, and I am all ears for that, baby. Not to sound too eager, but I've been trying to nail those guys on something for years. The stories I've heard about that church . . . whew. Well, I don't have to tell you."

Either this woman has already had a triple-shot espresso or she's the fastest talker I've ever met. I instantly like her. "No, you definitely don't. The thing is, I only have theories right now. I'm guessing you need proof before you can print anything."

Parker takes a sip of water, shakes her head, and twirls her hand in a *go on* motion. "Let me worry about that. You just tell me your story!

But first, do you want something to eat? Drink? Lindsay!" She gestures at someone behind me, and a waitress appears.

I glance at Finn, who is holding back a smile. Apparently, the talking-a-mile-a-minute thing is normal. We order coffees and sandwiches, and then Parker reopens her laptop.

"Do you mind if I record this? Just in case I miss something I want to go back to later. You wouldn't believe how quickly I forget stuff. It's a real hazard in my business, let me tell you. Luckily, I make up for it with kick-ass writing."

I chew my bottom lip. "I don't know . . . Did Finn tell you I don't want to be named? It's just, I have family still in the church, and even though we're not close, I don't exactly want to cause more problems for them."

"Oh, of course, of course. This is strictly for my records; no one will know you're talking to me. The recording won't be published."

Finn meets my gaze, gives me a small nod. Letting out a breath, I look back at Parker. "Okay. Sure."

"Excellent." She hits a few keys on the laptop. "Now, I understand you have reason to suspect that there might be more to the death of Lars Oback than a simple hunting accident."

"That's right."

I fiddle with the napkin as I continue. "I attended Lars's funeral because he was an old friend. An old ex-boyfriend, actually. But don't put that on the record because then everyone will know who I am. Right away, I had a weird feeling that we weren't getting the whole story. His parents said the police won't tell them who he was hunting with or how they know it was an accident. Plus, Lars was shot right in the chest from less than a hundred yards away, according to his dad. That doesn't sound like an accident to me."

When I say it all out loud, it sounds so logical. Pride swells up in me as Parker takes notes. I'm not good at a lot of things, but maybe I'm good at this.

The door to our secluded room opens, letting in a buzz of conversation and coffee grinding. Lindsay sets down our coffees, napkins, and silverware, then walks back out, shutting the door behind her.

"So, that led you to start asking questions around town, is that right?" Parker asks.

After taking a drink of my latte, I nod.

"Can you answer out loud just so I have it?" she asks with a smile.

"Oh, right." I laugh nervously. "Yes, I started asking questions. I went to a few different people who knew Lars—members of Messiah. They didn't give me a lot of information, but I started to suspect some things. I left a few years ago, but I still know Messiah pretty well. And I know when things are off."

My throat dries at the thought of what I'm about to say. Once I tell Parker this, there's no going back. Even if I am anonymous, Eve and Esha and Keith will all know that I'm the source. Maybe this is a bad idea.

"What kind of things?" Parker asks, encouraging me.

I take another drink to work up my courage. Finally, I say, "At the funeral, I walked past what was supposed to be an empty area of the church, and I saw Eve with another man. The associate pastor, Keith Rivers. Keith is a few years older than Eve, but we were in the same high school for a while, and everyone knew he had a crush on her. But we weren't allowed to date in high school, and by the time she graduated, she basically went straight into a relationship with Lars. Keith never had a chance with her. So, I thought it was pretty suspicious when I saw him whispering in her ear in a dark corner at her husband's funeral. And then I found out people in the church knew she and Lars were having problems. Marriage counseling is supposed to be confidential, but if you're one of the higher-ups in the church, you can find out just about anything about anyone."

Parker's eyes are alight when she looks up from her notes. "This is juicy stuff. What about Eve? She writes that super popular Noble Wife blog, right?"

"Yeah, and that's important. Say Eve was having an affair with Keith. A lot of people might ask why she wouldn't just divorce Lars to be with him. But the thing is, not only is divorce basically not an option in Messiah, she would never be able to stand that kind of hit to her reputation. She *is* the Noble Wife. Her marriage to Lars is supposed to be perfect.

Even having it get out that they were in counseling would have devastated her. She would have every reason to hide what was going on."

"And it would also mean Keith knew he had no real future with her," Parker says.

"Not as long as Lars was around, no." A painful knot forms in my throat at the thought of him being treated like an inconvenience, something to brush out of the way.

"So what's your theory?" she asks. "You think Keith and Eve were having an affair and Keith killed Lars to be with her?"

The words are so blatant, they seem to ring throughout the room. I look at Finn. His gaze is somber, but he doesn't say anything.

"I think it's possible. It might not seem like a big deal, but Eve hasn't posted on her blog for like two months, which is not normal. She used to write weekly, talking about how great her marriage was." Parker looks doubtful, but I press on. "All I know is that the church is covering for somebody. There's no way they don't know who shot Lars, and it would have to be someone pretty important for Pastor Rick to lend his protection."

"When you say 'they,' who do you mean?" she asks.

"The leaders. Or at least Pastor Rick and some of his elders. The sheriff. Maybe even some of the congregation."

"If they know Keith did it, though, why would they cover it up?"

"Are you a Christian?"

Blinking, Parker shakes her head. "Agnostic. Why?"

"There's this verse in 1 Peter, 'Love covers over a multitude of sins.' That was one of Pastor Rick's favorite messages to preach when he was talking about church unity, how we have to fight against the ways the world tries to tear us apart. Sins of individual church members are dealt with by the church, as much as possible. And often that means 'covering over' the sin, forgiving the person and pretending like what they did never happened. Especially if the person is one of the leaders of the church, and *especially* if exposing that sin would make the church look bad."

It doesn't always work that way, though. Whose sins get covered over and whose get exposed for the community to judge and condemn is usually left up to the church leaders.

"I see. So, if Rick Franklin's star Noble Wife influencer and his associate pastor were having an affair, that would be reason enough for the church to unite in covering it up."

"Right. And if Keith and Eve got rid of her husband so they could be together? Not even Rick could spin his way out of that one, so if that's what happened, they'd do whatever it takes to make sure no one else finds out."

Parker finishes a note, and the waitress comes back in with our sandwiches. "Eat, eat." She grabs a bite and continues to type. "Trust me, these things are way better hot."

I do as she says and take a bite of my Reuben. Finn is focused on his grilled cheese and tomato soup. After a few more bites, I say, "So, that's what I have. Nobody's made any confessions or anything to me, but I wouldn't expect them to. I just want the truth to come out. We—Lars's parents and I—just want to know what really happened to him. I think they deserve that, more than anything. But the church is tough to crack, and I don't know how much more I can do."

For pastors like Rick, the church isn't just a family or a community or a place of fellowship. It is first and foremost an institution, a fixture whose spiritual and emotional significance its leaders can leverage to gain power. And like any institution, it is excellent at protecting itself—especially when threatened with exposure by an insider trying to do the right thing.

Swallowing a mouthful of food, Parker grins. "Leave that to me. I'm a good little digger, and you'd be surprised the things people confess to journalists that they wouldn't tell their closest friends."

I play with a potato chip. "I don't know. Messiah is locked down pretty tight. Pastor Rick makes sure everyone knows they can't trust the media, and that means local papers too. He always says that they're biased and anti-Christian."

Parker snorts. "Hilarious. The talking points are always the same. Never mind that ninety percent of our masthead goes to church every Sunday. But hold on one second—I have some notes about Keith you'll want to know about." She clicks on something on her computer, scrolls for a second, then nods. "My source in the sheriff's department wouldn't tell me much, but I do know they interviewed Keith Rivers because he was one of the last calls Lars made on his cell phone."

I stiffen. If they were looking at Lars's cell records, that meant they would know he called me too. I wonder if they've told Eve.

Parker continues. "The deputy I talked to said Keith was hunting with a friend over ten miles away at the time Lars was killed. I'm not saying the part about his affair with Eve is wrong, but he couldn't have killed her husband."

I sit back in my chair. Finn looks just as stunned as I am, his hand gripping the table. "What? Are you sure?" he asks.

Her lips pull together. "Pretty sure. When you told me what Del was looking into, I checked with the friend, who corroborated Keith's story. He drove Keith that day. They were hunting on someone's farm . . . Hold on one sec." She scrolls again. "Bill and Angie Nilsen. They confirmed it. Even though they were in different parts of the woods, this guy said there's no way Keith could have made the drive to where Lars was. He had the keys to his car, and Bill and Angie left for the day shortly after they arrived, taking their car with them."

My heart sinks. I set down my sandwich, appetite gone.

"I'm sorry. That doesn't mean you're wrong about the affair, though! I will definitely look into that." Parker reaches out to pat my arm. "Hey, seriously, don't be so hard on yourself. I've been doing this for a while. You would not believe how many false starts I've made."

But I can't take any comfort from that. If after all this I prove that Eve had an affair but her husband really was just killed in a freak accident, what will I have accomplished? Showing that the Noble Wife philosophy is a scam? Making sure my former friend's life is just a little bit more destroyed?

Even if she brought it on herself, it's still spiteful. Vindictive. Exactly the kind of behavior Colette was always warning me against.

Exactly the kind of thing everyone here would assume I'd do. And I'm proving them right.

TWENTY-NINE

Noble Wife Journey: a blog
Title: Tribulation
Published: February 3, 2013

John 16:33 tells us, "In the world you will have tribulation. But take heart; I have overcome the world." Scriptures like this are a comfort to me in times of deep sorrow, and unfortunately, our Messiah family is going through just such a time now.

Last night, we wrapped up a three-day Noble Wife conference with the high school–aged girls in Messiah and all the best leaders in the church. It was a beautiful, challenging, enriching, precious time—and, of course, Satan and his demons would do anything to put a stop to that. Heartbreakingly, the Lord of Evil has attacked in a devastating blow.

On her way home from the conference, Pastor Rick's wife, Hillary Franklin, was in an accident. They believe a deer jumped in front of her on the highway and she swerved to avoid hitting it, sending her car off the road. It rolled several times before coming to a stop upside down. We are told she did not suffer—the Lord instantly called her home.

The passing of a beloved member of the Body of Christ is always bittersweet, as we know that they are now dancing on the streets of heaven, yet we miss their presence here in our lives. Mrs. Franklin was one of my greatest mentors. I can't imagine going to Messiah without seeing her.

I'm sure it will take readers of this blog time to process this tragedy as well. I invite any Messiah women to share stories about or prayers for Mrs. Franklin in the comments.

Before I leave you, though, I have to say one thing. He would not want me to make this about him, but I am just overwhelmed with the strength of Pastor Rick today. My family and I assumed that one of the elders would be preaching this morning, to give our senior pastor time and privacy to mourn. But when the last worship song faded out, there he was, walking onto the stage. I want to share what this moment was like with you, so that you can experience what faith looks like in practice, even in the most awful circumstances. I've dictated the words here, but you can listen to today's message on the church website if you want to hear it for yourself. I strongly recommend that you do.

"Our church is being tested." Pastor Rick said, his voice just as powerful as usual. "And we are found wanting. Satan has exploited a weakness in our faith, and now my wife is gone. But I will not allow her death to be in vain, no. I will be here every day, working with every Messiah member, to bring us in line with the Word and the Will of God."

He looked out at us, more furious and distraught than I've ever seen him. I watched him through tears, as I'm sure everyone around me did. I could hear the shuddering breaths, the stifled sobs of my community in mourning.

"I will not bow to you, Devil," he shouted. "I will not yield. This is my flock, and I am God's mouthpiece, and I will not. Go. Quietly."

Onstage, the band took up their instruments again, playing music to accompany our pastor.

"If God is for us, who can be against us?" he said. "No weapon formed against us shall prosper! If you are with me, stand to your feet. Lift up your hands to praise God." Around me, people rose, hands in the air. I stood with them. "And if you are not with me, now is the time to go. Our church is being tested, and I refuse to falter. I refuse to fail. Satan obviously hates the message being preached here, but do you think that's going to stop me?"

"No!" people said around me.

"No!" I agreed. Our voices rang to the heavens.

"No," Pastor Rick agreed. "He can't stop me. You can't stop me.

But if you are not ready to lose everything for the sake of this message, you are not ready to be part of Messiah Church. And we can't afford to have your weakness here. If you're going to go, go now. But if you stay, I want to see your full commitment to this church, to this Gospel, to this Jesus." He gestured at the cross behind him. "And I want to see your full commitment to the man God has anointed and placed at your pulpit."

The room was silent except for the melancholy tones of the piano and guitar.

For the first time, his voice broke as he said, "It's the least I can ask, now that I have sacrificed everything for you."

My mother took my hand, and I looked over to see Dad holding hers. I took Esha's next to me. As a family, we raised them in the air. "We are committed." My father's voice rang out across the auditorium.

Behind us, in front of us, all across the room, other families lifted their joined hands as well. Hundreds of voices of Messiah members built to support our pastor.

"We are committed. We are committed. We are committed."

In our devastation, in our grief, in our sorrow—Satan could not divide us. We are united in this fight for the truth.

THIRTY

"HE MUST BE LYING," I say as soon as we're in the car.

"What?" Finn asks, cranking up the heat.

"Keith's alibi. There must be a hole in it somewhere."

He pulls the car out of the parking lot, not saying a word. His jaw is working, like he's grinding his teeth.

I press on. "Parker seemed to believe me that Keith and Eve were having an affair. What are the chances that's true and it just so happens Lars really did die in a freak accident? It's too big a coincidence. He must have faked the alibi somehow. Got his friend to lie for him or something."

My mind is racing, trying to remember how many people I told my suspicions about Keith and Eve. I thought I was being cautious, but I know that I implied they were having an affair to multiple people—especially to Keith himself. I bring my freezing-cold hands to my face, trying to cool it down.

"You're quiet," I say after a few moments go by.

Finn's eyes are trained out the cloudy windshield. "What if you were wrong about the affair? Do you think that's possible?"

My lips part, but words escape me. It's like he knew exactly what I was thinking.

He eases to a stop at a red light, the wheels shuddering over a patch of ice. The sun is going down, and anything that melted during the day is now becoming slick and hazardous on the road.

I can't back down now. "Anything is possible, but I'm sure there was something going on between them. Plus, he would have set up an alibi for himself if he was going to kill Lars. Anyone smart would. But that doesn't mean it's airtight."

"I don't know." He still won't look at me. "Maybe he really didn't do it."

I clench my hands under my thighs. The light turns green, and he moves forward. "The police aren't looking at this case closely. They think it was an accident. They probably don't even consider Keith's story an *alibi*, because they're not accusing him of anything. Parker even said the only reason they talked to him was because he was one of the last people to speak to Lars."

"That's true," he concedes.

We crest the hill going toward the end of town, the pinks and oranges of an early sunset painting the horizon. The days are getting incredibly short, and I feel like I'm running out of time. How long am I going to stay here, playing investigator? I've got a job and a free place to stay, but I can't take advantage of the Obacks' generosity forever.

"Have you ever been in a serious relationship?" I ask suddenly. In my peripheral vision, I see him look at me, but I keep my gaze trained out the window. "It's just, we're talking about all these relationships between Lars and Eve and Keith, and I've never actually asked if you have been engaged or married."

We pass a florist, a used bookstore, a boutique that Esha loved when we were in high school. Finally, Finn answers.

"Engaged. To a girl who used to work at Elaine's. We met in high school."

"What happened?"

He's quiet for another long moment. "She cheated on me."

A burst of anger explodes in my chest.

When I say nothing, he continues. "She said once I graduated from high school, I got too busy with work. And I was too 'emo' when we were together."

I snort, then clap my hand over my mouth. "Sorry. It's not funny."

But he chuckles too, a little darkly. "No, it kind of is. We started dating in my senior year and got engaged when we were nineteen because that was the Christian kid thing to do, right? Stayed together until I was twenty. She's right, though. I did get emo. Those were about the worst years of my life."

My hand falls to my lap. "Oh? Why?"

He slows to a stop at a red light. "They just were."

"Okay." I don't want to push, but I need him to know that I understand. "I got cheated on too. When I was about the same age. We weren't engaged, but I thought that's where it was headed."

His eyes meet mine, a deep hurt and sadness glowing there. "I'm sorry."

"I'm sorry too." Feeling bold, I reach out and put my hand on his thigh. His hand settles on top of mine. My heartbeat picks up enough that I worry he can feel it through my palm.

After a moment, he says, "Maybe Keith hired someone to kill Lars."

The sudden right turn in the conversation catches me off guard. I pause, considering his suggestion. "I don't think so. That would require a decent chunk of money, not to mention the kind of underworld connections a pastor who grew up in a small town probably wouldn't have."

"Fair point. You have a different theory?"

"Let's assume his friend isn't lying for him, and so he really didn't have a car. There must be some way he could have made the trip in that time and gotten back before his friend noticed he was missing. We don't know exactly where the farm Lars was hunting on is, but Parker said he was about ten miles away, so he'd have to drive or have someone pick him up."

Finn bites his lower lip for a moment. "I doubt someone picked him up. That would mean he had to trust another person to be in on it and lie for him. Plus, it snowed right before hunting weekend. The roads were icy as hell, and I doubt he'd risk a high-speed drive on them."

"So, no car and no ride." We pass a snowy hill, carved up by narrow tracks. I point out the window. "What about a snowmobile?"

He follows my gesture for a moment before refocusing on the road. "That could work. If he was driving from one farm to another, it would actually probably be faster. He could cut straight across fields and not have to worry about speed limits. No one monitors those out in the country, not really."

Excitement fizzes inside me. Keith and his family had snowmobiles when I was growing up; most of the guys in church did. And I know Bill and Angie Nilsen do. Their son Levi was a year ahead of me, and he used to have a bunch of guys in his grade around for races in the winter. If Keith knew he had access to a snowmobile in their shed, it would be the perfect way for him to set up an alibi and still get to murder Lars.

As we pull into the parking lot of Elaine's, I say, "This would be a lot easier to figure out if we knew the farm where Lars was hunting. Without that, we can't even test whether the snowmobile route would work with the time."

Finn's expression has shifted from doubtful to confident over the course of the car ride. He's almost smiling when he says, "We don't need to test it. We just need to show that he could have done it that way. The rest is up to the police, if they ever decide to get off their asses and investigate. At least this way, we know the alibi could have holes poked in it."

At least this way, I don't know for sure that I'm wrong yet either. "To be fair, I think there's a reason the police aren't looking into this case. It's the same reason everyone in the church is going along with the accident story without asking any questions."

"Why's that?" Finn asks. The sun goes behind a cloud, dimming the light in the car.

"Pastor Rick." My hands clench when I say his name. "I don't know how, but he's involved in this. And that's going to make getting to the truth even harder."

He watches me quietly for a moment. Finally, he nods. "It certainly is."

I glance out the window, my fingers twisted up together. "I'm going to call the police when I get home. I just need to figure out how to make them listen to me."

He turns off the ignition, and I look at him. In the fading light, his eyes are dark as tar, and I could swear he almost looks impressed. "I'm sure you'll find a way. You're getting pretty hard to ignore."

Before I can respond, he smiles and gets out of the car.

THIRTY-ONE

Delilah's diary

JULY 4, 2013

Tonight, I watched the fireworks alone on the roof of my house. The spare bedroom window opens out onto the roof of our three-seasons porch, and from there, I can see the whole Independence Day display from Garfield Park light up the sky without any trees in the way. Someday, I want to bring a man here. Not just anyone. The one.

Things have been better since my confession. Even though I'm not able to do the drama ministry anymore, I'm allowed to attend my last youth camp in a couple weeks. Part of me doesn't really want to go, to be honest. Things have gotten mostly back to normal, but I still feel people looking at me all the time. I might be forgiven, but what I did won't ever be forgotten unless God decides to wipe the memories of everyone in Messiah.

I wonder what that would be like. Just one day of going to church where everyone has completely forgotten what happened. When people look at me, they would still see the same modest, pure girl I was before. They would once again be impressed by my acting skills onstage, rather than the ones I've had to use just to survive every interaction these past few months.

I think if I could flip a switch and make them all forget, I would. If it made me forget too, that would be even better.

I just have to get through six more weeks. On the 19th of August 2013, I will put my packed bags in the car and drive to Moorhead. My parents won't come with me. We'll say goodbye here at home—it's less dramatic. Plus, it's only twenty minutes away. I will drive that stretch of highway, every second taking me farther away from here, closer to my new life.

Moorhead Christian College is a destination spot for Messiah kids, so I know I won't be completely starting over. But none of my friends are coming. Esha is going to St. Paul, and Lily and Felicity are doing NDSU. Eve still has another year of high school before she'll join me in Moorhead. There are a few people from my class going to MCC, but no one I'm close to.

In that way, it's a new beginning. I can put everything that happened last year behind me.

And tonight, I celebrated that freedom, my own personal Independence Day.

THIRTY-TWO

WHEN I ARRIVE BACK AT Nathaniel and Susan's, there's a note for me on the counter.

Out for dinner. There are frozen pizzas if you're interested.

A night on the sofa in front of their huge TV sounds like exactly what I need after running around with Finn all day. I pour myself a glass of wine while I wait for the oven to preheat.

We didn't prove anything today, but the snowmobile theory does make sense. If we thought of it, maybe that means the police will too. But they haven't seemed interested in investigating this case at all. I know from true crime podcasts and TV shows that the police don't always get it right. When I grew up here, I basically thought they could do no wrong. Police, Republicans, evangelical Christians, the military—there were a lot of people I was raised to think were basically the good guys, always in opposition to the much bigger and much more powerful bad ones. We were David, and the secular world was Goliath, and just like the shepherd who would become king, we would prevail if we had enough faith. Anyone different, even if they claimed to share the same beliefs as us, was an outsider.

Difference was a threat, a potential disruption of their power. It's no wonder that Messiah looks the same now that it did five, ten years ago. Very white, very conservative, very straight. Even the faces I didn't recognize at Lars's funeral were familiar.

It has taken years to undo that us-versus-them thinking, and sometimes I think I'm still undoing it. It's why I haven't found another place I could go to church, even though I still believe in God. For me, getting away from fundamentalism has been like going on a cleanse. I had to stop consuming religion altogether, let the toxins leach from my soul until they're all gone. Maybe one day when they are, I'll find a way to reintroduce the healthier aspects of the church into my life again. Assuming I'll be able to recognize which ones they are.

The oven dings, and I take the frozen pizza out of the box, setting it on the middle rack. Perched on a stool at the kitchen island, I open my phone, searching for the number for the sheriff's office in Bower. I can't just sit here eating pizza when I know something that might be useful to the police. Keith is probably calm and comfortable at home right now, convinced he's gotten away with it. And if they're really buying that Lars was killed by accident, that means Keith is right.

"Green County Sheriff," a crisp voice answers.

"Yeah, hi, I'm wondering if I can talk to someone about a . . . um, do you have like a tip line or something?"

"This is the line, ma'am. We're a small office."

"Oh, okay." I fiddle with the hem of my shirt. "I'm calling about a case you got recently. Lars Oback. He was killed on a hunting trip."

"Yeah, I know the one. That was an accident, though. As far as I know, there's no open file."

I sigh. "That's what I want to talk to you about. I think you might want to look into something. You know his wife was rumored to be having an affair?"

There's a long pause. Then the woman on the line asks, "Who is this?"

My face flushes. "It doesn't matter who I am. I think you should look into Keith Rivers. He told you he was hunting ten miles away when Lars was killed and didn't have a car, but I know he had access to a snowmobile. He could easily have used it to make the drive and get back before his friend even knew he was missing."

"Ma'am, please identify yourself. I can't take down your tip if you don't tell me who you are."

I stammer for a moment, but then I remember something from those crime shows. "Actually, that's not true. You can accept anonymous tips. People do that all the time, especially in small towns where everyone knows everyone. Well, I'm giving this to you anonymously. You should look into Keith Rivers. Lars wasn't shot by accident. Goodbye."

I hang up, my lower lip between my teeth. It's easily the most disrespectful I've ever been to law enforcement, and it actually feels *good* for a second. Until I remember that I called from my cell phone, and they can easily trace that. She'll know who I am within minutes, if she doesn't already. But it's too late now. I've given them the information. I've done my part. And now I'll have to wait.

A soft chime sounds in the kitchen, and I look at the oven, confused. Only a few minutes have gone by since I put the pizza in. When it goes off again, I realize it's the doorbell. Leaving my wine on the counter, I walk to the front, my socks sliding on the wood floors. The porch light is on, but I can't make out the face through the textured glass window. It must be someone coming by to talk to Nathaniel or Susan. I open the door.

Keith Rivers pushes his way in before I have a chance to react. "Why did you come to Bower, Delilah?" He slams the door behind him, presses his back up against it.

Heart scaling my throat, I inch away from him. The foyer of the Obacks' split-level is small, and I end up in a corner near the carpeted stairs that go down to the basement. Keith doesn't appear to be armed, but his hands are curled into fists, and I've never seen the kind of rage that tightens his face. My pulse thunders as I try to calculate possible ways to escape him in a house I'm barely familiar with. He's got almost a foot of height on me; no way I could outrun him.

"I came back for Lars's funeral," I say, surprised at how strong my voice sounds.

"That was days ago. Why are you still here?" He stands in front of the door, as if he can sense how desperately I want him to move away from it. The gust of November wind he let in with his arrival sends a chill through me.

I meet his gaze for a moment, but the fury burning there makes me look away. He obviously knows I've done something, but I don't know how much he's aware of. No sense making him angrier than he already is. "Lars's parents don't think he was killed by accident. I don't either. So, I've been asking around, trying to find out if there was someone who might have benefited from him dying."

Keith's eyes blaze. I have made a mistake. He takes a step toward me, then pauses. "Like me? You think I benefited from him dying?"

"I . . . I didn't say that. I just want to know what happened to him. I know that the truth can sometimes get murky here."

"The truth is never murky. The truth is the truth. Who gets the privilege of knowing it—that's the part that people get confused about." He takes another step toward me, and my knees bend, ready to spring into action. "As a pastor at Messiah, I get access to certain information that the rest of the congregation can't know about. Sometimes it's to protect people's privacy, sometimes it's to protect spiritual revelation. But either way, I know who I can open up to and who I can't."

My breath comes out in tight, shallow bursts as he looms over me.

"You are not someone anyone should trust." His tone shifts from angry to condescending. "You abandoned your family. You are not right with God. Why you think anyone should listen to you is beyond me, but a yappy dog is still an annoyance even if they are not a threat. Stop going around town, stop talking to members of Messiah, and stop slandering me. Or I will press charges—against you and against the Obacks."

I swallow, but it does nothing to get rid of the dry knot in my throat. "I wasn't trying to—"

He puts up his hand, and I freeze, expecting a slap. Instead, his palm slams into the wall behind my head. I jump, a cry escaping my lips. "I suggest you leave. The Obacks are mourning, which is understandable, but they will come to see in time that the story of Lars's death is the truth, even if it's not satisfying. You, though. I have no hope for you. I don't waste my time on people who are blind to the truth."

After giving his words a moment to sink in, Keith turns and starts back to the door. When he opens it, suddenly I can't keep my words in. "I know there is something going on with you and Eve." His shoulders tense. "I might not have all the details, but you're more than just a pastor and a 'brother in Christ.' And I'm not the only one who knows. If there's an innocent explanation, I suggest you get ready to talk about it. Because pretty soon, I'm not going to be the only one asking."

He looks over his shoulder at me. Sweat breaks out on my neck. A loud buzzing pierces the silence between us—my pizza timer. He glances in the direction of the kitchen for a moment, then looks back at me. "No one wants you here, Delilah. No one wanted you at the funeral either. Your presence can only cause pain. For your sake and everyone else's, I hope you're gone by morning."

I'M SITTING IN *Pastor Rick's office, and the overhead lights are off. The only thing illuminating the room is the glow of his desk lamp, covered with a green glass shade. It casts his face in shadow.*

"Tell me what you did," he says.

I close my eyes. If I let myself, it's easy to pretend that none of this ever happened. I might simply fall asleep and wake up in a world where everything is right again—my parents look at me with pride, I am on the rotation to play keyboard for youth group worship, I get starring roles in our drama skits, and younger girls look at me with admiration. It might not be everything I want, but it's enough. I could be happy with that. I think now, knowing what I know, I could be content to go back to that Before Time.

"Repentance is an action, Delilah," Pastor Rick says, his voice cutting through my wishful thinking. "It starts with acknowledging the wrong you've done. Only by accepting the harm you've caused can you resolve not to do it again."

My throat aches with all the words trapped inside it. Finally, I whisper, "I don't want to say." The skin on my neck and face feels like it's a thousand degrees.

"If you want to get right with God, you don't have a choice."

As hot as it feels in this room, I know that hell is much worse. Tears fill my eyes as I focus them on Pastor Rick's face. I can do this. I can suffer this small moment of humiliation if it means finally being free of everything that's happened the past few weeks.

Lips numb, I say, "First of all, I never let him touch me."

An alarm goes off. I jolt upright in bed, bleary with the thick fog of sleep. My hands feel around in the dark of early winter morning, finally landing on my phone.

I had gone years without dreaming about Pastor Rick, but since I've been back near Bower, it's happened more than once. Turning my alarm off, I try to shake the image of his eyes glowing in the lamplight. That part wasn't accurate. His office was always fully lit when he made me do my confessions. More innocent-looking if anyone were to walk in on us, which they always could. He didn't have a lock on his door.

The dream clings to me as I roll out of bed. It's been almost ten years since I sat in Pastor Rick's office, telling him my sins, but the memory of them hasn't blurred. They play over in my head in the dark when I'm trying to sleep, in the quiet pauses between customers at work, in the few moments of intimacy I've had with men when my body has won out over the rules still infusing every romantic interaction I have.

I was still awake when Nathaniel and Susan returned home last night, but I didn't tell them about Keith accosting me in their house. I came here to be safe, but it's clear that will never be possible as long as I'm within thirty miles of Bower. At the time my motel room was vandalized, only a few people knew I was still in the area. Colette doesn't seem like the type to break and enter, but the verse written in lipstick on the mirror is right up her alley. Keith has already shown he's capable of threatening me, but I don't think he would have had time to mess up my room after I had just visited him at the church that day. At this point, though, it doesn't really matter who did it. Bower wants to reject me like a bad organ, but I'm not letting it cut me out as easily as it did last time.

After washing my face and combing my hair in the adjoining bathroom, I slip a hoodie over my head and wander downstairs for breakfast. The smell of French toast draws me into the kitchen, where Nathaniel is standing in front of a griddle, flipping four golden-brown slices. His freshly shaved face is serious with concentration, but when he sees me enter, he looks up with a broad smile.

"You're not at work."

I wrap my arms around myself. "Lunch shift today."

He flips the last piece, then opens a cabinet and hands me a blue mug. His chin juts toward the coffee maker. "Help yourself. Susan is out with a friend for brunch."

I pour my coffee, add a splash of milk, and take a drink. "Smells amazing."

"You haven't been here in the morning, so you don't know—I'm the breakfast master." He puts two finished pieces on a plate, sprinkles on sliced bananas from the cutting board, and slides it across the counter to me.

I take a seat on one of the stools and add a generous helping of the syrup and butter in front of me. The French toast is perfect: crispy on the outside; hot and soft in the middle. He looks for my reaction, and I close my eyes, nodding in approval. "Absolutely the breakfast master."

Looking pleased with himself, he dips four more slices in the bowl of egg mixture. The griddle sizzles as he places them on.

He turns back to me. "I was going to ask, did you happen to go out to my shed since you came here? It's no problem if you did. I was just out there this morning trying to find the salt for the driveway, and it seemed like a few things had been moved."

I frown. "No, I didn't even know you had a shed."

"Huh." He glances out the kitchen window, and I follow his gaze. A small metal structure sits against the line of trees in the Obacks' backyard, half-covered in branches. "You know, I told my neighbor he could borrow tools whenever he needed them. I'll give him a call."

"Is anything missing?" It's possible Keith went out there last night, but I have no idea what he would have been looking for.

"No, not as far as I could tell." He flips the toast, then smiles at me. "Anyway, how are things going? Any progress? Susan and I were thinking, maybe there's something in Eve's blog that we missed. Some hint that Lars was in danger or that she was worried about him."

I take another bite, talking around it. "I thought of that. Haven't been able to find anything, though." The image of Keith's furious gaze flashes through my mind. I avoid looking toward the foyer. Nathaniel's shoulders slump, and I rush on. "It's too early to say what, but I think I'm making progress. Obviously a few people aren't happy with me poking around. That must mean I'm getting close to finding something."

"You have a suspect?"

I feel a flash of embarrassment at his phrasing. I can't tell Nathaniel about Keith yet. If I do that, I'll have to tell him about last night, and I know he'll want me to report it to the police. Keith will deny everything, so it'll be his word against mine. Right back where I started.

"No, nothing yet." I drink my coffee, waiting for him to ask more questions, but he is silent. Finally, I say, "I'm sorry I don't have more answers yet. I don't want to overstay my welcome here if—"

"Don't be silly." Nathaniel slides the spatula under a slice of bread, checking the bottom. Then he meets my gaze. "It's nice having someone else in the house. Susan and I . . . Well, after you become a parent, the primary thing you talk about is your child. With Lars gone, we can't seem to figure out what to say to each other."

My eyes prickle with tears.

He clears his throat. "Of course, if you'd rather go stay with your parents—"

"No." I study the coffee in my mug. "We're not really talking much right now." I feel awful saying that to someone who just lost their child, but it's the truth.

There is no hint of judgment on his face. Instead, he offers me a small smile. "You are welcome here as long as you like, whether you find out anything about Lars or not."

On the counter next to him, his phone vibrates. He picks it up and swipes across the screen. "Hello." He continues checking the bread, phone clenched between his ear and shoulder. After a moment, he drops the spatula, hand flying to keep the phone in place. "What? When?"

My fork pauses in midair.

He listens for another minute. Finally, he says, "Of course. I'll be in right away." He pulls the phone away from his ear, staring at it for a moment before setting it on the counter.

"What happened?" The faint smell of burning bread wafts across the counter, but Nathaniel doesn't seem to notice. He's staring somewhere past me. I slide off the stool and walk around to his side of the counter, picking up the spatula to flip the French toast. Then I turn and put my hand on his shoulder. Slowly, his gaze shifts to focus on me. "Nathaniel, what's wrong?"

He blinks. For a moment, he looks old—much older than his fifty-something years—and confused.

"They arrested her," he says, blue eyes watering. "They arrested Eve."

THIRTY-THREE

Noble Wife Journey: a blog
Title: Him
Published: April 11, 2014

I have woken up in a new world.

I wonder if this is how my namesake felt when she blinked open dark eyes to peer up at the bright naked sky.

I am not the first Eve, but I am her daughter. I am flesh and breath and bone carved from man. I have light in my eyes and ambition to understand the mysteries of the world.

In those first few moments of Eden, I like to think she wandered. She stood on shaky feet with toes curled in thick warm grass, and she stared at the expanse of lush nature around her. In my mind's eye, she reached out to touch an orange hanging heavy and ripe on the branch, felt its knotted rubbery skin under her fingertips, smelled the burst of bitterness and sun-kissed citrus when she leaned in close. It was not one of the forbidden trees, but she knew nothing about them yet.

As she strode through the garden, the birds announced her presence with their glorious cacophony of song: *She wakes!*

Water bubbled up from the earth and soaked into the soil, hydrating the plants and the animals in the ancient method the world only knew before the Flood. Bees whirred from flower to flower, furry bodies speckled with yellow pollen, no stingers in sight. The world was too perfect for pain. Orange rays of sun lit the tight coils of her black hair, making her appear to the animals who bore witness as an angel walking the earth.

It would not be the first time.

She followed a line of trees until she came to a broad clearing, where she could see so far in the distance it appeared the sky caressed the earth.

That was when she saw him.

Adam tended to a lion, brushing burrs from his mane with long, slender fingers. His back was to her, lost in his thoughts about the deep sleep God had put him in the night before. He only realized her presence when the beast sniffed, raising his head at this strange new smell. Not quite a man, all soil and wood and rushing water. This was richer, more vibrant: jasmine and lightning and sweetgrass. The lion turned to look at her, and with him, the man.

From across the meadow, Adam looked into Eve's eyes for the first time, and the entire expanse of the universe focused into one infinitesimal point on the only two living souls within it.

That is how it felt last night, when I met the one my heart loves.

And today I've woken up in a new world.

THIRTY-FOUR

THE STATION IN BOWER ONLY has two small holding cells, so Eve is being kept at the Green County Jail in Elden. Nathaniel drives me, his anxious energy manifesting in jerky turns and heavy-footed accelerations as he relays what the sheriff's deputy told him on the phone.

An anonymous tip had been called in yesterday, which provided enough information for the sheriff's department to get a search warrant for the property of Eve's parents, Tim and Linda Thompson. Police conducted a targeted search of an old well in their backyard, one I remember playing around with Esha and Eve. We used to toss pennies inside and make wishes—the closest we ever got to dabbling in sorcery. I remember staring down into the inky pit, a damp chill blowing across my face. The depth of the darkness was as difficult to wrap my mind around as the concept of eternity. I imagined if heaven was a place forever glowing, then hell must be like this—the total absence of light.

That well was where they found a rifle registered to Eve Oback, a gift she'd received from Lars a few months earlier. A rifle that apparently was the same caliber as the one that killed Lars.

"So, they were supposed to go hunting together?" I ask.

Nathaniel drums his hands on the steering wheel as we wait at a red light. "That's what the deputy said. Eve had arranged for Emmie to stay with her parents for the weekend so she could join Lars on the hunting trip, but she backed out at the last minute. Said she couldn't be away from her daughter for that long."

The surge of excitement and vindication is making me light-headed.

I knew there was more going on with her than what she told me. I'm sure Eve did tell Lars she couldn't be away from Emmie, but I'm betting that's not why she backed out. She probably wanted an excuse to be with Keith.

As if guessing my suspicions, Nathaniel looks over at me. "Only thing is, she did drop the girl off with her parents after all. Saturday morning, early. I know that from talking to them. Didn't think it was suspicious before, but now . . ."

"It looks bad." I cross my arms, trying to hide the fact that they're shaking. It's looking more and more like I might have sat right across from a cold-blooded killer just a couple days ago. The only thing I don't know for sure is whether it was her or Keith. It could have been both of them together.

"Oh, God." His cupped hand rubs across his mouth. "Emmie. I hope she's with Eve's parents again. That poor girl."

I imagine her wisps of white-blond hair, her brown eyes I've seen only in photos. Eyes she got from her father. The Thompsons are good people. I know they will make sure she's taken care of, with one parent dead and the other in jail, but my heart is still crushed for her.

The light changes, and Nathaniel floors it. "They must think the rifle is the murder weapon. Otherwise, why arrest her?" I ask.

"I don't think they'd know that this early, but nothing else really makes sense."

If there's one thing I know from watching late-night forensic investigation shows with Jess, it's that crime scene testing takes a lot longer than they make it look in the movies.

A ringing sound comes through the car speakers. He hits a button with a phone icon on the steering wheel. "Susan?"

"Nathaniel, what's happening?"

He spends the rest of the drive repeating the details to his wife. When we pull up to the sheriff's station, she hangs up with a promise to be there in twenty minutes, and then we get out of the car.

We check in at the desk, and Nathaniel is met in the lobby by the deputy in charge of his case, who makes it very clear that the information he has is for family only.

Once they disappear, I sit in the waiting area, staring at a wall that looks like it used to be painted some kind of teal color that faded long ago. After ten minutes, I get up and start pacing the room. There are signs up admonishing people not to drink and drive, to report domestic abuse if they witness or experience it, and to comply with police if they're pulled over. Interesting that these warnings are posted here, where someone would only see them after already having an interaction.

My phone buzzes in my pocket. When I see Finn's name on the screen, I answer without greeting him. "They arrested Eve."

There's a short pause. "Ah. I assume that's why you're not at work?"

Crap—my lunch shift. "Finn, I'm sorry. We just got the news like an hour ago and drove straight to the station. My mind just went completely blank."

"It's okay, I understand. So they arrested her? Based on what?"

I quickly explain about the hunting rifle on her parents' property. "Anyway, so I'm at the station with Lars's dad. He's meeting with the sheriff's deputy to get more information, but I'm stuck out here in the lobby."

"Is that where they're holding Eve?" he asks.

"Yeah, why?"

"Oh, no reason. It's just she only got arrested a few hours ago, so she might not have a lawyer yet. And if she doesn't have a lawyer, she probably doesn't have anyone telling her not to take visitors."

The implication hangs in the silence between us. After a moment, I say, "You sure you can deal with lunch without me?"

"Definitely. Don't worry about us."

"Thanks Finn. I'll talk to you later." Before I even slide my phone back in my pocket, I'm at the reception window, talking to a grumpy deputy with a loose ponytail and rings under her eyes. "I'm here to see Eve Oback."

IT TAKES SOME convincing, but eventually, I'm led to a visiting room the size of a maintenance closet. In the center is a battered metal table with a steel ring welded to the top for attaching handcuffs. Eve isn't wearing any when she's led into the room. I don't know if that's because they think she isn't dangerous or because I've told them I'm a friend, so they assume she won't hurt me. Neither explanation makes me feel particularly at ease, but I do my best not to let that show on my face.

We both sit. The chairs are bolted to the floor; the thought of her trying to pry one up to throw at me almost makes me laugh. The way church girls fight has nothing to do with physical violence. We jab with devastating reminders of long-remembered wrongs, innocuous-sounding scriptural admonishments, and poisonous insults coated in the sugary glaze of a polite tone. If the guards really wanted to protect me from Eve, they would tape her mouth shut.

She stares at the table for several minutes. Although there aren't any tears on her face, I can see from her blotchy skin that she's been crying. She's still wearing her own clothes, so I don't get the satisfaction of seeing her in an orange jumpsuit. Not yet, anyway.

Maybe that's why I'm not enjoying this, watching her brought so low. The perfect Noble Wife, the famous Eve Thompson Oback, incarcerated and alone. It's the kind of image that would have made those first few months after I left Bower more bearable.

But I never could have imagined this. I wanted Lars to leave her, to wake up and see sense and come back to me. I didn't want him dead and her in prison.

Finally, I have to break the silence. "You want to tell me what happened?"

Her gaze slowly comes to focus on mine. A chill passes over my skin. I've seen that look before. In the photo on her blog, the one posted in her comments after Emmanuelle's dedication. The one where she looked empty, terrified, as she stared at her baby daughter being committed to God and Messiah Church.

"They think I killed Lars," she whispers.

"Did you?" I ask.

She blinks. "No."

"That doesn't sound super convincing."

"Let's be real, Delilah. You're never going to believe anything I say anyway."

"I wonder why that might be."

"Lars and I being together was God's will. I couldn't avoid loving him any more than I could avoid praying or reading the Bible."

I scoff. "That's a cool excuse you've come up with. Must have made it really easy to not feel guilty for taking him from me for all these years."

"I'm sorry you were hurt."

My fists tighten in my lap. I can't keep the sneer off my face when I respond. "You know as well as I do that's not repentance, Eve. An apology that puts the burden on me and my reaction to the way you wronged me isn't a real apology, just because it has the word 'sorry' in it."

She doesn't look ashamed, but she doesn't argue either. The silence stretches between us, heavy and tense like the sky before a storm.

Again, I'm the one to break it. "If you didn't kill Lars, then who did? Keith?"

Her gaze drops to the table, but she says nothing.

"The murder weapon was registered to you."

"Someone stole it. When I went to put Lars's hunting things away, I noticed it was gone."

"Why didn't you report it?"

"I was going to. I just hadn't had a chance."

I let out a frustrated sigh. "The rifle was on your parents' property, Eve. You must have at least been involved. Unless your dad did it."

She scoffs. "Don't be ridiculous."

She's right. Mr. Thompson is one of the gentlest men I know. Despite his being an elder in a church that glorifies toxic masculinity, I've seen the family photo albums that prove he never shied away from playing with his daughters. There are pages and pages of photos with him and the girls in fairy dress-up, having tea parties, and doing each other's hair. While I'm sure he knows how to shoot, I never knew him even to hunt.

"Speaking of your parents, I hope Emmanuelle is with them? Is there anything I can do to help?"

Eve's hollowed-out eyes settle on my face. "You've done quite enough, haven't you?"

"I just wanted to make sure she's okay. Because you know the Obacks would be happy to have her if you need—"

"She's fine," Eve spits. "My parents have her."

My fingers dig into my thighs. "Why do you hate the Obacks, anyway? Nathaniel and Susan are so kind. I can't imagine they've done anything to deserve the way you treat them."

"And how do I treat them? Enlighten me, Delilah, since you know everything despite having ghosted this town six years ago."

"I . . . They were just always so kind to me. Like second parents. I never doubted they loved me, even when Lars—" My voice falters.

After a moment, she speaks again, all the anger drained from her voice. "And that's your answer. I never doubted they loved you too. Loved you for him."

I gape at her. I assumed the obvious animosity toward Eve from Nathaniel and Susan was because they felt she was withholding information about Lars from them, but maybe I was wrong. If that's the way their relationship has always been, I can't blame Eve for being hurt, even if I feel a shameful swell of pride that they like me better.

An apology sits on my lips—a knee-jerk reaction to knowing I've caused someone pain—but I refuse to let it out.

At last, Eve ends the silence again. "What are you even doing here, Delilah? Keith's reputation is being ruined, and mine is completely destroyed, all because of the lies you've been spreading around this town like a plague. Did you just come to gloat?"

The self-pity sparks my anger again. It's so familiar—so *Eve*. As if I have no reason to think she has an inappropriate relationship with Keith. As if I didn't see them snuggled up together on the day she was supposed to be mourning the loss of her husband.

"I want you to tell me what happened to Lars," I say. "Before your lawyer cuts you a deal, or Pastor Rick and Sheriff Wilson concoct the story to feed to the media. Just admit what you and Keith did."

"We didn't do anything."

I lean forward. "You know I saw you two together at the funeral. The police are going to find out about your affair, if they haven't already. That will be your motive. They've got means with the weapon. All they need is opportunity. And you dropped Emmanuelle off at your parents' house Saturday morning. Unless you have an alibi, they're going to assume you did that so you could go to where Lars was hunting and shoot him without anyone knowing."

Now, the tears come. Glistening on her cheeks, dropping with a cinematic languidness. She looks at me pleadingly. "I didn't do this, Del. Lars and I were in counseling, that much is true. But I wasn't having an affair, and I didn't want him dead. I just wanted him . . ."

My breath tightens, but she doesn't finish the sentence. "You wanted him what?"

Her eyes squeeze shut, and she lets out a huff. "I just wanted him to be the man I thought I was marrying. I wanted him to adore me."

I stare at her, stunned. We're sitting here in jail, with her arrested for her husband's murder, and all she can do is complain about how he didn't love her enough in the way that she expected. Up until this moment, I didn't think she was really capable of hurting him. At least not being the one to pull the trigger.

But if there's one thing I know about Eve, it's that as high as her expectations were for herself, the ones she had in high school for her future husband were even higher. Six years of marriage was plenty of time for her to realize she wasn't going to get what she wanted from him. And if that realization hit her on the day they dedicated their daughter, the day the final pieces of the life she planned out slotted into place and it still didn't feel right, it would be no wonder that she looked horrified. After all the work she put into being a Noble Wife, God *owed* her. I grew up with people who felt like God owed them something and failed to deliver. When that reality hits them, there's no telling what they might do.

She's looking at me again, as if pleading with me to understand where she's coming from. I keep my face hard.

"You don't believe me."

I shake my head, jaw tight.

"I guess you don't have any reason to."

My teeth grind together.

"I guess you won't believe me, then, if I tell you I'm being set up."

"Sure you are, Eve."

Ignoring me, she presses on. "If I'm going to get out of here, I need someone out there who is willing to look at things a different way. Who isn't going to believe the company line everyone at Messiah is saying. I need you, Delilah. I need you to believe me."

When I don't respond, her eyes well up again. She flicks away a tear with one shaky finger. "I haven't met my lawyer yet, but he told me they record everything we say in this room. What I have to say won't go over well with some of the people who could hear it. You know the ones."

That wasn't what I expected. I lean forward. "The sheriff?"

She looks at me for a long moment. "I can't talk about it here. But I promise you there is more to this story, and you're going to want to know it. Everything you need to understand what's going on, you can find it in Galilee."

"Galilee?"

The door behind me opens, and a guard walks in. "Time's up."

Eve stands and offers her wrists, eyes on the ground so she doesn't have to look at me while she's being handcuffed.

"Eve, I don't know what that means. If you're trying to be poetic or something, this is a really bad time."

She looks up at me again, her expression blank. "You'll figure it out. You always were the best at memory games."

The guard puts a firm hand on her shoulder. Before I can respond, they walk out the door and down the hall, the shuffle of her suede boots and clink of handcuffs echoing behind her.

THIRTY-FIVE

Delilah's diary

AUGUST 19, 2012

Today, I did the thing that I promised myself I would never have to do. I gave a public confession at Messiah.

I had no choice. It's been months, and nothing else I tried seemed to work. After the Incident, everyone looked at me differently. Pastor Rick is always telling us that sin stains you, it clings to you like dirt, alters your appearance. He says once you get close enough to God, you can see sin on another person. That's what makes him such a good pastor—he knows exactly who he needs to talk to every Sunday morning, even if it looks like he's addressing all of us.

A public confession is different from the private ones I've done in his office. I wanted those to be enough, but after a while, it was clear they never would be. When Colette agreed to meet with me last week, I told her how desperate I was. How I just wanted everything to be wiped clean, a new slate that I could work from to rebuild my life. That's what salvation is, and I felt like I needed saving all over again. She was the one who suggested a public confession, and after she talked to Pastor Rick, it was decided.

This morning, I stood in front of everyone at Messiah Church and told them what I did. As Colette instructed, I made sure not to mention Noah by name. His role in everything doesn't matter; it was my decision, my actions, that have led to the consequences on my life. I told them what I had done, why it was wrong, and how I have worked to repent. I recommitted myself to the church and asked their forgiveness.

That was the hard part. The wonderful part was what happened after, when they stood in unison. I have only ever been the person out there in the congregation, standing up when someone else confessed, accepting them back in. I have never really realized how beautiful it is until that moment.

Hundreds of voices joined together, talking directly to me, and directly to God.

"You are forgiven."

It was the most wonderful thing I have ever heard.

Today, my life starts again. I am born new. No more walking with my head hanging low. I am pure again. I am wanted again.

I am forgiven.

THIRTY-SIX

WHEN THE DEPUTY LEADS ME back out to the lobby, Nathaniel still isn't there. All I really want is to go home to the Obacks' and enjoy a movie and some wine like I planned to last night. I was too anxious after Keith busted in to do anything except eat a whole pizza and cry.

But despite how much I want to celebrate that it looks like I was right—Lars's death was *not* an accident and Eve *was* responsible— fingers of doubt have dug into my brain. Eve was always a good liar. She wrote letters back and forth with my boyfriend for months without my knowing about it. I wasn't looking for deception then, but I am now.

And I didn't see any in that visiting room.

After waiting another fifteen minutes, I send Nathaniel a text saying I'll find my own way home—I can't hang around here anymore. I need to figure out what she meant by finding everything I need to know in Galilee.

Opening the station door, I nearly crash into my father.

"Ope, you okay?" He reaches out, steadying me.

"Fine, I'm fine." I straighten up, looking around for Mom, but she isn't here. "What's going on?"

"I was just coming in to see if you were here. Your mom called from work and told me the news."

"How did you even know I was still in the area?" He looks at me with a sheepish smile, and I nod. "Right. Messiah Lifeline." The phone chain of church wives who share news faster than CNN—under the guise of passing on prayer requests.

"I've been trying to find out where you're staying. Someone said you were at a motel in Elden, but the receptionist told me you checked out."

"I found a room at a friend's place."

He crosses his arms, nodding. It occurs to me that he might actually be hurt I didn't ask to stay with them. "So, so . . . how's it going?" he asks.

I let out a breathless laugh. "I mean, great. My ex-boyfriend was apparently murdered, and the police think the girl he left me for did it. I feel great."

All trace of discomfort flees my dad's face, replaced by concern. "Oh, honey." The words are powerfully familiar, the tone as full of care as it was when I got hurt as a kid. It makes me want to walk into his arms. It's been so long since I had a hug from my dad.

A bolt of sadness hits me so hard I sway on my feet. I wrap my arms around myself.

He notices. "I'm sorry, it's cold out here. Are you . . . Do you need a ride somewhere?"

"Actually, yeah. That would be great."

The corners of his mouth turn up, twitching as if he's trying not to show me how happy that makes him. He turns around and gestures at his blue SUV. "This way, m'lady."

Once I've directed him to the highway that will take us to the Obacks', I relax and crank up the seat warmer. Moments later, heat begins to seep into my skin, and my shivering finally calms. Neither of us speaks for several minutes.

Finally, at the last set of lights before we leave town, he looks over at me. "Your mom is worried about you."

"What else is new?"

"Delilah."

My face burns. "Well? Dad, she got after me at the funeral for not returning her messages, but she hasn't even called me in over a year. She can't be that worried about me."

He lets out a sigh—the special one he reserves for the topic of tension between me and my mom. We were fine in Boston, but as soon as we came to Bower, nothing I did was right. I've never been able to figure out if it's because we started going to Messiah or because I had just become a teenager. Suddenly, my clothes were too tight, and my attitude needed adjusting, and didn't I know that only *women of the night* painted their nails red? For a while, Dad acted as the referee between us, but eventually he just gave up.

"She is," he murmurs, staring out the windshield as he drives forward. "I know she has a funny way of showing it, but your mother loves you, sweetheart."

"You know, I never doubted that until junior year." It feels like a sinkhole has opened in my chest, and I blink back tears, turning my head toward my window.

Dad's hand comes to rest softly on my knee. He says, "I wish you didn't doubt it at all."

"How could I not?" I look back at him, wiping my cheeks with the back of my hand. "She chose the church over her own daughter, and you followed right along."

His expression is stunned, almost helpless. "Honey, I'm sorry. I . . . I know you had a hard time, but I thought everything got better after your—"

He won't even say the word. My public confession was the most humiliating thing I'd ever done, made even worse by the fact that it clearly mortified my parents. Like it or not, the Bible and the church held them responsible for the acts of their disobedient child. All was meant to be forgiven after I was forced to tell the whole congregation what I'd done, but it meant my parents' friends knew exactly how devious their daughter was. It took weeks for my mother to even look at me again.

"Turn right up here." I reach down for my purse and pull it into my lap, my hand on the door.

Dad follows my directions, but he stops at the top of the Obacks' long driveway. "Hold on a minute, now."

I grab the handle, but he puts his hand on my arm, holding me gently in place.

"Please, Delilah. What can I do to make things right? I miss you."

When I finally look back at him, his eyes are glistening. My dad never put on that fake tough bravado like some of the men in our church, but it was still rare to see him cry. Whenever it happens, I cry too. A fresh wave of tears floods my cheeks.

"I miss you too, Dad. But I don't know how things will ever be right again." I open the door and heave myself out, then slam it shut.

For a few moments, the engine runs behind me as I stalk toward the house. Then, the car turns off and feet crunch on the cold gravel as my dad jogs to catch up.

I stop, squinting at him in the afternoon sunlight. "Dad, what? It's been a ridiculously hard day, and I just want to be by myself."

"Okay, okay. I'll leave you alone." He stops in front of me, tugging the zipper higher on his coat. "I just thought you should know something." Color rises in his cheeks.

I wait for him to speak again.

He glances down, then back at me. "I think you might want to talk to Ronny James."

The name makes me flinch. "What? Why?"

His lower lip pushes out, and he shakes his head lightly. "Just . . . he's still pretty close to some of the people you've been talking to about Lars's death."

"How did you—?"

He raises his eyebrows at me, and I stop talking. Of course. Everyone in Messiah probably knows the rumors I've started by now.

With a deep breath, I offer him a small smile. "Okay. Thanks, Dad."

The lines in his forehead soften, and he smiles too. "I . . . I hope you won't leave without saying goodbye."

"I'll do my best."

His foot inches forward, as if he wants to reach for me, but stops short. We hold each other's gaze for a long moment. I wonder what I would say if he asked me to come home and have dinner with him and my mom. If he tried to give me a hug right now, I think I would let him—I would bury my face in his shoulder and close my eyes until things felt better again.

Instead, he starts back for his car, and I keep walking toward the Obacks' house.

THIRTY-SEVEN

Noble Wife Journey: a blog
Title: Him: Part 2
Published: April 14, 2014

I didn't mean to leave you hanging, lovely readers. But in fairness, I had no idea that this would be the week my world turned upside down in the most wonderful way possible. You have asked for details, many of which I can't yet supply.

You see, although I was certain the second we locked eyes that this man and I are going to be together forever, I still don't even know his name.

Let me explain.

Pastor Rick has been teaching us for years that God-ordained relationships require effort, but at the same time, they should be simple. He used to describe meeting his wife like trying on a pair of perfectly fitted jeans—they got more comfortable as time went on, but they were still right from the start.

For those who aren't filled with the Spirit, you might wonder how I could know something so important without ever having spoken a word to this man. But I have no doubt that others of you will completely understand.

Even though I can't tell you everything just yet, I can't hold back my excitement. This week, I had the chance to attend an information day at the college I plan to attend in Moorhead, Minnesota. It's one of the best Christian schools in the area, and a favorite of Messiah kids because we still live close enough to come home for church every week. Some people even keep living at home to save money, but I know I'll want to try out dorm life. It's a good opportunity to test my independent living skills before I have a house of my own to manage after I get married.

The day was spent exploring the campus and dropping in on a few classes: Old Testament Theology, the Book of Luke, Intro to Biology, and Communications 101 were the ones I chose. I didn't agree with everything the professor in theology was saying, but there was an active debate in class and he encouraged students to speak their minds, which I liked. One thing I know for sure after years at Messiah is that I'll be able to stand my ground on my beliefs, even when they're challenged by other so-called believers.

But it was that evening, the weekly Freshmen Fun night, when I saw him. He's not a freshman himself, that I could tell right away. He was one of the leaders, a junior or senior, I think, part of the band that performed a few Christian rock songs before we played games and someone delivered a short, thirty-minute message. The nights are more about getting to know fellow new students and staying connected than doing a deep Bible study, but I still enjoyed it.

Then again, I could barely stop staring at him the whole time, so that might be why I liked it so much. Let me tell you, it's a wonderful view.

I don't know what I'm going to do these next few months, while I wait to start college. It would have been too forward to introduce myself, to ask for his name or contact info. He had the same look in his eyes when he gazed at me that I know was in mine. The ball is definitely in his court. Still, every part of me now aches to wrap up this year and get started with the rest of my life. Up until now, I've had no problem being patient. But suddenly, it's hard.

I share this with you so you know that I'm also imperfect. Sometimes, my faith falters. But I know that by waiting, I am doing the right thing. By walking out of that room without approaching him, without offering my name, I am honoring my training as a Noble Wife.

If this guy is the man I think he is, he will find me. And if there are any obstacles in his way, I trust that he will find a way around them—or tear them down completely.

THIRTY-EIGHT

GROWING UP, RONNY JAMES WAS always on the edge of getting kicked out of wherever he was. Youth camps, game nights, lock-ins—no matter what activity we did, he found a way to goof off. He pulled pranks and messed around in the back row during sermons, cheated at games and snapped girls' bra straps. It didn't matter whether it was good or bad: any kind of attention was what he craved.

And because boys will be boys, he had no trouble making friends— one of whom was Keith Rivers. I think Keith was originally supposed to be like a mentor, since Ronny was a few grades younger. But once the youth leaders matched the two of them up at a boys' retreat, they were inseparable.

Ronny's construction shop isn't hard to find. It's linked to his social media account. A scroll through his timeline made it clear that I haven't missed out on anything by not speaking to him in years. Now that he's an adult, all that teenage rebellion has been refocused on mistrust of the government and a general derision for participating in a compassionate society. I turn off the road onto a gravel drive that leads past a used car lot and a tack shop. A white truck with a James Construction logo stuck to the side is parked out in front of a squat beige building. After pulling in next to it, I get out, boots kicking up dust.

"Help you with something?"

I look up to find Ronny standing in the open doorway of his shop. His worn Levi's and khaki button-down are covered in sawdust. A rolled red bandanna keeps the sweat out of his eyes, which he's shielding with a rough hand as he looks at me.

"Delilah?"

Stopping at the bottom of the short set of stairs into his shop, I squint up at him. My oversize coat and baggy pants do nothing to make me feel protected under his gaze. "Hey, Ronny. You got a few minutes to talk?"

"Sure." He looks around for a moment. "It's kinda dusty inside, but it's too cold out here. C'mon in."

It takes my eyes a few minutes to adjust to the dim light inside his shop. He's right: every shelf, table, box, and slab of wood is coated in layers of sawdust. Giant tools form imposing shapes all around the shop: some I recognize, others are completely foreign. Most of the light is coming from a bright yellow lamp with a white bulb behind a metal grate, to prevent it from being bumped and shattered, I suppose.

Ronny leads me on a path familiar only to him, through stacks of two-by-fours and toolboxes and trash cans filled with unusable scraps of wood. There's a tiny kitchenette at the back, right next to a closet just big enough to hold a toilet. Opening the mini fridge, he bends over and reaches for two bottles of water, holding one out to me. I accept with a nod, and he takes a stack of woodworking magazines off the one chair next to the kitchen, gesturing for me to sit. He seems content to lean against the wall behind him.

"So, what do you want to talk about?"

I can't just start by asking about Eve and Keith, so I look around the room. "Quite a shop you've got here."

He tries to hide a proud smile with moderate success. "Built it from the ground up. I've mostly done small projects: remodels, a few garages, fixing up places after a storm, that kind of thing. But I just won my first bid for a whole house. Bringing on a crew and everything."

"Sounds great." My fake enthusiasm sounds a little too bright, but he seems to buy it. "You work with anyone I know?"

Ronny takes several gulps of water. "Couple guys from the church you might remember. Josh, Shane, Paul. Keith is pretty busy with his associate pastor gig, but he sometimes helps out with bigger projects when he can get away."

Josh and Shane were in my class at school. In my mind, I see them huddled around Noah's desk, looking at his phone. Their flushed cheeks, their darting eyes. The sneering mix of lust and hatred when they looked at me.

Even though he wasn't in our class, Ronny made sure to let me know for weeks after that he had seen everything. I don't want him to think I can't handle being in the room with him. "You still go to Messiah, then?"

"Of course." His forehead wrinkles in confusion. "It's my home. I owe Pastor Rick for, like, my whole life."

Picking at the label on my bottle, I meet his gaze. "What do you mean?"

"He never gave up on me. I had a pretty rough time growing up. My parents couldn't afford Messiah High, so I went to the public school, remember?" His gaze drops to the floor. "Got in with the wrong kind of crowd for a while. I didn't stop coming to church because my dad would have beat the crap out of me for it, but my heart wasn't in it for a while. My grades were so bad I couldn't get into college anywhere, and I thought my life was ruined."

When he meets my gaze again, his eyes are glowing. Not with tears, but close. "Pastor Rick had been reaching out to me for years, trying to get me back on the right path. He saw my parents were doing nothing, so he took it upon himself to make sure I turned out okay. One day after church, he pulled me aside and told me if I stopped destroying stuff long enough, I could realize how much I loved building things. And he was right." He gestures at the room, taking it in. "He sent me to rehab in 2014, and when I came back, he'd bought me this shop. Can you believe it? Just handed me the keys, no questions asked. It started out with odd jobs, fixing things here and there, but eventually I got my license and now look at me."

Some of what Ronny's saying is familiar. I remember rumors floating around about him, about the kind of things he got into at the public school. He was struggling, acting out, and Pastor Rick bent over backward to get him on the right path. Church leaders could have seen his behavior as a sin and punished him for it, like they did me, but instead he was given countless chances to turn his life around.

Ronny gestures at me with the water bottle. "So, why'd you leave?"

He's messing with me. Like he doesn't remember the way he and the other boys tormented me. But his expression is completely sincere. What happened—what they did—changed the entire course of my life, but it wasn't even important enough for him to consider now.

There's no point being openly critical about Pastor Rick, much less telling Ronny that I could never attend Messiah again once Lars started going each Sunday with Eve instead of with me. I need to move past this conversation if I have any hope of talking about Keith.

"It wasn't any one thing." Which is sort of true. I lick my lips, taste salt. "I transferred to college in the Cities after sophomore year, so I wasn't really close by anymore."

Ronny nods, considering. "Yeah, I guess I remember that. You're just one of the few from our friend group who left, you know?"

I look at him. "Our friend group?"

"Yeah, you know. The other Messiah kids our age."

My fingernails dig into my palm, but I don't say what I want to say. "Right," I reply after a moment.

We're both quiet for a minute. Ronny taps the side of his water bottle and looks at me. "So . . ."

"Right. I just had a few questions for you. I'm . . ." For some reason, I didn't plan an excuse for coming here. The words tumble out of my mouth before I've considered whether they're wise. "I'm thinking about buying my dad a hunting rifle for Christmas."

Thankfully, Ronny's eyes brighten with interest. "Oh yeah?"

"Yeah, and I remembered you were pretty into hunting in high school. Are you still?"

"Sure, I was out last weekend."

I nod, trying not to look too interested. "Oh yeah? By yourself, or . . ."

"Nah, I always hunt with Keith."

Bingo. Ronny would be the perfect alibi for Keith. He'd never believe his best buddy capable of hurting someone, and even if he did, I don't doubt Ronny would defend him anyway. "That's right, he always went out the first weekend of deer season." I pause. "Still hard to believe what happened to Lars. I can't wrap my mind around it."

Ronny's eyes narrow. "Yeah, it was awful. Nowhere near us, though, if that's what you're thinking."

I put up a hand. "Oh no, not at all."

"Plus, I don't think this has made the news yet, but it sounds like it wasn't actually an accident." He leans forward, eyes gleaming with a familiar mix of wrath and mischief. "They arrested Eve for murder this morning."

"You're kidding," I say, my mouth open in what I hope is a convincing display of shock. "Eve? No way. Why would she kill Lars?"

He pushes his lower lip out as if he's unsure, but I can see he's got a theory.

"What?" I ask.

Rubbing the back of his neck, Ronny chuckles. "I don't know. Lars was a good guy, but that's not always enough, you know? There's something about the men in Messiah Church, the ones who grew up here. You know what I mean. We didn't grow up with any of that pansy liberal talk about feelings and togetherness. Pastor Rick raised us to be prepared for war, and I'll always be grateful for that. Look at the state of the world."

My hands tighten around the bottle, making it crunch. I loosen them with difficulty. "So you're saying Lars wasn't manly enough for Eve?"

"No, I'm not saying that. Obviously, they were married, so they should have stayed married. But I think there's a good chance Eve woke up one day and realized she should have married a Messiah man instead of finding one out there and trying to bring him in. She had her chance, though, and she missed out."

That has to be a reference to Keith. Anyone with eyes knew he was in love with Eve in high school, and I'm willing to bet he told Ronny about it.

Something he said is nagging at me, though. The idea that Pastor Rick was preparing the men in the church for war. He never went so far as developing a doctrine or a guidebook for the boys on how to be men of God, but he did rant about what he deemed the feminization of men in society, even in the church. He loathed any book or teaching that focused on men getting in touch with their feelings. It wasn't uncommon for his messages about sex and marriage to devolve into screaming at the boys in youth group to shape up, get a job, and learn how to protect their family. Girls were controlled through fear and guilt; to the extent that boys were influenced, it was through rage and humiliation.

Ronny is right. Marrying a man raised in that environment would be completely different from marrying one who came into it as an adult. Lars was not an overly feelings-driven guy, but he wasn't like the boys I grew up with—at least not before he became a member of Messiah. That was one of his best qualities.

Eve would have no reason to feel the same way I did, though.

"You make a really good point," I say, my throat tight with the strain of keeping my voice even. "I wonder if she ever wished she was with someone else."

For a moment, Ronny watches me, unscrewing and rescrewing the cap on his bottle. Finally, he says, "Couldn't tell you. All I know is, if she *was* given that chance, she would have jumped at it. Lars wouldn't have fought to stop her, and that was the problem."

I hum my agreement, but Ronny isn't quite done.

"A real man knows what to do with a woman like Eve Thompson." He smirks. "A real man would keep her happy. What happened to Lars, it's a shame. But I can't say I'm surprised."

THIRTY-NINE

Noble Wife Journey: a blog
Title: College
Published: August 17, 2014

Today is the day: a momentous one for me and more than a dozen of my
sisters who are part of the Noble Wife movement here in Bower. It was
the final Sunday at Messiah before we are released into the world.

Later this week, I leave for college. I'll be driving back for church most
Sundays, but the first will be spent at the campus youth ministry, where
I'll be looking to get involved, of course.

Pastor Rick was full of emotion today as he blessed the seniors in
the youth ministry and sent us off with final words of wisdom. "Hold
tight to your beliefs. Don't let anyone in the world talk you out of them.
No matter where you go, there will be some who will insist the way
you have been raised is wrong. That your teachers and pastors and
even your parents have lied to you. They will use painful, violent words:
brainwashed, *extremist*, *bigot*. No matter what they say, remember this:
You were raised in truth. You were fed solid food, not milk, as Paul says.
You can handle fundamental truths about the world that those far from
Christ cannot. If you hold fast to the teachings you have learned here,
if you stay vigilant against temptation, you will fulfill everything that is
planned for you. Stay strong, and do not be afraid."

What powerful words to carry us forward.

I'm sure many of you are wondering about the man I've told you about. While I've kept my blog up-to-date over the summer, I have intentionally not mentioned him again. Song of Solomon tells us over and over not to awaken love until the time is right, and this summer has been an exercise in patience as I wait for that time. While I've always been very open with you on this blog, I confess I have kept some things hidden.

He did indeed find me, after that night I visited MCC in April. I'm slightly embarrassed to say he found this blog too, but it only confirmed for him that I knew we were meant for each other too. Still, we needed time. So, rather than seeing each other this summer, we wrote letters. Every week, sometimes twice a week, I rushed to my mailbox like a wartime wife and pulled a soft envelope scrawled with my name.

We told each other about ourselves. We discussed our hopes for the future, our childhood dreams, our families, our faith. Slowly, like a flower unfurling its petals, I let him see my heart. It is the kind of romance I have always dreamed of, and I know now that God is rewarding me for all my patience and dedication.

Next week, we will see each other in Moorhead. There are a few things he needs to take care of before he can formally ask my father permission to court me, but we all know it's coming. And then, this dream, this adventure I have longed for my entire life, can begin.

I will show him that I am everything he wants in a wife, warm and sweet and full of devotion. I am the Proverbs 31 woman, and I want to be that woman only for him. I want to rise while it is still dark, bring him good not harm, have a noble character. I will be worth far more than rubies.

One day, he will praise me.

FORTY

NO ONE KNOWS HOW TO keep their emotions locked down like a food service worker. When your livelihood depends on tips, you learn pretty quickly how to slap on a smiling face and a chirpy voice no matter what kind of hell you're going through. To make up for missing my lunch shift, I came in for dinner service and have basically not stopped moving since I arrived. So far, I don't think I've messed up any orders, but I feel like I'm walking around in a haze.

Things finally start to slow down around eight, and I take the chance to relieve my aching feet by sitting on a barstool while I wait for Finn to make the cocktails for one of my tables. He looks up at me while measuring vodka and vermouth into a metal shaker. For just a moment, I let his warm smile distract me from my twisting thoughts.

"Hi," he says. "Sorry, I've been slammed back here all night, so I haven't had a chance to ask: How are you doing?"

"I'm okay." I dig around in my apron pocket until I find my small tin of mints, then pop one in my mouth. "It's been the longest day ever. I have so much to catch you up on." Our conversation with Parker at the café was only yesterday, but it feels like a week ago.

"Sounds like it. Did you get to talk to Eve? Did she admit to anything?" He shakes the drink while waiting for my reply.

"Not really. Just said she didn't do anything wrong and gave me some obscure biblical references. Typical Eve." I stretch my neck from side to side, sighing when it pops.

Finn chuckles as he grabs a chilled martini glass from the fridge, then strains the drink and sets it on the bar. While he starts on the next one, I skewer two olives with a little wooden sword and plop them in.

"Isn't that it, then?" he asks. "You said you were sure Lars didn't die by accident, and now it sounds like the police are too. They've arrested Eve, and if Keith helped her kill Lars, it's only a matter of time before they arrest him too. She might even turn on him herself."

I fiddle with the stem of the martini glass. "You're probably right."

Finn pours a margarita and sets it in front of me. I hang a sliced lime on the salted rim before looking up to meet his serious gaze. "You don't seem convinced."

"I want to be. I just can't shake the feeling that there's more going on. Something isn't adding up." I wipe my hands on my apron and sigh. "Anyway, I've gotta get these to table seven."

He opens his mouth like he wants to say something, but then his lips come together again, and he nods. On the way to my table, I yank up the corners of my mouth and try to think of a positive memory to put some warmth in my eyes.

An hour later, I finally get cut and start my side work. I'm a fast silverware roller, so my hundred sets are done in less than twenty minutes. My other task is to bring clean glasses to the bar, so I head to the dishwasher station. For a moment, I wonder if my unwillingness to accept the results of my little amateur investigation has more to do with leaving this job than anything else. Proximity to Bower aside, I have started to like it here. The food is tasty, the tips are good, and there's a guy who seems more than a little interested in seeing me every day.

Finn is right, though; this could probably be over if I let it be. I got what I wanted: a real investigation into Lars's death and a little bonus revenge seeing Eve exposed for the manipulative fraud she is. I could finish my shifts for the week and then head back to Minneapolis. I might not have much to go back for, but with the money I've stashed away, it won't take me long to get on my feet. If I knew what was good for me, I'd get as far away from Bower as possible.

I've never really known what was good for me, though.

The racks of clean bar glasses are stacked so high on the cart that I can barely see around them. I manage to get through the restaurant without crashing into anyone, and I'm rewarded with Finn's rich laugh when I finally reach the bar.

"I wasn't sure you'd make it." He comes in close, his tall body stretching up next to me. With ease, he lifts the top two off the stack, setting them on the bar. Still inches away, he looks down at me.

The warmth and scent of him make me bold. "What can I say? I'm used to dealing with a big rack."

He snorts, face reddening slightly.

You can always count on sexual humor to go over well in the restaurant biz. I start unloading the glasses. In between drink tickets, Finn helps me, and we work in companionable silence. It's weird that we've only known each other less than a week. I don't know if it's the fact that I've worked half a dozen restaurant jobs with guys like him, or if it's because he's never treated me like I was ridiculous for looking into Lars's death, but I am more comfortable with him than I've been with a man in a long time.

No, I really don't want to leave yet.

"You seem deep in thought," he says.

Hands full of pint glasses, I look up. Finn is leaning back against the counter, taking a long drink of water.

"Yeah, sorry. I've been trying to focus on work all night, so now I'm zoning out."

He shrugs. "Hey, that's okay. You've got a lot going on. Although, I guess I still don't get what you're wondering about. It seems pretty open and shut to me."

I stack the pints and put the empty rack back on the cart before grabbing the last full one. "I don't know. You're probably right that it was Eve and Keith working together. It makes sense. And as much as I want her in prison if she really did kill Lars, I hope she rats on Keith if he's the one who pulled the trigger. They should both be punished for it."

"Agree with you there. And at least you know that Parker will do her best to turn up any other dirt, if there's any left to find."

"It's Messiah, Finn. There's always dirt to find."

"Fair."

It's when I'm setting down the last clean margarita glass that something comes into focus. "Here's something I still haven't figured out: If he knew Keith and Eve were having an affair and suspected they killed Lars to get him out of the way, why would Pastor Rick cover for that? Why would he be so insistent that the police not investigate? It's bad for the church's reputation, sure, but not worse than getting caught up in a murder investigation if it didn't work out."

Finn's palm settles under his chin, elbow resting on his other hand. "Maybe he didn't know. Maybe he had nothing to do with it at all." His tone sounds almost disappointed.

"Then why would he be so sure it was an accident? It was clear from that first press conference with the sheriff—they were the ones who said it was an accident, but Pastor Rick was calling the shots. I know him. He's not above getting involved to make a crime go away, believe me. But he doesn't do it for just anyone, and there's always a way that doing so protects himself."

"I can't help you if you don't tell me everything, Delilah. The only path to repentance is total and utter transparency."

Was Eve utterly transparent with Rick? She would have had to confess everything in order to get him to help her, but that still doesn't explain why he would.

"Maybe you're looking at this the wrong way," Finn says, his eyes still focused on the restaurant. "I talked to Parker today. She's been looking into your claims about Eve and Keith, and even though she doesn't buy our theory about Keith's alibi, she's definitely suspicious of him. It seems like he had a lot more influence than she expected from a new pastor. If he planted the idea of it being an accident when he talked to police or when he spoke to Pastor Rick, that could have been enough."

"Giving Keith the chance to set the narrative from the start." I lean a hip against the counter, considering. Rick blindly trusting anyone, even his own associate pastor, is a bit of a stretch, but Finn doesn't know him the way that I do. Still, if Rick *acted* like that's what he was doing, it would give him plausible deniability if everything fell apart—the way it seems to be now.

When I look up, Finn is standing just a foot away from me, looking down with a gentle smile. "You're all finished up now, so relax and try not to think about it if you can. If there's anything else to find here, be-lieve me, Parker will find it. Especially if it implicates Rick Franklin in some kind of cover-up."

I let out a deep breath. "I just want to ask Keith about a thousand more questions."

He laughs. "I wouldn't be surprised if the police are doing that right now. If they're not, they probably will be soon. Now, clock yourself out so I can pour you a drink."

I chuckle, trying to hide how nervous what he just said makes me feel. If Keith is arrested, there's no way I'll be able to ask him anything else. My only chance of getting more information is to get it myself.

Seeing Ronny again was miserable, but at least I'd gained one thing: confirmation that Eve wasn't happy she hadn't chosen a Messiah man, and that Keith still held a candle for her after all these years.

Keith had no problem showing up unannounced at the place where I'm staying and scaring the crap out of me. I'm not nearly as intimidat-ing, but I doubt I'd be a welcome presence if I returned the favor.

So tomorrow, after work, that's exactly what I'm going to do.

FORTY-ONE

Tonight, he looked me in the eyes and told me my body was covered in sin.

Not just the parts that were exposed, but everything.

"Once one bit of you is defiled, the rest is ruined as well. It's not like cutting off a moldy corner of bread, Delilah."

That's right. I'm Delilah now. Delilah the temptress, Delilah the mistress of seduction.

With a name like that, what did you expect her to be like? That's what I imagine everyone thinking. The word is out: Lila, the innocent version of me, is gone.

On the table in front of me and Pastor Rick, there was a picture of me standing with Eve and Esha at last year's summer camp, only they were cropped out. It was just me there, standing in my swimsuit and shorts, wet from our race to the raft and back. Even though I was wearing a suit that passed Messiah's strict modesty guidelines, that was the photo Pastor Rick chose for us to examine.

We went over my body like an MRI, discussing its parts as if trying to diagnose a disease. This area causes eyes to wander, this one is prone to accidentally exposing skin, this will look promiscuous no matter what you cover it with. The shame made it hard to breathe. I don't understand why God would compose us of a thousand temptations for men.

At the end, we prayed, and I promised to consider how my movements and clothing choices impact the boys in our church.

When I got home, I told my parents all about the session, as I do every week. It's part of our agreement, to make sure we're all on the same page as I work to repair the damage I've done to my family's reputation in the church. For the first time ever, my dad looked upset. It was when I told him about the picture. He is never critical of Pastor Rick, since that would be challenging a godly authority, but I could see that he didn't like it. My mom didn't seem to notice. She just wants this all to be over with and keeps asking how much longer until Pastor Rick thinks we can move on. I told her I'm trying, but he doesn't seem to be in a hurry.

At least she still gets to talk to her friends. She and Dad might be uncomfortable on Sunday mornings, but they aren't being avoided. Mom still has all of her volunteer positions in the nursery and the catering club and the greeters team, and Dad goes golfing with his friends every Thursday afternoon. They were admonished for raising a daughter who did such a terrible thing, but the church seems to recognize that parents have only so much control over their children.

A few times a week, I catch Mom looking at me. I'll be eating at the dinner table or working on homework in the living room, and I'll notice her staring with that devastated, faraway look in her eyes.

"Why couldn't you have just done what we taught you?"

I never know how to respond. Sometimes, if he hears, my dad will say, "She's not the only one who made a mistake. The boy did the wrong thing too."

"But she could have said no."

She's right. I could have. Because I didn't, I've lost everything. In the two months since it happened, I got kicked off the drama team and all my friends stopped talking to me—Eve and Esha included. That was the worst of it all. I know they're just obeying their parents, but I can't believe they haven't even said two words to me. I go to church and sit with my mom and dad, standing during worship and listening to the sermon. Then I go wait in the car until they finish talking to people and we're ready to go home. I come to youth group on Wednesday nights and do the same, only I have an hour of private counseling with Pastor Rick afterward. Every minute of that feels like twenty, and by the time I'm finished, I leave his office with my heart a raw, gaping wound. At school, I go to my classes quietly and sit alone at lunch. The only good thing is that I don't see Noah anymore.

He's still here, of course. The pastor's nephew is not going to leave the church, and everyone seems to have forgotten his part in things quickly. He couldn't help his actions. No one could have resisted what I put him through, which should feel like a compliment, but I know it isn't. Pastor Rick smoothed things over with the sheriff so no report had to be filed. They said it was because they didn't want to ruin the boy's life, but I'm relieved too. It would have been unbearable to know that some kind of legal documentation existed about what happened, those photos preserved in a dusty police case box.

I know it's only been a couple months. I know it takes time to fix mistakes, to cleanse oneself from sin. But I'm getting impatient. Maybe over the summer it'll get better. Everyone will see how hard I'm trying, and they will welcome me back. There's always at least one radical night at youth camp, where everyone responds to the altar call and we all collectively rededicate ourselves to following God.

Right now, I might as well be dead. My friends look right through me. I imagine them talking about me at home, like I'm someone who isn't around anymore. I am a spiritual ghost, destroyed by sin.

I need a revival—I need God to bring me back to life.

If people see me at the altar, if they know how sincere I am about fixing all this, then things could get back to how they were again. I just want them back the way they were.

I'll do anything. Anything.

FORTY-TWO

I DRIVE TOWARD BOWER, SQUINTING in the glare of midmorning sun. My head is fuzzy and mouth sour. Finn invited me to stay for a drink after work last night, and one red wine turned into four. He was insistent on just one more every time I emptied my glass, and I couldn't suppress the joy it gave me that he didn't seem to want me to leave, so I kept drinking. It's funny, giving in to peer pressure when you're in your midtwenties. I feel like I'm finally having some of the experiences most people have in high school and college.

Somewhere in the night, I remember Finn leaning in close to me, his breath on my cheek. "You're amazing, you know that?"

I pushed him away. "Stop."

"No, you are." He reached out then and put his hand on the side of my face. Alcohol made the gesture slightly clumsy, but when his thumb brushed my cheek, I could barely breathe. "Nobody ever stands up to Messiah Church, but you're not letting them get away with any of this."

"I'm not going to stop until the whole truth comes out."

His forehead bunched as he looked at me in wonder. "What are you going to do?"

I swallowed the last of my red wine and set my glass down a little too hard. Thankfully, it didn't shatter. "I'm talking to Keith again tomorrow. I'm not going to leave until he tells me what happened. See how he likes it."

"Are you serious?" Finn's lips, inches away, were stained purple with Merlot.

"As hell," I said solemnly, and we both snickered like dummies as he poured me another drink.

Since my shift this morning started at four, I ended up catching a couple hours of rest in one of the booths at Elaine's rather than risk driving. A strong cup of sugary coffee got me through the hours of serving truckers who looked just as tired as I was, and thankfully things slowed down enough for Maxine to cut me early. I should go back to the Obacks' and get some proper sleep so I can confront Keith with a clear head, but I don't want to wait any longer.

Keith is smart. If the police do question him again, he'll be on guard. He'll probably even have a lawyer. The best chance I have to catch him slipping is if he doesn't feel threatened, and why would he think a girl from Messiah could do any real damage? If I can make him feel cocky—bold and fearless the way he and the other boys were raised to be—I might just be able to get him to say something incriminating. And my phone will be in my pocket, recording the whole time.

The sign announcing the next exit has something on it that I didn't notice before. Under the icons for food, gas, and restrooms there is another logo: the one for Messiah Church. Flicking on my blinker, I turn to drive into town. Once I reach the road that goes to the Mess, I look up at the sign. My suspicions are confirmed.

Messiah Way.

This was Main Street when I lived here. I hadn't paid attention the last couple times I was in town, but now it seems obvious that Pastor Rick would change it. Shaking my head, I drive toward the church.

The parking lot next to the office is empty. My car clock reads 9:45 a.m. Pastors don't necessarily keep standard business hours, so maybe he's still home. The Mess provides a parish house, but it was too small for Pastor Rick's taste. He bought himself a mansion on the edge of Bower, hugging the shore of a small lake. That would leave the modest two-bedroom free, and I'm guessing Keith is taking advantage of it.

When I arrive, there's a car in the driveway, but the windows in the house are dark.

With my phone recording, I get out of the car and stride up to the entry. My fist bangs on the door, ringing across the lawn. There's no response. Another forceful knock yields the same result.

Maybe he saw me coming, or he has a hidden security camera that shows it's me at the door. If that's the case, then he's a coward—but that would be no surprise. Not if he's letting his girlfriend take the fall for a murder I'm pretty sure he committed.

"Keith!" I shout. "I just have a couple questions. You're not afraid of me, are you?" Schoolyard taunts probably won't do any good, but you never know. Some guys never grow out of who they were at sixteen.

A few more moments pass in silence. I bounce on the balls of my feet, looking up at the window above the door, which reveals the top of a staircase and an open second-floor landing. Something catches my eye. Glancing behind me, I walk backward down the porch steps and then look through the window again. It's dim inside, but the morning sun provides enough light to see the banister, curving upward and deco-rated with hand-carved spindles. And attached to the banister at the up-stairs landing is the unmistakable coil of a thick rope, hanging straight down—tight, like it's bearing a sizable weight.

My knees buckle, and then I'm on the grass in Keith's front yard. It takes several moments for the flood of adrenaline to pass, the one that's telling me to bolt out of there. But I've been knocking and yelling, and there's every chance a neighbor has seen me. Possibly even called the police, as people around here often do to solve their problems. Running away will just make me look suspicious.

I finally reach into my pocket and pull out my phone. Shaky fingers hit three numbers I've been lucky enough to never dial before. The voice on the other end asks questions, and I answer numbly, hardly aware of what I'm saying. Except: maybe it isn't what I think. It can't be. He wouldn't.

We were taught that suicide is one of the worst sins, one that by its nature you can't repent of before you die. Like most of the damaging, in-flexible rules I grew up with, it's something I no longer believe. But Keith would. Even though I know it has happened before, I can't imagine a pastor taking his own life. Not unless the alternative—living with some kind of terrible truth about yourself exposed—was impossible to bear.

My head throbs as I stare through the window, unable to take my eyes off that rope. I imagine all the secrets about Keith and Eve, the truth about what happened to Lars, dangling at the end of it.

And I imagine Eve, sitting in her cell, finding out that another man she loves is gone.

PASTOR RICK HAD several signature rants, messages that I heard so many times during my time at the Mess that I could probably finish his sentences if I heard them again.

"We are at war, and the sooner the church realizes that, the sooner we can fight the way God intended us to. The Bible tells us to put on the full armor of God for a reason, folks! Because we are facing an enemy. And let me tell you something: sometimes that enemy looks just like the guys on our side. We need to be constantly prepared, shielded, ready to face whatever might come our way. Because if we're not, there are all too many people who are waiting in the wings, ready to exploit any sign of weakness."

I might not know the exact nature of Keith Rivers's weakness, but he lost his battle today. The police arrive less than ten minutes after I call, and I can't help staring after them as they break down the front door and enter the house. When I see Keith's bare feet, suspended in the air above their heads, I turn away and lose the contents of my stomach on the prickly dead branches of his rose bush.

Paramedics and sheriff's deputies seem to be everywhere. I don't want to see Keith's body, so I keep my gaze fixed on the ground. Eventually, someone comes to check on me. A young woman wearing some kind of uniform. Her gentle fingers test my pulse, concerned eyes looking into mine for signs of life. Eventually satisfied there is nothing physically wrong with me, she wanders away.

All this death. Keith has parents, siblings, probably aunts and uncles and cousins who will mourn his loss. Lars's murder blasted open this town, leaving shattered family and church members in a crater of grief. For a moment, I consider what it would be like if the paramedics were here for me instead of Keith. How few lives would be impacted if I were the one who had died.

A voice cuts through the thickness of despair, and I look up. Pastor Rick is standing by his shiny blue Audi in Keith's driveway. A sheriff's deputy strides over to him, and the two talk in low tones for a moment before Rick notices me staring. There's a small, almost imperceptible furrow in his brow, and then he approaches me.

"Delilah, I understand you made this tragic discovery."

The morning sun pierces my eyes as I look up at him. Pastor Rick isn't exceptionally tall, but I always felt like he towered over me. Being on the ground only adds to the effect. It's finally enough to get me to move. I push myself to my feet, brushing my hands across my backside to remove any grass and dirt.

"That's right," I say. The buzzing has been replaced with a low hum of panic.

He shakes his head in that textbook pitying way, gazing down for a moment before meeting my eyes again. He's always put on a convincing show, but I know what his eyes look like when they're lit up with emotion, and this isn't it. They are flat, icy.

I close my eyes, feeling dizzy.

I'm in his office again, sitting across from him. Pastor Rick is usually so friendly, so engaging. Now his eyes are cold.

My parents have just left, Pastor Rick asking for a few moments alone with me. They just walked out the door. They didn't even hesitate.

"This is an incredibly serious situation."

"I know."

"I need you to tell me everything that you did, Delilah. It's important to understand where the sin started so you know how to recognize it next time, so you never allow anything like this to happen again."

I swallow. "Well, Noah invited me to his—"

"Hold on. I asked what you did, and you immediately tried to blame Noah. Do you see the issue with that?"

"But that's how this all started."

"Now, Delilah, you know better than that. What am I always saying about sin? How does sin start?"

My voice trembles. "Sin . . . sin starts with a thought."

"That's right. And nobody can put a thought in your head. That is your responsibility—yours alone."

When I open my eyes, I'm breathing hard. Pastor Rick is watching me closely.

"What a difficult week for our family," he murmurs.

The family is the church. Two members dead and another arrested. I can't remember anything even close to this kind of tragedy happening when I was a teen. There were a few rebellious kids and an affair or two, and of course when Mrs. Franklin died, but nothing compared to this.

My arms cross in front of me, bracing against the wind although my shaking has nothing to do with the cold. Of course his first thought is how the people in the church are going to handle this news. Not Keith's family, not his friends. The body hasn't even been cut down yet, and he doesn't spare a thought for Keith himself.

Avoiding his gaze, I look at the sheriff's deputy stringing police tape around the yard. Several groups of people are wandering over to gather at the edges, ready to fulfill their roles as observers of tragedy.

Pastor Rick beat the neighbors here.

"News must travel even faster than I remember in Bower. I only called the police twenty minutes ago." I finally glance back at him.

His sad smile doesn't waver. "As you know, I have a good relationship with Sheriff Wilson. Of course he knew I would want to hear about this right away, and I came to say a prayer for Pastor Keith. Suicide is a terrible sin. I can only hope that God will have mercy on him."

I do too, but for different reasons, I'm sure. "But he's already gone," I say. "I thought our prayers couldn't help people after they were already dead. You always taught us salvation was only for the living."

He studies me for a moment, his well-worn brown leather Bible held firmly in his left hand. "I always visit the homes of recently deceased members to say prayers for them and their families. You'll remember I did the same for your grandmother." His gaze sharpens. "I am interested to find you here, actually. I spoke with Pastor Keith just yesterday, and he didn't seem particularly happy after we bumped into you at the Obacks'."

My heart thunders. I should have expected him to turn things around on me. "I can't imagine he would have been very happy to see me, considering the position I caught him in with Eve."

Pastor Rick's expression doesn't change. "Yes, he mentioned that you were making baseless, disrespectful allegations against him. Trying to ruin his name. In fact, he was pretty distraught about it."

I refuse to accept the guilt he's lobbing at me. "If he was so distraught, maybe he shouldn't have been having an affair with a married woman."

"Fascinating that you're the one critiquing the behavior of members of this church," Pastor Rick says. "I don't recall you being so pious. Quite the opposite, actually. It's sad to see someone who was shown as much mercy as you were fight to convict someone else without any evidence."

Face burning, I take a step back. He hasn't gotten any closer, but I suddenly feel afraid. "Mercy? Is that what I was shown? Because I seem to remember groveling in front of the entire congregation just to be given a second chance. And I do have evidence. I saw them together with my own eyes."

He looks unmoved. "You know as well as anyone here that the worst thing a woman can do to a man is make a false claim against him."

The words slice through me. It's not the first time he's said that to me.

"Noah made me do it, though! He made me feel like I didn't have a choice."

"That's a terrible, false accusation against your brother in Christ. Did he hold you down? Rip your clothes off?"

"No, but—"

"You lusted after Noah. Your infatuation with him is well known among your friends, even among the girls' group leaders. Colette has filled me in on the number of times she has pulled you aside, told you to stop trying so hard to get the attention of boys. Noah was obviously a particular temptation for you."

Tears run down my face. *"I liked Noah, yes. I thought he liked me too. He made me feel—"*

Pastor Rick's hand comes down hard on his desk. *"No one can make you feel anything. What did you do?"*

"I—" *The shame engulfs me, sudden and destructive as a tornado.*

"I wanted him to like me. I wanted him to know I would do whatever I could to help him be a good man. Just like you're always saying."

"And so you . . ."

"And so I tried to make up for how I tempted him. I thought if I could help him stop fantasizing, it would be okay. Because you said our thoughts can be just as sinful as our actions." The words sound so stupid, so obviously wrong.

At last, Pastor Rick seems satisfied. What I've told him is not a lie, but it's not the truth either. He's not interested in the truth.

"That's correct. Boys and men are most prone to sexual sin with their actions, but for women, these battles more often occur in the mind. Tell me, Delilah: Have you daydreamed about sex?"

The tornado of shame roars in my ears. I can't even look at him when I speak. *"Sometimes."*

There is a long moment between us. And then he clears his throat. *"Tell me about that."*

The memory snaps back, a rubber band released in my mind. Pastor Rick is standing in front of me, in front of Keith's house, not behind his desk at Messiah. I'm surrounded by police, not all alone. Still, I take no comfort from that.

"I did not make a false claim against him," I say, the tears evident in my voice. My anger often manifests in tears, but never has it been more inconvenient than now. I need to look strong, confident—assured. Instead, I am seconds away from bawling.

"If a man loses his reputation, he loses everything." As he says this, he gestures toward the house.

Behind me, I can hear the sounds of the police and paramedics maneuvering Keith's body off the banister. The weight of what has happened crashes into me as the flashbacks of Rick's office fade.

Keith is dead. Hanged in his own house, just days after I accused him of having an affair with a woman whose husband is dead too. It might have been guilt due to sleeping with Eve and murdering Lars, or it might have been despair at false accusations of impropriety. Either way, it will be clear to everyone that I'm to blame for stirring things up.

As if he can see the realization come over my face, Pastor Rick's tense expression shifts to one of pity. "It may be too late for Keith, but don't worry. There is still time for you to find forgiveness if you ask for it."

My dry lips part, but my mouth is too sticky to form words. The tears spill over onto my cheeks.

"You can still be forgiven. But it won't happen unless you repent, and part of repentance is voicing exactly what it is you have done."

He takes a step toward me, his other hand closing over the top of his Bible. "You might be thinking, how can he forgive you? Sometimes, I wonder the same thing. Some sins seem so egregious, so terrible, that I don't understand how he can wash them away. But he can, if you let him."

"This is not my fault," I whisper. It's what has repeated in my mind for the last decade, what I wish I had the courage to say all those nights in his office.

Pastor Rick's lips purse. "Still unwilling to take responsibility for anything. Some things never change."

"This is *not* my fault!" My voice rings shrill across the yard. Pastor Rick's eyebrows rise, and he looks over my shoulder. Slowly, I turn to see the sheriff, two deputies, and two paramedics holding a stretcher with a black bag on top. They're all frozen, watching me.

For a moment, I'm frozen too. The sting of humiliation radiates from my body, the same way that it did during my public confession nine years ago. I want to vomit and scream at the same time. Instead, I do the only other thing I feel physically capable of.

I run.

FORTY-THREE

Noble Wife Journey: a blog
Title: Mine
Published: August 27, 2014

I am my beloved's, and my beloved is mine.

Those words, spoken by the wife of Solomon thousands of years ago, are now constantly on my lips. As you well know, I have bared my soul and innermost thoughts on this blog for three years. I have told you about what I learned in Pastor Rick Franklin's Noble Wife classes, how I have absorbed and been transformed by this one particular chapter of the Bible: Proverbs 31. I have memorized it word for word in at least four translations, taking every sentence to heart as though it was written to me.

And now, sisters, my reward has come.

It might not seem like much, the time between seeing this man across the room to now, when I can shout about our love to the rooftops. But the road to get here has felt long, full of hope and yearning and self-control.

All of it, worth it.

After months of letters back and forth, after weeks of talking on the phone to preserve my modesty and ensure our connection was more than physical, last week he went to my father and asked his permission to pursue a relationship with me. Yesterday, we went on our first date. And there is no doubt in my mind, not that there ever was. I am my beloved's.

And Lars Oback is mine.

FORTY-FOUR

ONCE I'M OUT OF BOWER, I drive around for a while. As the adrenaline from my encounter with Pastor Rick fades, exhaustion burns in my eyes. I want nothing more than to take a hot shower and crawl into bed, but going back to the Obacks' will mean facing more grief, more questions. I just can't do that yet.

After taking several backstreets and random turns, I see a sign for the Elden Library and park my car. I walk through the door, breathing deep the smell of old pages and printer ink. I don't read as much now as I did in college, but I still love visiting libraries. They are some of the last places on earth where you can sit for as long as you like and nobody will ask you to buy something. I find an empty table near the back and sit down.

For a while, I scroll through social media. News of Keith's death hasn't broken yet, but it's only a matter of time. There is nothing for me here, just snippets from the lives of people I no longer really know.

This is a waste of time. If I don't do something, I'm going to spiral. On the desk by the catalog computer, there is a bunch of scrap paper and miniature pencils to write down references. I grab a stack and settle back at the desk.

It's time to take stock of what I do and don't know.

I still don't know who Lars was hunting with, or where. I have to assume the rifle found on the Thompson property was indeed the murder weapon, but that doesn't prove they or Eve knew it was there. There was obviously something going on between Keith and Eve: an affair being the obvious choice, but at the very least, something they didn't want anyone else to know about. Eve had been acting strange for months, and she didn't trust the sheriff enough to tell me what was going on where she might be recorded, which is odd by itself. Lars's parents said he was feeling down the last few times they talked to him. And now Keith is dead, and Pastor Rick is keen to place the blame squarely on me.

Pastor Rick, who seems to have his hands in every business, family, and secret in Bower. Pastor Rick, who was at Keith's house in record time after the police were called. Pastor Rick, who had everyone convinced Lars's death was an accident until it became impossible to deny the truth. I hate that I know nothing more about his involvement in all this, except that he had to leave a conference early to get back when Lars was killed. He would say he rushed home to be with the families and provide comfort, but I wonder if it was so he could do damage control. Eve might be able to give me some clues, but I doubt her lawyer would let me in to see her again.

All I have to go on is what she said when I visited her in jail, which I haven't had time to properly think about.

"Everything you need to understand what's going on, you can find it in Galilee."

Galilee was the birthplace of Jesus, but I also remember it being part of a rhyme that Eve, Esha, and I made up to help us remember the reference for the story of Jesus's baptism.

Jesus came from Galilee
in Matthew 3.
Verse 13, wanted baptism
but John said 'No,
you baptize me!'

It wasn't perfect, but it helped us remember the verse and we used to chant it at each other until it was stuck in our heads so bad we couldn't stand it. After a few months, Esha finally begged us to stop so she wouldn't hear it in her dreams. Eve joked when she set up her email account that she used it as a password because it was the only thing she knew she'd never forget.

Her email account. I wonder if that's what she was pointing me to.

After gathering up the pieces of paper with my notes, I go to the front desk. I have to get a library card to use the computers, which requires about ten minutes of paperwork and some negotiation over which address to use given that I'm basically homeless. Finally, the librarian points me to computer #3, and I am logging in to their internet.

Eve's email is listed on her blog; one of her claims to fame was that she never removed it, no matter how many thousands of messages she got. Once I have that, I try logging in to her account. It feels invasive, but then again, I have been digging into her life for the past week. What's one more thing?

The first few combinations don't work. I do variations of *Galilee313*, *galilee3*, and *GalileeMatthew3* with different letters capitalized. Finally, the email says I have one more attempt before I'll be locked out. I sigh, closing out the browser tab.

Eve's blog sits on my screen, open to the contact page. In the top-right corner, there's a link to log in. I click on it, enter her email in the username field, and try one of my password guesses there.

Incorrect information.

This is pointless. Even if I'm on the right track, there are a hundred variations Eve might have used, and I would never be able to try them all before getting locked out. Then I remember something Colette used to say after our chant caught on in the youth group. When she saw Eve, Esha, and me coming, she would say, "Ah, here come the Galilee Gals!" Esha and I thought it was super cheesy, but Eve always laughed. I guess because she liked being on Colette's good side.

I type in *GalileeGals313* and hit enter. The page loads for a second, and then I'm in the admin section of Eve's blog.

It worked. It worked, but now I don't know what to do. Eve told me the answers I need are here, but what does that mean? The answers about her affair? About how Lars died?

Like most people my age, I've had a blog before, although I'm pretty sure that no one besides internet bots ever visited it. It took the place of my diary after Lars and Eve got married and was so full of bitterness that I'm relieved I deleted the whole thing years ago. Before I did, I'd read back over a couple of the old posts. Trying to grasp that rage and hurt through my own words was like trying on an old pair of glasses—familiar, but hazy all the same.

My former blog was on the same platform as Eve's, so I know where to look. Nothing seems out of place in the pages section: the standard "About Eve," the contact information, the affiliate links to Pastor Rick's books. I navigate to the blog posts section next.

There are dozens of pages in the archive, spanning the hundreds of blogs Eve wrote over the decade she's been doing this. Rather than going through each of them, I try to think about what she might want me to find. There could be a hidden code in one of the posts—maybe something I'm supposed to realize is connected to me, like the one where she tells her readers she met Lars. The first time I read that, I had just gotten home from an innocent date with him, having no idea who it was about. The worst part is, I was happy for her. At the time, I still wanted her to get the things she worked so hard for.

I go to that post, but nothing seems amiss. I even scan the alt text of the images she included, just in case there's some hidden message there, but no. Nothing.

When I click back, I see a post just above it. The title is "Draft: At Peace." I open it.

According to the metadata, Eve wrote this on April 27, 2014. That was when the post was last updated, but it was still in draft form. Which makes sense, because I would have remembered this.

God promises to fulfill his will in us, but he doesn't promise that we won't face obstacles. These might be tests from him or a result of the sinful world that we live in, but either way, we must overcome if we are ever to see the blessings he has in store for us.

Today, I faced the first and biggest obstacle to my forever story with Lars. He had told me, of course, that he was seeing someone. That he wanted to honor his commitment to her and pray about whether they should stay together. That's why we have only been writing letters. I would never have done even that, of course, if I didn't believe that we were truly designed for each other. I knew—I still know—that this bond between him and the other woman will be broken, and he will commit himself to me very soon.

But I did not know who she was until today.

When he walked into church with Delilah Walker, I was stunned. He'd never mentioned that the girl he was seeing was from my town, from my church. Maybe he worried that I would know who she was right away; or maybe he thought that the church was big enough that we might not be friends.

Either way, I have taken all day to process this. You would think I had to recover from seeing them together, but that isn't it. I love Delilah, but she is no competition for me. She is not right for Lars. He deserves a different caliber of woman, and now that I know what I'm dealing with, I will be sure that he knows it too.

No, what I needed to recover from was hearing him sing in the worship service. I was two rows away, but his baritone was unmistakably new and too rich to be covered by the worship team and their microphones. Lord help me, I could not focus on a word I was singing. In that moment, I was even more confident than before that I would marry him. There is no other, there is no one better.

Whatever it takes, I will make sure he leaves her by the time summer's over. When I go to MCC in the fall, I don't want anything standing in our way. I am meant for him, and he is meant for me. Anyone who suggests otherwise is just an obstacle we will overcome together.

I push the keyboard away and sit back in the creaky library chair, arms crossed. Eve's entitlement disguised as some divine calling is no surprise—it's the kind of crap she pulled all the time. But seeing her write it down like that feels worse than usual. The fact that she didn't publish this means she knew on some level that she was in the wrong. She knew she would be criticized. Lars being with another woman when they met would disrupt the version of her love story that she wanted everyone else to believe.

My existence was inconvenient to her narrative.

The draft flowed just like her other blogs did, although it was a little less flowery in the writing. I wonder if there are others. Returning to the posts page, I filter for drafts only.

More than twenty results come up, dating as far back as the second year of the blog. When I see the date on the most recent one, my heart rate shoots up. She hadn't posted on the blog in weeks, not since the dedication. But this draft was written three days before Lars died.

Fingers shaking, I click on it.

I tried to talk to him about our plans this morning, but he said he's still trying to figure some things out. I want us to be in agreement before we make any moves. He's finally told me part of what he's so concerned about at work, some potentially criminal irregularities in the account he helps manage, but I can tell he's still withholding from me. My voice should matter to my own husband, but apparently it doesn't.

The Bible prepared me for this. Pastor Rick prepared me for this. Being a wife sometimes means sitting back and supporting your husband without question, without interruption. Even when you know he's wrong—or in my case, not as right as he can be. He's got his own concerns about the church. Whatever they are, they were big enough issues for him to finally raise at the elder board. Even after they dismissed him from service, he wouldn't tell me what happened. You would think that, knowing we are both concerned about what's happening in Messiah, he would want to work with me. This could bring us closer together again, give us something to unite behind. But no. Keith is the only one who seems to care about my perspective.

I sit closer to the screen. This is it. This is where she's going to confess to sleeping with Keith.

Yesterday I told Keith I'm ready. What happened with Bella Schmidt was the final straw. If we hadn't have gotten her away from her house, she would probably have ended up in the hospital—maybe worse. Pastor Rick told her to go home to her husband, to treat him with kindness, to honor his wishes. She tried to do everything the right way, and now she's in a motel on Keith's credit card, sharing a bed with her three kids while Brian Schmidt roams around looking for her like a wolf stalking a chicken. She's the fourth woman in our church who's confided in me just in the past month. Saturday morning, I'm dropping Emmie off with my parents and driving Bella to the airport so she can go to her sister's.

I've had ten years to listen to the people who told me stories like Bella's, but I didn't want to hear them. It was easier to block the comments on the blog and continue on believing that for ninety-nine percent of people, the Noble Wife philosophy works out. How can I say that now, though? I'm in couples counseling because my husband and I can't communicate, and now I'm helping other women escape their terrible marriages—something I never thought I'd do. Thousands of people all over the world have read my blog, taking on this lifestyle because I told them it was the right one. They listened to a dreamy-eyed teenager because I wrote with passion, and I told them something they wanted to hear.

What if I was wrong? What if all this is wrong?

Maybe I should listen to Keith. He thinks I should come forward now. I could hit publish on this blog right this second and be done with it. No matter what it would do to Lars, to my family, to the only home I've ever known.

I should just . . . I should hit the button. It would be the right thing to do.

FORTY-FIVE

Delilah's diary

MARCH 3, 2012

I have destroyed my life.

I was too ashamed to write about what happened on Wednesday, mostly because I'm still convinced my mom reads this journal. But she already knows now. Everyone knows.

If enough people tell you something is the truth, it gets harder and harder to deny. But I know what happened, and I'm going to write it down so I never forget.

Noah has been talking to me after youth group every week for the past month. There's this little corner between the back door of the church and the basketball hoops where you can kind of be alone, and when I walked by it on my way to watch the guys play horse, I felt a hand on my arm. He pulled me so close I could barely breathe—it's the closest I've ever been to a boy.

"You look amazing," he told me, and I could feel his breath on my face. It smelled like overchewed peppermint gum, but it wasn't the worst thing. "You should come hang out with me."

We're not really supposed to leave the church grounds during youth group, and the after-service activities count as part of that, but I wasn't going to say no to Noah Franklin. If he was asking me to do it, I thought it couldn't be wrong.

So, I went with him. He led me to his truck, and I felt like I had been chosen for something special. I know how much Noah likes that truck. It was a gift from his dad when he turned sixteen, and he talks about it like a pet. When he opened the passenger door for me, I stepped in like a princess.

For the first little while, we just listened to music on the radio and talked. He asked me what I'm most excited about for college, and I asked about his plans to become an electrician. We compared favorite bands and playlists, and he let me have a drink from his Mountain Dew. Every second of it felt like the most exciting thing I've done in my life. I know we're not supposed to be alone with boys, but we were just talking. I thought it would be okay.

Then he suddenly got serious. "Lila, you've probably noticed how much you've had my attention the past few months. You have become a real distraction."

My face got warm. It wasn't necessarily a positive word, but it felt like a compliment. "I have noticed, yeah."

He reached out and touched my cheek, and his finger felt both cool and fiery hot. I didn't know a body could respond that way to someone else's touch. Every part of me lit up. He leaned in close, and I stopped breathing. He would never kiss me—that was wrong. That was a clear breach of the rules. And he didn't, but he said the words that changed everything.

"You are my biggest temptation."

For a minute, I just stared at him. I shouldn't have felt pride, I shouldn't have felt joy, but I did. No guy had ever even given me a second glance, and here was one of the hottest boys in our class—the most eligible senior in Messiah—and he wanted me. Mom, if you can't understand anything else, I hope you get that. I have always felt plain and ugly next to the other girls in our church. Especially when compared to Eve and Esha. This was the first boy who ever made me feel wanted, and even though it might have all been a trick, it didn't feel that way at the time.

Finally, I did the only thing I could think of. I said I was sorry. Because that's what we're supposed to do when we cause another person to stumble, right? All the Noble Wife teachings have drilled that in. I'm not supposed to cause a brother to stumble.

When I said I was sorry, he smiled. "I forgive you. But there is something you could do to help."

Of course, anything I could do to make life easier for Noah, I wanted to. Should I stop wearing the shirts from Aunt Georgia? Wear less makeup? I only have mascara and tinted lip balm on most days, but I don't need those things.

"What can I do?" I asked.

He looked hesitant then. Guilty. Like he was asking too much.

"Tell me."

His eyes locked with mine. "This is so embarrassing. I just can't stop imagining what you look like underneath that shirt. It's so tight, I spent all night thinking about it."

I felt like he'd slapped me. It was my clothes. The one thing Colette and Pastor Rick are always saying we need to watch out for, the thing that acts as a stumbling block. I was shocked no one else had said anything to me. I didn't think what I wore was that revealing, but apparently I was wrong.

"I'm so sorry, Noah," I said. Embarrassingly, I started crying. "I didn't mean to cause you temptation. I'll stop wearing them. Can you ever forgive me?"

He ran his fingers through that wavy hair and stared out the windshield. "I can, I think. But the image of you in them is stuck in my head. You know how my uncle is always saying that men have overactive imaginations? Like, that our minds create images of naked bodies when we see a girl in revealing clothes, imagining what she looks like underneath?"

I nodded.

"Well, I've been thinking. There is one way I could stop doing that, and it's if I knew what you actually looked like."

That made me pause. I was confused. He couldn't be asking what he was asking. "Are you saying you want to see me without the shirt on?"

Noah met my eyes, and there was so much pain and frustration in his gaze, I felt like the worst person in the world. I did this to him.

"It's the only thing I can think of. Otherwise, you'll just keep cycling through my mind, and I'll never be able to move past this. I've been praying for weeks to stop seeing you like this, but I just can't. I think if you show me, even just for a second, it'll help. And then we never have to talk about this again."

I should have gotten out of the car and stormed away. But since I know everyone thinks this is my fault, let me just say: you can't blame me more than I blame myself. All I wanted in that moment was to right my wrong. I had worn shirts that were immodest, and I had caused one of the most godly boys in our youth group to stumble. If he thought this was the way to help fix that, I didn't feel like I could disagree with him.

I did hesitate, though. I don't even like changing in front of girls at camp, so I can count on one hand the number of people who have seen me shirtless.

Or at least I used to be able to.

But finally, after a few more convincing words from Noah, I agreed. I looked out the windows of his truck, but the sun had set, and we were far enough away from the parking lot lights that no one would be able to look in. I didn't want to go slowly. If I was going to do this, I wanted it over with, like getting my ears pierced. I unbuttoned my shirt, holding it closed until the last button was undone. My bra had a front clasp, which I quickly undid. If he needed to stop imagining what I looked like naked, I thought he would have to see it all.

"Can you close your eyes?" he asked. "It feels too weird if you're looking at me, and that's not the point of this."

That seemed sensible to me, so I did. I didn't hear him pull out his phone. I didn't know about the pictures. It was five seconds that I held my shirt open, and then I buttoned it back up and left the truck. The only thing I said to him was that I was sorry.

That was all. I went home and I felt like a fool. I prayed for forgiveness, both for tempting the boys in Messiah by wearing those shirts and for showing Noah my chest, even if it felt like the right decision at the time. I cried until I was too exhausted to cry anymore, and then I fell asleep.

The next day, I went to school with more makeup on than usual, just to cover how red and blotchy my face was. That's why I thought everyone was looking at me funny at first. I walked through the halls and said hi to Eve, but she turned away. I thought maybe she didn't hear me. But then I got to my first class, and all the boys were gathered around Noah's desk. He had his phone out and they were all laughing, but as soon as I walked in, everyone went quiet.

I knew what happened then, before I ever saw the photos on Instagram. They got taken down a few hours later, but by then the damage was done. Everyone in school—everyone in the church, it seemed—had seen them. And it doesn't matter that I didn't know they were being taken, or why I had my shirt open in the first place, or that someone obviously violated my privacy by sharing them for the whole world to see.

All that matters is they were out there for hours, and there are probably screenshots on dozens of phones, and no one will ever look at me the same way again—including my own father.

I can only say I'm sorry. It sounds stupid, but I thought I was doing the right thing at the time. I did. I swear that I did. I'm sorry. I'm sorry.

I'm so sorry.

FORTY-SIX

SOMETHING BUZZES AGAINST MY THIGH, and I jolt awake. For a moment, I can't place myself in time. I'm reclined in the driver's seat of my cold car, the warmth from the afternoon sun long gone. My stomach is empty, and I have to pee.

I fumble around until I find my phone. The call from an unfamiliar local number goes to voicemail. It's 9:17 p.m. There are dozens of notifications on my screen, mostly missed calls. My mom, Nathaniel, several unknown numbers, Finn.

With a groan, I rub my fingertips over my eyes. They're still swollen from crying. Eve's blog drafts had put me in a state of panicked despair. I read through them all, looking for any hint that she and Keith were involved romantically, but there was no confession to be found. They may have been attracted to each other, but Eve's stories about him were all related to marriage counseling or helping abused women in the church.

Unless she was so ashamed of her affair that she denied it even in what seemed to function as her secret diary, then I had been wrong the whole time.

"The worst thing a woman can do to a man is make a false claim against him."

Eve was not cheating on Lars. The only thing she and Keith seem to be guilty of is working together to undermine Pastor Rick's authority. Keith was innocent, and now he's dead.

I had stayed in the library until it closed at 5:00 p.m., and when I came back out to my car, I was too tired to drive. I must have fallen asleep within minutes of closing my eyes.

Sniffling, I navigate to my voicemail. I can hear the sounds of the bar in the background before Finn's voice comes through the speaker. "Hey, Del, just checking in on you. I hope you're all right. Call me." He called twice more after that but left no messages.

As I hang up, the phone vibrates with another voicemail, this one from the call I just missed. It's Parker. "Del, I know about Keith Rivers. I think you and I need to talk. Can you give me a call?"

My heart rate spikes. Parker is supposed to be looking into Lars's death, but the suicide of Messiah's associate pastor is much bigger news. The fact that he was being accused of having an affair, and potentially killing the man whose wife he was sleeping with, is much more salacious—even if everyone would have written it off as the baseless accusations of a bitter ex-member. Now that he's dead, I have put myself at risk of becoming the focus of the church's wrath once again.

I hover over the callback button for a few seconds. Maybe I should get on top of it this time instead of letting everyone draw their own conclusions like they did when I was sixteen. I'm not some naive teenager anymore. I have a voice, and everything I've done the past few days has been with a good reason. But no one in Bower will see it that way. Keith might have been the one to take his own life, but as far as everyone else will be concerned, I tied the noose for him.

There's only one person who has been on my side this whole time. Conveniently, the one who didn't know me nine years ago. Chewing on my lower lip, I tap Finn's name.

He picks up on the first ring. "Hey! Are you all right?"

The concern in his voice makes my chest ache. I wipe away a tear with the back of my hand. "Not really. It's been a rough day. Are you working?"

"Yeah, but I can finish up early. Want to come in for a drink and tell me about it?"

Despite everything that's happened, I smile. "Make it two drinks, and yes."

After a quick stop at a gas station to use the bathroom and grab a burrito, I head to the restaurant. Finn's at the bar, and he passes me a Jack and Coke as soon as I sit down.

"You look like you've been through hell."

"I'm not sure I believe in hell anymore, but if it exists, it can't be far off from today." I take a few gulps and stare past his shoulder at the bottles lining the shelves. When I finally meet his gaze, I can see he already knows what happened. "So. News travels fast."

He winces. "Yeah, Parker called me a couple hours ago."

"I got a call from her too. I haven't returned it."

"Why not?"

I raise my eyebrows. "Seriously? You know how this looks. I accused Keith of having an affair and possibly murdering his mistress's husband, and four days later he's hanging from his own banister." Another gulp of alcohol makes its way past the lump of tears in my throat.

"There's no way you could have known."

Even though I shouldn't have expected anything else, that response still stings. Part of me hoped he would say it wasn't my fault, help alleviate the crushing guilt compressing my lungs. But I don't deserve that.

"I just thought he was angry with me. Which, obviously, he would be since I was trying to expose what he and Eve were doing. I never expected . . . I thought *I* was the one he was going to hurt."

The expression on his face is hard to read. He reaches behind him, picks up a glass filled with clear liquid, and takes a drink. "You should talk to Parker. She's got to follow this story, and if anything, what Keith did just makes him look more guilty. I talked to her about our snowmobile theory. She's more willing to buy the idea that he was involved in Lars's death now."

If that's true, it would certainly take some of the heat off me. There's only one problem: they don't know about Eve's blog drafts. If I could trust what Eve wrote, considering she didn't think anyone would ever read it, then the only thing she's guilty of is going against the senior pastor's teachings. She even provided a reason for why she dropped Emmanuelle off with her parents the morning Lars died—she was taking a woman to the airport to escape town.

Then something occurs to me. If challenging Rick was all Keith did, he would have every reason to keep working to clear his name. I'm nobody in this town. My theories and accusations wouldn't be devastating to someone as respected as Keith—at most, they were obnoxious. Certainly no reason to take his own life.

For the first time in hours, I feel like I can take a full breath. I sit forward on the barstool, my elbows on the counter and chin on my hands.

"What's wrong?" Finn picks up a ticket from the printer and starts mixing a drink.

"Just something that's been bugging me." I swirl the liquid in my glass, the ice cubes clinking together. "Pastor Rick showed up at Keith's house only a few minutes after the police. He lives fifteen miles away. I don't think he could have made it in that time, even if the sheriff called him right after I phoned it in."

The corners of Finn's mouth turn down. "Maybe he was already nearby."

I nod slowly. "Maybe. I mean, it's no secret that Rick knows everything going on in Bower. That part's not a surprise. It just bugs me how fast he got there. It's almost like . . . like he knew what happened before even I did."

The liquor bottle in Finn's hand dips, sending a slosh of vodka over the side of the glass. He quickly redirects the stream, then sets it down and looks at me. "Are you saying Rick knew Keith killed himself? Like maybe Keith called him before doing it or something?"

"I hadn't thought of that." Truthfully, my theory was much darker—but also much more outlandish. Considering how off base it seems I've been so far with everything happening in Bower, I should probably keep it to myself. But liquor and desperation for another explanation for Keith's death loosen my tongue. "I was just thinking, we don't actually know it was suicide. That's just how it looked."

Finn's eyebrows shoot up. "Are you serious?"

"I'm just saying. They'll have to do an autopsy, right? They won't just assume it's suicide—they have to prove it, don't they?"

"I don't know. Everything I know about police investigation is from TV."

"Same, to be honest." Which explains why I'm so bad at it. My heart flip-flops in my chest as I recall Pastor Rick's expression when he saw me. Contempt, sure—always. But there was something else. A word I know from the Bible but have never had reason to use.

Haughty. He looked absolutely haughty.

"Hear me out." I take the final swallow of my drink. "I've found out more about what Eve and Keith were doing, at least according to her. They were both unhappy with the way Pastor Rick was forcing some women to stay in abusive marriages, and they helped a few of them get away from their husbands." I decide to avoid explaining about the blog drafts, just in case he thinks that's too tenuous.

Finn crosses his arms, leaning back against the bar fridge. "Okay."

"I know you don't like Rick either, but I don't think you understand what a big deal that is. No one in the church ever questions him, especially the leaders. Eve wouldn't be allowed in leadership because she's a woman, but she was the closest one of us could ever get. She's the reason the Noble Wife movement gained such huge traction. She's the reason he became a bestselling author and got so many people to pay attention to his messages. Rick gets offers to be senior pastor at big-city churches all over the country, but I think he stays in Bower because that's where he has the most control. Messiah is nondenominational. They don't have to answer to anyone. He knows if he goes to another church, he'll have to face an elder board that actually holds him accountable."

Finn looks like he wants to say something, but I press on. "It would be bad enough for the associate pastor and the face of the Noble Wife movement to be having an affair, but what if they were doing something worse? What if they were trying to change the way Pastor Rick runs the church? He would never let that pass without doing something about it."

"So what are you saying?" he cuts in. "That Keith didn't kill himself? Someone else killed him?"

Hearing the words aloud, I know how ridiculous they are. "I don't know. I just can't shake the feeling that there was something off about the way Pastor Rick acted at Keith's house this morning."

"Are you sure you're not just trying to find another explanation that makes you feel less guilty?"

He might as well have smacked me. A silence stretches between us like a sore muscle. Finally, I whisper, "That's not what I'm doing."

He takes a breath and nods, his expression apologetic. "Okay. I'm not saying you *should* feel guilty, by the way. It's just . . . you said Parker wanted to talk to you about this. If you're going to mention this stuff about Rick, just make sure you have some real evidence to give her. Not just a gut feeling. She can't report on that. You're only going to get one shot at taking him down—you've got to make it count."

Real evidence. That's what I've been lacking this whole time. Maybe I'm reading too much into Pastor Rick's behavior this morning. I hate him so much it's easy to imagine him being evil enough to kill someone, but that doesn't mean he's actually capable of it. I've never even seen him physically hurt a person; he prefers to inflict pain in ways others can't see—ways that keep you awake at night years after the fact.

When I don't say anything, Finn reaches across the bar and puts a hand on mine. His palm is warm—rough, but not in an unpleasant way. "I'm sorry. I know this day has been shit, and you don't need my help to feel worse."

I sigh. "You're right, though. I keep throwing out these theories, and so far, none of them have been true. Parker can't write about any of it unless I find some proof."

"SO, WHAT DOES this mean? Did he leave a note?" Nathaniel asks.

We're sitting at the kitchen counter, empty breakfast plates in front of us. It took a whole plate of pancakes and two cups of coffee for me to talk him and Susan through everything that has happened in the past forty-eight hours. My eyes ache from crying, and I'm tempted to go upstairs and crawl back into bed.

Instead, I pour myself another cup from the French press. "I don't know. I stopped by the sheriff's department on my way home last night because they'd left me like six messages. I talked to one of the night-shift deputies. He asked me to go through what happened when I found Keith, but they didn't give me any more information about what they found at his house."

Susan is studying her empty mug thoughtfully. "He must have been having an affair with Eve," she says. "It's the only thing that makes sense. Why else would he end his life?"

"Surely it's more than that." Nathaniel rises from his stool, fury clear in his voice. "An affair is bad, but it's nothing a pastor hasn't done before. It must have something to do with Lars's death." He looks at me. "What did Eve tell you when you saw her?"

"Nothing. She denied the affair. She said she didn't kill Lars."

"Of course she did. The sheriff's deputy we spoke to was pretty clear, though. They're confident the rifle they found on the Thompson property was used to shoot Lars, although they have to wait for the official ballistic results to come back. And if someone called in an anonymous tip, that means at least one other person knew she killed Lars. An accomplice, maybe, or a confidant."

I blow my nose, crush the tissue, and wipe under my eyes. "You think Keith ratted on Eve?"

"Maybe he thought turning her in would relieve his guilt, and when it didn't, he decided to end it all."

It's possible. I want to believe I'd be able to tell if Eve was lying to me, but maybe I'm putting too much faith in myself.

"We knew something was different with her the last few months or so, didn't we, Susan?" Nathaniel is pacing now. "We thought it was because of Emmanuelle—some kind of delayed postpartum depression or something. But this . . . she could have been planning this for weeks."

Susan shakes her head, her face crumpling into tears. "My boy. Why couldn't she just divorce him if she was so unhappy?"

I wrap an arm around her shoulders as they shudder with sobs. Nathaniel pauses his stride and looks at his wife but does not approach. I know the death of a child, even an adult one, can drive the strongest couples apart.

"I guess that's it, then," Nathaniel says, his eyes wet.

Stroking Susan's back, I look between the two of them. Lars used to tell me his parents' marriage was the one he looked up to most, the one he wanted. "They genuinely like being together," he would say. "I don't think they've spent more than five nights apart my whole life."

Seeing them now, quietly burning with grief on their own, is unbearable. I want to give them answers. Keith's death just creates more questions. He was angry when he showed up here the other night, but there was something more than rage in his eyes that I didn't want to see at the time. He was desperate. He wanted me to stop digging. So that I wouldn't find evidence he was cheating with Eve, I had assumed. But now I'm less confident.

"Did the police tell you anything else when you were there?" I reach for a box of tissues on the counter, offering one to Susan.

As she blows her nose, Nathaniel says, "Well, they did finally tell us who Lars was hunting with. Now that Eve is in jail, they're less concerned about him being wrongly accused of being part of this."

I take a sip of coffee, wait for him to continue.

"It was a friend of his. You might know him? Noah Franklin."

The hand holding my drink goes weak, sending scalding liquid into my lap. I jump up, biting back a curse.

"Oh, honey, are you okay?" Susan grabs a wet cloth from the sink, runs it under cool water, and hands it to me. Nathaniel mops up the coffee on the counter and refills my cup. For just a moment, the miniature crisis seems to snap all of us out of our stunned grief.

My skin doesn't feel too tender under my pant leg, so I don't bother to check for a burn. I have to make sure Nathaniel just said what I thought he did. "You're sure it was Noah Franklin? Pastor Rick's nephew?"

Nathaniel's eyes widen. "I assumed they must be related, but the police didn't say. Why, do you know something about him?"

They both watch me intently. I suck in a tight breath. The Obacks are as close as they might ever get to a resolution on their son's death, even if that means their daughter-in-law is convicted of murdering him to be with another man. I know they don't want that to be true, but the last thing they need is for me to give them false hope.

"I . . . I do know him, yeah." I stall by adding a splash of milk to my coffee. "We grew up together. I just didn't realize he was friends with Lars. It's good the police are telling you more now."

Susan seems to accept this, stacking our plates and turning to load them in the dishwasher. But Nathaniel has not broken eye contact. He knows I'm not telling him the whole story. Swallowing a bubble of guilt, I hold up my coffee. "Um, is it okay if I take this to go? I've got to get to work."

"Sure, darling." Susan pulls a travel cup out of the cabinet and hands it to me.

"Thanks. I'll see you later." I smile at both of them, feeling the weight of Nathaniel's gaze as I walk out of the room.

FORTY-SEVE

WHEN MY SHIFT IS OVER, I slump in an empty booth and count my tips. Nothing amazing, but probably better than I deserve considering I was so out of it the whole time. My mind has been racing, inventing and discarding theories, ever since I learned Noah was the one hunting with Lars.

After stacking the bills together, I look up at the TV behind the bar. We keep the volume off except when a Timberwolves or Vikings game is on, but the captions run all day. Eve Oback's name catches my eye. There's a group of four men standing outside a brick building that I recognize as the sheriff's office in Bower. A man with a rusty brown mustache and pockmarked skin is speaking into a cluster of microphones on a cheap plastic podium. It's been years since I saw him sitting in his usual row of chairs at the Mess, but I recognize Deputy Mike Tyler immediately.

"Can you turn that up?" I ask Maddy, the lunchtime bartender.

She picks up the remote.

" . . . extremely confident we have apprehended the right person for this horrible crime, and the tragic passing of Keith Rivers does nothing to shake that confidence, no."

Off camera, I hear a voice I'm ninety percent sure belongs to Parker. "Any comment on the rumor that Eve and Keith were having an affair and that may have had something to do with Lars Oback's homicide?"

I sit up straighter. It's weird to hear a journalist ask about a rumor I'm responsible for.

Tyler shakes his head. "I can't comment on that, Parker, but surprised to hear you peddling in gossip and fantasies. It's ex-that sort of thing that makes it easy for everyone in this upstanding wn to disregard you and the rag you write for."

I swallow hard. It's no surprise hearing a police officer have such disdain for the media, but the deputy seems to particularly hate Parker.

She doesn't respond, and he moves on to another question. A man's voice asks if there's any physical evidence against Eve, and the deputy holds up a hand.

"I'm afraid I can't discuss the particulars of an active investigation. Suffice to say we are confident in the case we're building against Mrs. Oback."

Parker speaks up again. "Does that mean you've cleared Noah Franklin of any wrongdoing?"

My body goes rigid.

Deputy Tyler's eyes flash before his face settles into a carefully neutral expression. "Like I said, we are confident we have our killer in custody. Now, if you'll excuse me, we've got a lot of work to do." He turns and walks toward the building, closely followed by the three men in uniform behind him. The cameras stay on the empty podium for a moment before the channel transitions to an overly made-up blond behind a news desk.

It took Parker some guts to say the last name Franklin in connection with a crime, even if she does work in another town. Pastor Rick will be furious. That thought puts a genuine smile on my face for the first time today.

I open Facebook on my phone and search for Noah's name. I unfriended him years ago, but his profile is public. He graduated from trade school in Moorhead and works as a senior electrician for the same power company as my dad. I'm surprised by the stab of jealousy I feel when I see pictures of him with his wife and two daughters. Jealousy mixed with horror, at both the first emotion and the thought of him raising girls. I wonder if he'd accept a boy doing to one of them what he did to me.

Pastor Rick's brother—Noah's dad—owns a farm fifteen miles out of town, and Noah always talked about how he'd build his own house right across the highway one day. He is the kind of person who gets everything he wants, so I'm sure that's where he lives now.

Noah Franklin, the golden boy. The one nothing sticks to. Pastor Rick always protects his family. I'm sure that's just a coincidence.

It's just a coincidence that Rick made sure everyone treated it like an accident at first. It's just a coincidence things only started to spiral out of control the second Lars's parents and I refused to believe the Messiah party line. It's just a coincidence he let his Noble Wife evangelist take the fall for her husband's death after she started to question his authority.

Sliding out of the booth, I say goodbye to the shift manager and walk out to my car. Once there, I'm not sure where to go. My whole body is buzzing with the need to do something. To tell someone.

Finally, I pull my phone out of my purse and call Parker.

She answers after the second ring. "Hey, I was beginning to think you forgot about me."

"No, sorry. It's just been a wild couple days."

"No kidding. Finn said you found Keith Rivers's body? That must have been horrible. I wouldn't put it past the guy to have planned it that way. Make you feel super guilty like all this was your fault instead of his after he slept with a married church member. Just remember you had nothing to do with this. Don't let him win by making you feel bad, okay? Del?"

A shaky laugh escapes me. "I'm here, I just couldn't get a word in."

"Oh right, sorry. I do tend to yammer on. Just tell me to shut up if it gets annoying; everyone else does. Anyway, I assume you're returning my call? Unfortunately, I had to file the story about his body being found. I wanted to interview you about it, but the news doesn't wait, you know?"

"That's okay. I actually . . . I have kind of a crazy theory. And no offense, but you seem like the kind of person who would listen to that."

Parker barks a laugh. "Offense taken, but you're not wrong. And if it's about Messiah, then I'm even more likely to hear you out. Nothing could be more ridiculous than some of the stuff I already know is true. That church has done every bonkers Pentecostal thing I've heard of except letting vipers bite them to prove God's healing power."

"Believe me, there are some members who have wanted to do that. I think the only reason they didn't is Rick didn't want the bad publicity if it went wrong."

"*If?*"

I chuckle. "Right, when. Sorry."

"Don't apologize. So anyway, they might let me write another story if you have anything to add. Do you want to tell me what happened?"

I briefly recount the reason I went to visit Keith and the way I found his body. It's mostly stuff Parker already knows from her contact in the sheriff's department. But when I get to the part about Rick showing up so fast, she stops me.

"Hang on, I didn't know he was there."

I look out the windshield of my car, shifting the phone to my other ear. "Yeah, like extremely quickly after it happened. I told Finn I thought it was impossible for him to get there so fast unless he was already on his way over, but he thought I was being overly suspicious. But it's still bothering me. Especially since I—"

My mouth goes dry. This is a bad idea. Once I say the words out loud, I can't take them back. And I've seen what happens when I start throwing around accusations without proof.

Parker lets the silence go on for only a moment. "Since you what? What happened?"

I clear my throat. "I just watched the press conference with the Green County Sheriff. You asked about them clearing Noah Franklin. I assume that means you know he was the one Lars was hunting with?"

"Yes. I got my law enforcement source to finally spill the beans." I can tell she's swallowing about a thousand other words, waiting for me to keep talking.

"Right. And do you think you can take their word for it that they've cleared him?"

"Are you kidding? Police lie even more than politicians."

I smirk. "Good, because I think I've finally figured something out. It was clear Pastor Rick wanted everyone to believe Lars's death was an accident, so I started wondering who he was covering for. It had to be someone important to him. When I thought it was Keith, it made sense because he was the associate pastor. But that was before I knew Lars was with Noah Franklin when he died."

"And why does that matter?"

"Well, I'm sure it won't surprise you to know that Rick Franklin will do anything to protect his family."

"It would not."

"Even covering up a crime."

"You think Noah killed Lars?"

For a moment, I stare out the window with my mouth open. I'm not sure if I'm ready to say it, even though it suddenly feels so obviously true. Maybe I can ease into it.

"Not necessarily on purpose. Maybe it was a hunting accident after all, but Noah was being negligent. It's the kind of thing he might do. He was always messing around, acting invincible. Because in our town, he was. He could do whatever he wanted, and his uncle would make sure he didn't face any consequences, even if his actions were illegal. Even if he hurt people."

"Do you have evidence of that?"

I rub my fingers on my collarbone. "Just my own story."

"And what is that, if you don't mind me asking?"

"I'll tell you, I promise. But right now, I'm only asking you to look into it. Don't stop investigating Noah Franklin, no matter what the police or Messiah Church tell you. There's something there, and whether he did it on purpose or not, there's no doubt in my mind Rick would help him cover it up if he really did kill Lars. Even if that meant framing someone for the murder."

There's such a long silence that I'm sure Parker has hung up on me in disbelief. When I pull the phone away from my ear, the call is still connected.

"Hello?"

"I'm here," Parker says. "I'm just thinking. What if it wasn't an accident? If your theory is true, they are framing Eve for the murder. That's more than just a cover-up. Do you know any reason Noah might want to kill Lars? Maybe he knew something about Noah or the Franklins that he shouldn't?"

I pause, remembering something Eve said in her blog drafts. "Eve mentioned that Lars was worried about some stuff he was finding at work, issues in the account he was assigned to. It was taking up all his time. I talked to Lars's boss at the accounting firm, and he said Lars was hired to work on one of their biggest clients." That fact hadn't even made it onto my pieces of library paper, but it now seems like it could mean something. "Noah's a senior electrician at Emerald Power. They would be a huge account if Prosperity manages their money—maybe there's a connection there?"

"Now, that is interesting. I'll look into it."

"You will? You don't think it's too ridiculous?"

"Trust me, Del, no one wants to get the real story more than I do. I've been trying to expose Messiah for years. It's the kind of thing that could finally make my editor take me seriously."

For the first time, I hear a sour edge in Parker's voice, and I wonder about her passion for this case. It doesn't feel like the kind of thing I can ask about without sounding suspicious.

"Sex and adultery are one thing, but accounting irregularities? He'll eat that shit up. What I need now is documentation. I'll do my own digging, but it would help to have a Messiah insider getting information too. When you're ready to tell me your story, is there anyone I can talk to who would back you up?"

Twisting the hem of my shirt around my finger, I close my eyes. "Yeah. I think so. I just have to convince them to talk."

"Great. Call me when you do."

I REMEMBER THE house where Noah grew up. We had the occasional birthday or snowmobile party out there when I was a teenager. His dad had farmed the land since before my mother left town the first time. Twelve years his brother's senior, Todd Franklin was part of the reason Rick took the job in Messiah when he was offered it. Close to family, good cost of living, and all the power an ambitious young pastor could want.

Across the highway from his childhood home stands Noah's house, built exactly where he planned in high school. It's more like a mansion, three stories with floor-to-ceiling windows taking in the scenery of his fields. I drive past, scanning the countryside. Noah wouldn't be dumb enough to hunt near his house, and there's almost no shelter for deer in the vicinity.

I slow as I round the bend, spotting a gravel road that almost blends into the dead grass and snow on my left. In the distance, I can see a large grouping of trees. Flicking on my blinker, I turn onto the road. The entrance is just far enough down a hill that I can't see the house behind me. Hopefully, that means Noah can't see me either.

Minnesota is known for lakes more than forests. The thickest woods are clustered up north, swathes of evergreen popularly used as campgrounds in the summer. Around here, most of the trees were cleared in favor of farmland more than a century ago. Deciduous forests are reserved for state parks and hilly or swampy areas where the soil couldn't grow crops. Here and there, you'll find small patches of woods like these, where the deer congregate to hide from the icy wind and eager rifles every winter.

On Noah Franklin's property, this is where they go to die.

The sunken land puts the trees out of sight of the farm. It doesn't look like much, but it's the only place I can see that would work for deer hunting. As soon as I start walking through the trees, the temperature and light both drop. The branches are thick, and I almost miss the path. I'm sure Noah only comes here a couple times a year, during hunting season. I keep my eyes peeled for anything that looks like a stand, but for several minutes, all I see are fallen leaves and branches like skeletal fingers reaching for me as I pass.

After ten minutes of trudging through the underbrush, I stop, panting. I'm in what feels like a small clearing, maybe fifteen feet square. Nothing looks out of place on the ground level. It's a cloudy day, and the weak afternoon light is already fading. Although not especially thick, the trees are overgrown enough to make it hard to see. I could wander around here for hours and not figure out where they were hunting, and even though I'm hoping Noah didn't see me drive in here, I don't feel like I have that kind of time.

Besides, I don't know that I'd learn anything by seeing the place where Lars died anyway.

Nathaniel said he was shot from less than a hundred yards away. If it was just the two of them out here, it had to be Noah who shot Lars. There would be no other hunters around. Maybe he got too excited, mistook Lars for a deer rustling in the branches. It was early in the morning, both of them probably sluggish and cold. It could be that he just wasn't being careful and his rifle went off.

Or maybe, just maybe, Noah Franklin wanted Lars dead.

On some level, it doesn't matter why. Not right now. Sitting here, looking down at the forest floor so close to where Lars took his last breaths, I can't bring myself to theorize about why Noah would want to kill him. All I can do is imagine him lying somewhere in these woods, lungs gasping for icy air, dying in the cold, alone.

I don't care why Noah did it. There is no bringing Lars back from the dead. The only thing I can do now is make sure that he gets justice.

For once, I'm going to make sure Noah Franklin pays for what he's done.

FORTY-EIGHT

[DRAFT]

Noble Wife Journey: a blog
Title: Mafia
Last updated: August 20, 2016

I remember the first time I lied to my husband.

It was before we were married, before we were even really in a relationship. He wanted me to come to the Bible group where I first saw him, this time as a full-fledged student and his almost-girlfriend. It was the night I had been waiting for since we started writing letters four months earlier.

He beamed at me when I walked in, lifted a hand in a small wave. I had told him we should just act like acquaintances here. I didn't want anything to mess this up. He hadn't asked my father's permission yet, and we couldn't truly be together until he did.

After a quick hello, his co-leader announced we'd be playing Mafia. They split us into three separate groups, and Lars joined mine, squeezing in between two of the boys after a glance in my direction.

The skin from my collarbones to my ears flared at his presence, but I knew how to be demure, to squash down feelings and temptations in favor of modesty. We were dealt cards, and in the first round, I was a nobody—an innocent villager who sat back while the ones with face cards got to play a role in either killing or saving us.

I was very good at Mafia, mostly because I have excellent hearing and could almost always pick up on the rustle of clothes from pointing or popping of gums from mouthing words. When people have played a role in the circle, they don't react to the light upon opening their eyes the way the villagers do. If I saw someone squinting after the moderator said, "Mafia, wake up," I usually ruled them out.

But the real reason I was good at that game is because I paid more attention than most to the way people lied. After a while, it was easy to notice the trends. The people who looked down, avoided meeting other people's gazes—those were the ones I could detect easily, the ones I knew I could trust in real life. The people I needed to watch out for had completely neutral expressions, their gazes steady even as they accused someone else of being the Mafia without flinching. The game required you to lie for yourself, but I drew the line at throwing other people under the bus.

When the moderator dealt another round, I held a joker.

We were told to go to sleep, and then I awoke, making eye contact with my fellow Mafia hit man. I nodded towards one of the girls— someone I had seen eyeing my man before. His chin dipped once, agreeing with my choice, and we went back to sleep.

The doctor lucked out and saved the right person, but neither of us were caught. The next few rounds were more successful; we managed to pick off three other players, one of whom was the detective. The villagers accused my partner and he defended himself, but his voice was shaky and the remaining players voted that it was him, ousting him from the game. The next round, I was on my own. I looked around the circle, caught the moderator's eye, and pointed at the last guy left besides Lars.

When everyone woke up, accusations started flying around. People pointed the finger at a girl who was trembling all over, obviously innocent.

"I think it's Eve."

Lars's voice cut through the group, making everyone sit up straighter. He had barely spoken throughout the game, letting everyone else hold votes without his input, other than a raised hand. Now, he was looking at me like he was trying to see inside my mind.

I couldn't let him catch me. "It's not."

He continued. "She's an excellent bluff, but I think it's her."

I returned his gaze without blinking and smiled, my shoulders lifting in a casual shrug. "It isn't me."

His eyes were locked on mine for what felt like five solid minutes before he finally said, "Okay." And he voted for the other girl.

I won. Everyone in the circle applauded, patted me on the back, congratulated me. Lars looked annoyed at having been tricked, and I felt a cloud of doubt, wondering if I shouldn't have played the game so well. But then he smiled and laughed, and days later, he asked my father's permission to date me.

It was just a game, but it took me weeks to stop feeling guilty for lying to him. I vowed never to do it again.

It didn't last. We've been married less than a year, and I quickly realized in order to fulfill my role as a Noble Wife, I can't be one hundred percent honest with my husband. If he wants a happy refuge to come home to, it means I sometimes don't tell the truth. They never explicitly taught us that in our lessons at Messiah, but there is no other way. Be charming, be peaceful, be lovely. Don't cause strife. Submit.

So, I lie.

That doesn't bother me. Of course, do what you want. Baby, I'm so happy.

Yes, this is all I ever wanted. Yes, yes, yes.

FORTY-NINE

FOR FIFTEEN MINUTES, I'VE BEEN parked outside the house where I grew up. It's hard to know what to call it. It's not my home, but there was a time when it felt like one. The playhouse is still out front—Eve, Esha, and I spent hours in there when we were in junior high. The pink paint has faded to an ugly tan, and the cluster of flowers my mom stenciled over the doorway looks more like a spiderweb from a distance. It's smaller than I remember it, but I didn't hit my full height until I was sixteen, and by then we had long since grown out of spending time in there.

For the third time, I reach for my phone, thinking I should call my mom and ask if it's okay that I come over. And again, my finger freezes on the screen. What kind of daughter needs to ask permission to visit her parents?

"This is stupid," I say. With one last look in the mirror, I get out of the car.

The path to the house is neatly swept. A smattering of snow dusts the dead lawn, not a fallen leaf in sight. My dad always keeps the yard in pristine condition. It's his go-to move when things get tense in the house; I always knew when he and my mom were arguing by the sound of the back screen door slamming as he made his way to the shed. The month after the incident with Noah, I saw him on his knees in the dirt after midnight, like he was trying to catch the weeds as they sprang up in the dark.

The garden is dormant now, but in a few months it'll be bursting with life again. Tomatoes, cucumbers, carrots, beets, green beans, and sugar snaps. Once or twice, he let me help with the harvest. Most of the girls my age would have hated the hours bent over the plants, dirt under fingernails, but it was the only time I really spent with my dad outside of church. It's my fondest memory here.

My stomach turns as I approach the house. It feels wrong to knock, even worse to ring the doorbell. But I can't just walk in either. Finally, I settle for peering through the window into the living room. My mom is sitting in her favorite chair, Bible open on her skinny thighs. I tap the window with a fingernail and she jolts up, her hand over her chest. When she sees me, her mouth sets in a line. She lowers the recliner and stands up.

A moment later, the front door opens. "Nice of you to stop by," she says, like I'm an inconvenient neighbor.

"It's nice to see you too, Mom." The smell of coffee drifts out on the warm inside air. "Do you have a few minutes?"

"I'm just doing my reading."

"I saw." I lick my lips, my mouth suddenly dry. When she doesn't step aside, I cross my arms. "I promise this won't take long."

"All right." The words come out on a sigh. Finally, she turns and lets me in. "Would you like some hot chocolate?" No matter how unwelcome the guest, May Walker doesn't have it in her not to offer refreshments.

"I'm all right, thanks." Declining is part of the ritual.

"Don't be silly. It'll only take a minute." She gestures at the couch and then walks off toward the kitchen.

It's a strange thing, being treated like a visitor in a place where you used to live. This is the same furniture I grew up with, the same pictures on the walls, the same scratchy carpet with the subtly darker ring in the corner from an overwatered potted plant. But there's no warmth here, no memories I want to reach out and cling on to. I feel like I've stepped into a photograph of my home rather than the place itself.

Between the clanging of spoons on dishes and the kettle boiling on the stove, I hear my mom murmuring. Praying for wisdom, no doubt. For strength to deal with her wayward daughter.

Familiar footsteps sound on the wooden stairs. A moment later, my dad walks into the room. He pauses when he sees me. "Delilah."

"Dad."

"I thought I heard voices."

"You did."

"Mm." He studies me for a moment. "It's good to see you again."

"You too."

A dish crashes in the kitchen, and he looks in that direction. "She making you tea?"

"Hot cocoa."

A smile tugs at his lips. "Let's see if she puts marshmallows in it. Then we'll know if she forgives you."

My neck burns, but I return his smile. I'm the one who needs to forgive her, but neither of them will see it that way. I walked out on them—never mind that I had good reason. "She's slammed like three dishes since she went in there."

He sits across from me in the recliner opposite Mom's. "Maybe not." After putting a bookmark in her Bible, he shuts it and sets it on the side table. "What brings you here?"

"Yes, you didn't say." My mom enters the room with a small serving tray. There's a cup of hot chocolate and two small cookies on a plate. No marshmallows.

I cut my eyes at my dad, and he pretends to wipe his mouth to cover his smile. Wrapping my fingers around the mug, I hold it up. "Thanks."

She settles back in her chair, hands folded between her legs. "Now. What's wrong?"

The hot chocolate is bland. She always makes it with water instead of milk and half the recommended amount of powder to reduce sugar; I drink it anyway. Despite sitting in the car for twenty minutes before I came in, I actually don't know where to start. It's probably best just to come out with it. "I wanted to talk to you guys about . . . about what happened when I was sixteen."

Instantly, my dad's head drops and he sits lower in his chair. My mom, however, looks at me blankly. "What do you mean?"

"Come on, Mom, you know."

Lower lip pushed out, she shakes her head. "Know what?"

I sigh. "What happened with Noah Franklin. The pictures."

Splotches of red are creeping up her neck, but she still tries to maintain a neutral expression. "I would rather not. Once we've forgiven something, Delilah, we're supposed to put it in the past."

"Well, that might work for you, but it doesn't work for me. I can't just pretend it didn't happen, and you shouldn't be able to either." My tone is more shrill than I want. It's like I'm sixteen again, sitting across from an artificially clueless mother and painfully silent father. There is nothing there—no sadness, no hurt, no rage. Only the slithering tendrils of shame.

When neither of them says anything, I continue. "Noah got off with a slap on the wrist because the church protected him. Pastor Rick protected him. I never asked you this, but I've always wondered why . . ." I swallow, trying to keep my voice steady. "Why you didn't protect me."

My mother's eyes blaze. "Did we not raise you with every bit of wisdom you needed to avoid that situation? Did we not show you how to be a godly young woman, bring you up in the church?"

"What happened to me *happened* in the church," I say.

"It did not happen in the church. You left and wandered off with a boy to be alone, which you knew would lead to temptation," my mother says. Next to her, my dad is still sitting with his head bowed, studying his hands. If it weren't winter, I'm sure he would have escaped to rake or mow the lawn by now.

Taking a deep breath, I stare at a spot on the table rather than meet my mother's eyes. "This isn't why I came here, to fight." I laugh mirthlessly. "In fact, I don't know why I came here at all. I should have known you would still defend Messiah before you would ever believe me."

"Believe you about what?"

My mom and I both look at Dad with a start.

"About . . . about Pastor Rick. About how he's covering up what really happened to Lars Oback." My mouth is sticky, so I take another sip of hot cocoa. "Did you know Lars was shot when he was hunting with Noah Franklin? Don't you think that's weird, that the police immediately ruled it an accident and tried to keep the identity of his hunting partner a secret? Why would they do that if there was nothing suspicious going on?"

"This is a small town," my mother argues. "They probably just wanted to make sure no one thought badly of Noah."

"Why would they think badly of him if it was an accident? If he wasn't doing anything wrong, why not just tell everyone what really happened?"

"What really happened is that Eve killed Lars," she says, tears spilling over. My mom has always been an easy crier. "It's horrible, and it's absolutely devastated all of us at Messiah, but that is the truth. She's been arrested, Delilah."

"That's right, she's been arrested. Not convicted. And even if she had, that doesn't make her guilty."

She stares at me for a moment. "Are you seriously suggesting Noah had something to do with this?"

"I'm suggesting that there's a reason Rick Franklin didn't want the public to know that Lars was killed on Noah's property. He's protecting his nephew again, and you know better than anyone that he's willing to do that even if Noah committed a crime."

My dad's gaze falls to his lap again, but he speaks before my mother can. "You think what happened to you was a crime?" His voice is sad rather than derisive.

"I know it was," I murmur, looking at him to avoid seeing my mother's expression. "I didn't realize it at the time, but I've looked it up. I was underage when those photos got taken. What Noah did would be classified as distributing child pornography."

A strangled sound emits from my mother. "Delilah! What a horrible thing to say."

Not *what a horrible thing to happen*. I look at her, trying my best to return her fierce gaze with my own. As much as I wish I didn't get anything from her, I know my chin is lifted defiantly just like hers. "It is a horrible thing. A horrible thing to accuse someone of, so I would only do it if it were the truth. Noah took pictures of me in a sexual manner and posted them online, sent them to his friends. I was a child. I know you think I should have known better, and at the time, I did too. It's only in the past couple of years that I've realized how messed up that is. I was the victim of a sexual assault. He might not have touched me, but he violated me. He did, and then Pastor Rick made sure he didn't face any consequences for it. I had to spend a year begging forgiveness from people who clearly didn't care about me at all."

Tears are running down my cheeks, but I refuse to look away from my parents long enough to find a tissue. My mother's face is red with anger or embarrassment—I'm not sure which—and my dad is studying his jeans like they hold a sacred message.

"I came here because I hoped you might finally see things the way they really were after all this time. I know you were just trying to do your best to raise me the way the church wanted, but because of that, you never questioned how Pastor Rick interpreted what happened. You never questioned the way he chose to handle it. And I'm telling you, something like that is happening with Lars Oback, only even worse because a man is dead. Two men, if you count Keith Rivers. Two people are dead, and Pastor Rick is making sure everything gets tied up as neatly as possible without attracting any negative attention. You should wonder why that is."

The silence in the room is a crushing weight. I don't know what I expected. My parents never apologized to me growing up; there was no reason to expect them to now. But still, I had hoped . . .

Setting down my mug on the coffee table, I stand. I'm halfway to the front door when my dad finally speaks.

"Wait."

I turn to find him standing in front of his chair. "What do you want us to do?" he asks.

My lips part to take in a shuddering breath. Looking past him, I see my mother cover her mouth. She doesn't try to interrupt. I don't know what that means, but it feels like something. My gaze shifts back to my dad.

"Well, I came here because I hoped you might back me up if I finally tell my story to a journalist. But I know that might jeopardize your membership in Messiah, so . . ." I take a deep breath, holding back a sob.

"You know what I really want? I want you to believe me. That's all. You're my parents. You should be on my side."

Neither of them speaks. After a moment, my dad crosses his arms, his mouth tight with regret. Swallowing more tears, I nod. I tug on my boots and coat and walk out the door without looking back.

FIFTY

"YOU'RE GOING TO THINK I'M a lush, but I need the strongest drink you can pour me." I sit on the barstool across from Finn.

Without a word, he turns and picks up one of the large cocktail glasses. "Long Island, light on the juice?"

"Done."

He's generous with the spirits, and I appreciate that in a man. For someone who never touched alcohol until I was of legal age, I sure do know how to knock them back now.

"Another rough day?" He sets the cocktail in front of me, and I take a long drink. I'm instantly filled with déjà vu. I've only known him a week, and I've lost count of how many times he's served me booze. He's going to get the wrong idea about me, but I can't help it. The alcohol doesn't fix anything, but it numbs me just enough to make it bearable. In that way, I'm glad I didn't try it when I was a teenager.

"You joining me?" I ask.

He looks around. There are only a handful of customers in the building, and we're ten minutes from closing. For a guy who sat down and had a few drinks with me the night we met, he's acting strangely reserved about bending the rules. I wonder if one of the staff told his parents what he was doing. I have yet to see them in here, but my understanding is they still keep a close watch on the business, even with Finn ostensibly running it.

Then he grins. "Why not?" He quickly mixes himself the same drink but stays standing behind the bar while he sips from it. "You going to tell me what's wrong?"

"It's just . . ." The events of the day come crashing down on me. I take another drink to swallow the knot of tears in my throat. "You ever think you're doing the right thing, only to have literally everything that happens in a twenty-four-hour period insist that you're not?"

He purses his lips on the edge of his glass, then nods. "Sure. Once, my friend's dog had a litter of mutts, and he was trying to give them to good homes so they didn't end up in the pound. I adopted one, which is how I found out I'm allergic to dogs—also that everything in my apartment is chewable."

Despite everything, I laugh. "Chaos?"

"Oh, utter chaos. Within six hours, my furniture was in tatters, and I could not stop sneezing. I had to give the dog back. Luckily, he found her a new home."

My laughter fades as I take another pull of the Long Island, and without warning, tears well up in my eyes.

Finn's hand rests on my arm. "You know, you're putting a lot of pressure on yourself. What you're trying to do, investigating Lars's death like this, it's not something anyone should expect of you."

I study my hands. "I know that. But it's not just Nathaniel and Susan. I want to find out what happened to him too. I owe him that."

Finn is silent for a moment. I suck on the straw, then examine my glass. The drink is already almost gone.

"Do you still love him?" He studies my face for a reaction. My lips part, but I can't think of anything to say. "I know you said it had been a few years, but it seems like . . . you know . . . like those feelings hadn't gone away." Turning his focus to a task, he grabs a rag and starts wiping down the bar.

It's not too much to hope that he's asking because he wants the answer to be no. I might be insecure, but I'm not ignorant. Finn looks at me like he sees something new and intriguing every time, like I'm a work of art. Ever since the night we met, he's made it clear he's interested in me. The subtle hand on my hip as he passes me in the kitchen, the playful glances across the restaurant when I'm dealing with an annoying customer.

Some of my best hookups have been with guys at work. Restaurant staff rosters are basically just dating lists, and the stockroom of every one I've worked in has served as a make out zone to half the staff.

The purity culture I was steeped in at the Mess has kept me from casual sex, if nothing else. But the way I'm feeling right now, the way he's looking at me with those hooded but vulnerable eyes, I'm open to anything.

"I'm not in love with him anymore." And it's true. I think. I'm fairly sure it's true.

The corners of Finn's mouth turn up. He leans across the bar. I can smell the sweet spice of cola on his breath. "Yeah?"

"Mm-hmm." Boldly, I sit forward until I'm just inches away from his face. The warm buzz of alcohol and attention makes me dizzy. "Lately, I've been thinking about somebody else."

"Lucky guy," he says.

"If he wants to be." I press my forehead against his for a second, then pull away with a grin. This is the kind of life I wanted, the feeling I was always told I shouldn't chase. A man trying to soak me in with his eyes, entranced by the thought of being with me, unable to look away. I spent so much time trying to convince Messiah that I wasn't the person they said I was, the seductive temptress. Maybe, instead, I should have just surrendered to it. If everyone believes you're consumed by sinful pleasure, you might as well be getting some.

"I'm going to wait outside while you close. Will it take long?"

Finn's eyes darken. "Twenty minutes, tops."

"Make it fifteen."

It only takes him ten. He finds me sitting on the hood of his car. The night is bitterly cold, but I'm so flushed and warm that my coat is unzipped. His hands part the fabric, gripping my waist to pull me close. I wrap my legs around his hips as our mouths come together.

Some kisses fill you with tender affection, others with warm desire. This isn't either. This is the kind of kiss that ruins a person, and tonight, I want to be destroyed.

He presses himself hard against me, and I lean back until I'm flat on the hood, his body over mine. The November wind is metallic with cold, but his fingers are warm as they slip under my shirt.

I've only had sex three times. You don't grow up hearing about the evils of fornication every week without being affected, even if you later decide that teaching is at best overemphasized. It was with the boyfriend I had before Dan, the only other guy besides Lars that I thought I could love. Even though we had been together for months by the time I caved in, I felt horribly guilty after every time. Since then, I've mostly stuck to the "everything but" strategy.

But I've never been kissed like this before. Finn is holding me like I'm a tether keeping him from drifting into outer space, like he's been wanting to do this for years instead of days.

I look up at the stars and feel a sudden gust of shame. On this cold, clear night with the lips of a man I'm infatuated with on mine, I feel more alive than I have in years. Even with so much death around me. Lars will never feel this way again; Keith will never hold a woman the way Finn is holding me. I close my eyes, and a vision of his body, dangling from a rope, is waiting there. I gasp, but then Finn's hand closes around my breast, and the memory is zapped from my mind like a pesky fly. When I moan at his touch, I imagine how ashamed my mother would be if she drove by and saw her daughter stretched out on a car with a man.

Then Finn's mouth presses into my neck, and I stop thinking about anything at all.

FIFTY-ONE

[DRAFT]

Noble Wife Journey: a blog
Title: Secrets
Last updated: April 10, 2021

Lars has been obsessing over something at work for weeks. Whatever it is has changed him, consumed him.

For Emmanuelle, he is the doting father. At least that will never change. He swoops her into his arms, lets her play in the bath until the water gets cold, and pulls her soft blond curls into pigtails every week for church. While we're there his face is a tight mask, his greetings stilted and awkward, his laugh obviously fake.

Men think they are so good at covering up their emotions.

At night, he is supposed to be mine. We always promised to lay down the troubles of the day and be with each other, at least for ten minutes—whatever that looked like. When I reminded him of that, he told me I don't understand what he's going through at work. I said I couldn't understand if he didn't tell me, and then he stopped talking again. Every time I try to help, I make it worse.

There has not been a night this week that I didn't fall asleep under the blue light of his laptop, listening to him sigh and click and type until exhaustion took me.

People warned me about the newborn days: the sleep deprivation, the hormones, the isolation. Women at church told me kindly that "nothing you say to each other after 9:00 p.m. counts" because that's when our fatigue would be at its peak, and we might snap at each other in ways we never imagined before.

But no one told me what to do if my husband just stopped telling me anything. He is cordial with me. Not a day passes without a small kiss on the lips when he leaves and another when he comes back home. That is the best I can hope for. He is either too busy or too tired for more. I simultaneously long for physical intimacy with him and am repelled by it, disgusted at the idea that he could want only my body and not me. So, he gets neither, not for weeks now. It feels like he's barely noticed.

I am the one who gets up with Emmanuelle when she cries. I am the one who literally drains my body to keep her alive, sets aside every desire in favor of her.

All I ask is that Lars do what he promised on our wedding day. He said he would spend every day of his life finding new ways to love me. Instead, I sit here in the dark, unable to sleep after waking once again to breastfeed our child, typing on my phone to no one.

Married to the man of my dreams, I am the loneliest I have ever been.

FIFTY-TWO

MY BREAKFAST SHIFT AT ELAINE'S passes in a haze of maple syrup and waffle-iron burns. Finn is on the night shift today, but just the thought of him proves to be a distraction. Every time I glance outside at the spot where we kissed last night, I feel a surge of excitement followed quickly by raging guilt. I haven't lived by the Messiah purity pledge rules for years, and yet they're always there, ready to torment me the second I break them. We didn't do anything more than make out and fumble around under each other's clothes, Finn being ultracareful to not push any boundary. But by the Mess's standards, I am a filthy sinner.

Not much has changed.

I wish I could just enjoy what happened. I finally got together with a guy who treats me well and seems really interested in me, and all I can think about is the glue and construction paper bodies from Pastor Rick's object lesson.

Once I'm cut from the floor, I call the Elden jail and ask if I can visit Eve. I'm placed on hold for fifteen minutes before the bored admin comes back on the line. "Mrs. Oback has retained legal representation, who has instructed us to say that she is not taking any visitors without him being present. If you want to see her, you'll have to call his office. Want the number?"

I let out a breath, holding my free hand up to the warm air starting to drift through the vents of my car. "No, that's okay. Thanks anyway."

"It's my pleasure." Sounds like it's anything but.

When the call disconnects, I stare at my phone. If I can't talk to Eve,

I need to speak to someone who knows her inside out. I can only hope Esha has the same cell phone number she did in high school.

It rings three times before someone picks up. "Hello?"

"Esha. Is that you?"

"Delilah."

"How did you know?"

"Your number changed, but your voice hasn't. Plus, I've kind of been waiting for you to call."

I turn the heat dial three clicks until it's on full blast. The frost on my windshield starts to disintegrate. "Yeah? Why?"

"I knew you would once you realized you were wrong."

The words are both an accusation and a sigh of relief. Esha is my age, but she sounds a decade older. I can't imagine what the last week has done to her.

For a moment, I chew on my bottom lip, considering how to respond. Finally, I say, "Don't you want to know why I changed my mind?"

"Does it matter?"

"Yeah, it kinda does. I think we should talk."

She's quiet for a moment. Then: "I'm going for lunch at Selma's. Meet me there?"

"Sure," I say, shifting my car into gear. "I'm on my way."

SELMA'S CAFÉ IS bustling. The oval-shaped, brick-walled space features a coffee counter and cases of pastries in the middle, with spirals of tables and chairs flowing out from that. Every one of them is taken, but I'm relieved to see Esha beat me here and got us one.

When she sees me, Esha lifts a hand in a gentle wave. I weave between tables until I'm across from her. The metal chair shrieks against the polished concrete floor when I pull it out.

"Haven't been here in years," I say by way of greeting. This was our favorite lunch spot when we went thrift shopping in Moorhead as teenagers. At the time, it was one of the cheapest cafés in the city—a little hole-in-the-wall that we felt we discovered. Looking around, it seems word has gotten out.

"Me neither. The food hasn't changed, but the prices sure have." Esha holds up the menu.

"Geez, it's just as bad as Minneapolis—but I guess you know that."

Esha's gaze flicks to the side, then back at me. "Sorry I never got in touch. It seems silly we live probably twenty minutes away from each other and never hang out."

"Yeah, it does." I lick my lips and rub them together. "Guess we both were busy with college, and then, you know . . ."

"Life."

"Right."

A waitress in denim overalls and a red-and-gray-checkered shirt stops by our table, setting two glasses of water on the wood surface. "Hi there! You two ready to order?"

Esha nods. "I am. Delilah?"

"It's just Del now." I look back at the menu. "And sure. Can I just have a latte and a ham and cheese?"

Esha orders a grain salad, and the waitress walks away.

Not sure where to start, I reach for some easy small talk. "So, what are you up to these days? I know you got married. He's a banker, right?"

"That's right. Felipe." Esha's eyes glow. "And I'm an interior designer at a small firm."

"Just what you always planned." I smile. "Any kids?"

"No. Neither of us really wants them." She sets her mouth in a line, as if waiting for me to object. When we were younger, the three of us made dream wedding plans and talked about how many kids we wanted. No Messiah girl says she doesn't want any at all.

"Fair enough," I say. "Sometimes I don't think I want any either."

She lets out a breathless laugh. "Right? It seems like so much fun when you're a teenager, but I think after I became an adult, I realized how much work they are. How about you? Married? Kids?"

"No, none of that. And don't ask about my job." My laugh comes out phony instead of carefree. "It's embarrassing. You've got your life together, which is great. I'm still trying to figure mine out, I guess."

"Do you ever wonder if Messiah did that to us on purpose?" she asks after a moment. Her brown eyes are solemn when they meet mine.

"Did what?"

"Stunted us. Tried to make sure we weren't prepared for the world."

I had never thought about it that way. "Why do you think they would do that?"

She chews on the corner of her lower lip. "I don't know about you, but when I went to college, I felt . . . I felt like I could take a full breath for the first time in my life. There is something about that place: everything is hot and close and stifling. Every time I drive back into town, it feels like walking into a sauna with my clothes on."

She looks unsure for a moment, so I nod encouragingly. Never in a thousand years did I think one of the Thompson sisters would criticize the Mess. I feel like if I say anything, I'll shatter the moment and Esha will go back to using the churchspeak we all grew up with.

Respect authority. Submit to leadership. Obey God's will.

Thought-terminating clichés, a book I read about cults calls them. Designed to make you feel confident that the leader has a plan and you don't need any more detail.

After taking a sip of water, Esha continues. "When I got to St. Paul, I was able to just be myself: still a Christian, but one who liked secular art and magazines and didn't feel the need to be at church three times a week. But my second year, when I moved out of the dorms and into my own apartment, my power got turned off because I didn't know I needed to pay for utilities. Nobody ever taught me what bills to expect, how to check the oil in my car. I knew how to be a wife—that's it. There was so much about life they didn't tell us."

I stare at her for a moment. "I always thought I was a failure. I did okay in college—not great. But I had no idea what to do with an English degree, and I've basically just been bouncing around minimum wage jobs since I graduated. At least you built the life you always wanted."

She plucks the wedge of lemon from the rim of her glass, squeezing it into her water. "I did. I got connected with a really good Christian college ministry, and they helped a lot. They also took me to the church where I met Felipe. It's a great community there. Totally different from—"

"The Mess."

Esha snickers. "Right."

I wish I could just sit and think about this for a while, the fact that maybe my entire adult life being a catastrophe isn't one hundred percent my fault.

As if she can tell where my head's at, Esha reaches across the table and puts her hand on mine. "Look. You were dealt a bad hand. And then they reshuffled and dealt you an even worse one. I know I should be mad at you because of what you said to Eve the other day, but to be honest, I can't blame you. I never told her that what she did was wrong, even though it so obviously was. I made sure you knew Lars had been writing to her while you two were still together, and even that felt like a betrayal. Eve and I, we went through a lot together as kids, and she was the only one who even partially understood what it was like to grow up adopted in Bower. I felt like I couldn't be disloyal to her, even when she was being such a—" She cuts herself off. "Anyway. I'm sorry that it took this whole terrible thing for us to talk to each other again, but I'm glad we are. I missed you."

My chest swells, and I squeeze her hand. "I missed you too."

She squeezes it back, then pulls away. "And at least now you don't think Eve killed her husband anymore."

I let out an awkward laugh.

"Want to tell me what changed your mind?"

"I'll get there, I promise." I run my finger through the condensation on my glass. "This might be a dumb question, considering what you just told me. But how do you feel about Pastor Rick now?"

"I think he's a gifted man."

The words are more diplomatic than I expect, but her hard expression gives her away.

"He's a gifted speaker, but he's also a gifted manipulator."

"What do you mean?"

"You know exactly what I mean. The whole Noble Wife thing. He's got thousands of people, probably hundreds of thousands, convinced that his teachings about marriage and the roles of men and women in relationships are gospel. I know I thought they were. You did too, at one time, and obviously so did Eve." She starts to tear thin strips off her napkin, her eyes focused on the task. "When a pastor tells you to do something and points you to a Bible verse that seems to agree with him, it's hard to argue. What they don't teach you in church, or at least what Messiah never taught us, is that spiritual leaders are just people too. They can be wrong. Sometimes accidentally, sometimes on purpose."

"Yeah." My brain searches for something more intelligent to say, but I can't come up with anything. Esha has *thought* about this. She has taken time to process and grow and change. While I've been avoiding church altogether, she seems to have found one that is actually healthy.

Our food is placed in front of us. "You need anything else?" the waitress asks.

"I'm good," I say, and Esha nods. I pick up my sandwich and take a bite. "Go on."

She scoops some salad onto her fork, studying it. "Do you remember Samantha Woodly?"

I wipe my buttery fingers on a napkin. "Uh, yeah. She was a year ahead of us."

"That's right. Do you remember how much they used to nag her about what she ate when we were at youth camps?"

"I haven't thought about that in ages, but they really did give her sh . . . crap." I chew my food, remembering a time Colette snatched a grilled cheese sandwich out of Sam's hand and gave her a piece of celery instead.

"I told you, if you feel hungry, I want you to pray."

Esha's gaze is far away, as if she's thinking about a similar incident. "They were so awful to her. Plenty of us ate the same food she did, but because she was fat, they were always scolding her about gluttony. They never explicitly said this in our classes, but part of being a Noble Wife was also being like 1950s-housewife thin. In fact, 1950s housewife was the model, wasn't it? Mrs. Franklin was like June Cleaver, with every hair in place and perfectly pressed dresses. Skinny, fragile, and white— that's what we were supposed to be. Never mind that the Bible was written by brown people."

I set down my sandwich, appetite gone. "You're right. It's not the kind of thing they would ever say, but that's only so they could have plausible deniability. The implication was there."

"Pastor Rick is a master of making his beliefs crystal clear without needing to express them outright, especially if they are actually contrary to what the Bible teaches."

A wry smile pulls at my lips. "It's funny how we both still call him Pastor Rick. Calling him by just his first name feels wrong, even now."

She chuckles around a bite of salad. "True. I still call all the adults I grew up with Mr. and Mrs. too."

Something she said sparks an idea. "You're right, though. Pastor Rick is more than capable of getting people to do what he wants without needing to even tell them directly. Especially the people most loyal to him." My arms tingle with goosebumps.

"What?" Esha sits forward, her gaze latched onto mine. "You just realized something. Is it about Pastor Rick?"

"It might be nothing," I say. My brain is still trying to pull the threads of an idea together. "But it seems like he was clearly turning on Eve."

For a moment, we sit in silence, eating our food. Esha obviously doesn't view Messiah through rose-tinted glasses, but I'm not sure how she'll feel about my theories about the Franklins.

Setting down her fork, Esha clears her throat. "I'm not supposed to tell you this, but a couple months ago, Eve called me and asked about my church for the first time. She said she realized that she was committing her daughter to the same set of rules and restrictions we had growing up, and that didn't seem like something she wanted to do anymore."

I think of the photo on Eve's blog from Emmanuelle's dedication ceremony. The faraway, unhappy look on Eve's face as she watched her daughter be committed to the church.

"How did Lars feel about that?" He may not have grown up in Messiah, but he seemed as committed as the rest, especially once he became the worship pastor. I had always felt like Eve ruined him, but for the first time, it occurs to me that maybe Messiah did. And I'm the one who brought him there to begin with.

Esha's eyes are guarded. "She never told me, but I have reason to believe he would have been more supportive than you might expect."

I take the leap. "Would the reason be related to why he was kicked off the elder board?"

"How did you know that?"

"His dad told me. He never got a chance to let his parents know why it happened, but Nathaniel seemed to think it was because he said something to challenge Pastor Rick."

She continues fiddling with her napkin. "That's probably true. Eve hasn't told me exactly what happened. You know how we were raised; intimate discussions in a marriage aren't for other people's ears, not even your family." Her eyes meet mine again. "I know she was upset when he quit as worship pastor, but as far as I know, that was more about money than anything else. Not many people know this, but Eve and Lars had to do a bunch of fertility treatments to get pregnant."

That's one mystery solved, then. I feel a sliver of guilt for blaming Eve's extravagance for Lars quitting, back when I visited her house.

Esha continues. "Now, tell me what you realized before. What made you look so freaked out."

I was hoping she forgot. I've said some controversial things about the Mess in my life, but this would easily be the worst. But I've dragged this out long enough. Esha's sister is facing life in prison for something it seems like she didn't do. If she's ever going to be receptive to what I have to say, it's now.

"I think . . ." I clear my throat, lower my voice. "I think Pastor Rick could be involved in what happened to Lars."

Esha's perfect dark brows rise. "You think he killed him?"

I pinch the fabric of my jeans between my fingers. "No, when I came here, I was going to tell you I thought Noah Franklin had killed him, either by accident or because Lars was looking into him for embezzling money."

Recognition lights up her face. "The problems at work. Eve knew he was looking into some kind of irregularities on a major account, but he never told her what."

"Right. And I thought if he did kill Lars, Pastor Rick was covering for him. You know he's done it before."

A shadow passes over her face. "Yes."

"But then something you said made me think. Pastor Rick is good at convincing other people to do things for him without explicitly saying so. We know that Eve and Lars were having issues with the church. The former worship pastor and the Noble Wife movement's most famous ambassador leaving? That would have been devastating, something not even Pastor Rick could write off without an explanation. Noah is an elder. He would know what was going on, assuming Pastor Rick was concerned enough to tell the board. Maybe Noah got the idea that it would be better for the Obacks to be silenced instead of getting the chance to leave."

For several moments after the accusation leaves my lips, we sit looking at each other, the buzz and clang of the café the only noise between us. Now that I've said it aloud, I feel sweat tickling under my arms and between my shoulder blades. I remember exactly what happened the last time I demanded Noah Franklin face some kind of accountability.

In the days after he shared those photos, my parents and I had multiple meetings with Pastor Rick and Colette. I endured an hour of the adults going back and forth talking about what I had done and how they were going to address it.

Finally, I asked, "Isn't anyone going to punish Noah?"

The way they looked at me is branded on my mind. Pity from my father, annoyance from Pastor Rick, but the worst was my mother and Colette. They both just looked confused. The very idea of holding a teenage boy accountable for anything was unfathomable.

That's not how Esha is looking at me now. Instead, her eyes are gleaming hungrily. "So, Lars had recently challenged Pastor Rick at an elders' meeting, and he ended up dead. Eve was starting to question the pastor's key philosophy and the abuse it led to for dozens of women, and she's in prison for murder. You're right, that does seem pretty convenient for Pastor Rick."

We are both quiet for a long moment. If I'm right, the implications are catastrophic, for both Messiah and Bower as a whole. But that would require someone to actually believe me.

Esha is clearly thinking the same thing. "We need to find a way to hurt Pastor Rick's reputation."

"Messiah seems like it owns half the businesses in town now. He's protected by the police and the elders," I say. "No one would believe a bad word against him. I don't know how we change that."

She stares at her plate, tapping her fork against the side of it. Then she looks up at me. "What about what happened to you?"

Heat rises, starting in my neck and spreading to my face. "Everyone already knows about that. No one cares."

"Does everyone know what he did afterward?"

I stare at her.

"The sessions in his office."

My mouth opens and closes, then opens again. "How do you know about those?"

"Everyone knew, Del. We might not have known the details, but we knew you had to see him every week. Talk about what happened. As a teenager, it didn't faze me, but now I think . . . I mean, they can't have been appropriate."

I swallow hard. "They weren't."

"I'm sorry," she whispers. "Did he . . . touch you?"

"No." The answer is sharp, like it's been punched out of me. "He didn't have to."

This takes a moment to sink in. Her eyes lower. "You weren't the only girl who had to have one-on-ones with Pastor Rick. I knew of at least a few ahead of us who did, and definitely some in Eve's grade. All these girls forced to visit his office regularly, talk about their sexual sins. Don't you think that's something the elder board should know about?"

I take a long, shuddering breath. "Maybe they already do and it doesn't bother them. Like I said, he never touched me, and I'm guessing he didn't with the other girls either. You and I both know pastors get away with actual sexual assault all the time. This isn't even going to rate."

Her eyes blaze. "That was actual assault, Del. Being compelled to talk explicitly about sex and sexual fantasies with an adult—don't downplay that."

"I'm not trying to, but I'm just saying, they won't care."

"Maybe. But I bet there are hundreds of stories like yours, like the women Eve has helped—other girls and women who were negatively impacted by Pastor Rick's teachings. Who faced abuse, excommunication, maybe even worse because of the Noble Wife movement. If we could gather those stories together, we might have enough to get the board to doubt him, maybe even to suspend him and do an investigation. If that happens, *that's* when we tell the police about your theory. Especially if you can find any evidence Noah really did kill Lars."

"The thing is, neither of us is part of the church anymore. Do you think you could talk to Eve? Try to find out the names of other people we could contact?"

Esha shakes her head. "I've already tried that. The few women she helped escape either went off the grid or have no interest in talking to me. I can't really blame them. Some of them are hiding from their ex-husbands."

I clench my hands on the table in front of me, my mind racing. There has to be a way we could reach out, try to find other victims of Messiah Church's warped theology. The sheriff's department is obviously in Pastor Rick's pocket, but maybe if we got enough people to draw media attention, we might get them to take a closer look.

"I know!"

When I look up at her, Esha's face is beaming. "What?"

"There's one channel Pastor Rick doesn't control. Something he's always considered his personal mouthpiece, because for all intents and purposes, it was." She crosses her arms, satisfied with herself. "But not anymore."

It takes me a minute, but then I grin. "Oh. He's going to hate this."

FIFTY-THREE

Noble Wife Journey: a blog
Title: Your Stories
Published: November 18, 2021

"We each have it within us to be a Noble Wife."

That is how this movement began: a statement of fact and a call to action, all in one. Whether you came to this blog searching for answers, hoping to find romance, longing for comfort, or wanting something to hate-read: you are here, and you have followed Eve Oback's journey as a Noble Wife.

It's a journey that seems very near a catastrophic, abrupt end. As many of you know, Eve was recently arrested for the murder of her husband, Lars. He was killed in the woods two weeks ago, and the police are saying she did it and tried to make it look like a hunting accident.

While that certainly makes for a dramatic story, it is not true. She is being set up.

You see, just a few weeks before her husband's death, Eve was doing something Noble Wives aren't supposed to do. She was having doubts. She was asking questions.

The Noble Wife philosophy teaches us that women are both delicately fragile and impenetrably strong. We are told we're the weaker vessel, and yet also that our bodies have the power to bring about the destruction of men. That is why we must keep ourselves hidden—our sensuality, our desires, our ambitions. Submit at all costs. Like the Proverbs 31 woman, we are known for how we never tire, the way we never break.

It took years, but Eve had begun to notice that some of these teachings weren't lining up with the Bible she was reading, with the God she knew.

She isn't the first one.

There is a pattern at Messiah Church of people, especially women, being punished for asking questions. One way or another, anyone who challenges the status quo is silenced.

When Eve started this blog, she did it with the best of intentions. She felt moved by the teachings of her pastor and wanted to share them with anyone who found her little site. There's no way she could have known the global reach, the enormous impact, her words would have. She had no idea she was becoming an ambassador for a theology that she would one day have grave concerns about.

What led to those concerns? The voices of women: women in the church and, I'm sure, readers like you. Just like hers, your words have the potential for tremendous impact. Your experiences matter. And we want to hear about them.

If you've ever felt silenced, stripped of agency, smothered, or otherwise limited by Messiah Church or the Noble Wife teachings, we want to hear from you. Email us through the blog contact form or leave a comment below. Your anonymity will be preserved, but your story will be shared.

And to everyone who's been harmed by the teachings shared in this blog, the unwitting manipulation of Scripture to suit a patriarchal system it was never intended to uphold, we are sorry. Eve is sorry. She can't be here to share it, but we know she would want us to.

We want to prevent this from ever happening again, and the only way to do that is to refuse to allow it to go on. So please, be bold. Be courageous. Be loud. We want to hear your stories.

FIFTY-FOUR

I'VE NEVER DONE DRUGS. AS many of the rules as I've broken from my upbringing, that was one that I just couldn't. But if I could bottle the high I feel after hitting publish on the post Esha and I wrote on the Noble Wife blog, I would be sure to make millions. We sit in front of the screen, refreshing every ten minutes for over an hour, but nothing happens. No comments, no emails.

People are scared. I get that. No one wants to go first, so that will have to fall to me. Commenting with my full name, I write my story under the post. My diaries are in a box in my car, so I take pictures of the entries I can bear to make public, tell my side of the story about what happened with Noah Franklin, talk about my uncomfortable private sessions with Pastor Rick, and detail how I was ostracized from the church until I made a public confession where I took full responsibility for my own assault. Esha holds my free hand when I take a deep breath and press submit.

After that, the stories come rolling in: at first a small trickle, then a tsunami. We cry as we read them, horrified to know so many of our friends and classmates had stayed quiet while going through similar issues. There are even emails from those I thought of as the good girls—the ones like Eve—who still go to the Mess. All of them are trusting us with their stories, the worst things that have ever happened to them. It's an enormous responsibility, but it makes me feel almost giddy.

We are actually going to accomplish something.

I'm still buzzing as I walk through the door at Elaine's, tying the short black apron around my waist.

Finn grins when he sees me, juts his chin toward the alcohol storage fridge. Making sure no one on the staff will notice, I open the thick metal door and slip inside. It's cold and the bluish-white fluorescents do nothing for my complexion, but when he comes in after me a moment later, my skin is hot and I feel recklessly attractive.

"You're in a good mood." His fingers wind through the strings on my apron, pulling me close. Then his hands close around my hips as he pushes me gently against the fridge wall. My shirt rides up, and I gasp when the cold metal hits the exposed skin on my back. A curl slips over his forehead as he bends his neck to kiss me.

After a moment, I pull away. "Even better now."

His eyes are fixed on mine. "Care to share why?"

"Oh, you know." I lift one shoulder and drop it in an exaggerated shrug. "Secretly making out in a beer fridge will do that to a girl."

Finn chuckles. "I'm flattered, but you seemed happy when you walked in too."

I stretch up on my toes and kiss him again, then settle back against the wall. The cold feels good now that my whole body is overheated. "Well, that's the main reason, but I've figured some stuff out with the case too."

"Oh? That's great." He brushes a thumb on my abdomen and then steps back. "Like what?"

"Well, I know you still have your doubts about Pastor Rick's involvement in all this, and I get it. So I'm trying to get some evidence together. We may not be able to prove that he had anything to do with Lars's death, but we know that he's covered up crimes in Bower, and we know he is especially fond of helping abusive husbands keep their wives around under the guise of spiritual obligation. He's hurt a lot of people just in Messiah, not to mention the sway he has over the thousands who have read his books."

Finn nods, his arms crossed. I try to ignore the way his rolled-up sleeves hug the tops of his forearms and keep talking. There will be time for lust later.

"Everyone in the Christian community only seems to know the good things he's done. The marriages he's apparently helped, the people who found his teachings life-changing in a good way. There's a reason for that. I'm sure you've seen it yourself if you've ever been to Bower. Messiah Church is wrapped up in almost every local business, and people can't afford to be on his bad side. The church was just a small local congregation until he came along, and now it's the closest thing to a megachurch you can get in a town that size. Their income would be in the hundreds of thousands, probably millions when you factor in his book and teaching series sales. They can't afford negative publicity, so any time someone tries to say anything against him, they get shut down."

"Shut down how?"

It might be that I'm sensitive from the last time we had a talk about my suspicions of Pastor Rick, but I feel like I can hear the doubt in Finn's voice. This time, though, it doesn't make me feel anxious that I might be wrong. It makes me even more determined to show him I'm right.

"Oh, they have a few different methods. Eve's sister and I were able to get into the admin page of her blog, and we made a post last night asking women to come forward with their stories about how the Noble Wife teachings have hurt them. We've already gotten over a hundred comments and emails. Most of them are about how the philosophy harmed them generally—kept them with abusive and controlling partners for far too long, made them feel worthless for being single, convinced them not to pursue certain degrees or careers. But there have been a few about Pastor Rick in particular."

His eyebrows raise, and I see him shiver. The cold air is starting to affect me too, so I rush on.

"One woman says her husband went to him upset that she was working a part-time job instead of staying home all day with their kids. She was a paralegal at a firm in Bower. The next day, she was fired, and she couldn't get a job anywhere else in town. She's convinced Pastor Rick made it happen."

He shakes his head in disbelief, pulling my hips closer as I continue.

"There are a few women who said they told their husbands they wanted a divorce, and then the church offered to pay the legal fees for their husbands in the custody battle. All but one of them opted to stay, afraid they'd lose their children otherwise. Another woman says her son was bullied throughout high school, and instead of consequences for the bully, Pastor Rick told her it was because he was too effeminate."

"Geez."

"Yeah." My body is trembling. "We've gotten at least twelve stories about girls who were accused of being promiscuous or sexually misbehaving in some way, all of whom were given one-on-one counseling with Rick. Their sessions weren't observed or chaperoned in any way, and many of them talk about how he persuaded them to confess not just things they had done, but any sexual temptation or fantasy they had ever had. I . . . I was one of them."

Something sparks in Finn's eyes, and I wonder if it's the same rage I felt when I read those emails. The familiarity of them made me sick to my stomach. I wasn't the only one who'd been forced to sit for hours in that chair across from Pastor Rick. When he'd asked about any imaginary scenarios I had concocted, about Noah or any other boy, I thought that was part of what I needed to do to confess all my sin. According to his teachings, the fantasies were just as wrong as my actions. Like the Bible said, if you even look at someone with lust in your heart, you have already committed adultery with them.

We weren't Catholics. The confessions weren't about saying every sin I'd committed so I would be told what I needed to do to be forgiven. Pastor Rick told us that repentance was an action, and part of that action was expressing the thoughts and wishes I'd had that were contrary to the Bible.

I never told my parents how much he seemed to enjoy hearing about them.

"Del, I don't know what to say." Finn reaches out again, a gentle hand on my shoulder. I lean in, and he pulls me against his chest. I feel him trembling as he wraps his arms around me. "I'm so sorry."

For a moment, I soak in his embrace. Then I laugh. "We need to get out of here before we freeze."

He chuckles, pulling away. "We do. But I'm sorry that happened to you. To all those women. It sounds like he . . . I mean, it kind of sounds like he got off on it."

The words twist something in my gut. When I was younger, that thought had never even occurred to me. But over the last several hours, as I read the stories coming in, it seemed almost impossible that it wasn't true. Pastor Rick Franklin, the self-appointed champion of female purity, was defiling the girls in his congregation. And he did it without ever touching us.

Which, unfortunately, makes it even less likely that anyone will take us seriously. But we have to try.

As if he can read my thoughts, Finn asks, "So, what are you going to do with all these stories?"

Reluctantly, I pull away from the warmth of his embrace. "On Monday, we're taking everything we have to the Messiah elder board. Hopefully, we can show the pattern of abuse and misbehavior Pastor Rick has had for years. And if we can convince them to put Pastor Rick on suspension, that might be enough to loosen his grip on the town and give the sheriff's department a chance to investigate him and Noah."

"So, you don't think Rick killed Lars himself?"

"Apparently, he was a couple hours away at the time. In Bemidji, I think," I say. "Plus, it just seems so perfect the way he took Noah's mistake and turned it into a win for himself. It's exactly the kind of thing Pastor Rick does."

Finn traces my cheek with his finger. "Do you have any actual evidence against either of them?"

I shiver. "Not yet. But unless he has at least a small fall from grace, there's no way the sheriff's department will even consider it. I've got to start somewhere."

He nods. "It's a good plan."

The fridge door opens, and the very harried face of Denise the head waitress peers through. "There you two are! We've got fifteen drink tickets on the printer and, Del, you just got triple-sat. This is the longest quickie I've ever seen."

I open my mouth to protest, but Denise has already disappeared. Face heating up, I turn to Finn and find him holding back a laugh.

"Shut up." I retie my apron, ducking my head to hide a smile as I walk out the beer fridge door.

FIFTY-FIVE

MY PALMS LEAVE A DAMP trail as I wipe them on my pant legs. We've been sitting in the halls of Messiah next to the elders' meeting room for twenty minutes. Any man in the church is allowed to request a special meeting with the board, and after we explained everything we had found, Mr. Thompson agreed to do so. He is currently in the room laying the groundwork, and then Esha and I will go in and present our findings.

All told, we have twenty-seven stories that we were able to verify in some way. Former Messiah attendees, women who took the Noble Wife pledge through the form on Eve's blog, ostracized family of church members. We wanted to make sure the elders couldn't wave away our concerns by saying it was just strangers talking on the internet. If we had included those, the stories would have numbered in the hundreds.

"You ready for this?" Esha asks. Her jaw is set, but I can see the thin sheen on her skin, the slight tremble of her top lip.

I nod once, sharply. "As I'll ever be. You?"

"I'm ready." The fury in her voice gives me a shot of courage. The elders of Messiah Church aren't ready for the collective anger of dozens of women. Not when they're used to our silent obedience.

Footsteps echo on the hallway tiles as someone approaches. A moment later, Noah Franklin strides into view. I knew to expect him here, but I wasn't prepared to see him before I even went in. He's running late. His face turns ruddy when he sees us, and he ducks his head before going into the meeting room.

Esha is watching me when I look her direction. I open my mouth to say something, but then Mr. Thompson is in the doorway. His face is grim, but a smile tries to cover it. "Come on in, girls."

As one, we take a deep breath and stand. I force myself to walk in with my head high.

Around the table are twelve men. All of them white, varying in age from twenties to seventies, wearing the same stony expression. Todd and Noah Franklin sit next to each other, a few feet away from me. My eyes skip over them, my heart thundering even harder. I can feel waves of hostility as we sit in the two empty seats. My gaze sweeps the rest of the table. I recognize Henry Tanner and a few others who have been around as long as the church has.

These are the men I was taught to revere without question, and I'm about to do what they will deem the most disrespectful thing imaginable.

Challenge their pastor.

"Ladies." At the head of the table, the overhead lights gleam off the bald head of Louis Herschell, casting shadows under his fierce blue eyes. He is the lead elder, the second most powerful man in the church after Rick Franklin. And he does not look impressed by our presence. "Tim says that you have some important information for us about the welfare of women in our church. Of course, we take that very seriously. Protecting women is one of the highest callings for a man of God. If you have any real evidence of wrongdoing, we want to see it."

Real evidence. The dismissive phrase rips through me, but I refuse to take a loss before we've even tried. I look at Esha, sitting next to me.

"We have more than enough evidence for anyone willing to consider it," she says, her tone carefully even. I nod for her to continue, my throat suddenly too dry to talk. She pulls out the folders we have put together, one for each elder, and passes the stack to the man beside her. "As you know, my sister, Eve, ran a blog for more than a decade promoting Pastor Rick's Noble Wife teachings. She reached hundreds of thousands, probably millions, of people around the world. Four days ago, we posted on that blog, asking for anyone to come forward if they had stories about how Pastor Rick or his teachings had harmed them. We had reason to believe that there would be many, and we were right."

The elders each take a folder and open it, finding our printouts of the stories we verified.

"There are no names here," Louis says.

"That's right," I reply, my voice husky. "Unfortunately, for what I believe are legitimate reasons, most of the women felt unsafe sharing their stories. They would only do so if we promised to keep them anonymous, although there are several that I'm sure you will be able to identify once you've read them."

"I gather this board is not unaware of what has happened to many of these women," Esha adds.

A murmur goes around the table, and I see Mr. Thompson's shoulders inch up. Still, he nods at us encouragingly.

I continue. "For example, on page three there's the story of a woman who was locked in a room in her house by her husband for six weeks. She was only allowed to leave to come with him to church, and he stayed by her side every moment to make sure she didn't say anything. She managed to tell someone what was happening during a bathroom break. It took another week for that person to tell one of you, and the following week, she was finally released and able to go about her normal life."

It's impossible to keep the anger out of my voice. I can hear it rising, becoming more shrill. Under the table, Esha squeezes my hand. I clear my throat before I go on. "We know that at least one elder was aware of what happened, and he must have talked to her husband, convincing him to release his wife. He kept her imprisoned in her own home, not because he thought she was having an affair or was going to leave him—although that would still be unacceptable. He did it because, as he said, she was spending too much time with her friends. Fellow women at Messiah Church. For that reason, he decided she shouldn't be allowed to leave the house without him. We also know she is still married to him, still fears that he might do this again. He faced no consequences before, so that fear seems reasonable to me."

Louis closes his folder and looks at me. "If this is true, why hasn't she reported it to the police?"

A snort emits from Esha's mouth. The righteous fury in her eyes makes me giddy. "The police in Bower? The ones who attend church every Sunday and have a direct line with Pastor Rick?"

"Now, there's no reason to get emotional." Louis clears his throat.

"I disagree with that, actually," Esha says. "I think anger is the correct response when our sisters in Christ are being attacked. We have several stories of women in this church being physically or emotionally abused by their husbands. They were told to go to counseling, where they were only advised to be more respectful and loving of their husbands. We know of three people who came out to Pastor Rick or one of the youth leaders and were sent to a conversion camp, which he has partial ownership of, by the way. And at least a dozen young women had one-on-one counseling sessions with Rick, where he forced them to tell him details of their sexual fantasies, with the excuse that it was a form of confession."

She looks at me. I take a deep breath. "I'm one of them. Many of you know what happened when I was sixteen. Afterward, I spent an hour every Wednesday night trapped in his office, told I needed to relay every sexual action and daydream I'd ever had in order to repent and purge the sin."

Louis's eyebrows come together. "Talking? You're upset about talking?"

Even though I prepared myself for the disregard, it still makes my stomach turn. "It might not matter to you, the way he humiliated me and stripped my mind bare. But if you have daughters, ask yourself: Would you want a man to compel them to vocalize every sexual thought they've had, alone in his office? You think that is an appropriate use of pastoral authority?"

No one in the room speaks. A couple of the men look uncomfortable.

Despair claws at my throat. They have to react. They have to care. We knew they might not, but seeing it actually happen is devastating. I hold up my folder. "Another woman reached out to us. Her family are still members here, but she left when she went to college. She told us when she was twelve years old, her twenty-year-old cousin started molesting her. It went on for years, every time he got the opportunity. He even tried to get help once. Visited Pastor Rick." The fury I felt when I first read this email is even stronger now. "Rick stopped him as soon as he realized what the man was saying and told him not to say another word."

"That's an obscene accusation," Louis snaps.

Rage blazes through me. "Rick is a pastor, and he is obligated to report instances of child abuse. He chose to pretend the confession didn't happen. He protected the man instead of the child he was assaulting."

Across from me, a man lowers his eyes. The story is deidentified in the folders we passed around, of course, but I know. I know this man is the girl's father. I look straight at him as I finish. "That's right. Rather than getting the young man any kind of therapy or intervention or helping the girl escape his abuse, your beloved pastor told him to pray for forgiveness and did nothing else. She continued to suffer for years."

Pages are being turned now, a few whispers shared. Louis looks around the table, as if in warning, and the murmuring stops. Then he looks at me. "That is a serious accusation to make, young lady."

"I know." I refuse to lower my gaze.

"There are many more," Esha says softly. "Whether directly or indirectly, these teachings have ruined lives. Even people who never went to Messiah. We know about a woman from Colorado who took the Noble Wife pledge on Eve's blog when she was seventeen. She was sexually assaulted a year later and died by suicide because she believed she was no longer 'pure.' The Noble Wife philosophy might have started with the right intentions, but surely you have to agree that it's done incredible harm as well."

Angry tears blur my vision as they continue their stony silence. "All of those are acceptable to you, then?" I ask, forcing myself to take slow breaths. "You say protecting women is the highest calling the church has, but none of you care about these stories? Maybe it's time to admit that the church doesn't protect all women equally. You only save the ones you deem worthy; no one ever wants to talk about the ones you sacrifice."

Louis is glaring at me, but several men around the table won't meet my gaze.

Pushing out my chair, I stand up. "But Eve Oback, she's one of the good ones," I say. Next to me, I see Esha's head bow. "She's the kind of woman you're always holding up as the standard. The champion of your pastor's Noble Wife philosophy, the poster girl for submissive Christian women. She took Pastor Rick's teachings to heart in every possible way, and she used her writing and youthful optimism to reach the hearts of thousands. Every dollar that lines the pockets of Rick Franklin and the rest of Messiah staff is, on some level, because of her. And the second she had doubts, the moment she started to wonder if this was the right path— the actual godly path—to a healthy marriage, what happened? Her husband was killed and his murder was pinned on her. How convenient."

That breaks through. Several of the elders mutter, their faces turning red, and Louis stands himself. "That is enough." His hands plant on the shiny table, his eyes locking on mine across the surface. "The Bible says that we are to be wise as serpents and gentle as doves, but you have taken after the snake of Eden. A crafty, manipulative voice trying to deceive the people of God."

Those words would have destroyed me as a teenager, but now they only toughen my resolve. "You know, I was raised to believe that you would watch over us. We were told that we had to submit and obey our husbands. In exchange, we would be sheltered and loved and cherished. If we were the soft, pliant caretakers of the home, then men were the strong, fierce warriors who would guard our hearts with their very lives."

I look at Esha. Her eyes are glowing with rage, with hurt, mirroring my own. Her lips part; she has found her voice again. "If that were true, then most of what Pastor Rick taught us in the Noble Wife classes would actually work. The Bible does say we are supposed to submit, but it also says you're supposed to lay your lives down for us. Giving up your life doesn't always mean dying. Sometimes it just means sacrificing what you want for the ones you love. But the men here aren't told that part, are they? And the women aren't told to expect it in exchange for all that we're taught to do. You know what it took for me to hear the verse interpreted like that?"

Mr. Thompson's cheeks are red as he watches his daughter. Esha locks eyes with the head elder. "I had to go to a different church."

Louis's brows come together, but other than that, his face betrays no feeling.

I look at each of them, daring them to stay silent. "So you're really going to do nothing? You're going to read the stories of these women, you're going to watch Eve Oback take the fall for a horrible crime she didn't commit, you're going to see your own associate pastor die under mysterious circumstances, and still you're going to do nothing?"

"Enough! These wild accusations and attacks on Pastor Rick are unacceptable. The scripture is clear. You do not touch the Lord's anointed ones. And what we do or don't do in this church body is none of your business." Louis's voice is cold steel. "You are not members. You are not family. You are branches that have been cut off from the vine, bearing no fruit."

The reference to the verse written on my motel mirror knocks the wind out of me. Esha lets out a stifled sob. After everything, that is the thing that breaks me.

"You clearly have a personal vendetta against this church, Delilah," Louis continues. "You were right about one thing. Everyone in this room knows what your relationship to Messiah is like. You are like a toxic weed, choking the life out of anything near you whenever you spring up." Then he looks at Esha. "Mrs. Prescott, you left Messiah on much better terms, so I'm sad to see you come under the influence of someone like her. You and your father have been deceived. But you could be forgiven for desperately trying to find a way to make your sister seem innocent. It's a terrible thing she did."

"Go to hell," Esha says, her voice low but steady. I bite my lip to hold back a smile.

Louis's eyes widen. Several of the men suck their teeth, as if a woman using slightly foul language is the worst thing that's happened here today.

"I have to believe they will," I say to Esha.

Mr. Thompson puts his arm around his daughter, his chin lifted high. "We're leaving." Tears glisten in his eyes. "For good."

After decades with the church, the Thompsons are no longer members of Messiah. Sadly, his words seem to make more of an impact than anything we have said.

I look Louis Herschell directly in the eyes. "The Bible does tell us to be wise as serpents and gentle as doves. But there's another verse right after that."

His face contorts in a grimace.

"It's the Scripture I live by now." I look at every last elder in the room until my gaze lands on Noah Franklin. "'Be on your guard against men.'"

WHEN WE WALK out of Messiah Church, the fires of my rage and bravado disappear, extinguished by a heavy blanket of hopelessness. It's all I can do to keep the tears at bay as I storm toward my car.

"Del, wait! What are we going to do?" Esha calls after me.

I whip around. She's standing next to her father, his arm wrapped tight around her. A wave of jealousy rocks me. "I don't know. I'm done."

Esha looks like I've slapped her. She takes a few steps toward me, the wind yanking at her long black hair. "What about that journalist you told us about? You said you would share everything with her if this didn't work."

"Parker, right." My brain feels foggy. As much as I had prepared myself for the disregard of the men in that room, I hadn't actually believed they would be so unmoved.

"I know you're upset, Delilah. I am too. What Louis said . . . it wasn't right," Mr. Thompson says. "But we can't give up now. For Eve's sake, we have to make sure those stories get told."

I rake my fingers through my hair. "What good is telling those stories if the elders won't hold Pastor Rick accountable? We might go through all this effort, Parker might publish an exposé revealing all the ways Pastor Rick has harmed women, and nothing will happen."

Esha takes a step toward me. "What are you talking about? Don't you remember how it felt to read all those stories together, to realize bad things were happening to other people besides you? We don't know how many women in the congregation haven't seen our blog post yet or were too scared to come forward. There might be hundreds more stories out there. They deserve to be heard, Del."

"Don't you get it, Esha?" Tears stream down my face. "They *heard* us. Everyone in that room heard what we had to say. Some of them even looked a little upset. But they didn't do anything."

Her lips tremble. "Then we need to be louder."

"That's right," Mr. Thompson says, putting his arm around his daughter again. "We tell the media. Make sure the whole community knows what's been going on. This was your plan, Delilah, and it's a good one."

I back away. "I just . . . I need some time to think." My whole body is rejecting being here. I look at the church office, flooded with the same sensation as the day Lars and Eve got married. I want to run and run and drive and drive. I want to never have to look at this place again.

"Del, come on! We can't wait." Esha wraps her coat around herself, her face tight with exasperation. "If you're not going to do it, I'll contact Parker myself."

"Fine! Do it. But you're kidding yourself, Esha," I snap. "As long as Louis Herschell backs Pastor Rick, there is no chance of the elders turning against him. And if they can convince themselves the stories we've gathered don't matter, they can easily sway the congregation too. Pastor Rick and the elders will stick to their usual narrative about the media and petty ex-members trying to keep Messiah from doing God's work, and everyone else will eat that up. A few people might leave, but it won't make a difference."

"You don't know that," Mr. Thompson says, but I can hear the doubt in his voice.

"I do. I know." I turn away.

"Del. Delilah!"

I keep walking.

"What about Eve?" Esha cries. "What am I supposed to say to her?"

Finally, I stop and look back, my eyes stinging from the cold wind and tears. The words tumble out before I can stop them. "Tell her I hope Lars was worth it."

The horror on their faces is printed on my brain as I run to my car.

FIFTY-SIX

[DRAFT]

Noble Wife Journey: a blog
Title: Therapy
Last updated: July 2, 2021

Today, we started marriage counseling.

It was inevitable that we'd get here. Inevitable, but no less humiliating.

Messiah has always had a strong focus on marriage and the family unit. Pastor Rick says it's his greatest calling, helping couples stay together. There is a marriage retreat each spring, and Lars and I have gone every year since we got married except this one, since Emmie was still so young. I wonder if that's what we were missing.

He seemed genuinely shocked when I told him I thought we needed help. I must be better at acting happy than I thought I was. To his credit, he put up very little resistance.

After a private conversation with Pastor Rick last Sunday, we were called the next day and scheduled to come in for our first visit with Pastor Keith. I thought it would be awful, talking about our most intimate problems with someone I used to be in high school with, but I knew as soon as Pastor Keith sat us down in his office that I had misjudged him.

It was just like having a conversation with a friend. He asked about Emmanuelle, about how she was growing, whether she was crawling yet. He told me they missed me in the office but made sure I knew to take as much time away as I wanted. My position is being covered by one of the other young ladies in the church. Truthfully, I haven't even thought about work since Emmie was born, but as soon as he mentioned it, I missed it. The organization, the planning, the schedule. I liked how everyone in the church office relied on me; I liked making their lives easier. I liked working with adults instead of a little being who can't tell me what she wants or needs, only that she demands it *right now*. Every day with a baby is simultaneously impossible to predict and exactly the same.

Jesus, forgive me, I feel horrible even typing this.

Pastor Keith asked how we were doing. How we felt about being parents. I did all the talking. Lars sat quietly, nodding along to what I was saying, contributing nothing. The minutes ticked by, and I felt my anger rising. But if the pastor wasn't going to say anything about it, I certainly couldn't.

So, finally, I just surrendered. I let myself talk to Pastor Keith, who seemed genuinely interested in what I had to say. I told him how I felt that Lars was withdrawing from me, that he didn't trust me enough to confide in me when he was going through something hard. Lars responded that it was his responsibility to shoulder the burdens of work, especially in this first year of Emmanuelle's life, and that he didn't want to make me anxious by telling me about things I couldn't control.

Pastor Keith responded to my concerns and complaints with sympathetic murmurs, his eyes never leaving my face to look at his computer or check his phone. He gave Lars credit for trying to protect me while encouraging him to look for opportunities to tell me how he was feeling.

At the end of the hour, he said he would have us in his calendar the same time next week.

We were silent the whole way home. Lars parked the car, and I put a hand on his arm. My parents were in our house, probably watching a television show while Emmanuelle slept in her nursery. I couldn't go inside without trying one more time.

"So, how did you feel tonight went?" I asked, meeting his gaze in the dim light cast by our porch.

"Fine. You?"

"Fine." I paused, my emotions cartwheeling between anger and grief. "Lars. I . . . I love you."

"Love you too, babe." He squeezed my hand and tossed me a small smile. Then he got out of the car and walked into the house.

FIFTY-SEVEN

RUNNING FROM BOWER IS WHAT I do best. When the streetlights of the town fade behind me, I know that I will never see them again. I'm done.

If I could, I would keep driving to Minneapolis like last time. But I need to get my things from the Oback house, and I can only pray that they're out for the evening. I'm not sure I have it in me to explain why I've failed to find justice for their son.

Of course, the lights inside are glowing when I pull into the driveway. Wiping the remnants of tears from my face, I check my reflection in the car mirror before stepping into the bitterly cold night. December is not far off, and I can smell a blizzard in the air. A white Christmas looks promising this year. As much as I hate snow, it never really feels like the holidays without it.

Christmas. For the past few years, I've spent it with various friends and roommates' families, but I don't have anyone this year. I need a job when I get back to the Cities, so I might as well go for something seasonal and get extra pay to work the holiday. Let people with families enjoy it; for me, it can pass like any other day.

When I open the front door, I hear Nathaniel and Susan talking in the dining room. The house smells like roasted meat and vegetables. They turn and smile at me when I walk into the room, but Susan's expression quickly falls.

She stands up. "What's happened?"

Nathaniel has a glass of wine in hand, paused halfway to his lips. "Are you all right?"

"I'm fine." Not believable in the slightest. "I just need to go. I'm sorry."

"You're working?" he asks.

"No, like I need to get out of here. Out of Bower, out of Elden, out of anyplace where I could possibly run into someone from Messiah at the grocery store." I shake my hands, breathing too fast. "I need to get out. I'm sorry."

They both take cautious steps toward me. "Something happened. Are you hurt? Did someone attack you again?" Nathaniel asks.

I had all but forgotten the motel ransacking, the scratching on the door. Who did that? Keith? Colette? Louis Herschell? His reference to the vines and the fire was suspicious, but I can't imagine him doing something so immature. I will probably never know.

"I'm sorry, I know you wanted me to find out what happened to Lars, but I just can't. I've done my best, but every theory I've had has just hurt someone else. I thought it was Eve and Keith, and now both of their lives are destroyed. Then I thought maybe Pastor Rick had something to do with it, helped his nephew cover up an accident, but . . ."

"What?" Susan's voice is shrill. "You think Rick Franklin had something to do with this?"

"No! I don't know." Tears are bubbling to the surface again, and my entire body is aching to get away. "Look, I can't help you anymore. I'm sorry. I loved Lars; I love—"

Nathaniel puts a hand on my shoulder, and I sob, collapsing against him. He's not my father, and I don't deserve this, but it's all I want right now. Strong arms around me, keeping the world out. I'm breaking his heart, and he's got me anyway.

Soon, I smell Susan's perfume, and her arms wrap around me as well. She's trying to keep them quiet, but I can hear the shallow sound of her sobs.

I stay there longer than I should, soaking in the grace and love I've done nothing to earn. Three broken people, holding each other up.

It's the closest I've felt to church in a long time.

I HAVE A shift at Elaine's in the morning, but I'm not going to make it. Part of me wants to skip out without a word, not deal with the drama of saying goodbye. It wouldn't be the first time I've left a job with no warning. The only benefit of working in the service industry is that because places treat you like crap, it's expected you'll do the same back.

But for once, I don't want to piss off the manager. In fact, I'm kind of hoping Finn might be the one good thing that came out of all this. Wishful thinking, probably, but I've got to at least give it a chance.

It's after 11:00 p.m. when I pull up to the restaurant. The parking lot is empty save for a few trucks and the staff cars around the back. I spot Finn's blue sedan, and my heart jumps.

He'll be annoyed with me for leaving, not because of us but because he'll be down a waitress again. Proximity is what makes these kinds of relationships work.

I've gotten in my own head now, and I'm about to turn around when I remember the way he pulled me close by the strings of my apron. The way his hands felt on my body. The way his eyes light up every time I talk about what I'm doing here, as if he's actually interested in my ideas and theories.

Finn hasn't always agreed with me, but he's never made me feel stupid for looking into Lars's death. He gave me a job and a place to brainstorm, and I owe him at least one more conversation.

"Hey, gorgeous," he says as soon as I walk through the door. One eyebrow rises. "Aren't you on the early shift tomorrow? I would have thought you'd be asleep."

My face strains to make a smile. "Yeah, about that. I'm really sorry, Finn, but I've got to head back to Minneapolis."

Surprise flashes across his face. "Really? I thought . . . What happened?"

"Nothing, it's fine. I've just stayed here as long as I can stand is all. It has nothing to do with you. If anything, you've made it much more bearable." I laugh, swiveling side to side on a barstool. "I know I'm leaving you high and dry for my shifts."

"Don't worry about that." He leans across the bar. The smell of his shampoo makes me want to climb over the wooden surface and wrap myself around him. Instead, I just swallow hard. "What about your investigation? Did things not go well with the elders?"

"You could say that." I run my fingers along the back of his hand. "I appreciate that you've always made me feel like I could do this, but I think it's time to admit I'm in way over my head here. I'm not a cop, and I'm not a journalist like Parker. Maybe Lars really was killed by Eve. I know from reading drafts of her blog that she wasn't happy. They found the gun on her property, and she's unaccounted for at the time of the murder. It makes sense."

Finn turns his hand over, his palm sliding against mine. "But you don't believe it."

I look at our fingers threaded together. A spot between my ribs aches, thinking about leaving here. Leaving him. "It doesn't matter what I believe. I've done everything I can to get the people with actual power in town to take a closer look at this case. The sheriff's office is sure they have the right person in jail, and the elders don't give a damn about what Pastor Rick does as long as he keeps bringing in money for the church."

Blinking back tears, I meet his gaze. "Anyway, I wanted to let you know in person. And I also wanted to say . . . um, well, you've got my number. If you want to use it, I would love that." He's quiet, and I stammer on. "I mean, if you want. No pressure obviously."

His forehead smooths out, and I realize with a pang that I know that expression.

He's relieved. My heart sinks.

Gently, Finn squeezes my hand. "I had a great time with you, Del, it's just . . . you know, I'm here. My business is here. If you can't stand even being close to Bower, I don't know how it would ever work with us."

It makes sense. That doesn't make it hurt less. I try my best to plaster on an understanding, relaxed smile. "You're right. No problem."

As I slide down off the stool, my phone rings. Esha's name flashes on the screen. Below it, I see I've had several missed calls from her in the past hour.

I answer, my finger over my free ear. "Hey, Esha, I'm just leaving a restaurant. Can I call you when I get on the road?"

A woman's urgent voice responds. "Delilah, it's Linda Thompson. I'm at the hospital in Moorhead. You need to get here right now—Tim and Esha were in an accident."

IT'S PAST MIDNIGHT by the time I run up to the nurses' station, out of breath. "I'm looking for Esha Prescott's room."

"Visiting hours end at eight." The nurse on duty looks up at me, and I recognize her. Bianca, a friend of my mom's from Messiah. "Oh, Delilah, it's you."

The words pour out of me. "Hi, Bianca. I'm sorry, I know it's late, but Linda Thompson asked me to come right away. I think she needs help managing with the baby. Her husband and daughter were just in an accident."

After a moment, Bianca nods sharply. "Room 208. If anyone asks, you're family."

I race down the hall before she can change her mind.

Esha is still unconscious. The skin around her closed eyes is swollen, an oxygen mask strapped to her face. Her mother is sitting by the bed, her head resting on the back of the chair. Emmanuelle straddles her lap, asleep on her shoulder.

"Mrs. Thompson?"

She opens her eyes to look at me, and I hold back a gasp. Mrs. Thompson was always one of the most joyous people I knew. Her heart-shaped face glowed, and when someone was talking, she looked at them like they were the only person in the room.

That woman is gone now. The last two weeks have hollowed her out.

"Delilah." Tears run from her eyes without effort, without notice. "They're saying . . . they're saying she'll be okay. Several broken bones, including a rib that punctured one of her lungs, but she's out of critical danger now."

"And Mr. Thompson?"

Linda straightens up in the chair, cups the back of Emmanuelle's head to keep her in place on her shoulder. "He's all right. A broken arm and quite a few cuts and bruises, but it could have been so much worse. It's a miracle they're alive. They hit a tree going sixty."

My knees feel weak. I stagger to a nearby chair and drop, staring at Esha. Her waves of black hair splay out from her head, as if she's underwater. Smears of blood mar her face and neck. One leg is elevated in a long cast.

"How did it happen?"

"They don't know for sure." Linda puts a hand on her daughter's arm, strokes it gently. "Esha was the one behind the wheel, and she still hasn't woken up. Apparently, Tim was too upset after the meeting, so she offered to drive. Of course, now he's blaming himself for it."

"I need to go talk to him." Something flickers inside me, a spark threatening to become a wildfire. This town, this church—it makes me feel unhinged. My mom always said I thought everything about the church was some kind of conspiracy, but the destruction is getting to be too much to ignore. Lars and Keith are dead. Eve is in jail for murder, and now Esha and Tim Thompson are in the hospital after a terrible accident.

The Obacks and I are the only ones left who have been asking questions, trying to point fingers at the church. It's starting to feel like our days are numbered too.

Linda gestures to the left. "Tim is three doors down, room 212. Unless he's resting, it should be fine for you to go in. He asked me to call you."

Bracing myself, I stand up. "I'm so sorry, Mrs. Thompson."

She shakes her head. "If anything else happens, I don't—" A pause. Then she clears her throat. "I certainly don't know how Job dealt with everything he did. Losing all his children, his whole life, within just a few days."

I never understood that story. It was one of the many that made me start to question who God really was, what he was trying to tell us about himself. Would he really let the devil completely destroy someone's life just to prove they were loyal to him? What did Job ever do to deserve losing everything and everyone he loved, except love God more? I was raised to believe every word of the Bible was dictated by God and therefore one hundred percent true. The story of Job is one where I kind of hope the writers used a little creative license, but any suggestion of that would probably get me labeled a heretic.

Now is not the time to talk about questioning faith, though. I put my hand on Linda's free shoulder. "I don't know either. But you haven't lost everything. Esha and Mr. Thompson are going to be okay."

Eve, I'm not so sure.

Her hand reaches up to cover mine, giving it a squeeze. "Go. I'll be all right."

The door to Mr. Thompson's room is open, and he's sitting up in a hospital bed. The man I don't remember ever seeing in anything but a plaid shirt and jeans now looks back at me wearing a faded blue hospital gown. He's not frail by any means, but the difference is striking.

"Del, come in." He gestures with his good arm.

"Mr. Thompson, are you okay? I'm so sorry." I perch on the chair next to him, sitting forward. One of his bare legs is peeking out from underneath the rough hospital blanket. I do my best to avoid looking at it. "Your wife said Esha was driving. What happened?"

He's silent for a moment, until I meet his gaze. Esha might be his adoptive daughter, but when they're angry, the same fire burns behind their eyes. "Someone messed with the car, that's what happened. I told the police, but they're skeptical. They think Esha just lost control around one of the turns on the way to our house. You know how the road is windy out there."

I shake my head. "Esha's driven that road a million times, though."

"That's right. I tried to tell them that this was no accident, but they think I'm being paranoid." Mr. Thompson shuffles up in the bed, wincing. "We were on the highway near our house when Esha switched off the cruise control so she could handle the turns. Only thing is, the cruise wouldn't switch off. She tried braking, but that didn't work either. The car kept going sixty, and there was nothing she could do to stop it. She was yelling at me, and I was trying to think what to tell her, how to avoid an accident, when we hit the first curve. She did her best, made it through three or four of the bends before we got to that sharp one out by the Pattersons'. We left the road and rammed straight into a tree."

I shudder. "It's a miracle you survived." The people I grew up with overuse that word, but in this case, I really believe it.

"I told the police exactly what happened, and where we were right before we got on the road. We were fine driving to Messiah. I used cruise most of the way there once we got on the highway. Someone had to have messed with the car in the lot, and you don't do something like that unless you want people to die."

His voice cuts off on the last word. For a moment, he breathes hard, gathering himself. When he looks back at me, tears are in his eyes. "The stories you collected were horrible enough. What the church has been doing to people, to women—" He shakes his head. "I believed it, but I didn't really believe it, you know? Didn't believe it was intentional. Just bad application of good theology. But what's been happening lately, all this death and chaos . . . Lives are being destroyed. We could have been killed. Almost our entire family, wiped out in less than a month."

"Mr. Thompson, I don't want to downplay what you've gone through. But you have to understand, Messiah has been killing people for years." My fingers twist together in my lap. "Every ousted member, every frozen-out backslider. We have a social death. It might not seem as extreme as murder, but when you're completely cut off from everyone you know and love? Trust me, it's the closest thing I can imagine to dying."

He rubs the stubble on his jaw, his eyes downcast. I wonder if he's thinking about what he's participated in, he and his family. He and Esha might have survived this time, but there's no guarantee whoever did this wouldn't try again. And even if they didn't, the accident was a pretty clear warning. We had stepped over the line.

Then I remember. "Noah was late to the meeting."

Mr. Thompson sits up straighter. "He was. I remember."

"And he's an electrician. He would know how to mess with the car's electronics, make the cruise control malfunction."

His face blanches. I feel my heartbeat vibrate on my ribs.

We were on the right track. Noah and Rick are bound up together in this.

Mr. Thompson shakes his head. "Do you really think he would try to kill us? He would have had to tamper with the car before he even knew what we were going to say."

"He knew." I meet his gaze. "Everyone in that room had to know when you requested that meeting that you were going to call Pastor Rick's authority into question. Their wives read Eve's blog. I'm sure at least some of them told their husbands what we were doing."

I can't stay sitting any longer. I cross the room to his chart on the wall, then look away, not wanting to take in the private information. "I wasn't just trying to get a reaction from the elders, Mr. Thompson. Esha and I told you that we were there to tell the stories that came through the blog, and that was true. But we really do think Noah and Rick Franklin are connected to killing Lars and framing Eve."

"Why would they do that?"

"We're still trying to work that out. Parker is looking into it. We know Lars was handling a big client at his accounting firm, and we think it might have been Emerald Power. Noah's a senior electrician there."

Mr. Thompson rests his head back on his pillow. "Eve mentioned he was upset by something at work. He'd been doing overtime at home for months. She never knew what it was about, though."

I nod. "He apparently found some discrepancies, numbers that didn't look right and had been ignored by other members of his firm. Lars had changed a lot since I knew him, but he was still an honest man. Noah was his friend, but if he was doing something wrong—embezzling money or something—I know that Lars would have confronted him about it. Maybe he did it on the day they were hunting together. He told Noah what he knew, and rather than face the consequences, Noah shot him to keep him quiet. Then he called his uncle. Pastor Rick tried to get everyone to believe it was an accident and keep Noah's name out of it at first, but when that didn't work, he decided to frame Eve for the murder. She had started having questions about his teachings, helping women in the church leave their husbands. Framing her would take suspicion off Noah and silence her at the same time."

"Why didn't you say any of this earlier?"

"Are you kidding?" I shake my head. "We had corroborated stories of a decade of abuse and control, and the elders treated us like we were just a bunch of whiny women. I have no proof for any of this, Mr. Thompson. Esha and I were hoping the elders would look into the stories we had, maybe even suspend Pastor Rick for a week or two, and that would damage his reputation enough that we could talk to the sheriff about our theory. Right now, there's no way he'd even consider it."

He's quiet for so long I wonder if he's fallen asleep. When I look over, his face is pale, but his eyes are open. Finally, he says, "A few days ago, I never would have believed you. But now . . . now I think that anything is possible. You've got to expose this, Delilah. I know it's not fair to ask you, but I can't. We can't. I need to focus on helping my family get through this. Please, go online, go to the media, use Eve's blog. Whatever you need to do."

My skin suddenly feels too hot. I walk from one side of the room to the next, shaking my hands as if I could jar the anxiety off my body. "I've tried. I've been trying for so long to find a weakness in Pastor Rick's empire, but there isn't one. The stories are all over Eve's blog already, but she's bleeding subscribers since we posted. People don't want to believe the promises of being a Noble Wife were a lie. I sent Parker everything we have after Linda called me about your accident, but even if she does publish something, you know he'll just spin it as yet another secular media attack on the work of God."

"He will, you're right." Mr. Thompson studies his lap for a moment, then grips the blanket in his fists. "He will deny wrongdoing when it comes to the lives he destroyed through his Noble Wife teachings. No matter how bad the stories make him look. What you need is proof he was involved in framing Eve for Lars's murder. That's something he can't spin. There's only one person who could confirm it, and we both know he's not as smart as he thinks he is."

My mouth is too dry to respond.

"Delilah, I hate to ask this. But if anyone could get it out of him, it's you. You need to talk to Noah."

FIFTY-EIGHT

[DRAFT]

Noble Wife Journey: a blog
Title: Help
Last updated: July 30, 2021

As Christians, we know that we cannot save someone who doesn't want to be saved. We are lifeguards, paddling the stormy seas on our rafts, looking for outstretched arms to grab hold of. We can do nothing for the ones who don't reach for us.

I think it's like that in other aspects of life too. Today, Lars showed that he is content for us to tread water in our marriage. He might not feel like anything is wrong yet, but one day we will grow tired and slip beneath the surface. These past four weeks, Pastor Keith has invited us into his office, throwing us a line. I have lunged for it, doing everything I can to help get us back on firm ground. Lars has barely said a word, and when he has, it's only to defend himself. This afternoon, he didn't even show up.

It's probably my fault. Last night, I let my anger get the best of me. We were in bed, and I tried to playfully push his laptop away so we could be together. He asked me what I was doing and pulled it back onto his lap, covering the part of him I was trying to get access to.

"What are *you* doing?" I snapped. "Don't you love me anymore?"

I felt dramatic saying it—foolish and immature. But I never thought I would have to deal with sexual rejection from my husband. I was told that *I* would be the one who had to make myself available even if I didn't feel like it, that he would always want me physically.

The only education Messiah gave us about sex was how important it was to save ourself for our future spouse. I always assumed that as long as I stayed pure, some kind of switch would flip once I got married, and my husband and I would know exactly how to please each other. Instead, I was so nervous on our wedding night that I couldn't even fully bare myself to him, and he was completely unaware of what he needed to do.

But that was before. Once we grew more comfortable with each other's bodies and figured out what we liked, it was better. We had a rhythm. But now, Lars is withholding himself from me.

For a moment, in his stunned expression at my outburst, I saw the boy I fell in love with seven years ago. Then his features rearranged, and the Messiah Man Mask shifted into place. Strong, confident, calm. Prepared for battle.

"Of course I love you, Eve," he said. "I would do anything for you. I would die for you."

"I don't need you to die for me, Lars. I need you to talk to me!"

His gaze left his laptop for a moment to settle on my face. "What do you want to talk about?"

I couldn't think of anything to say in reply—at least not anything that I wouldn't later regret. Instead, I just turned over and closed my eyes. Soon, he was typing again.

So it wasn't really a surprise when he didn't show up for counseling today. Pastor Keith invited me in, and he asked where Lars was. The carefully constructed wall—the one holding back my anger and sadness and desire—crumbled into dust.

I told him everything. About Lars's distance, his obsession with work, his coldness. Our years trying to get pregnant, how he got a better-paying job to afford fertility treatments, the way he seemed to like being a dad better than being a husband these days. He never physically hurt me, no. He never manipulated me. It just seemed like he had worked so hard to become the man I wrote about in my blog, a Messiah man, that I didn't notice it changing him until it was too late. My creative, ambitious worship pastor had slowly been eaten away by this stressed-out corporate grouch.

It wasn't supposed to be like this. I held up my end of the bargain: I gave him a comfortable home, a beautiful baby, plenty of delicious food, as much intimacy as he wanted. Why wasn't anyone reminding him what he owed me?

When I finished, I had a stack of wet tissues in my lap and my heart was racing.

I love my church. I love my husband. I love my life.

I repeated all those things, just to make sure Pastor Keith knew. I had this fear he would call in Pastor Rick, tell him that I had been disrespectful. When he was quiet for so long, I started to cry again, panicked I had overstepped in an unforgivable way. I had spoken negatively about my husband, about the church, and in front of a pastor! What was I thinking?

Finally, Pastor Keith met my gaze. To my shock, his eyes were wet too. It was like a shield had dropped. I hadn't been looked at that way in years. Desire, adoration, longing. Regret.

"I'm so sorry, Evie."

That name. He was the only one to call me that in high school. It was his little rebellion, his way of showing he liked me even though we weren't allowed to be together.

"You deserve better."

He cleared his throat. I stood up. We looked at each other for a moment, and then I left.

When I got home, Lars was in his study with the door closed. I drifted into the nursery, hovered over my daughter's sleeping form, placed a kiss on her perfect forehead. And then I came here to write this down in the only place I know it won't be found.

Keith and I will never be together. I will never be unfaithful. But I can't disagree.

I do deserve better.

FIFTY-NINE

I SLEEP ON THE SPARE bed in Esha's hospital room, the beep and whir of machines connected to her body jarring me awake all night. She doesn't stir. By noon, I am antsy and wired on terrible hospital coffee, and Linda pushes me out the door with a promise to call when Esha wakes up.

Unable to put it off any longer, I start the drive to Noah's place. I'm a mile away when my cell phone rings. My car is too old for Bluetooth, so I press the speakerphone button and keep driving.

"Hello?"

"Hey." Finn's voice is tinny and distant. "Sounds like you're driving. Are your friends okay?"

I had rushed out of Elaine's after getting the call from Linda, only offering him a muttered explanation about a car accident. The fact that he's checking in is a pleasant surprise.

"They're all right, I think. Esha was still unconscious when I left, but Mr.—Tim is fine. Cuts and bruises. They were very lucky."

I can hear my mom's voice in my head: There's no such thing as luck—only blessings.

"Glad it wasn't worse. I swear, something is in the water in that town."

"Oh, I don't think the water is the problem."

He's quiet for a moment. "So, are you heading to the Cities now?"

"Not yet. It wasn't an accident, Finn. Someone messed with the Thompsons' car. I know I said I was leaving, but I can't let him get away with it."

"Let who get away with it?"

"Noah Franklin. I'm on my way to see him now."

There's a long pause. Then: "Del, this is a bad idea."

I grip the steering wheel harder. "Maybe, but I am done letting the men in this town chase me away. Every time I go, they get to carry on with their lives and pretend like nothing bad happened, and I'm the one who loses out."

"That's a fair point, but you can't go to Noah's alone. You could get hurt. Let me meet you."

"And you know what? That goes for you, too, Finn. I know we just got together, but we had a good connection. Then, as soon as you found out it would be slightly less convenient to be with me, you acted like it meant nothing to say goodbye. You don't get to be all concerned and protective now."

"Del, I'm sorry. There's some stuff going on in my life. I want to explain. Please, just pull over and let me meet up with you." There's a shuffling sound, like he's putting on his shoes.

"We can talk later. Don't worry, Noah is not going to see me as any kind of threat. I'm just going to talk to him, and I'll be recording the whole conversation with my phone in my pocket."

"So, what, the police will be able to hear him hurt you after the fact?"

I swallow hard, knowing that's at least a moderate possibility. "Fine. I'll stay away from his house, but I'm going back to where he and Lars were hunting at least. There's got to be some evidence out there the police missed."

"Delilah, you're not a cop!" Finn's voice roars over the speaker. "You're not an investigator."

For some reason, those words hurt more than anything else he could have said. I blink back tears, then turn onto the gravel drive leading to Noah's hunting spot.

Finn continues. "Your theory is that Noah murdered one person and tried to kill two others, and you're just going to his property without a plan. Do you even have a weapon?"

Although I've been here once before without getting caught, I still feel that electric wave of nerves as small rocks spit out from under my car. I pull up to the edge of the woods, shifting the car to park.

"You're right, Finn. I don't know what I'm doing. I'm not a detective," I say, looking at the dead branches through my windshield. "But none of the real detectives care about the truth in this case. None of them are here. I am."

Then I hang up. For the first time in days, I feel like I'm back in control.

The sun has started its descent, but the weather is still in the midforties, and it's brighter than the last time I was here. I leave my coat in the car, knowing I'll be too hot hiking around in it. Even so, halfway down the trail I am already sweating with exertion. Stopping in the clearing I found last time, I pull out my phone.

Parker answers after two rings. "Hey, stranger. Boy, have I been busy. That was a hot tip you gave me about Lars working on some big accounts. I am knee-deep in emails and text messages. It took a little convincing, but Eve is so insistent she's innocent that I got her lawyer to agree to open up their records to me. I've got all her and Lars's comms from the last year and I've been sifting through. Do you know how many random text messages married couples send each other? I'm serious, evangelicals are so repressed I thought I'd find a bunch of weird sex photos in their media folders, but like ninety percent of it is just random pictures Lars sent her from the grocery store to make sure he was picking up the right thing."

For the first time in what feels like days, I laugh. "Parker, hi."

"Damn, hi, sorry. What's up?"

"Just a quick question. You seem to know Noah's side of the story for what happened to Lars. Can you tell me what it is?"

"I can only tell you what my contact at the sheriff's office let slip. He said Noah told them they were both hunting up in the tree stand, and Lars needed to pee. So he walked off on the trail a ways to make sure he was downwind from where the deer might approach them. A few minutes later, Noah heard a shot. He assumed Lars had gone for a deer, so it took him a while to realize something was wrong. He climbed down and went looking, and by the time he got there, Lars was dead."

Phone clutched to my ear, I look back at the path I came down. I have no idea if that was downwind on the day they were hunting, but without much else to go on, I'll have to assume. The thicker part of the woods is in the opposite direction, so that's where the deer would be coming from. Now I just need to find the tree stand.

"Okay, thanks."

"You're doing something, aren't you?"

She doesn't say *something stupid*, but the implication is there. "Nothing you wouldn't do."

She barks a laugh. "That's hardly comforting. Oh, hey, I've been meaning to call you, actually. There's no way to put this delicately, but because I have Lars's phone records, I see he called you a few days before he died. Do you mind telling me what that was about?"

A swell of guilt builds inside me. "I wish I could tell you. He left me a voicemail, and I never called him back."

"What did he say?"

"Just . . . 'You were right.'" I can hear his voice in my head as I say the words. "He said, 'You were right. Call me.' No explanation. I've been trying to figure out for two weeks what he meant."

"Well, I might be able to help with that, actually."

My fingers tighten on the phone. "Really? How?"

"I probably shouldn't share this, but since it seems like he wanted to tell you anyway, I'm thinking it's okay. After that call, he texted Eve. I'll read you what it says. 'Called Delilah. Left a message. She deserves to know she was right about Rick and the church. She was right not to trust them.'"

I blink, and a tear slips down my cheek. I wish, more than ever, that I had taken that phone call. But at least I won't have to wonder forever what he was going to say. "Parker, thank you."

"You're welcome. Good luck out there. Let me know what you find."

I put my phone in my pocket. I could sit and think about that text for hours, regretting that I never got my final conversation with Lars. But the best thing I can do right now is what I came here for—I can try to honor him by finding out why he died.

Noah's story is simple. Hard to poke holes in, especially when no one is trying to. But there must be something.

I start to walk in a circle around the clearing. Tilting my head back, I peer up into the branches. It takes several minutes, but finally I spot a two-by-four nailed into the side of a thick oak. Following it down, I see another and another.

A ladder.

I scramble to the spot, take a quick look around, and climb up. It's not much to look at, but this has to be the tree stand they were in. From here, I can see several yards in every direction. The trees are close together, but an animal or a person walking down the path would surely be visible.

Noah was never a very good liar, and I know that most lies have a kernel of truth. Maybe he was up in the stand when Lars went down. Maybe he was able to see him from here, take a shot.

But looking around, there's no view of the path I walked down. The trees are thick in every direction, and it takes a minute for me to even remember which way I came from. I wonder if Noah walks a different way every time he comes out here, or if it's just because they're only hunting a couple times a year that the path isn't more well-worn.

No matter where he went to pee, though, I'm sure Lars would have walked farther than a hundred yards away. Noah would have had to follow him.

"What the heck are you doing up there?"

The voice instantly makes my heart race. Somehow, Noah Franklin has walked through the woods without a sound, and he's standing just below me, red-faced and furious.

Even though I'm not that high up, looking down with no barrier between me and the forest floor makes me dizzy.

"Uh, just looking around," I say.

"Well, get down. This is private property. You can't just come and go as you please, Delilah."

"All right, sorry." I am always apologizing. Stupid, stupid.

This isn't how I planned it. I wanted to find something to confront him with, something that didn't add up. The only way I'm going to get the truth is if I can talk him into telling me. Before I climb down, I pull out my phone and press record.

Noah looks even angrier up close. His body has thickened since we were younger, wiry frame replaced with ominous muscle. But the hair he took such pride in has thinned, and that gives me a perverse pleasure.

It's short-lived. When he takes a step toward me, I flinch and then immediately hate myself again. Gathering every ounce of anger and disdain inside me, I straighten up.

"Seriously, did you think I didn't know you were here?" he asks. "I've got cameras at every entrance to my property. I saw you here a few days ago, but I let you be since you didn't come to the house. But this isn't okay."

Oh, now he's got boundaries. I see. My fists are pins and needles, squeezed tight against my body. I force myself not to give in to the automatic need to apologize. "I'm just trying to figure out what happened to Lars."

"You're a detective now? Is that what you did when you ran off to the big city? Became a cop?"

His words are an echo of Finn's, but they make me feel angry rather than ashamed. "No. Just a concerned citizen."

His laugh is just as derisive as I remember. My stomach rolls at the sound. It's the way he laughed when he held up his phone, the pictures of me there for everyone to see. It's the way he laughed when I screamed. Without thinking about it, I cross my arms over the front of my body.

"I see. So, you trespassed on private property to solve a case that's already been solved and you found . . . what exactly?"

I open my mouth, but no words come. Even after everything he did to me, all the retorts and things I wish I'd said that I wrote in my journals as a teenager, I can think of nothing. Something about Noah breaks my brain. What happened between us was ten years ago, but it might as well have been days. Even though I saw him every week in church—and almost every day in school—after it happened, I never spoke to him again. I haven't talked to him since he assaulted me.

He assaulted me. I repeat that in my mind. That's what he did—it was assault. Then he was able to move on, go to college, get married, have kids. Maybe I'm the only girl he ever hurt, but there was nothing to stop him from leaving a string of us in his wake, damaged women who shouldered the blame for his misdeeds.

The church protects boys like Noah because it believes they will grow up to be good men. Their teenage boyhood is just a temporary rough patch they have to get through on the way to an otherwise upstanding life. But they judge a man's behavior by what they see on Sunday mornings—the most polished version any of us presents of ourselves. The church is so good at monitoring the lives and actions of women: Are we involved in enough Bible studies, contributing enough meals to the potlucks, volunteering at enough church activities, bearing and raising enough good Christian children?

Nobody ever checks on the men.

"Delilah, are you on something? What are you doing?"

I blink, realize that I've been staring somewhere past his shoulder. My eyes focus on him. All the hesitation, fear, and vulnerability vanish. He needs to pay. It's not enough to believe in hell, the potential for eternal damnation. I want Noah to face consequences here.

"I know you killed Lars. You might be able to fool everyone else, Noah, but I know exactly what you're capable of. You killed him and your uncle Rick helped you frame Eve, didn't he?"

His eyes widen. "You've really lost it this time. Get out of here before I call the police."

"Go ahead! I'll tell them they should take a look at the cameras on your property. I bet they'll prove that no one else came in or out of these woods that day. You're the only one who could have shot Lars, and if they weren't so wrapped around your uncle's finger, I bet they would have figured that out by now."

For a moment, he just stares at me. Then an unbearably familiar smile creeps over his face. Cocky and cruel, certain of who has the power in this situation.

"You always were a city girl at heart. The police already know about my cameras because every farm around here has them. They got the footage on day one, and it doesn't show anything, but Eve obviously knew about them too. As long as she avoided the main road in here, it would have been easy to pass them by. You would know that if you knew anything at all."

My teeth grind.

He studies me closely. "Why are you really here, Delilah? Are you still so obsessed with Lars that you can't let it go? You need to move on. You should have moved on when he married Eve six years ago."

Okay, so I was wrong about the cameras. That doesn't mean I'm wrong about this. I try another tack. "Why were you late to the elders meeting, Noah?"

"What?"

"Someone tampered with Tim and Esha's car while they were in the church. Someone who knew a lot about electronics. And you were late getting inside. Did you think we wouldn't put that together?"

Noah is shaking his head now, his anger giving way to confusion. "You really are just saying whatever pops into your head, aren't you?"

"Go ahead and mock me all you want. I know exactly who I'm dealing with. You might have convinced the police you're innocent, but I know better than anyone what a liar you are. I will not stop until I prove what you did."

Noah crosses his arms. "You keep saying that. What are you talking about? What did I ever do to you?"

I gape at him. "Come on."

"No, seriously. I know we kind of flirted in high school, but I was never that into you. Sorry if that ticked you off, but—"

"You're messing with me." But the expression on his face is genuinely clueless. I stare at him for a long moment, and then a harsh sound escapes my lips—somewhere between a laugh and a scream. "You have no fucking idea, do you?"

He clicks his tongue in performative disgust at my language.

"The pictures, Noah. The pictures you took of me and posted on social media, sent to all your friends."

"Oh, that? Geez, you really can't let anything go, can you? It was just a bet."

My throat constricts. "A bet?"

"Yeah, like a prank. I was supposed to get you to flash me, and a bunch of the guys bet five bucks I wouldn't be able to. When you did, I had to prove it, so I took a picture. It wasn't my fault it ended up on Instagram. That was all Robby."

Robby. I sat across from him and never said anything. He probably doesn't even remember either. Why would he? Why would any of them? They never got into any trouble. For them, my humiliation was just one in a series of jokes and antics that decorated the absolute freedom of their teenage years.

Finally, I find my words again. "What you did was a crime. What Robby did was a crime. I was underage. You took pictures of my naked body without my consent and distributed them. You could have gone to prison, if anyone at Messiah had cared about actually letting you face consequences for your actions."

For the first time, he looks less than absolutely sure of himself. His eyes dart to the side, confused. In that moment, I see him for what he is: a stunted man who never met a boundary that wasn't soft enough for him to break.

"You know what? I actually feel bad for you." I take a step back, laughing bitterly. His glare only spurs me on. "Yeah, I do. What you did to me was horrible, but because of it, my eyes started to open. I got to see that the church wasn't the benevolent institution of protection I was raised to think it would always be. Not when it's run by men who refuse to hold each other accountable—men who can sit in the same row Sunday after Sunday, lifting their hands to God and then going home to lay those same hands violently on their wives and kids. I let what happened with you and then Lars sour me on church as a whole, but really, it shouldn't. Because I still believe in the God I grew up reading about. And because of that, I know that all of you are going to regret what you did."

His lips are a hard line, his arms crossed over his wide chest.

"Because of what the church did after what happened between us, I had to grow up. But for the same reasons, you've stayed the same immature, reckless boy you always were. What a pathetic waste."

"That's enough. Get off my property."

"Not until you tell me the truth. Like you said, no one thinks anything about my opinion anyway, so why not just tell me what happened? Tell me how Lars died."

"Eve killed him. Don't you watch the news?"

I shake my head. "You know something. Tell me, and I'll go away."

"I don't know anything." He lets out a harsh sigh. "But if it'll get you to shut up." He digs in his pocket, pulling out his phone. "Here."

A video is open on the screen. I press play. It's clearly taken from up in the tree stand, focused on a young doe picking her way through the dead branches on the ground.

"She's a beaut," Noah's voice whispers on the video. "Too bad I don't have a doe permit this year. Lars does, but the dummy has a bladder the size of a golf ball—"

A shot crashes through the speakers, and the video shakes. "Whoa. Must have got something!" He waits, and thirty seconds or so pass before he speaks again, louder this time. "Lars? What'd ya get, buddy?"

The video stops. I'm too frozen to hand it back to him, so Noah takes it from my grasp.

When I finally meet his gaze, his eyes are glassy. "That's why the police never looked at me. Not because I'm being protected by my uncle or because we made some kind of shady deal, but because I have absolutely no idea who killed Lars. All I know is it wasn't me."

For a long moment, I look at the sky between the branches of the trees. It's innocently light gray, but I know the clouds are just moments away from opening up and releasing mounds of snow. I blink once, forcing the tears back. Then I look at him.

"I told you, I'm innocent," he says.

My gaze stays on his, steady and furious, until he finally looks away. "You might not have killed Lars, but you will never be innocent."

SIXTY

[DRAFT]

Noble Wife Journey: a blog
Title: Others
Last updated: September 24, 2021

I am not alone. That's the first thing Keith made clear.

For years, I worried that I was just ungrateful. The worst kind of sinner. The Lord has blessed me with so much, and I couldn't be happy with it. Every hurt, every complaint—I swallowed it, crammed the words down my throat until I was so filled to the brim with discontentments that I wondered when they would all spill out.

After talking to Keith today, I realized two things: I am not alone, and I am not even close to the worst story he's heard. Lars never physically hurts me. He doesn't control where I go, how I spend my money. He doesn't demand his dinner or belittle me in front of our friends. Some of the women Keith told me about despise their husbands; I just want mine to be more loving and affectionate.

Lars only missed the one session of therapy. Since then, he's been coming every week, and we are making progress. I am learning to voice my concerns in the moment rather than letting every disappointment fester. Lars is learning that being the man of the house doesn't mean protecting me from every concern or possible stress.

We are talking. It's better. I only occasionally catch myself sinking into the words Keith says or basking in the way he watches me as I talk. It has remained unspoken, but we both know how the other feels—just as we know that nothing will ever come of it.

But today, Keith asked me into his office at work. I sat down across from him, and he asked if I would be open to helping him with something confidential. Of course, I said yes. I had transferred him a call from a troubled woman a half hour earlier, and without telling me who she was, Keith explained that she was a Messiah member who has been trying for months to leave her husband.

They met last week with Pastor Rick, after several unsuccessful months of counseling with Keith. Although he doesn't hit her, thank goodness, he seems to enjoy humiliating her.

Throwing the food she makes him against the wall, telling her coworkers she suffers from a variety of embarrassing ailments, calling her names in front of their kids, taking unflattering pictures of her without her knowledge and posting them online. Over the years, his actions have gotten worse and worse, and now she feels like she has no dignity left. The man says he's just a funny guy. She needs to learn how to take a joke.

Today, apparently, was the last straw. When she got to her office this morning, her entire desk was covered in dirty underwear. The dirty underwear from her own hamper. It's been over a week since she had time to do laundry, and of course her husband doesn't even know how the washing machine works. This was his way of hinting that she was falling behind. You know, in a funny way.

Her coworkers sat at their desks, unable to look at her as she sobbed and shoveled panties into the garbage can before running out.

"She told me if she doesn't go today, she worries about what she'll do to him," Keith told me. "I need to get her out of there."

"Why hasn't she left him before this?" I asked.

The way he looked at me, I knew what a stupid question it was. We don't leave our men here. Constant degradation is not biblical grounds for divorce. He wasn't unfaithful, he didn't beat her. So, she stayed. Being with him isn't a threat to her life, but now it seems like it might be a threat to his.

Then Keith said the thing that absolutely pulled my life apart. "She feels ashamed for not making it work. She's tried so hard to follow the Noble Wife way. Apparently, your blog has really helped."

My blog. This place where I've waxed poetic for years about how to be the perfect Noble Wife, as if I knew anything about marriage or commitment when I was sixteen years old. Of course, I have thought before about the responsibility I owed my readers as my audience grew. But I have always shrugged off any negative attention or angry emails, convincing myself the people writing in just weren't as dedicated as I was to the truth.

But this woman is a member of our church. She and her husband are here every week, and this has been happening to her for years. I asked Keith then, even though I was afraid of the answer.

"Are there . . . others?"

He looked at me for a long time, like he was deciding whether to tell me. But he finally nodded. There are. There are plenty of others.

The weight of what I've done hit me at once. As proud as I've felt about *Noble Wife Journey* for the last decade, I now feel the same level of shame. I have no idea the damage I've caused.

I could run and hide from that, continue on my usual path of disregarding negativity and focusing on the positive. But I just can't anymore, and I told Keith that today.

I told him I want to help.

SIXTY-ONE

"DON'T STAY TOO LONG. BLIZZARD'S coming."

With that warning, Noah leaves me in the woods, standing under the tree where he sat while Lars was killed. All the righteous fury has drained out of me, and I'm suddenly bone tired.

I've been here for two weeks, and I'm no closer to finding out who killed Lars than when I started.

All I know for sure now is that it wasn't an accident. Not with Noah being in the clear and the rifle showing up.

There's still a chance that Pastor Rick knows who did it. If Eve was responsible, he might have tried to cover it up at the start. Protect her reputation, and his by extension. When it became clear that wouldn't work, he stepped back, taking his influence with him.

"Then what about Keith?" I say aloud to no one. He can't have killed himself because of me. If Eve really did murder Lars, it has to have been so she could be with Keith. He might not have had anything to do with it, but he would at least partially blame himself if he found out Eve did it for him. For them. And then, when faced with the prospect of the church learning the truth after she was arrested, he decided to end it.

A strong gust of wind cuts through the trees, and I gasp. I can smell the snow, probably only minutes away now. I should go.

When I turn to start down the path, Pastor Rick is blocking the way.

My pulse thunders. He's wearing a thick wool coat and stocking cap, his sharp jaw obscured by a scarf. To someone else, he might appear casually distinguished, nonthreatening with his hands tucked in his pockets.

But here in these woods, standing between me and my car with none of his Sunday morning sheen, he looks terrifying.

"Delilah."

The way he says my name makes me feel filthy. Always has.

"We're going to need to do something about that."

"What are you doing here?" I ask.

"This is my nephew's property. I have more reason to be here than you do."

"Noah knows I'm here. He's fine with it."

He shakes his head. "It's a shame you and the truth still haven't gotten better acquainted."

I wrap my arms around myself. "It's cold. I'm going home, anyway. So if you could just—"

Pastor Rick pulls something out of his pocket. It takes me a solid five seconds to register that it's a gun.

"What?" I whisper.

"No one wanted this," he says, taking a step toward me. I stumble back, barely keeping my footing on the uneven ground. "I tried so many gentler ways to get you to leave, but you just wouldn't listen."

As he speaks, he comes closer. I am breathing in tight gasps, my heart thrashing like it wants to run. Like it knows that Pastor Rick Franklin is about to put a bullet through it.

The idea that he might kill me is something I can't wrap my head around. He is manipulative, abusive, terrorizing—sure. But he never touches us, never makes us do anything physically.

He gets off on broken souls, not bodies.

When my mind catches up from the shock of it, I know: I'm not the first person to stare down the barrel of a gun held by Pastor Rick in these woods.

"But you were in Bemidji," I say stupidly.

His face betrays nothing, that practiced calm never wavering.

None of us ever checked, because why would he lie about something that was so easily verifiable? A surge of anger builds in my gut. He lied because he lies all the time, and he knows that nobody will ever call him on it. Even I underestimated him. Of all my scenarios, all my theories, the idea that Rick would kill Lars himself seemed impossible.

"You shouldn't do this," I say. "You don't have to do this. Another person shot out here will make people ask questions, even the people you have always convinced to look the other way."

Rick smiles, exactly the way he does from the pulpit on Sunday morning. "Oh, I'm not going to shoot you. I'm not going to kill you." He lowers the gun slightly.

I let out a sigh, resting my back against a tree. "You're not?" Drifting snowflakes have begun to filter through the branches above, which means the snowfall is even heavier outside these woods.

His face is completely pleasant, devoid of anger or malice. "Of course not." He tosses something to me. I catch it without thinking: a bottle of pills. "You're going to do that yourself."

It's an orange prescription bottle, the label torn off. The capsules inside are white. Panic claws at me from the inside. "The whole state is watching what's happening in Bower. I know another murder is worse, but I don't think another suicide is going to be easy to explain away either."

Another suicide. Bottle clutched to my chest, I sink to the forest floor. The back of my sweater scrapes against the tree bark. Numbly, I look up at him. "You did this to Keith too, didn't you? You made him kill himself."

Rick waves his gun. "Go on, Delilah. No point in delaying things, trust me."

I throw the bottle of pills at him. "Why should I? You can't make me swallow these. If you want me dead, you're going to have to get your hands dirty again, Pastor."

For a moment, I feel a surge of vindication at the ripple of surprise on his face. I wonder how many people he's tried to control have actually fought back.

Then he sighs. "I see. I guess I'll have to use this after all." He holds up the gun, makes a show of checking the clip and sliding it back into place. "Good thing it's borrowed."

Snowflakes sting my face. The weapon is dark and menacing in the fading light. I know he wants me to ask who he borrowed it from, but I won't. I want to hold on to this moment when I still think I have a chance, when I still have it in me to fight.

After throwing the pills back to me, he points the gun at my chest. "Let me make this clear: If you don't take those right now, I will shoot you. In the stomach, in the arm, in the knee. It will not be quick. I want you to suffer. Because when the police find your body, they will search the area. And just a few hundred feet away, they will find this gun poorly hidden in a bush. They will quickly learn that it's registered to Nathaniel Oback. He'll be in jail by tomorrow morning."

"Why do you—?" The shed. Nathaniel had said someone moved things around in his shed. Pastor Rick must have taken his gun days ago, just like he'd stolen the rifle from Eve. "They won't believe it. They won't believe he would kill me."

"But, Delilah, didn't you know that Nathaniel came to see me this morning, in serious distress about your little amateur investigation into his son's death? Didn't you know that he was worried you were taking advantage of him and his wife, trying to insert yourself into their lives, pretending you were their daughter? Didn't you know he was wondering if he had been wrong to trust you?"

My eyelids close, pushing two tears out. "That's not true."

Rick's head tilts slightly to the side. "It is true, Delilah. Nathaniel could see that people who were talking to you were ending up hurt or dead, just like his son. In fact, Lars called you just a few days before he was killed. Do you really think Nathaniel believed that was just a coincidence?"

Something strange is happening inside my body. I want to stand, to scream at him, to call him a liar and run away—dare him to shoot me in the back. Because it can't be true. This has to be another one of Rick's lies. Nathaniel and Susan held me in their arms just last night. They wouldn't have done that if they thought I had something to do with their son's death.

But the police will buy it. That's all that matters. I shouldn't be surprised. I've sat through enough of Pastor Rick's sermons to know—true or not, he always has a convincing story.

I look at the gun, and then at the pills in my hand. Maybe it will just be like going to sleep. Who will really miss me if I die? No job, no boyfriend, family that barely speaks to me. My life has been short, and half of it has been taken up by this man and the sanctimonious garbage he teaches. All things considered, this is a gentle way to go.

If he succeeds in killing me, I can at least make sure he doesn't get away with it. I just need to keep him talking.

Popping the lid on the bottle, I glare at him. "So, you're going to watch me die. Just like you did with Keith Rivers, just like you did with Lars Oback. Only you were a little more hands-on with them, weren't you?"

Rick steps closer, throws me a bottle of water. "Here. That'll make them go down easier."

"You even tried to kill Esha and Tim Thompson, didn't you?" I pour a few pills into my palm. "We asked for it to be confidential, but I'm sure Louis told you about that meeting. You tampered with their car while we were all inside."

He pushes his lower lip out, as if he's not sure whether it's true.

I need him to say something. One verbal acknowledgment of what he's done, the other lives he's ended. I don't want there to be any chance of him getting off easy. "There's just one thing I don't know. And since I'm about to die, maybe you could indulge me. Why did you kill Lars? Was it always the plan to frame Eve and discredit her concerns about the Noble Wife movement?"

He strokes his smooth chin. "That's an interesting theory."

"You definitely had me fooled. I was sure Noah shot Lars and you just helped him get away with it. I know how much you love covering for him." When Rick still won't say anything, I press on. "At least for Noah I had what I thought was a solid theory. I was sure Lars had caught him embezzling from Emerald Power."

If he wasn't so good at maintaining his cool, I might have missed it. But even a minor slip in Rick's demeanor is noteworthy. His eyebrow rises for just a moment, and that's when the answer finally becomes clear.

"The big account Lars was working on wasn't Emerald Power." My voice is hoarse, tension and bitter cold drying out my throat. "It was Messiah."

I really am the worst investigator. Everything makes sense now: why Lars was so withdrawn from Eve about his concerns at work, what made him realize I was right not to trust the church, even why he was kicked off the elder board. He must have tested the waters, posing questions about the church's finances. I have no concept of the kind of income Rick brings in, but with the way he has monetized every aspect of his "ministry," I wouldn't be shocked if it was in the millions. And if he tried to claim that was all the church's money, he'd avoid paying a dime in taxes.

I laugh, so suddenly it hurts. "Of course you had to kill Lars. You can cover up a lot of stuff—battered women, child abuse, sexual indiscretion—but fraud? Tax evasion? Those are federal crimes. Your pals at the sheriff's department wouldn't be able to help. Countless women and children can suffer and no one bats an eye, but you can't lie about what you're doing with your money."

"Very good," he says, as if I'm a puppy that just peed on the grass. "You can die knowing you worked it all out. Now take the pills, Delilah."

It's as close to a confession as I'm going to get; hopefully, the recording app on my phone caught it. But I'm not quite ready to give up and die just yet. The edges of a plan start to form in my mind. I grab a handful of pills and pretend to toss them all back, swallowing only a few. The others, I let pour down my sleeve. It's clumsy, though, and he sees one bounce out.

"You can delay all you want, but I'm staying here until you're dead."

"No, you're not."

Finn's voice rings out from the trees. It's only when he steps into view that I realize how much the woods have darkened with the storm, with the coming night. But he's here now, and the relief is so staggering my knees shake.

"Finn!" I scramble to my feet, tears icy on my cheeks. "Careful, he has a gun."

He looks at me, his expression unreadable in the dimming light. Then he turns to Pastor Rick. "You're not killing her."

Rick keeps the gun trained on me. "It's not for you to decide what happens here. Go."

"I'm not leaving."

Finally, Rick looks at him. "Don't be ridiculous."

Finn's nostrils flare. "If you do this, I will tell everyone what I know."

"Then so will I."

I look back and forth between them. My mind battles through the fog again, trying to find purchase on something familiar. "What's going on?"

Rick's lip curls in a sneer. "You think she will want you after she hears the truth? No one is going to take the word of a kill—"

"Don't. Don't say anything else." Finn glances at me for a moment, panic in his eyes. Then he lets out a breath, hanging his head. "She's recording you on her phone."

I STARE AT Finn. I replay the words in my head, trying to get them to make sense. "Finn, what are you doing?"

He refuses to look at me, his head bowed. It's only when he takes a step back from Rick that I realize he's not going to save me.

"Why?" I stay on my feet, looking up at the sky through the trees. I feel suddenly, horribly small. "You . . . you hate him."

"I do," Finn says. "Trust me, I wasn't lying about that."

Rick claps Finn on the shoulder, and then he comes toward me, gun first. "Give me your phone."

It might be the sleeping pills already kicking in, or the heady relief followed by instant betrayal of Finn's presence, but all the fight has gone out of me. If I don't take the pills, he's going to shoot me and frame Nathaniel. He might even kill Finn too. I can't have more ruined lives on my conscience. Rick has been the one pulling the trigger, but Keith was only in the line of fire because of me. Eve might not even be in jail if I had just let the accident explanation be.

I throw my phone in the opposite direction as hard as I can, which is pretty pathetic. It lands in a thick mess of dead grass thirty feet away. Rick doesn't even spare me an annoyed glance as he walks over and digs it out. A few swipes, and the recording that has been going for the last hour is gone. He turns the power off and tosses it up into the tree stand.

Finn's head is still bowed. I take a step toward him. "Why are you doing this? Have you been lying to me this whole time?" Grief and rage threaten to split me apart. There is no proud smirk, no flushed cheeks from staring at my nakedness. Some boys look a girl in the eyes when they tear her apart; others hang their heads. But the slap of betrayal feels the same.

His eyes stay on the ground.

I look between him and Rick. "What does he have over you?"

That gets Finn's attention. When his gaze meets mine, I am hollowed out by the sadness there.

"Young Finn Walsh," Pastor Rick says, watching both of us with something like amusement. "He was part of Messiah back when I first came on as the youth pastor. That was a few years before you arrived, Delilah. The Walshes were devout members, pillars of the Elden community who made the twenty-minute drive every Sunday to be with their Messiah family. Mr. and Mrs. Walsh . . . and their two sons."

Finn's eyes fill with tears. He's mentioned his parents before, but he never said anything about a brother.

I suddenly want—more than I have ever wanted—to make Rick stop talking.

"I really don't need your help with this, Finn," he says. "You've done your part by letting me know Del was here."

My head spins.

Pastor Rick smiles. "You thought he was paying such close attention because he cared about you. No, I needed someone to tell me what you were doing. Who you were talking to. That is, when his attempts to scare you away didn't work."

I feel like I'm falling. "The motel . . . You broke into my room. You made those calls."

Finn's mouth trembles; he wipes his face, sucking a wet breath through his nose.

Everything that has happened in the past two weeks plays across my mind. All our chats in the bar, brainstorming theories about the case. The flirtation, the instant connection. Bad-mouthing Messiah and Rick Franklin was just to get me to trust him, to confide in him what I was learning. It was all for *him*.

"Take those pills, Delilah."

"Fuck you." The words aren't as ferocious as I'd like, but just saying them to a pastor feels powerful. I unscrew the top of the pill bottle and throw it behind me, the capsules scattering across the snow.

Rick sighs, taking stock of our location. "All right, then. Change of plans." He grabs my wrist, turns me around, and shoves the gun into my spine. His mouth comes up next to my ear.

"Walk," he commands.

I push back against him, but my feet move forward to keep from falling when Rick pushes me in return. As I pass him, I try to catch Finn's eye.

"Please, Finn. Please don't let him do this. There's still time to stop it."

"Move." Rick knows where he's going, and I'm nearly running to keep up with his pace, stumbling every few feet over a fallen branch or a divot in the ground. It's marshy and sunken in this section of woods. The water is frozen, which keeps me from getting soaked every time I fall, but the ice cracks hard against my knees.

A few minutes later, we stop. In front of me, the ground drops away for ten feet or so. It's as if a large hand has reached down and grabbed a chunk of the earth. At the bottom of the pit, branches and dead wet leaves poke through a light layer of snow. The roots of a nearby oak jut out of the side a few feet away from me.

And I know exactly what Rick is going to do.

When his hands shove against my back, I'm ready, but it doesn't help. There's a sickening moment when I'm flying through the air, my limbs thrashing. I land on my feet, but my right ankle turns badly, and I crumple onto my stomach. Mercifully, most of my body is numb from the cold already, but I still feel a dull shot of pain. When I cry out, dirt fills my mouth.

"Actually, this is better, thank you," Rick says from above me. "You went wandering in the woods, in search of some ridiculous shred of evidence that Eve was innocent, and you stumbled and fell into this pit. Likely as a result of taking too many sleeping pills to soothe your anxiety. Tragic."

I groan, pull my knee up to check my ankle.

"Let's go."

"No." Finn's voice is fierce. "I'm not going to just let her die."

I turn my head, peering up through the fading light. Finn's face is almost unrecognizable, etched with fury. Rick grabs his coat, pulling him in close to say something I can't hear. After a moment, he steps back, and Finn's shoulders sag. My heart drops with them.

Rick stares down at me for several seconds. I refuse to look away. "What a waste," he says, nearly spitting on the last word. And then he turns and disappears from the edge of the pit.

SIXTY-TWO

[DRAFT]

Noble Wife Journey: a blog
Title: Bella
Last updated: November 2, 2021

I don't think I've ever been truly afraid until tonight. It's after two in the morning, and my heart is still hammering. Every time I close my eyes, I see the rage on his face again.

Bella Chase was one of my mentees. A short, prim girl with a narrow face and thick blond hair. I've known her since she was born. When she was fifteen, I had just gotten married to Lars and she approached me, asking if I would be her accountability partner and mentor on her Noble Wife journey. Of course, I was delighted.

I watched her grow from a tiny slip of a teenager into a beautiful, demure, strong, virtuous young woman. I watched the boys in Messiah gawk at her no matter how she covered herself, and it was no surprise when she had a handful of offers the moment she turned eighteen.

Why she chose Brian Schmidt I will never know. I told her what I thought of him, as gently yet directly as I could. But she was in love, and he was the handsomest boy in her grade, and they were inseparable from the moment it was allowed. They married at nineteen, both of them sharing their first kiss at the altar, just as we were told it should be. It was perfect, storybook.

Except she didn't tell anyone he was hitting her.

I know now that it started two months before their wedding. She wrote it off as sexual frustration, sure that he would stop once they were able to consummate their desire for each other. He didn't. But then she got pregnant almost immediately, and he started taking better care of her. She relaxed, thinking they had just been through a rough patch and now he would be better.

Instead, he found other ways of controlling her body. After twenty-six hours of labor and a vicious delivery of their son, he announced they were going straight home. He didn't want her or their child to stay overnight in a hospital. She was exhausted, scared, in pain, and overwhelmed with the hormones of new motherhood, and she didn't want to fight. Luckily, nothing terrible happened to her or the baby.

From his perspective, that only proved he was right. He decided when she would stop breastfeeding, when they would get pregnant with another child, who was allowed to babysit. She had two more kids in three more years, and his violence only seemed to increase with each one. Like as soon as he got what he wanted and wasn't happy, he took it out on her.

She told me all this last week, and I had to force myself not to react. I wanted to scream and sob. I wanted to ask her why she didn't tell me sooner. It would only have made things worse. I know why she felt she couldn't, and I will have to find a way to earn her forgiveness one day.

Today, Brian burst into the church office and charged past my desk. He screamed at Keith, accused him of trying to ruin his marriage. Somehow, he had found out that Bella was speaking to Keith. Pastor Rick came out and managed to calm him down enough to coax him into his office. I kept my expression pleasant behind my desk, even as I listened to the senior pastor tell this violent man that his frustration was understandable. When they were gone, Keith looked at me from his doorway, and his expression told me everything I needed to know.

It was time to get Bella out. I ran to my car. The Schmidt house is only ten minutes from the church, but I sped the whole way there like Brian was directly behind me. When Bella let me in, the left side of her face was purple and swollen. Her eyes were feral, panicked, darting around as if her husband would jump out from behind me and attack her at any moment.

I told her we had ten minutes. I threw as many of the kids' clothes into bags as I could while she packed her own. Eight minutes later, she had the baby strapped to her chest and the toddler on her hip, while I grabbed the hand of her oldest and made our way out the door. We were just getting them in their car seats when the garage door started to open.

Brian was home.

Bella started humming, a high-pitched, terrified sound, and her hands were shaking too much to do up the last strap. I shoved her into the passenger's side, clipped her son in, and jumped into the driver's seat. I hit the automatic lock and waited until her husband had pulled his car in far enough that he wouldn't be able to block us.

Then I reversed as quickly as I dared.

Their garage opens out into an alley shared by everyone else on their block, so I had to turn on a right angle. He came bounding after us, shouting words that I'd never heard in my life but knew were profane. Bella clapped her hands over her mouth, trying to keep her sobs from her children.

The car stopped as I shifted it from reverse to drive, and he yanked on the handle of her door. When that didn't work, he threw himself in front of us. I looked at Bella, told her I was sorry, and hit the gas.

He jumped out of the way, because if there's one thing I know about Brian Schmidt, it's that he cares about himself more than anything else. The kids were crying by the time we got onto the main road, which gave Bella something to do. She focused on calming them down while I took a few random turns until I could be sure he wasn't following us.

We left town. Keith met us at a hotel in Dilworth, and he used his card to put them up for the next couple nights until we figure out what to do. When I left her, she was exhausted but more relaxed than I've seen her in years.

I don't know what happens now. We have to figure out how to get her away from here.

I've been writing about this for years, and it only just occurred to me that I have sold the Noble Wife ideals not just to women but to men. We know what we're striving to become, but the men in Messiah—the men who read my blog—they know what they can expect. There is no instruction for them here, no behavioral guidelines. Only a list of the virtues they should seek in women: chief among them, subservience.

I don't think Brian will come after me, but only because I'm not what he wants. He wants what he thinks he earned, the pure and submissive wife who will give in to his every whim.

And while I think Pastor Rick is mostly to blame for that, I can't pretend I didn't play a role. All those years I mentored her, all those times I encouraged her to respect him no matter what. Bella has to figure out how to rebuild her life away from the man she loved with three small children she never expected to care for on her own.

I could have helped her sooner. I could have seen what was happening if I had been willing to look. I could have realized this blog was acting as a shopping list of qualities for selfish men who have no interest in upholding their end of the biblical marriage bargain.

The fact that I didn't—that's on me.

SIXTY-THREE

FOR A WHILE, I JUST lie here. My instinct is to curl up on my side, hug my knees into my chest for warmth, so that's what I do. At least, down here in the pit, I am sheltered from the worst of the wind.

I know that won't save me, though. I did not dress warmly, thinking I'd just be outside for a half hour at most, and that was when the weather was above freezing. The sun is dropping fast, taking the temperature with it.

When I finally lift my head, I see that my body is covered with thick, flossy snowflakes.

There are two kinds of blizzards in Minnesota. The first is like an apocalypse, icy pellets of snow blowing so hard they're like needles on your face. Winds cold enough to freeze the snot in your nose and the tears on your eyelashes. They howl through the countryside, blowing drifts the size of tractors and making it impossible to see two feet in front of you. Blizzards like that kill people, every time.

And there are the ones like this, the deceptively beautiful. Fat blankets of snow cover the world to make it look like a fairy tale. During the day, temperatures are balmy, and kids run out in their suits and boots to pelt each other with snowballs.

Then the night comes. Everything that has melted suddenly freezes, the roads becoming a maze of slush and black ice. Winds pick up and temperatures fall, and anyone left outside is faced with a cold so damp and bitter it drives all the warmth of the day straight out of you.

I am numb to my bones, and further in. Numb to my soul. Finn turning on me shouldn't be a surprise. It's clear I have terrible taste in boy-friends, but I didn't expect one to eventually preside over my death.

"Are you going to say anything?" Finn sounds far away, even though the drop is probably only eight feet down. The sides of the pit are all dirt and thin roots—impossible to climb even if I didn't have an injured ankle.

"I feel like Joseph." I roll onto my back, chuckling bitterly. "Of course Pastor Rick would find a way to kill me that looks like some kind of bib-lical metaphor. Joseph got thrown into a pit because his brothers didn't like how he flaunted his coat and his dreams. I'm here for flaunting my knowledge that Rick Franklin can't be trusted."

Above me, Finn's face peeks over the edge. He shivers, but at least he's got on a warm coat, hat, and gloves. He'll be fine for a while, but I don't know why he's still here. Whatever Rick said to him before he left, it was enough of a threat that he's not trying to save me.

"So, if you're just going to sit there and watch me die, do you mind at least telling me how all this happened?" My voice is slurred, and I feel oddly calm. Every part of my body is comfortingly heavy, and the pain in my ankle has settled to a dull throb. Guess that handful of pills will make this whole thing easier.

Finn looks away for a moment. Then he sits down, his legs dangling into the pit. "What do you want to know?"

I sit up and shuffle to the wall. I'm vaguely aware of dampness seeping through my jeans, but there's no avoiding it. At least this way, I don't feel quite as vulnerable. I keep my knees pulled into my chest, trying to hold my bad leg up to avoid too much pressure on my ankle.

"How long have you been working for Pastor Rick?"

"I'm not working for him."

"Come on, Finn. You were the only one who knew I was coming here. You shouldn't even know where Noah lives, but here you are. You're involved in this."

He's quiet for a moment. "I swear I didn't know about him killing Lars. I thought you were right, that it was Eve and Keith, and Rick was just covering it up at first. I wanted you to find the truth, finally expose him for who he is. Why do you think I introduced you to Parker?"

"Cut the crap, will you? You're sitting there, doing nothing. You might not be pulling a trigger, but you're responsible for this too."

"That's not true. This is on him; it's all on him."

The wind sends a spray of snow from the ground into the pit. I blink, rubbing my eyes.

"You scared me," I say, trying not to cry. "You ransacked my room and freaked me out enough to run away from my motel in the middle of the night, and then you acted all concerned when I told you about it later."

A fresh surge of hurt wells up as I think about him pushing me against the hood of his car, kissing me like I was the only person he could think about. For all my claims about no longer trusting men after what happened with Lars, the truth is that I still give myself to them freely, clinging to every new scrap of male attention with the hope that he will be the one.

I hate everything I was taught about being a wife, and yet part of me hasn't let go of the idea that I will finally feel whole if I become one.

"I'm sorry, Del." Finn's voice is raw. "I didn't have a choice. He's blackmailing me."

I peer up at him. "Over what?"

"Does it matter?" His heel kicks the side of the pit. "The point is, I don't want you to die thinking I did this because I wanted to. I did it because the only other option was to let him ruin my family."

"So, you're going to watch me die."

He looks up. On nights when it snows, even in the country, the sky maintains an orange glow that doesn't disappear for hours. That's why I can see the snowflakes catch on his hat, melt on his face. That's why I can see the tears on his cheeks when his gaze returns to me.

"I killed my brother when I was seventeen." A gust of wind blows the curls peeking out from his stocking hat. His eyes look black. "It was an accident. Or at least that's what it looked like. But I could have stopped it. I could have . . . I could have helped him, and I chose not to."

My throat is tight with questions I don't dare ask.

After a moment, he goes on. "Erik was always the good kid. He was a good student, but he was an even better musician. A prodigy, everyone said. He was on the Messiah worship team from the time he was four-teen, and he already had offers for scholarships at creative arts colleges by the time he was sixteen. Meanwhile, I was a year older and getting ready to graduate, and I could barely keep my GPA up enough to get in anywhere. My parents basically told me I was just going to take over Elaine's. They knew I wasn't capable of doing anything else."

"What happened?" I finally ask.

"We were ice fishing. The winter of my senior year, just a few months before I graduated. It had been warm for a couple weeks, but then we had another cold snap, and everyone said the ice was still okay. So we went out. Even though we didn't get along much, that was one thing Erik and I liked to do together. We'd been out for a half hour, and we didn't have much to say to each other. Erik had auditioned for a summer pro-gram at some fancy school, and he walked back to the truck to get his phone and check his email. We had a rule when we were on the ice—no phones. But I told him it was fine since it was special circumstances."

Finn pauses, looking down at me. I know I've started to slump against the wall. My arm muscles ache from holding up my ankle, and the drugs in my system are making everything hazy. But I can still hear his voice, see his face in the bronze glow. "Are you still awake?" he asks.

"Still here. So, what, he fell through the ice?"

"When he went outside, he saw the truck was sinking. He called for me, and I came out. I told him to leave the truck, that we had to run. But he'd just bought it a few months before, and it was like his prized posses-sion. He was sure he could jump in and back it off the ice really quick be-fore it broke. I told him it was a bad idea." Finn shakes his head. "Once Erik got something in his head, he didn't let it go. I think that's what made him such a great musician. When he wanted to conquer some-thing, no one could talk him out of it."

He licks his bottom lip, shaking his head. "The ice cracked as soon as Erik got in the truck, but he kept going. I yelled at him to get out, but he started the engine and put it in reverse. He got part of the way off the spot. Then the ice gave way, and the whole front of the truck sank. He opened his door and tried to get out, but the edge of the ice was block-ing it. I had a rope in the icehouse. I had time to run and get it, try to help him get out through the window. He looked at me, standing there, and he yelled, 'What are you doing?' But I just . . . didn't move. I was so mad at him for not listening. For thinking he could just do whatever he wanted. I thought, 'Maybe if he gets doused with some cold water, he'll realize he's not invincible.' And then the ice cracked more, and the water swallowed the truck whole."

I don't know how long I sit there. My tongue feels swollen in my mouth, my whole body strangely warm. I know this means I'm getting hypothermia. I know this means death is terrifyingly close. And I know that what Finn just said should shock me, but it feels impossible to connect any emotion to my brain at all.

"He managed to get out of the truck at some point, but he must have gotten lost in the water. They didn't find his body for two days. My parents were devastated, obviously. And the whole church, the whole town, mourned him like he was a martyr. I felt like everyone blamed me, even though no one knew what had happened."

There is a prickling of familiarity to this story now. Someone in high school talked about a boy who drowned after breaking through the ice. It was used as a warning to keep us off the lake when we were at a weekend retreat out at the Franklins', I think. No one mentioned his brother was with him, at least not that I remember.

Finn continues. "For a while, I was able to deal with the guilt on my own. I didn't want him to die. I thought if he fell through, he would get out and I would lay across the ice and pull him up, and I would be a hero for once instead of just the stupid older brother who couldn't do anything right. But he never came up. I think I was numb for weeks, but once that wore off, I had nightmares. I was consumed by guilt. Telling my parents wasn't an option. I knew they would never forgive me. So finally, when I felt like I couldn't stand it anymore, I asked Pastor Rick if I could talk to him in his office. And I told him everything."

I know as well as anyone what that confession would have looked like. The hard stare, the open promise of forgiveness if you would just make sure he knows every last thought that was in your head as you committed the sin you can't shake loose. Pastor Rick would have feasted on Finn's confession like carrion.

"*Leave out no detail. You know that saying, 'The devil is in the details.' Do you want the devil in you?*"

"He told me he was obligated to report what I said to the police." Finn hangs his head. "Then he said that he wouldn't do it, but only if I swore to never tell another soul, and only if I would remember that I owed him. If I would do those two things, I could be forgiven. I promised, and he kept his word. For a while, I kept going on Sunday, but I felt like every message Rick preached was directed at me. All his talk about brotherly love and honoring your parents—it was like he looked me in the eyes every time he said those things. Once I graduated, I left and never went back. And for more than a decade, I thought it was over."

"Until I came to town." The words are mealy, sticky in my mouth. I am so, so tired.

"He didn't know right away. The connection you and I had, the offer of the job—it was real." He looks down at me, trying to catch my gaze, which feels impossible to focus on for more than a few seconds. "I don't know why, but I feel like you should know that. He came to me the day after you got to Elden, and he said he was calling in his favor. He wanted me to get you to leave town."

I blink. "You did a good job."

For a moment, he hangs his head. "He told me about you, what happened when you were sixteen. Not all the details, but enough that I knew you would be insecure about being a backslider, just like I was. That verse in John was one he used on me a dozen times. Then when that didn't work, I resorted to the old horror movie tactics."

Knowing it was Finn now, the heavy breathing on the phone seems ridiculous. I can't believe I let it freak me out so much.

"And then you became his spy? Told him all the theories I was talking through with you so he would know what he needed to cover up, who he needed to get to before me?"

Pursing his lips, Finn nods.

Then my mouth falls open. "Did you tell him I was going to talk to Keith?"

"When?"

"That night we got wasted. I told you I was going to his house the next day to get him to confess. Did you tell Rick?"

His guilty silence is answer enough.

"That's why Rick killed him."

The color drains from Finn's face. "No."

"It is. That was right after Eve was arrested. If Keith was ever going to be ready to talk, it was then. He would have told me what he and Eve were doing, and I would have tried to convince him to tell the police. That would have messed with Rick's plan."

Elbows on his knees, Finn buries his face in his hands. "I never thought he would do this. I didn't know he was *capable* of this."

"How many more people have to die, Finn?" I ask. "You could go to the police now, tell them everything that's happened."

"He'll pin everything on me," Finn says. "That's what he told me before he left just now, when I said I was done helping him. I don't know how, but you know as well as I do that Rick always has a backup plan for his backup plan. And he has me on tape, confessing to killing my brother. My parents have already lost one son, and my mom is sick. This news would kill her."

My eyes close. Every breath has started to hurt, a dull ache in my chest. I imagine my lungs are freezing even though I have no idea if that's possible.

The desire for sleep is all-consuming. It would be easy to just fade away. To surrender to Pastor Rick's manipulation, one more time.

I was always told women would never be stronger than men. That was why we had to put our lives in their hands.

If you are willing to let him hold your dreams and worries, to lay your body down for him—you can trust that any decision he makes for you is the right one. That's the Noble Wife way.

But I'm not a Noble Wife. And I'm not ready to give up yet.

I look back up at Finn. His head is buried in his hands. He looks so miserable, this man who's letting me die—who wrote a Bible verse in lipstick on my mirror. I don't know if it's the medication or delirium from hypothermia, but it suddenly strikes me as incredibly funny. Too tired to restrain myself, I let out a hysterical giggle.

Finn gapes at me.

I snort, then cover my mouth, knowing I should be embarrassed but too far gone to care. "He's making you do the same thing you did to your brother."

"What?"

"He's making you watch me die when you could prevent it." I shake my head, laughing some more. "Don't you get it, Finn? He knows that what happened to Erik was an accident. You might think you could have stopped it, but you probably would have drowned too if you had tried to help him. That wasn't murder. It probably wasn't even manslaughter, and you were a minor. Even if it did come out now, there's almost no chance you'd be charged with anything."

He shakes his head. "No, I've looked it up. When you and I . . . the night we kissed, I told him I was done working with him. He said the police could charge me as an adult. I was almost eighteen, and my actions showed 'intentional disregard for human life,' he said. With my confession on tape, I could be looking at twenty years in prison."

I snort again. When he glares at me, I clear my throat. "Sorry. It's just, I'm so used to being the one who falls for Rick Franklin's BS, it's funny to be hearing it from the outside." I take a deep breath, trying to hold back my laughter as I wipe away tears. I feel outside myself, knowing none of this is funny but unable to control my reaction.

Finally, I can speak again. "When you're alone with him, listening to what he says, it all sounds so real. So threatening. But think about it, Finn. You warned your brother about going to the truck. You told him to get out when the ice started to crack. And you were probably bigger than him, right? If you had gotten closer, trying to help, the ice would have just broken faster. The only thing you're guilty of is choosing to save your own life instead of making your parents lose two sons."

"That isn't true."

"I know you think that." The air down in the pit is so stuffy. I'm jealous of the wind I see lifting Finn's hair. Sliding my sleeves down my arms, I lift my sweater over my head.

"Don't do that. It's freezing."

I giggle again. "Isn't that the point?"

"You're getting hypothermia. That's why you feel hot."

"Well, then, I guess you can just leave. I'm not going to last much longer." In just my long-sleeved shirt, I sit back against the wall with a sigh. Finn's hat is coated with freshly fallen snow, but not much has made its way down here. I'm sad about that. It looks so soft. When I was a kid, I used to love lying in a fresh snowdrift, closing my eyes. Pretending I was a bear about to hibernate.

"Don't worry," I say, my voice dreamy. "This isn't so bad. There are worse ways to die." Then I realize something. "That's why you got Parker involved, isn't it? You wanted her to find something on Rick that had nothing to do with you, so he could be discredited without your secret coming out."

Finn lets out a sharp breath. "I thought you were on to something with Keith and Eve, and I figured if she could get dirt on them, it would come back to Rick somehow anyway. Win-win."

"Mm. Except apparently, we all lose."

We're both quiet for a long moment. Then, Finn stands up. "He really is manipulating me, isn't he?"

"Yep." I yawn. "Don't feel bad. He's very good at it."

"And if you die, he has something new to hold over me."

His words cut through the fog of drugs and hypothermia. I force my eyes to focus on his, as much as I can in the burnished glow of the snowy night sky. "That's right."

Finn paces at the edge of the pit.

With great effort, I sit up straighter. "Finn, Rick Franklin has hurt a lot of people. He's killed at least two. We know that. We might not have evidence, but we can testify to what he told us. Only I can't do that if I'm dead."

"If you don't die tonight, he'll just find another way."

I pause. "You're right. Who's going to believe us?"

"He said he's already set me up for all of this: Eve, Keith, everything."

"He might be lying. He does that, you know. Very un-Christian of him." My acerbic joke falls flat. After a long moment, I say, "Don't you get it, Finn? He's never going to stop."

He looks down at me. Without another word, he walks away from the pit.

Fear grips me. I know that I'm going to die now, but I didn't actually think I would be alone. As awful as it is, having Finn watch over me as I faded away felt comforting somehow. I wonder how long it will take for someone to look for me. I wonder if anyone ever will. My body might lie in this pit forever, until I become dust that blows out into the universe. I guess that isn't so bad.

I close my eyes, trying to relax.

HOURS, OR MAYBE seconds later, something rough hits me in the face.

My eyelids are heavy, but I can see Finn is back, holding something in his hands. "I had to get this from my car. Sit in the loop I made and hold on."

Dumbly, I stare at the rope. "You're saving me?" I ask.

"Delilah, I don't know how much longer you have. Will you just do what I said?"

My ankle spasms with pain when I try to stand. Gasping, I shift onto my good side and use my arms to heave myself forward until I can sit in the ring. "Okay," I say, gripping the upper part of the rope in my hands.

After a few false starts, I get the hang of balancing, and I feel my body lift off the ground. Above me, Finn grunts with effort, but I make fast progress. A minute later, I am at the top of the pit, peering over. Finn has used a thick branch as a pulley so he can yank down on the rope with his full body weight. He looks back, seeing me at the edge.

"Hang on." He ties it tightly to another tree to avoid losing progress, then runs to the pit. Grabbing me under the armpits, he pulls me over the side. I start to lumber into a standing position, but he quickly sweeps me into his arms. "We've got to get you some heat."

Instead of running back to the clearing, he takes off in a different direction. There's no path, but he seems to know where he's going. A few minutes later, we're out in a field, where I can see a car running with the lights on low.

"Cameras," I mumble.

"Yeah, Rick told me about them, so I drove in on the field." He dumps me in the passenger seat of the car. The heat is already cranked up. "Don't warm your hands. Hold your chest up to the vents, otherwise all the cold will move from your limbs to your heart."

I cut my eyes at him. "I grew up here too, dummy."

In the red glow of his car dashboard, Finn smiles. "Glad to see you're still with it." Then he shifts the car into reverse, and we're on our way.

SIXTY-FOUR

THE FIRST THING IS BEEPING. A slow, melodic chime. That's what brings me out of whatever darkness I've been in.

I'm in the hospital. That sound and the smell of disinfectant are unmistakable. It takes a few minutes to remember how to open my eyes. When I do, the room glares white. I squint, trying to make out the shape next to me.

"You're awake!" I recognize Susan's voice before her face comes into focus. Deep shadows sit under her red-rimmed eyes, but she looks thrilled to see me.

"I guess I am," I rasp.

There's a sharp pinch, and I look down to see a cannula in the top of my hand, which she's currently clenching between hers.

"Ow."

"Oh, sorry. They told me a couple hours ago that you would probably come to soon, so I've been anxious at how long it was taking."

"You're up!" Nathaniel strides into the room, holding two cups of coffee. The smell jogs some life into my senses.

"Is one of those for me?" I ask.

He looks embarrassed, but Susan takes a cup out of his hands and gives it to me. "It is now. I hope you don't mind it black."

Nathaniel steps closer. "Should we ask the nurse—"

"It's hot, right?" Susan says, tucking a short strand of hair behind my ear. "She needs warming up."

I chuckle and take a sip. It's hospital coffee, but it tastes like heaven regardless. After another drink, I set it on the table stretched over my bed and look between the two of them. "What happened?"

Nathaniel sits in the chair on the other side of my bed. "You're being treated for severe hypothermia. The hospital staff says someone carried you into the emergency room, told everyone you had been out in the cold for several hours, and then ran off as soon as he saw you were being treated. You've been unconscious ever since, but they stabilized you within a few hours."

"So, I'll be okay?" It seems impossible. I remember Finn yelling at me to stay with him, driving through the night at speeds I was sure would kill me before the cold did.

"That's what the doctors have told us." The sound of my dad's voice makes me sit up straighter. He's standing at the door to my room, calm as ever. But I can see the relief in his eyes when he looks at me. "They've given you warm intravenous fluid and used heat packs to bring up your body temperature. Your right ankle got a bad sprain and you're a little dehydrated, but you'll be fine."

Tears collect in my eyes.

"I should go get your mother," Dad says. He hesitates at the door. "She's just grabbing lunch."

Susan stands. "No, you sit. I'll get her."

"Mom's here?" I ask as Susan hurries out the door. Dad takes her place, gingerly putting a hand on mine. Suddenly, I want him to wrap me up in his arms more than anything in the world.

"Of course she's here," Dad says. "We were so worried, honey." And then he leans forward, responding to my wish without even knowing it. Careful not to disturb any of the machines connected to me, he pulls me in for a warm, gentle hug.

I could not have described the way my dad smells, but my body has not forgotten it. The scent of his soap curls around me, bringing me home. We're still sitting like that when Susan returns with my mother.

My chin is hooked over my dad's shoulder as she walks into my line of sight. Reluctantly, I give him one more squeeze and pull away.

"Delilah." For years, my name has been a disappointment on her lips. Today, it's a relief. She stands at the end of the bed, holding two paper bags that are already spotted with grease. The smell of toasted bread and melted cheese makes my stomach grumble.

"Mom."

She shifts her weight from one foot to the other. "The police were here, but they left a few hours ago. They want to know who the man was that brought you in."

I chew my bottom lip. I don't know what crime he committed, but I'm guessing dropping a half-dead woman in the ER and splitting is illegal somehow. "I don't know," I say after a moment. "It's all a blur."

She studies me for a moment, in that way she did when I was younger and she was trying to decide if I was lying. I rarely lied to her, though. There was no point, and the guilt of being dishonest wasn't worth saving myself from whatever trouble I wanted out of.

"We should give you some time." Susan sends her husband a pointed look, but I can tell Nathaniel has questions he's dying to ask.

"It's all right." The weight of exhaustion pulls at me again. It's worth answering all their questions now if it means I can avoid telling the same story multiple times. "What do you want to know?"

Nathaniel leans forward in his seat. "What happened? Eve's dad said you went out to Noah's farm. Did you get stranded? I wish you would have told me; I would have gone with you."

"Nat . . ." Susan starts.

"No, it's okay." My gaze falls to my hands, curled in my lap on top of a thick stack of hospital blankets. "I thought I could convince Noah to confess. I was sure he killed Lars, but it turns out I was wrong."

I can feel my mother looking at me, but I know if I see the expression on her face, I might be tempted to stop. I sit for a moment, building up courage.

"When the police come back, I'm going to tell them what happened, so you might as well hear it from me first. You probably won't believe me, but I've got to try."

"Del, after the day we've had, I am pretty ready to believe just about anything," my dad says.

The use of my chosen name gives me the extra courage I need. I take a deep breath. "Pastor Rick killed Lars and Keith. He admitted it, right before he tried to kill me too."

Their faces register varying levels of shock, but no one protests, so I continue. "I went to Noah's hunting patch to see if I could find evidence he was lying about what happened the day Lars was killed, and Rick came out of nowhere, holding a gun on me. He said he was tired of me bothering his family and the church, and he forced me to take drugs and pushed me in a pit, leaving me to die." I hadn't thought about how I was going to keep Finn out of this, so I try to invent something on the fly. "At some point I lost consciousness, and then I remember being in a car. Someone must have found me and taken me to the hospital."

I know Nathaniel and Susan will be on my side, so I don't even look at them. My mother is clearly fighting the temptation to say something, but it's the expression on my dad's face that cuts through. He's not watching me with disbelief—just incredible, tremendous sadness. He must think I've lost my mind.

I sit up, my heart hammering. "It's true, okay? I know it sounds crazy, but I would never lie about something like this. That's what happened."

"Oh, honey," my dad says. He looks at my mom and then back at me. "I believe you. It's just . . . well, you should know that Pastor Rick was killed in the middle of the night at his house. Someone shot him."

I blink, sitting back. When I look at Nathaniel, he nods.

My dad continues. "The police haven't said whether there are any suspects, but if all this happened with you just before, they're going to have questions."

It feels like my blood is still sluggish and cold, not quite bringing oxygen to my brain as fast as it should. Obviously, I'll be questioned. At least my near-dead state will back up my story and make it clear to investigators I was in no condition to go murder somebody, but if they can't find anything to connect Rick to Lars's and Keith's murders, they're going to assume whoever killed Rick did it because of what he did to me. And the list of people who love me enough to bother with revenge is painfully short.

My mom has tears in her eyes. I know Pastor Rick and Messiah mean a lot to her, so I try not to be angry at her sadness. Assuming she believes me at all, she's not just mourning him—she's mourning the man she thought he was.

Nathaniel clears his throat. "A few hours before Rick's body was found, a story was released in the *Daily Chronicle* about the corruption and abuse he perpetrated at Messiah. Of course, they couldn't have known how bad the timing would be."

Parker came through. Yes, the timing looks bad, but it's actually perfect. All the dirt coming out about Rick, and no Rick to spin it for his benefit.

"We expected it to be the usual vague accusations about cult behavior, but this one is different," my dad says. "There's so much evidence. I'd heard some stories, but seeing them all together like that—it's shocking. Apparently, Lars had raised concerns with the elders about the church's financial reports and Rick's tax returns. He discovered Rick was using the church's charity, Messiah Ministries, to grant himself large housing allowances. But Pastor Rick owned his house outright, and the allowances went far above what he needed for property taxes and utilities, so it looks like he just treated the money as tax-free income. He also had a credit card in the ministry's name that he used to make purchases for himself, writing them off as supplies for one of the businesses they owned. The journalist found emails between Lars and his boss, where he detailed the crimes Rick and the church could be charged with if he was to report them."

I rest my head back on the pillow, trying to absorb it all.

"Are you okay?" Susan asks. She looks like she's holding herself back from coming over to rest the back of her hand on my forehead.

"I'm fine," I whisper, then look at my mother. "You believed me. When I said that Rick tried to kill me. Is that why? Because of the story?"

Her head drops, a light sob escaping her chest. "I didn't want to take the article seriously when I read it. You know how the journalists are around here; everyone is always trying to find a reason to hate Messiah. I'm a woman in the church, and I never had any of the problems those ladies were talking about." She takes a long, shaky breath and meets my gaze. "I know how awful that sounds. But at the end of the piece, there was a video. They think it was taken right before Rick was killed. He admitted to everything."

"Oh." I don't know what else to say. All those stories of battered women and financial deception weren't enough to convince my mother. She had to hear it from the mouth of the man himself. At least that finally broke the spell.

My dad's eyes are wet. Anger and defiance war on Nathaniel's face, and my heart twists at the tears pouring down Susan's. They don't say anything, but I know they're relieved. They finally know what happened to their son. It won't make losing him easier, but hopefully it will answer some of the questions that have tormented them.

Dad takes my hand. "This has been a day of grief, but also incredible gratitude. You're still here. We came so close to losing you. You were right, when you visited us the other day. Everything you said. We should have listened sooner."

I look at my mother, to see if he really is speaking for both of them. She sets down their lunch and steps toward us, standing next to my dad.

"I don't know what to think," she whispers. As if annoyed at herself for crying, she rolls her eyes to the ceiling. "I still can't understand why he would do anything like this. But here you are. And right now, I'm just glad you're okay."

Finally, her hand rests on my thigh, squeezing it through the blankets.

A sob builds in my chest. I close my eyes, letting it out. Gently, they both lean in to hold me. When they pull away, I notice Nathaniel and Susan have slipped out of the room.

I take a deep breath through my nose, sniffling. "How's Esha? And Mr. Thompson?"

"They're both recovering," my mom says, shaking her head. "Such a horrible accident. Honestly, this used to be a quiet town."

I won't tell her—not yet. She's on the edge, and I feel like one more outrageous accusation about Rick might flip her back into protective mode.

After a few more minutes, I can't hold back my yawn any longer. My mother immediately assumes the role of caretaker, something I haven't seen in years. She tucks the blankets in tight around me and shoos my dad out of the room. They switch off the overhead light as they leave.

I should close my eyes and go to sleep, but the exhaustion won't take me yet. For a long moment, I stare at the ceiling, relief and guilt wrestling in my mind. Rick is dead. He can't hurt anyone ever again. If Finn gets caught, it means Rick succeeded in destroying his life after all. But at least it will be the last one.

I should be thrilled. Instead, a creeping sadness is taking over. The article coming out on the day Rick was killed isn't as perfect as I first thought.

Because I know what's going to happen now. Rick Franklin was an expert at getting people on his side, at turning his congregation into mercenaries, willing to go to battle for him even when he wasn't present. I think of those elders, turning away from two women begging them to care about what had happened to so many. The financial crimes might be enough to get the police involved, or at least take a closer look, but the story will get twisted by Messiah leadership all the same.

Pastor Rick Franklin, a martyr—killed in his own home after being coerced into confessing to something he didn't do. His name dragged through the mud by the biased media on the very day of his tragic death. Eve might go free—enough reasonable doubt to sway a jury—but I doubt Rick will lose a drop of power, even in death.

Whoever takes over at the Mess will face not a repentant elder board acknowledging the harm they've allowed, but a group of men more certain than ever that their leader was a prophet in his time. And just like biblical prophets, he faced overwhelming forces fighting against him until he was ultimately silenced.

Rick Franklin is dead, and some members like my parents might finally have their doubts about him. But Messiah leadership will do everything they can to make sure the man's legacy lives forever—untarnished and above reproach.

SIXTY-FIVE

I HAVE A STRONG SENSE of déjà vu, walking into Eve's living room with her and Esha. Esha was discharged from the hospital yesterday, a few hours before Eve was released from jail. It took a couple weeks after everything happened with Rick, but all the charges have finally been dropped. To avoid the obvious conflict of interest with Sheriff Wilson, the Clay County police are now investigating the crimes Rick admitted to on video, as well as the accident that killed his wife eight years ago. We were always told she must have swerved to avoid hitting an animal, but clearly he had the ability to tamper with a vehicle—and to kill someone he professed to love. From the outside, Hillary Franklin was the perfect Noble Wife, but if she stood in the way of him and his ambitions, that would have been enough to make her his first victim.

We may never know how many lives Rick chose to snuff out, in one way or another.

As the least injured one among the three of us, Eve sets about making tea while Esha and I chat about our recovery. My ankle is still tender and weak, but I have started putting weight on it again and only need the one crutch to walk. Esha will have a much longer journey. Her broken leg will lay her up for a while, but she and her husband are driving back down to the Cities tomorrow. Understandably, after weeks in Bower, she wants the comfort of home.

On the floor in the corner of the room, Emmanuelle sits with a stack of blocks and a purple plastic car, playing quietly. When she glances up at me with those familiar brown eyes, I have to take a steadying breath. I don't know if I will ever stop missing Lars.

"I saw your blog post last night," I say, as soon as Eve hands me my tea and sits down. "That was fast."

Her fingers trace the rim of her cup. "I wrote and rewrote it in my head a hundred times while I was in that cell," she says. "I should have written it a month ago."

Not surprisingly, it went viral on Facebook and has already been viewed over two hundred thousand times. It's one of Eve's longest posts, detailing her months of questioning and deconstructing the only Christian theology she's ever known.

"The point is, you wrote it now." I sip my drink. "It might not convince too many more people at Messiah, but you will help a lot of women who were sucked in by the things you wrote rather than Rick himself."

A shadow passes over her face as she nods.

"Dad said a few people told him they were leaving after last Sunday." Esha's voice is still croaky from days without use. "Louis Herschell spent like twenty minutes attacking all of us from the pulpit instead of making any attempt to discredit the findings in the article."

"Of course he did."

Louis was installed as interim pastor, but I'll be shocked if he isn't eventually granted the position full-time. They can't take a chance on bringing in an outside leader—too much risk he'll see Rick's corruption for what it was and clean house. As of right now, my fear has proved correct. I've listened to the messages online from the last two Sundays since Rick died. From the pulpit and on all the official Messiah platforms, he is being spoken about only with the greatest reverence.

But at least he's not speaking anymore.

After taking another drink of my tea, I set it down on the table next to me. "I won't stay long. I know you're still recovering from everything, but I wanted a chance to say goodbye." I take a deep breath. "And I also wanted to suggest something."

Eve and Esha sit close to each other, Eve being careful not to touch any of her sister's injuries. Their faces and bodies are more mature, narrower in places and fuller in others, but they are still every bit the girls I became best friends with in high school. I hate that it took Lars's death to bring us back together, but I'm glad we're speaking again. One day, when we're all a little less fragile, I hope we can all pile onto a couch again and watch a dumb movie, eating candy and gossiping like we did back then.

"What is it?" Eve asks.

I've been silent for a beat too long. I clasp my hands in my lap, leaning forward. "One thing that always bothered me is how Rick profited off all the work you did writing the *Noble Wife Journey*. It was his doctrine, but you were the one who made it palatable, appealing. You did all the hard work of creating an audience, and he was the one who got all the money and recognition when his book was published."

Esha is quiet, her forehead creased as she listens. Eve's lip curls in disgust. "I don't want any of the money or recognition for Noble Wife now."

"I know that. But you have a style that people—particularly Christian women—want to read. And now you have a pretty compelling story. When you feel ready, I think you should write about it. Not on the blog, though. A guy I went to college with is an editorial assistant for a publishing house in New York now. I reached out to him last week with a link to your blog and Parker's article. He's interested in meeting with you."

She opens her mouth, clearly ready to reject the suggestion, when Esha puts a hand on her arm.

"You should do it."

Eve looks at her sister. "What? No. I don't know how to do that."

Esha chuckles. "Eve, you've probably written enough blog posts to fill five books in the years since you started. Del is right. You've got a story people will definitely want to read. But it's more than that." Her fingers drift up to her face, gently caressing the lacerations on her cheek from the car accident. "A viral blog post and a couple stories from a small-town newspaper are one thing, but this would be a chance for you to tell the whole world. Tell them what happens when you tie the life or death of people's eternal souls to one man's theology, when you endow him with the kind of spiritual authority that makes him impossible to disobey."

I sit at the edge of my chair. "Exactly. A book would give you the room and the reach not just to help the women Rick and the Noble Wife theology hurt, but to warn people about other men like him. Right now, you have a voice and a critical message. It's time to give you a megaphone."

Eve looks at me for a long moment, conflicting emotions on her pale face. A crash shatters the awkward silence, followed by a squeal of laughter. Emmanuelle gathers the blocks that have just fallen, starting to stack them again. Her face glows with mischief, little lips pursed in concentration.

When I look back at Eve, she's watching her daughter too. Her mouth slowly curves into a smile. She meets my gaze, a lightness in her eyes for the first time since I came back to Bower.

"How do I get in touch with your friend?"

IT'S LATE ON a Saturday night, several weeks into my new bartending gig, when I turn around and find Finn sitting on a stool in front of me. It's the first time I've seen him since he left me at the hospital six months ago.

At the insistence of my parents, I stayed in Bower for a couple months, getting back on my feet and trying to rebuild our relationship. The sheriff's department questioned me several times, obviously not believing that I couldn't remember who had pulled me from the pit and brought me to the hospital. They had no reason to suspect the person who rescued me had also killed Pastor Rick, but I wasn't about to give them Finn's name regardless. As soon as the lawyer Nathaniel had hired said it was okay, I made a swift exit, and I was too nervous to stop at Elaine's to say goodbye.

When I didn't hear from him, I assumed that was it.

"Hi," Finn says.

"Hey, that's my spot." My eyes flick to the stool, then back to his face.

He chuckles. "You're looking good," he replies. His eyes are red and shadowed. I wonder if he has trouble sleeping. It causes a flicker of guilt every morning when I wake up, but I am better rested now than I have been in a decade.

I hold up his favorite rum. "You look like you could use the bottle."

He grins, recognizing the first words he ever said to me. "I could. But I'll start with a glass. And add some Coke."

"Classic." I scoop in ice, pour a generous shot, and fill it to the top with cola. I grab a cloth to make it look like I'm cleaning in case my manager makes a sudden appearance. "I wasn't sure if I'd see you again."

"It took a while to figure out what I should do."

I nod. "That's fair."

"I didn't want to leave town too quickly, especially since I wasn't sure about Parker."

Avoiding his gaze, I wipe underneath the rubber mat where I set drinks for the servers. "She got the video anonymously, though." From an encrypted messaging app on a phone now at the bottom of an abandoned well.

Ice chimes against his glass as he stirs the drink. "Still. She has to suspect."

A small ripple of anxiety. I push it down.

"I heard Eve got out," he says.

I nod. "She moved down here with Esha last month. We actually see each other most Sundays."

One eyebrow rises. "Church?"

"Hard to believe, isn't it?" I chuckle. "Esha managed to find a place that's nothing like the Mess, and she finally convinced me to check it out when I got back." Sometimes the sound of a particular worship song or a familiar turn of phrase from the pastor still makes me sweat, but it gives me more peace to attend than abstain, so I find myself driving there every Sunday morning anyway.

"I'm glad for you, though."

"Thanks." I don't know if Finn will ever see church the same way, but then again, I didn't think I would either. That's the thing about God: he never leaves, even when we do.

"I never got to thank you," I say. The garnish tray is fine, but I set about replenishing it anyway. I pull containers of chopped lemons, limes, and oranges out of the fridge and start spearing them with cocktail umbrellas.

"For what?"

"You saved my life."

"Yeah, but you were only that close to dying because I let you stay down there as long as I did."

"Let's not pretend like that had anything to do with you." Our eyes meet. "So, you're in Minneapolis now? Or just visiting?"

A smile tugs at his lips. "I got into business school, actually. A few months ago."

"Finn, that's great. When do you start?"

"Next week. I just signed a lease on an apartment in Fridley."

"Oh, wow." It's only a couple suburbs over from me. I debate whether to tell him that. He obviously knows where I work. For the first time, I wonder how that is. I don't post about my job or private information on social media, and besides, we never connected there. I could ask, but it doesn't really matter. I don't have any reason to be concerned.

Finn is not a cold-blooded killer.

A ticket comes up on the printer, and I turn to make the drink. When I look back at him, he's watching me quietly. There's a raw longing in his gaze that wasn't there before, when we worked together in Elden. I wonder how much he held back his emotions, conflicted about what he was doing to me.

"I'm sorry, Del," Finn murmurs, stirring his drink. "I don't even remember if I ever said that to you. But I am. I wish we could start over."

Running my tongue across my lower lip, I study his face. I've thought about this a lot. I knew that if he came to find me, I wouldn't turn him away. I don't need the attention of a man to be happy anymore. But despite everything that happened between us, I want his. There are things I don't have to tell him, things I know that no other guy I will ever meet could understand.

"I don't." I reach across to put my hand on his. "I want us to be able to pick up where we left off. Something binds us now. I don't think that's a bad thing."

His other hand closes over the top of mine. The warmth of it shoots up my arm, makes me want to jump over the bar. I can tell the touch affects him, too, but there's a flicker of shame in his eyes as well.

"Do you regret it?" I murmur.

It could be any number of things. Giving me the job, trying to scare me out of town, hooking up with me, working with Rick, trying to kill me, saving my life. Ending his.

I want to know all of it, but I'm afraid to be more specific.

He looks at me for a long moment. "No. Do you?"

His answer fills a gap inside me, a crack in my mind that had been leaking that question over and over for the past six months. The din of the bar fades. Visions of that night wait for me every time I close my eyes—but they're not the sharp daggers of a nightmare, rather the warm glow of a triumph. The drive down the dark highway, the sound of Finn's frantic voice, the shot of adrenaline as the heat made its way into my skin and revived my vital organs. His insistence that he drop me at the hospital, my stronger demand that we do it together.

Legs shaky but determined on the icy sidewalk. The early Christmas lights guiding our steps to the door of the mansion. The sound of Finn's fist on the door.

Then footsteps, shuffling and innocent, slippered feet to guard against the chill: an unexpected touch of vulnerability. The door opening, my phone in his face—camera on—both Finn and the gun out of frame but in his line of sight.

And the words I wanted to say to him from the moment I knew what he'd done.

"*Confess to me.*"

My eyes focus on Finn's again. It's the crack of the bullet I hear as I'm lying in bed each night—the sound of finality, of terror ending. A sound that would scare anyone else lulls me to sleep.

No more backup plans, no more manipulation, no more surprises. Just a voice that needed to be silenced.

I tell him the truth. "No. I don't regret anything."

ACKNOWLEDGMENTS

I wrote the first draft of this book in year one of the COVID-19 pandemic. On the advice of my editor, I completely rewrote it while pregnant with (and then raising) twins. I edited it in snatched time during naps, when my husband was home, or when one of my generous family members let me sneak out to a café while they stayed with the babies. It is the hardest thing I have ever done, but it is the best thing I have ever written, and I am grateful to every person who helped me see it through.

My editorial team at William Morrow shaped this book's journey in so many ways: Jaime Levine, who encouraged me to focus on the religious abuse at Messiah and write the story I really wanted to tell; and Liz Stein and Ariana Sinclair, who offered the enthusiasm and support that are essential to any book's success. Everyone in the publishing house who worked on this book, from design to sales to marketing to publicity and beyond: you have my eternal gratitude.

Thank you to Victoria Marini for your advocacy, encouragement, and excitement for my work; and to Sharon Pelletier for your years of support.

Bethany C. Morrow is my first reader, my best friend, my most admired author, and my confidant in every way. I would not have had the courage to write this story the way it is, to critique our Christian family the way I did, without your inspiration and your refusal to let me take the easy way out.

Several wonderful people offered early thoughts and critiques on this book, shared feedback on cover and title ideas, or just listened to me while I bemoaned the difficulty of writing as a new mom. Libby

Hubscher, Megan Collins, Marjorie Brimer, Ryan Licata, Amina Akhtar, Jesse Sutanto, Nekesa Afia: you are all wonderful friends and incredible writers—thank you. Swati Hegde, thank you for your careful review and thoughtful notes on Esha's character. Sheyla Knigge, your critical eye at a moment's notice was so appreciated.

The crime-writing community keeps me coming back to social media, even when I should definitely be writing my next book. There are too many people to name and I can't stand the idea of leaving anyone out, so thank you all for being my friends and liking my random tweets. Special thanks to the incredible authors who provided such generous quotes of praise.

Finally, I couldn't do any of this without my family. My husband, Peter, has believed in my writing from the first time I told him about it, and every quiet hour he makes sure I get now that we have toddler twins running around is critical to making sure I have time and space to write. Emery and Asher, you are exhausting and exhilarating in equal measure, and I hope you don't look at me funny when you're finally old enough to read my books. My parents, my parents-in-law, and all my siblings, cousins, aunts, uncles—I really couldn't ask for a more supportive family.

Acknowledgments are hard. Authors are always worried about leaving someone out, so if you know you had an impact on this book, thank you.

ABOUT THE AUTHOR

Amy Suiter Clarke is the author of the psychological thriller *Girl, 11*. Originally from a small town in Minnesota, she completed an undergraduate degree in theater in the Twin Cities and earned an MFA at Kingston University in London. She currently lives in Melbourne, Australia, with her husband and twin sons.